W9-DES-928

Harlequin Books is proud to offer classic novels from today's superstars of women's fiction. These authors have captured the hearts of millions of readers around the world, and earned their place on the bestseller lists with every release.

As a bonus, each volume also includes a full-length novel from a rising star of series romance. Bestselling authors in their own right, these talented writers have captured the qualities Harlequin is famous for—heart-racing passion, edge-of-your-seat entertainment and a satisfying happily-ever-after.

New York Times and USA TODAY Bestselling Author

SUSAN MALLERY

Completely Smitten

HARLEQUIN® BESTSELLERS

Recycling programs
for this product may
not exist in your area.

ISBN-13: 978-0-373-60588-0

COMPLETELY SMITTEN

Copyright © 2011 by Harlequin Books S.A.

The publisher acknowledges the copyright holders
of the individual works as follows:

COMPLETELY SMITTEN
Copyright © 2003 by Susan Macias Redmond

HERS FOR THE WEEKEND
Copyright © 2004 by Tanya Michna

This edition published by arrangement with Harlequin Books S.A.

For questions and comments about the quality of this book, please contact us at CustomerService@Harlequin.com.

® and TM are trademarks of the publisher. Trademarks indicated with ® are registered in the United States Patent and Trademark Office, the Canadian Trade Marks Office and in other countries.

Printed in U.S.A.

CONTENTS

To my readers, with thanks.
And to my former editor, Karen Taylor Richman,
who always loved this book.

COMPLETELY SMITTEN

New York Times and *USA TODAY* Bestselling Author

Susan Mallery

SUSAN MALLERY

is a *New York Times* and *USA TODAY* bestselling author of more than ninety romances. Her combination of humor, emotion and just-plain-sexy has made her a reader favorite. Susan makes her home in the Pacific Northwest with her handsome husband and possibly the world's cutest dog. Visit her website at www.SusanMallery.com.

Chapter One

All Kevin Harmon wanted was a beer, a burger and a bed, in that order. He'd had the kind of day designed to make a man rethink his career choices. He'd been bit, he was stuck in the middle of Kansas on a night that was practically guaranteed to produce twisters, and he'd just been offered a promotion. Not one thing was going right with his life. For once he wasn't looking for trouble, so of course trouble came looking for him.

He'd been around long enough to know that when a pretty, wide-eyed blonde walked into a seedy roadside bar, somewhere, somehow, there was going to be hell to pay. Kevin was determined to stay out of the way. No matter what.

He turned his attention from the petite blonde back to the bartender. "Burger," he said, pushing the plastic menu back at the man. "Extra fries."

The bartender nodded and wrote something on a pad

of paper, then set a frosty mug down on a once-white coaster advertising the local grange.

Kevin took a long drink. He'd just spent the better part of the day transporting a convicted felon across state lines. The process had not gone smoothly, which explained the bite on his arm. The skin hadn't been broken, but he really hated when there was trouble on the road. If he hadn't drawn the short straw, he would be down in Florida, helping with a drug raid. But no, he was stuck in Kansas where the air was so thick you could practically stand a spoon up in midair. The pressure was rising—or maybe falling—he could never remember which one caused storms to spin out of control and become tornados.

He'd grown up with twisters, back when he'd lived in Texas, and he'd never liked them. They always seemed to show up right when he was supposed to be whipping the crosstown rival at a baseball game.

Kevin thought about tornados and Texas. He even tried to remember if he needed to buy milk when he flew home the next day. Anything to keep from turning to watch the progress of the blonde. It wasn't that she was so attractive that he couldn't resist her. Far from it. Sure, she was pretty enough, but pretty was a dime a dozen.

Instead, what made him determined to stay out of it was the nervousness he'd seen lurking in her eyes, and the hesitation in her step. She belonged in this bar as much as a dog with mange belonged in church.

The bartender flipped on a small television. Instantly the sound of a ball game blasted into the half-full room. Kevin continued to drink his beer, while he stared determinedly at the screen. He ignored everything else, even the half sly, half defiant male laughter behind him.

Bullies moving in for the kill.

He swore under his breath as he set his mug on the bar and pulled off his cap. The one with U.S. Marshals embroidered on the front. He was hot, he was tired, he was hungry. The last thing he wanted tonight was a fight.

Since when did fate pay any attention to what he wanted?

He turned on the bar stool and surveyed the situation. The blonde stood between two big guys with more tattoos than sense. A third, smaller man, had his hand on her arm.

She was of medium height, maybe five-four or five-five, with short hair and big eyes, more blue than hazel. There wasn't a speck of makeup on her face, but she was still attractive, with full lips and a stubborn-looking chin.

Her clothing choices made him wince. The shapeless short-sleeved dress she wore fell nearly to her ankles. It looked ugly enough to be embarrassed to be a dust cloth— with a white lace collar and some god-awful flower print. What was it about women and clothes with plants on them?

Kevin approached the quartet. The blonde struggled to break free of the little guy's hold. When she looked up and saw him, relief filled her eyes.

"You with them?" he asked, getting more tired by the second.

She shook her head.

Kevin turned his full attention on the man holding her arm. "Then, son, you'd best let the lady go."

One of the big guys took a step toward him. Kevin flexed his hands.

"I've had a bad day, gentlemen. I'm hungry, tired, and not in the mood. So you can walk away right now, or we can move it outside. I feel obliged to warn you that if we take this to the next level, the only one walking away will be me."

Haley couldn't believe it. She felt as if she was in one

of those Clint Eastwood Dirty Harry movies her dad liked so much. She half expected to see the dark-haired man pull out a .357 Magnum and ask someone to make his day.

Instead, the skinny man with rabbit teeth who'd been holding her arm let go. He took a step back, holding up his hands and trying to smile.

"We didn't mean nothin'. Just thought the lady would like some company."

His two friends nodded. They were big. Bigger than her rescuer. A couple of their tattoos had interesting swear-words woven into the designs. She'd been trying to read them when Mr. Rabbit Teeth had grabbed her.

The three of them threw some bills on their table and left. Haley breathed a sigh of relief.

"That was something," she said earnestly. "I didn't know what to do. I mean, when he wouldn't let go. I thought about screaming, but it's kind of embarrassing to have to do that. I didn't want to make a fuss."

The man who had come to her assistance didn't say anything. Instead, he headed back toward the bar and slid onto his stool. She followed.

"Thank you for rescuing me," she said.

"Make a fuss," he said, reaching for his beer.

She sat next to him. "What?"

He took a long swallow, then stared at her over the mug. "Next time you get in trouble, make a fuss. Better yet, next time stay out of bars."

Haley reached out to tug on a strand of her hair, only to remember too late that she'd cut it all off the previous afternoon. Instead of a long braid nearly to her waist, she had short bits of fluff flying around her head.

She smoothed what was left of her bangs, then nod-ded. Stay out of bars. It was probably good advice. "I just can't," she said with a sigh. "Not yet."

The man stared at her. "You have a death wish?"

She laughed. "I'm not going to get killed. I just need to handle things better." She scooted a little closer and lowered her voice. "Can you believe that until two days ago I'd never been in a bar before?"

Her rescuer stared at her in shock.

"I know," she said. "I've led a very sheltered life. It's pathetic. I mean, I'm twenty-five years old and I've been living like a nun." She shrugged. "Not that I'm Catholic. We're Baptists. My dad's a minister at our church."

The man didn't say anything. He turned his attention to the baseball game on the television. Haley studied his strong profile. He was handsome, in a rugged, cigarette-advertisement sort of way. There was an air of strength about him. He looked people in the eye when he spoke and she liked that. He wore his dark hair short.

She reached over and picked up his U.S. Marshals cap, then ran her fingers along the stitching. "So you're like a cop?"

"Sort of."

"I'll bet you're a good one."

He turned his attention back to her. She noticed he had brown eyes the color of chocolate, and while he'd yet to smile at her, she liked the shape of his mouth.

"How the hell would you know that?" he asked, sounding gruff and annoyed.

His tone made her spine stiffen just a little, while the swearword startled her. He'd said the H-word. Just like that. She would bet that he hadn't even planned it. The word had just come out.

One day she was going to swear, too. She would casually drop the H-word or the D-word into conversation. But that was all. Swearing was one thing, but really bad words were just ugly.

He waved a hand in front of her face. "Are you still in there?"

"Oh. Sorry. What was the question?"

"Never mind."

She put his hat back on the bar. "I'm Haley Foster." She held out her hand.

He stared at it for a long time before taking it in his and shaking. "Kevin Harmon."

"Nice to meet you, Kevin."

He grunted and turned back to the television.

Haley shifted slightly on her stool and took in the ambience of the location. There were several posters of various sports, some advertisements for alcoholic beverages. The floor was dirty, and some of the tables looked as if they hadn't been wiped off in a while. Except for a woman with an incredibly large bosom in the corner, she seemed to be the only female in the place.

She glanced at her watch. It was nearly eight. "Why aren't there more women here?" she asked.

Kevin never took his gaze off the game. "It's not that kind of place."

"What kind of place?"

"This isn't the kind of bar where you bring a date."

There were different kinds of bars? "How do you know that?"

"I just know."

A not very helpful answer.

The bartender walked over. "What can I get you?"

Haley eyed Kevin's beer. Yesterday she'd had her first glass of white wine ever. To be honest, she hadn't really liked it.

"A margarita," she said.

"Frozen or on the rocks?"

The only liquor question she knew the answer to was James Bond's, "Shaken, not stirred." Okay, rocks were ice. On the rocks would mean over ice, which wasn't how she pictured margaritas.

"Frozen," she said. "Oh. Do you have any of those little umbrellas to put in the glass?"

The bartender stared at her. "No."

"Too bad." She'd always wanted a drink with a little umbrella.

She watched as the man poured various liquids into a blender. He added a scoop of ice, then set the whole thing to whirling and crunching. When he finally put a glass in front of her, the light green concoction looked more like a slushy drink than anything else.

"Thanks."

She took a sip from the tiny straw the bartender had dropped into her glass.

The first thing she noticed was the cold. The second was the flavor. Not sweet, but not bitter, either. Kind of lime, kind of something else.

"It's good," she said in surprise. It was sure better than that wine she'd had the previous night. She turned her attention back to Kevin.

"So why are you here?"

He turned slowly until his dark gaze rested on her face. He was really very handsome. She found herself wishing she hadn't been quite so quick to cut off all her hair. Allan had always said it was her best feature.

Allan. She took a long drink of her margarita. She did *not* want to think about him. Not now. Not ever.

"Are you asking my spiritual purpose in the universe?" Kevin asked.

"Only if you want to tell me. I was thinking more of, do you live around here? What are you doing in the bar? That sort of thing."

He finished his beer and pushed the glass across the

bar. "Another," he called before turning his attention back to her. "What are *you* doing here? In this bar. Today."

"Well..." She took another long sip. "I'm driving to Hawaii."

Kevin wished he'd changed the order of his wants back when life had still been sane. If he'd wanted a *bed,* a beer and a burger, he would now be in some hotel, ordering room service and watching the game in peace. Instead, he was having a conversation with a woman who had left the functioning part of her brain back in her car.

"Hawaii?"

Haley beamed at him. "Okay, so I know you can't *really* drive to Hawaii, but I'm going to get as close as possible."

"That would be California."

"Right. I'll figure out the rest of it when I get there."

"Where are you driving from?"

"Western Ohio. I'm—"

But whatever she'd been about to confess was cut off by the arrival of his dinner. Haley stared at the large plate containing a burger on a bun—the top of the bun covered with lettuce, tomatoes and onion—along with a mound of fries that threatened to fall onto the counter.

"You can get food in a bar?" she asked, incredulous. "For real?"

He remembered walking to school years ago and seeing a starving dog. The dirty brown-and-white fur ball had been hiding in an alley. Kevin had taken one look at its shivering, skinny self, then he'd handed over his sandwich. He'd gone without lunch for two days before finally taking the dog home.

"You're broke," he said flatly, wondering when his luck had gotten so bad. He pushed the plate toward her. "Eat up."

She took another drink of her margarita. "Broke?" She swallowed. "No. I have money."

She put the glass on the bar, then pulled a small purse that had been dangling off one shoulder onto her lap and opened it. Inside was a wad of bills.

"I cleaned out my savings account," she said, then lowered her voice. "I have the rest of it in traveler's checks. It's really much safer that way." The purse closed with a snap.

She took another drink, then gasped and slapped her hands over her face.

"Ouch. Oh, yuck. It hurts. It hurts." She shimmied on the bar stool, alternately cupping her nose and mouth and waving her hand back and forth.

Kevin pulled his plate in front of him, then nodded at the bartender. "Could we have a glass of water?"

The bartender filled a glass and passed it over to Haley. She gulped some down. After a couple of swallows, she sighed.

"Much better." She put the glass down. "I had one of those flash ice headaches."

"We all knew that."

She half stood, stretched over the bar and snagged a small plate. "Want to share your fries?"

"Why not?"

She scooped several onto her plate and crunched the first one.

He was in hell, he decided, watching her. Somewhere in his day, he'd died and this was God's way of punishing him for all the screwing up he'd done in his life.

"So I'm from Ohio," she said with a smile. "Western Ohio. A little town you've never heard of. Have you been to Ohio?"

"Columbus."

"It's nice, huh?"

"A wonderful place."

She nodded, not coming close to catching the sarcasm in his voice.

Why him? That's what he wanted to know. There were probably twenty other guys in the bar. Why had he been the one to come to her rescue? Why hadn't someone else stepped in?

"Like I said, my dad's a minister." She ate another French fry, then drank more of her margarita. "My mom died when I was born, so I don't remember her. The thing is, when you're the preacher's kid, everybody feels responsible for keeping you on the straight and narrow. I didn't have one mother—I had fifty. I couldn't even think something bad before it was being reported to my dad."

"Uh-huh."

Kevin turned back to the game and tried not to listen.

"So that's why I don't know the bar thing."

"What bar thing?" he asked before he could stop himself.

"That this isn't a bar people bring their dates to. I'm practicing being bad."

That got his attention. He swung back to face her. "Bad?"

"You bet." She finished her margarita and pushed her glass to the edge of the counter. "I'd like another one, please," she said, then beamed at the bartender. "It was great."

She turned back to Kevin. "I just wish I could have a little umbrella."

He didn't care about that. "Tell me about being bad."

"I haven't been. Ever. So that's what I'm doing on my drive to Hawaii." She glanced around as if to make sure no one was listening. "This is only my third time in a bar."

"You're kidding," he said, more because he was hoping she wasn't telling the truth than because he didn't believe her.

"When I left home three days ago, I'd never even had anything alcoholic to drink. So that first night, when I stopped, I went into a bar." She bit into another fry and wrinkled her nose. Humor crinkled the corners of her eyes.

"It was horrible," she said when she'd swallowed. "I felt so out of place and when a man smiled at me, I ran out the door. Yesterday was better."

He gave up. There was no point in avoiding what was obviously his fate. "Your second time in a bar?"

She nodded. "I had white wine, but I have to tell you I didn't like it at all. But I did almost speak to someone."

Great.

The bartender finished blending the margarita and set it in front of her. "Want to run a tab?" he asked.

Haley pressed her lips together for a couple of seconds. "Maybe," she said at last.

"Yes," Kevin said. "Run her a tab. You want your own order of fries?"

"Okay. Extra salt, please."

The bartender muttered something under his breath, then wrote on his small pad.

"A tab," Kevin said when they were alone, "means they keep a list of what you've ordered. You pay once at the end of the evening instead of paying each time."

Haley's blue-hazel eyes widened. "That's so cool."

He had a feeling the world was going to be one constant amazement after the other for her.

He studied her pale skin, her wide smile and trusting eyes. This was not a woman who should be let out on her own.

"You need to think about heading back to Ohio."

"No way." She took a long drink of her margarita. "I've spent my entire life doing what everyone else has told me to do. Now I'm only doing what I want. No matter what."

Her expression turned fierce. "You can't know what it's like," she continued. "I never get to voice my opinion. If I even try, I get ignored. No one cares what I think or what I want."

"That's why you're running away?"

"Exactly." She picked up a French fry, then put it back on the plate. "How did you know I was running away?"

"You're not the kind of woman to come to a place like this on purpose."

She glanced around at the seedy clientele, then shrugged. "I want new experiences."

"Like little umbrellas in your drinks?"

"Exactly."

She smiled. He had to admit she had a great smile. Her whole face lit up. She'd said she was twenty-five, but in some ways she acted more like an awkward teenager than a grown woman. No doubt being the daughter of a single father minister had something to do with it.

He thought about suggesting that next time she find her new experience at a more upscale bar, but then he reminded himself he wasn't getting involved. He had enough problems of his own without adding her to the list.

"It's not that I don't like the *piano*," she said.

"What?"

"The piano. I play. It was expected. I can also play the organ, but only a few hymns and not very well."

"Okay." He started eating his burger.

"The music is great. But I wanted to be a teacher."

"Your father objected?" he asked before he could stop himself.

She sighed. "He would never come out and tell me no. That's not his way. But there was subtle pressure. In a way that's a whole lot harder to resist. I mean, a direct statement can be argued, but hints and nudges kind of sweep you along until you suddenly wake up and find yourself in a place you don't want to be."

She took another long drink of her margarita. The bartender appeared with a plate of fries. Haley smiled her thanks.

Kevin finished his burger and thought about making his escape.

"You want me to replace what I took?" she asked, motioning to his plate.

"No thanks."

She shrugged, then munched on another fry. "So you're a U.S. Marshal. What are you doing here?"

"I just delivered a prisoner to the federal penitentiary up the road."

Her eyes widened. "There's a prison here?"

"Didn't you see the signs about not picking up hitchhikers?"

"Sure, but I thought it was some kind of joke. You know, a local gag on tourists."

"This isn't a real tourist haven. Most of the folks are passing through or here to visit relatives."

She glanced over her shoulder, then leaned close and lowered her voice. "People here know men in prison?"

He groaned. "Haley, have you ever been outside of your hometown before?"

"Of course. I spent four years at the Southern Baptist College for Young Women."

Just perfect. "And after your college experience?"

"I went back home, where I got my master's in music and finished up the courses I needed for my teaching credentials. I graduated with honors."

She reached for her glass. Her hand missed the stem by about three inches. She stretched out her fingers, then curled them into her palm.

"My skin feels funny," she said. "My cheeks tingle."

Kevin swore silently. He glanced at the nearly finished second drink, then turned his attention to the bartender drying glasses with a dirty towel.

"Doubles?" he asked.

The old man grinned. "Thought you might want to get lucky."

Perfect. Just perfect. In less than forty minutes the nondrinking preacher's daughter had just consumed the equivalent of four shots of tequila. The full effect of the alcohol wasn't going to hit for about twenty more minutes. He would bet a week's salary that she would be on her butt about thirty seconds after that.

He slapped some money onto the bar and stood. "Come on, Haley. I'm going to get you out of here while you can still walk. Have you got a hotel room?"

She blinked at him. "I can walk."

"Sure you can. Why don't you try?"

She wore the ugliest beige shoes he'd ever seen, but at least the heel wasn't too high. When she slid off the stool, she stood straight just long enough to give him hope. Maybe he'd overreacted. Maybe—

She swayed so far to the left, she nearly toppled over.

"Am I drunk?" she asked, sounding delighted as she managed to stand straight. "The room is spinning. Wow. This is so cool."

Yeah, everything was cool to her. "Do you have a motel room?" he repeated, speaking slowly and deliberately.

"Yeah. The pink one. I liked the color. It's over there. Outside."

She pointed to the exit and nearly fell on her face. Kevin gritted his teeth.

"Put your arm around my shoulders," he instructed as he wrapped an arm around her waist.

His first impression was of heat; his second, of slender curves that got his body's attention in a big way.

Instead of following orders, Haley simply sagged against him. "You smell good," she said as he half carried her toward the door.

"Thanks."

He would get her to her motel and leave, he told himself. She would probably pass out in a matter of seconds and wake up with a hangover big enough to cure her of ever wanting another margarita. She'd made it this far without him, she would get to wherever she was going without his assistance.

Kevin knew he was trying to convince himself that he wasn't responsible for Haley. Unfortunately he wasn't doing a very good job.

They stepped into the sultry evening air. Haley sucked in a deep breath, then turned to look at him. As she was leaning against him, her face rested on his shoulder. Her mouth was inches from his. One of her wisps of blond hair brushed against his cheek.

"So," Haley said, licking her lips. "Is this where you take advantage of me?"

"What?"

She blinked slowly, then smiled. "I don't think I'd mind."

Chapter Two

She wouldn't mind?

Kevin did his best to ignore the sexual desire that slammed into him the second she spoke the words. His unexpected attraction to Haley couldn't begin to matter. Not with circumstances being what they were. She was drunk, alone, out of her element and, with his luck, a virgin. Thanks, but not tonight.

Lightning cut across the sky, as if warning him the Almighty was keeping tabs on the evening's events. With that in mind, Kevin ignored the curves pressing against his body and the way those curves made him feel. She might be a little slimmer than he'd first realized, but she seemed to have everything in the right place under her ugly dress. Not that he was going to be checking her out.

"Did you say a pink motel?" he asked, looking around at the motor inns on both sides of the highway.

"Uh-huh. There's flamingos." She blinked at him. "I like birds."

"Good to know."

He spotted a low, two-story structure that matched her description. He mentally cringed at the plastic flamingos stuck into the cement. If the place looked this bad at night, what did it look like in the light of day? Of course, there was no accounting for taste.

At least they didn't have to cross the highway to get there. The motel was only a couple hundred yards up the frontage road.

"Let's start walking," he said, still supporting most of her weight.

A second bolt of lightning illuminated the sky.

"Look!" Haley said, pointing at the heavens. "Don't you love lightning? Don't you wish it would rain?"

"Sure."

Because a douse of cold water might cool him off. Drunk women begging to be taken advantage of were nothing but trouble. He had to keep reminding himself of that as Haley's soft blond hair brushed against his cheek.

He got them moving in the direction of the motel. Haley was still upright and remotely mobile, but he had a feeling that was going to be changing in the next few minutes. At least she was still managing full sentences.

"Do you know your room number?"

Rather than answer, she sighed. He felt the soft puff of air on his cheek.

"You never answered my question," she said instead.

"What question?"

He made the mistake of looking at her face—at her blue-hazel eyes and the curves at the corners of her mouth. At the knowing expression that heated his blood and made him consider possibilities.

"No way," he muttered more to himself than to her. He was *not* going there with her.

She pushed away from him and tried to stand on her own. She was nearly successful. With her feet firmly planted, she swayed back and forth, stumbled a step, then regained her balance by holding her arms out a little on each side.

"What is it about me?" she demanded. "Why don't men want to take advantage of me? Am I ugly? Is my body hideous?"

Did they really need to be having this conversation now? He eyed the night sky—thick with clouds and the promise of rain. More lightning flashed in the distance.

"We're going to get soaked in about thirty seconds," he said.

She glared at him. "I mean it. What's wrong with me?"

"Nothing's wrong with you."

"So why don't you want to have—"

For a second he thought she was actually going to say "sex" but at the last minute she pressed her lips together and stared meaningfully. At least he assumed that's what she was doing. That and tipping over.

He grabbed her around the waist and hauled her against him.

"Walk," he commanded.

She started moving.

"Tell me," she demanded. "What's wrong with me?"

"Like I said—nothing. It's not you." Hell, why not just tell her the truth? "It's the whole preacher's daughter thing. No one wants to spit in the eye of God."

She considered that while they crossed the rest of the bar's parking lot and stepped onto the motel parking lot.

"What about forbidden flute?"

The flute thing threw him for a second. "Do you mean 'fruit'?"

She nodded vigorously and nearly collapsed. "My head is spinning," she said, sounding as thrilled as a kid at a carnival. "The sky's spinning, too."

"Great."

"I can be fruit," she insisted.

"If that's what you want."

"Don't you think of me that way? Aren't I a temptation?"

He was impressed she could manage a three-syllable word. Unfortunately, while her verbal skills remained intact, her motor skills were fading fast. He had to support more and more of her weight to keep them moving toward the motel.

"Room number," he said.

"Look at what happened with Eve and the apple. That could be me. I could be an apple."

"I'll bet you could even be a plum. Keep moving."

"Plum? Who wants to be that?"

They had reached the building. Kevin paused to lean against a column supporting the overhead walkway around the second story.

"I need your key," he said. "I'm going to take it out of your purse."

She smiled brightly. "Okay."

He opened the clasp and dug around until he came up with a key attached to a plastic pink flamingo. The number three had been painted on the flamingo's wing.

At least they weren't going to have to negotiate the stairs.

She shifted her weight just as he closed her purse. The action caused her to slide against him, which pressed her right breast into his side. Instinctively he wrapped both his arms around her to hold her upright. She turned until they were facing each other. Pressed together. Close. Too close.

Her slightly unfocused eyes half closed. "You're very strong," she murmured.

"Don't even go there," he told her, trying to figure out where he was going to find room number three.

"Strong and sexy."

Before he could stop her, she reached up and pulled off his cap and stuck it on her own head. Of course she looked completely adorable.

"I've never thought about a man being strong before," she continued with a sigh. "It's nice. As for the sexy part." She covered her mouth with her fingers. "I've never thought about a man that way before, either."

"All right, Haley. Let's go."

He got them moving toward the row of doors, each labeled with a number. There were seven on each floor.

"Do you think I'm sexy?" she asked.

They passed seven. He didn't answer.

"Kevin?"

Six. Just three more doors and then they were home.

"Can I at least be an apple?"

Bingo. He stuck the key in the door and pushed it open.

"In we go," he said, helping her over the threshold.

"Not even an apple," she murmured, sounding tragically sad.

He told himself that speaking the truth would only get them both in trouble. In her current state there was no telling what she would do if she figured out that she was exactly like forbidden fruit and he was a man who had been starving for years.

He followed her into the room, which was typical for a cheap roadside motel. Full-size bed, small dresser, a couple of chairs and a door leading to a white-on-white bathroom. It looked clean enough, he supposed, a little surprised to find himself wanting Haley to have something nicer than this. What did he care where she stayed? As long as it wasn't with him.

He pulled the key out of the lock and closed the door. Haley continued to hold on to him. He moved them both toward the bed so that when she finally did let go, she wouldn't have very far to fall.

Speaking of which, once he really noticed the bed—wide, covered with a blue spread and very empty—he found it hard to notice anything else.

Sexy, willing women and beds just seemed made for each other.

He had to admit he liked the feel of her pressing against him. She was warm and seemed designed to fit him. He allowed himself a brief but meaningful fantasy, then put it firmly out of his mind. For one thing, he didn't take advantage of anyone, ever. For another, his track record wasn't exactly the greatest.

He dropped the key onto the small table between the chairs and put his hands on her shoulders.

"Why don't you sit down?" he suggested. "The bed is right behind you. If you're still, the room will stop spinning."

She smiled. "I like it spinning." She blinked and when she opened her eyes, her gaze lasered in on his mouth.

"Do you know that I've only ever been kissed by three men. Well, only one man, really. The other two were boys in high school." She frowned. "Or were they young men? When do boys become men?"

When they finally make it with a woman, he thought but didn't say. "Haley, you need to sit down."

Her gaze didn't waiver. "If I was fruit, you'd kiss me."

It scared him that her comment almost made sense.

"In college I didn't date much," she continued, swaying slightly so that he was forced to release her shoulders and grab her around the waist to keep her from falling. "There weren't that many boys around and the ones who were never seemed to notice me."

Then they were idiots, he thought. "Haley—"

She interrupted with a soft sigh. "I like how you say my name."

He swore silently. They were standing too close for comfort, at least for him.

"Maybe I was too good."

He stared at her, taking a second to put the statement into a logical framework. "At college?" he asked.

She nodded vigorously, then blinked several times. "I never did anything wrong."

"I'll bet."

"I don't mind doing it now." She tilted her head. "Something wrong, I mean."

"Oh, I got that." He reached up and pulled her arms from around his neck. "Sit," he said firmly.

She sat.

Her eyes widened when she hit the bed. She was eye level with his waist, which he could handle, and she seemed delighted, which he could not.

She laughed. "Okay."

Okay? Okay, what? Then he decided he didn't want to know.

Kevin pulled out one of the straight-back chairs and set it in front of her. He sat and wondered if he had a prayer of reasoning with her while she was this drunk. Regardless, he had to try.

"Haley, I need you to listen to me."

"I like listening to you talk."

"Great. But pay attention to the words, too."

She sighed and nodded.

He had a bad feeling he was screaming into the wind. "You can't go around trusting people. You're drunk and vulnerable right now. That's dangerous. You can't let strange men into your motel room."

Dammit all to hell if she didn't laugh at him. "I trust you," she said.

"You shouldn't."

"Yes, I should. You're a nice man."

Nice? Perfect. Just perfect.

"Fine. I'm nice. But the next guy won't be."

"I don't want the next guy. You're my best shot at being bad."

"What?"

She shrugged and nearly toppled onto her back. He shot out a hand to steady her.

"You're nice but you're bad, too." She lowered her voice. "I can tell. I want to be bad." She leaned in close to him. "Don't you want to help me?"

What he wanted was to know what he'd done to deserve this.

She shifted on the bed, suddenly moving closer. Too close. Her gaze settled on his mouth again.

"Don't you want to kiss me?" she asked, sounding mournful. "I'd like you to, but I don't know if I'm very good at it. I've always wondered. But how do you ask? I mean, is anyone going to tell the truth? Would you tell me?"

He had no idea what they were talking about. Despite the ugly dress and her crazy, trusting personality and the fact that if he even *thought* about touching her he would be zapped by lightning, he suddenly wanted to kiss her.

He wanted to know what she would taste like and how she would respond. He wanted—

She suddenly turned from him. Her legs bumped against his as she struggled to get away. He stood, pushing the chair back, and she bolted for the bathroom. The door slammed behind her, the toilet seat went up with a clatter and two seconds later came the sounds of her being violently sick.

Kevin winced in sympathy. He was guessing this was the first time she'd been drunk, so it was probably the first time she'd been sick with alcohol. Not a fun way to end the day.

He glanced at the door, then hesitated as the need to do the right thing warred with his desire to bolt for freedom.

He compromised by deciding to stay until he knew that she was all right. At least he no longer had to worry about his virtue. There was nothing like barfing one's guts out to break the romantic mood.

Twenty minutes later it was all over but the moaning. Kevin walked to the bathroom door and knocked softly.

"Tell me you're still alive," he said.

A groan came in response.

He pushed the door open and found Haley curled up on the bathroom floor. Her eyes were closed, her skin the color of fog. The soft strands of blond hair now lay plastered against her forehead.

"I'm dying," she gasped.

"It only feels that way."

She shook her head, then groaned again.

"Come on," he said, crouching next to her. "Get up and take a shower. You'll feel better."

She opened one eye. "I'm never going to feel better."

"Hot water works wonders."

Her eyelids fluttered shut.

"Come on, little one," he said, slipping his arm around her and pulling her into a sitting position.

She kept her eyes closed until she was upright, then opened them slowly.

"Is the world still spinning?" he asked.

"A little. It's not as fun as it was before."

"I'll bet." He shifted so he could unbuckle her ugly shoes. "You're probably done throwing up."

"So now I can pass away in peace?"

"Not on my watch." He pulled her up until she was sitting on the edge of the tub. "How about a change of clothes for after your shower? Do you have a robe or something?"

"I have a nightgown in the top drawer."

"Stay here. I'll go get it."

Kevin walked into the bedroom. He wasn't sure what he expected when he slid open the drawer, but any visions of lace and satin were quickly squelched when he saw the high-necked, long-sleeved, cotton granny gown.

He returned to find her sitting right where he'd left her.

"Can you stand?" he asked.

"Why would I want to?"

He chuckled.

She glared. "You should have a little more respect for the dying."

"Death is a long way off, Haley. You only wish it wasn't."

He pulled her to her feet. She swayed a little. He shifted so she had a clear line to the toilet, but she didn't bolt, so he figured they were both safe.

After pulling the plastic curtain halfway closed, he turned on the water until it was steaming hot, then adjusted the temperature to just below scalding and pulled the knob to start the spray.

He stepped back. Haley didn't budge. He gave her a little push toward the water.

"You can get in dressed or undressed," he said. "Your choice."

One hand fluttered behind her before falling back to her side. He sighed heavily, then pulled down the zipper of her dress. As he did so, he was careful not to look at anything more interesting than the sink he could see over her shoulder. He stepped back and headed for the door.

"Holler if you need anything."

"Okay."

He heard her dress hit the floor. His imagination supplied a perfect picture of everything he hadn't seen. He had a feeling the real thing would be even better.

"Kevin?"

He made the mistake of turning around before he realized the potential for disaster. Haley stood facing him, now clutching her dress to herself, but behind her was the small mirror. It reflected a slender back, narrow waist and gentle curving hips. Cream-colored perfection.

He made himself look only at her eyes. "What?"

She swallowed. "Thanks."

"No problem."

He retreated to the bedroom where he was tortured by the sounds of her in the shower. Reminding himself that she had just been sick, and probably felt less appealing than a fur ball, didn't help.

He paced restlessly for ten minutes, then forced himself to sit on the edge of the bed and click channels until he found the ball game. It was tied in the eighth inning and damned if he didn't care at all.

The shower finally went off. There were more sounds he couldn't identify, then the bathroom door opened.

Haley stood dwarfed by her cotton nightgown. The fabric hung to the floor and concealed every single curve and womanly feature. She was pale, but she no longer looked quite so desperate. Her wet hair stood up in spikes.

She'd said she was twenty-five, but right now she could pass for twelve.

"I still feel pretty awful," she said.

"That'll teach you to suck down margaritas at the speed of sound. The good news is you got most of the alcohol out of your system tonight. You'll be fine in the morning."

"I hope you're right."

He stood and pulled back the covers. She slid into bed, sitting up against the pillows instead of lying down.

"You need plenty of water," he told her, filling a glass from a bottle she had on the small table. "You want to stay hydrated."

She nodded as he put the glass on the nightstand. "Are you leaving?"

Her eyes seemed bigger than before. Her mouth trembled slightly and her voice shook as she spoke. She looked like a drowned kitten.

Good sense insisted that he head out now that he knew she was all right. There was no point in staying. In the morning she could get back to whatever it was she'd been doing, and he would catch a flight back to D.C. where he was expected for a two o'clock meeting.

He stared at her, then the door. Her fingers twisted the sheet. "I'll be fine," she whispered. "You've been really nice and I don't want to take advantage of that."

He called himself eight different names, none of them fit for her ears, kicked off his shoes and sat on the bed.

"I'll stay for a little while," he said, shifting close and putting an arm around her.

She snuggled against him, resting her head on his chest where her damp hair quickly soaked his shirt. Oddly, he didn't mind.

He told himself looking after her was like caring for

a child. Except she didn't feel very childlike in his arms. Nor was his reaction to her even close to paternal.

"You know all about me," she said after a few minutes. "What about you? Where are you from?"

"A place you've never heard of. Possum Landing, Texas."

She glanced up and smiled. "Possum Landing?"

He nodded. "Lived there all my life. My brother and I were born in the Dallas area."

"You have a brother?"

"Fraternal twin. Nash works for the FBI."

She sighed. "I always wanted a sister, although a brother would have been nice. Sometimes it got quiet, what with there only being me."

"Your father never remarried?"

"No. He and my mom were really in love. He used to tell me that no one could ever take her place. When I was little I thought that was really romantic, but as I got older, I thought it sounded lonely."

Kevin agreed. His mother and stepfather had a good, strong marriage, but if something happened to one of them, he would hate to think the other was destined to a solitary life. Not that he was in a position to talk. After all, he'd managed to avoid matrimonial bliss for all of his thirty-one years.

"You're a pretty young woman," he said. "How come you've only kissed three guys?"

She raised her head and looked at him. "You think I'm pretty?"

"Fishing for compliments?"

She smiled. "If you knew how seldom they came along, you wouldn't be asking the question."

He didn't like the sound of that. Why weren't people complimenting her? Then he remembered the ugly dress and even worse-looking shoes. Maybe it wasn't such a stretch to think she'd been overlooked.

"Yes, I think you're pretty," he said. "Tell me about dating."

"You mean, not dating." She dropped her head back onto his shoulder. "I can't really explain it. Some of the reason I never went out much was because I was busy with school activities and different things at church. Some of it was my dad. He used to lecture me on the importance of setting an example and doing the right thing. Plus everywhere I went in town, I knew people. They reported back any hint of unacceptable behavior."

She shifted slightly, as if getting more comfortable. The covers slipped, and instead of touching layers of sheet and blanket, he suddenly found his hand resting on her hip. Only the voluminous cotton nightgown kept his fingers from touching bare skin.

He could feel the heat of her body and the arc of the curve. Ugly clothes or not, she was a woman, down to her toes. An attractive woman who, for reasons he couldn't explain, appealed to him.

Touching her hip made him think about touching other parts of her body...such as her breasts. Need flared inside, bringing his own male heat to life.

Down boy, he told himself. Not this night, not with this woman. Still, a man could dream.

"Sometimes it seemed easier not to go out," she continued, apparently unaware of the change in circumstances. "Not that there are all that many guys beating down my front door." She glanced up at him again. "I'm sure you dated a lot."

"Some."

Color flared on her cheeks. "You've probably even... you know."

Uh-oh. He deliberately moved his hand away from her body and rested it on the mattress.

She cleared her throat. "You've probably been with a woman before."

He stared at her. "Are you talking about sex?"

She blushed fiercely and nodded.

Hell. Why were they talking about this? "I've had my way with a woman or two," he said.

"What's it like?"

Now it was his turn to groan. "We are *not* having this conversation."

"I know it's not appropriate, but just once I would like someone to give me some details."

She wouldn't be getting them from him, that's for sure.

Haley sat up and looked at him. "You've been really nice, but I'm feeling much better after the shower." She yawned. "I guess I'm tired. You don't have to stay if you don't want to."

"I know." He thought about leaving and realized he wasn't all that much in a hurry to go. "I'll head out in a little while."

She smiled at him, then. A warm, welcoming smile that stirred something in his chest. Something he hadn't felt before. Then she picked up the remote on the nightstand before settling back against him.

"Do you know they have cable here? We never had cable. There's lots of really cool channels. Even one of those shopping shows."

"Great," he muttered. "Maybe we could finish watching the ball game instead."

"Wouldn't you rather shop?"

"Not really."

She laughed. "Okay. Baseball, then shopping. How's that?"

"Sounds good."

* * *

Kevin didn't remember falling asleep, but suddenly he came awake. Several bits of information flashed into his brain at once. First, he was in a strange bed, on top of the covers. He knew the woman in his arms, but not how she got there. Second, a man on television was holding up what looked like a pair of diamond earrings and listing all sorts of reasons one should purchase them. Third, his cell was going off.

He flipped on the lamp on the nightstand and pulled the phone from its spot on his belt. The emergency message chased the last clouds of sleep from his brain.

He listened to the information, swore, then hung up. Haley had stirred enough to ask what was going on.

"I have to go," he said as he pulled on his shoes. "There's a riot at the prison. I need to get there now."

Haley's blond hair had dried in spikes that stuck up all over her head. She blinked sleepily.

"A riot?"

"Yup."

Which was exactly how his day had been going. He paused and bent long enough to scribble a number on the pad by the phone.

"This is my cell number," he said as he straightened. "Leave me a message in the morning to let me know you're okay. Agreed?"

She sat up and nodded. Her big eyes studied him. "I didn't thank you for everything."

"Thank me on the phone. I gotta run."

Kevin was out the door before Haley could think of anything else to say. She clicked off the television, then slid over to turn out the light. His side of the bed was warm. She curled up in the dark and thought about all that had happened in the past few hours. She smiled as she realized she'd finally slept with a man. All things considered, the experience had been pretty wonderful.

Chapter Three

Haley woke with the sensation that she was late. Before her eyes had focused she was trying to figure out if it was choir practice or her morning to visit the shut-ins or—

Then she blinked and realized she didn't recognize her bedroom.

In the split second it took to view the unfamiliar dresser, the window in the wrong place and the television, the events of the previous evening flashed through her mind like a silent music video. The montage included her entrance into the bar down the street, those scary men who had tried to get her to sit with them, and her rescue by Kevin Harmon. From there she recalled the margaritas, her reaction to the drinks and—

Here the memories got a little fuzzy. Or maybe it was just that she didn't *want* to remember, because honestly, it was too embarrassing to think that she'd actually thrown herself at a man. Worse, he'd turned her down.

Haley groaned and buried her face in her pillow. The

exact sequence of events wasn't clear, but she definitely recalled something about wanting to be forbidden fruit, then having to throw up. They hardly combined to make a good first impression. And through it all, Kevin had been perfect.

She sat up suddenly and brushed her too short bangs off her forehead, then stood cautiously and waited to see what her stomach was going to do. But except for an icky taste in her mouth, she felt fine. Certainly a whole lot better than she'd felt the previous night. Lying on that bathroom floor had been the closest she'd ever come to wishing for death. At least for herself.

Okay, she thought as she crossed to the bathroom, last night had been both good and bad. The good had been meeting Kevin. He'd taken care of her, treated her wonderfully, had brought her back here and stayed to make sure she was going to survive. More than that, he'd spent the night with her.

She smiled at the memory of falling asleep in his arms. Romantic things like that didn't happen to women like her.

She'd also found a drink she liked—although maybe two doubles were more than she could handle—and she'd actually spent time in a bar. If she kept this up, eventually she would be worldly.

Haley paused in front of the bathroom sink to pin back her hair, only to remember that she'd cut it all off on her way out of Ohio. She used a headband from her small cosmetics bag to hold her bangs off her face, then turned on the water.

The bad things about last night had been getting sick and throwing herself at a man who obviously didn't find her attractive. As she splashed water on her face, she tried to figure out if she could have said or done something to make herself more appealing to Kevin. Was it something specifically about her, or was she not his type? Not that she knew what being someone's type meant. She didn't have a type that she knew of, except for "not Allan."

She straightened and pulled the hand towel from the rack. Kevin had been nice and had stayed until he'd gotten called away. So he couldn't have disliked her too much.

"There is no way you're going to figure this out," Haley told herself as she started the shower, then stripped off her nightgown. "The inner workings of the male mind are a complete mystery."

That decided, she stepped into the warm spray and contented herself with the memory of him holding her close as they stretched out together on the bed.

Thirty minutes later Haley was dressed, packed and eating a breakfast consisting of coffee made in the in-room pot and a granola bar she'd brought with her. She would have liked something more substantial, but she hadn't seen any fast-food places on her way into town and she hadn't worked up the nerve to eat alone in a regular restaurant. Plus, she wasn't sure how her stomach was going to react to a big meal just yet. Maybe it would be better to take things slow.

She sat on the bed and peeled back the wrapping on her breakfast, all the while staring at the phone number written on the small pad. Kevin's cell number. Before he'd left he'd asked her to phone to let him know she was all right. Part of her wanted to hear his voice again, but part of her was still pretty embarrassed by everything that had happened. He'd done more than enough. She shouldn't bother the poor man.

Indecision made her shift on the bed. As she nibbled on the bar, she reached for the television remote and clicked on the TV to distract herself. A well-dressed, thirty-something woman spoke directly to the camera.

"We'll go to that footage in a moment. Our live shots

confirm what the authorities are telling us. The prison riot seems to have ended."

Haley stared at the screen. Prison riot? Hadn't Kevin said something about delivering a prisoner?

"As you can see from this video taken last night, several prisoners started a riot that turned violent. There were over two dozen injuries, including at least three gunshot wounds. One U.S. Marshal was taken to a local hospital at about five this morning."

As the woman spoke, the camera panned over heavily armed authorities trying to subdue angry prisoners. From there, the shot focused on a man on a stretcher. The camera zoomed in on his face. Haley dropped her granola bar and came as close to swearing as she ever had in her life. Despite the blood on his face and the thick, blood-soaked bandage around his leg, she recognized the man being rushed to the ambulance.

It was Kevin.

Okay, she was an idiot, Haley thought an hour later as she paced in the hospital waiting room. What had she been thinking when she'd decided to check on Kevin at the hospital? Or *had* she been thinking?

One second she'd been stunned by the live news report and the next she'd been loading up her car and asking the guy at the motel's front desk how to get to the hospital. Now that she was here, what was she going to do? She didn't know Kevin. Not really. He was a competent grown-up who didn't need her checking on him and probably wouldn't appreciate her visit.

She crossed to the door and nearly left, then turned back and walked the length of the room. Okay, she was here. The nurse said she could see him in a few minutes. She would go into his room, thank him for the previous night and duck out while she still had some small measure of dignity.

"Are you here to see Kevin Harmon?"

Haley turned toward the speaker and saw a nurse standing in the doorway.

"Yes." Haley approached the woman. "Is he all right?"

"Actually he's doing surprisingly well, for a man who was shot." She smiled. "He's in Room 247. Right down at the end of the hall."

"Thanks."

Haley clutched her purse to her stomach and headed down the hall. As she walked, she tried to figure out what exactly she was going to say. After "Hi," her brain sort of stalled. She supposed she could pretend he was just another sick parishioner. She'd visited hundreds of them over the years.

Yes, that was it. She would think of Kevin as just one more member of her father's congregation. Not the man who had rescued her and then turned down her offer of carnal knowledge of her person.

The hospital door stood open. Haley knocked softly as she entered. There was only one bed in the room. The man in it turned his head as she entered, giving her a clear view of his face. Her feelings of concern turned to dread as she took in his bruised face and the bandage around his head. Where it wasn't bruised, his skin was pale in contrast to his thick, dark hair. His eyes were only partially open. One leg was propped up on a pillow and a thick bandage encircled his thigh.

"Kevin?"

He managed a slight smile. "You should see the other guy."

She bit her lower lip as she approached. "You look really beat up. How do you feel?"

"Like I was shot."

"I saw you being taken away on television. That's how I found out what happened."

"Thanks for visiting." He motioned to a straight-back chair against the wall. "Take a load off."

She pulled the chair closer and settled next to him. Without thinking, she took his hand in hers and squeezed. His fingers were warm and strong, and more than a little distracting.

"Is there anything I can do to help?"

His mouth curved up again. "Yeah. Don't talk to me about being fruit."

She remembered bits and pieces of their conversation of last night, when she'd wanted to be forbidden fruit. Embarrassment flooded her, making her cheeks burn. She quickly dropped his hand and stared at the floor.

"Yes…well, I wasn't exactly myself."

"For what it's worth, I liked whoever you were."

She raised her head and stared at him. "Really?"

"Absolutely."

"But I was an idiot."

"You were charming."

"I was drunk."

"A charming drunk."

Their eyes locked. Despite the bruising and the bandage, Haley found herself getting lost in his gaze. Her insides shivered slightly. Her heart beat faster. A strange, unexpected yearning filled her and while she couldn't say for what, she ached with need.

The powerful sensation frightened her, so she did her best to ignore it. She forced herself to look away from Kevin's face. Instead, she focused on the bandage around his head.

"Was the riot the reason you were called away last night?" she asked.

"Yeah. They knew I was still in the area. All available personnel were summoned. By the time I got there, the riot had already turned dangerous."

"What started it?"

"It seems the prisoner I delivered yesterday had a lot of enemies in residence. A few of them got together and tried to kill him. They jumped a guard and took his gun." He touched his injured leg. "I got caught in the cross fire. Just dumb luck."

Haley didn't know what to say. Kevin spoke matter-of-factly, as if this sort of thing happened every day. "Have you ever been shot before?" she asked.

"Nope. And let me tell you, it hurts like a sonofa—" He caught himself and grinned. "It hurts a lot."

"You can swear. I don't mind. In fact, I plan on learning to swear."

"You're kidding."

She shook her head. "I don't want to do it a lot and there are some words I'm not interested in using. Once I learn to do it, then I can figure out if I like it or not. I was thinking of mostly the D-word or the H-word."

Kevin closed his eyes. "I've never heard anyone call it 'the D-word' before."

"I can't actually say it here."

He opened one eye. "In my room?"

"I'm in a hospital."

"That's not exactly like being in church."

"I know, but serious things happen here. Sometimes people die."

He opened his other eye. "You can't swear where people are dying?"

"No. Death is a sacred experience."

He rubbed his forehead. "You're from another planet, aren't you?"

"Sometimes it feels like I am," she admitted, thinking

how different her world was from his. "I did very well in my classes at college, but none of them prepared me for this sort of thing."

"Are we talking about swearing or prison riots."

"Both."

"Uh-huh." He closed his eyes again.

She took the opportunity to study him. Even with his injuries, he was a tough-looking man. She supposed he should have frightened her, but he didn't. She knew that underneath the power and muscles beat a good and noble heart. He wasn't the kind of man to take advantage of a defenseless woman. Which was just her bad luck.

"How long will they keep you in the hospital?" she asked.

"Overnight. They want to make sure my head injury isn't serious. Somebody nailed me with a metal chair. I ducked, but not fast enough." He fingered the bandage. "There's some bruising around my inner ear, so I'm a little wobbly."

After last night, she knew the feeling.

"What about your leg?"

"It was a clean shot. Through the meat. It'll need regular changing, but it's just a matter of letting it heal."

He'd spoken without opening his eyes. Haley had the feeling that he was getting tired. She knew she should go and let him rest, but first she had to thank him for all that he'd done for her. And apologize.

"Kevin, I—"

A faint ringing interrupted her. He opened his eyes.

"Dammit, that's my cell phone," he mumbled, turning his head toward the sound. "It's in my jacket pocket. Probably in the closet. Would you get it?"

"Sure."

She rose and crossed to the small closet. As she opened the door, the ringing got louder. She pulled the phone out of his chest pocket and carried it to him. Kevin pushed a button.

"Harmon," he said, his voice brisk and all business.

A little shiver went through her. He was competent, she thought. So in charge. Not like any man she'd ever met, certainly nothing like Allan.

She crossed to the window and tried not to listen, but when he chuckled and said, "Hi, Mom," she couldn't help tuning in to the conversation.

She wouldn't have thought of him as someone with a mother. Not that she'd assumed he'd hatched from under a rock or anything, but for him to have a family meant he was just like everyone else. But now that she thought about it, she remembered him mentioning a brother. That part of last night was still a little blurry.

"Nothing much," he said, his words filled with warmth and affection.

Haley recognized the emotions and they warmed her. She liked that Kevin cared about his mother. Some people didn't get along with their folks. She'd never understood that. Didn't parents always do their best?

Her own father sometimes made her crazy, but she knew every action was motivated by love. Her need to get away wasn't about her father—at least not completely. There was also Allan, and her need to grow up and be independent.

"No, I'm okay," Kevin was saying. "What? I'm in the hospital. I was shot."

Haley couldn't help glancing over her shoulder at him. He held the phone away from his ear and gave her an "aren't parents a pain, even though we love them" look that made her feel as though she was part of the in crowd.

The momentary connection lightened her spirits. She'd never felt it with a man before. She'd thought that sort of thing only happened with girlfriends. It had certainly never happened with Allan, but a lot of things hadn't happened with him.

"No, you don't have to come get me," Kevin said. "I'll be fine. Yes, I'll be home in a couple of days. You're sure it's not an emergency, Mom? Promise?"

He listened for a couple of minutes, then sighed. "Mom, you don't have to worry. No, they don't think I'll have a limp, but I'll have a scar and you know how chicks go for scars."

Haley turned her attention back to the window and tried not to think about the scar on Kevin's leg. Would she find it attractive? She was female, but she'd never thought of herself as a chick.

"Okay. I'll keep you informed. I love you, too. Bye, Mom."

She heard a high-pitched *beep* as he disconnected the call.

"How did she take it?" she asked, turning back to face him.

"Not bad, considering. She's distracted. Apparently a family situation has come up in the past couple of days."

"What does that mean?"

"Hell if I know. She says it's not an emergency, but she also told me we have to talk. What is it about women and conversation?"

Haley was momentarily distracted by his easy use of the H-word. It took her a second to respond to his question.

"Men have conversations, too."

"Maybe, but we never start them with the words 'we have to talk.'" He shuddered. "Four of the most frightening words in the English language."

She laughed. "Why?"

"Because they usually mean the guy has screwed up somewhere. He's in big trouble and she's about to tell him everything he's going to have to do to make it right. Who wants to hear that?"

"I see your point," she said, which reminded her of her own. She crossed to the bed.

"I don't want to stay too long. I know you need your rest. But I did want to thank you for last night."

He brushed aside her comment with a wave of his hand. "No big deal."

"It was to me. You were very considerate and I appreciate that." She clutched her purse tightly in both hands. "I'd never been drunk before."

"No kidding."

She shifted her weight from foot to foot. "I didn't really mean for that to happen."

"I don't buy that for a second, Haley. You were ordering margaritas, so you meant for something to happen."

"I guess you're right." She circled the bed and sank down into the chair. "Life is very confusing right now. I have a lot of decisions to make about my life. I thought the drive would give me time to think things through."

"Long drives always work for me." He smiled at her. "It's only been a couple of days. Give yourself a break. You'll get it figured out."

His faith in her made her smile. "Thanks. What about you? What are you going to do?"

"First, take advantage of the very generous hospitality here. I'm off duty until I'm cleared by the doctor. It could be three or four weeks."

"Will you go home?"

"As soon as I can."

"Do you want me to take you to the airport?"

He shook his head, then winced and touched the bandage. "You don't have to stick around for me. Besides, I'm not flying home."

"Why not?"

He pointed to his bandaged ear. "Until the swelling goes down, I'm not allowed in the air. Something about pressure and elevation."

She glanced at his injured leg. "So how will you get there?"

"Drive."

"How?"

"I'll wait until I'm well enough."

Haley didn't know that much about gunshot wounds, but she didn't think they healed all that quickly. Not when the bullet had gone all the way through his leg.

A thought occurred to her. It wasn't as if she had an appointment or anything. Driving was driving. So what if she got to California a few days late? She could offer to take him home.

She glanced at him, then away. Maybe that wasn't a good idea. Kevin had been really nice and everything, but he obviously didn't find her attractive. Would he want to spend that much time in her company? Still, she owed him. She should at least offer. It was the right thing to do.

What she refused to acknowledge, even to herself, was the sense that she didn't want to say goodbye. There was something about being around him that made her feel good about herself.

"I've taken several first-aid classes," she said cautiously. "We offer them at the church and in the past couple of years, I've been teaching them. So I have some basic first-aid knowledge."

He watched her without speaking. Haley cleared her throat.

"My point is, I could probably change your bandage."

"Thanks, but if I can't do it myself, I'll just make my way to the hospital."

"I didn't mean I would stay here. I was offering to drive you home."

It seemed that he was still inviting trouble into his life, Kevin thought as Haley spoke. She detailed all the reasons it made sense for her to help him, concluding with, "I owe you for last night. For not, um, well, taking advantage of me."

The last couple of words came out as a mumble. She ducked her head and he could barely make out what she was saying. Still, it was enough for him to remember helping her back to her room. Even drunk and practically incoherent, she'd been appealing. Too appealing.

There was no way he could spend that much time with her. Shot or not, even with his head pounding, even with her in another hideous floral-print dress that looked more like a tent than a fashion statement, he wanted her. Yup, right here under the scratchy sheet, with the painkiller coursing through his veins, his groin throbbed with an ache that had nothing to do with recent injuries.

Spending time with Haley, even the day or two it would take to get to Possum Landing, would be a level of torture he didn't deserve.

She was too sweet, too innocent, too...everything. She deserved way more than the likes of him.

"I don't want to hold you up," he said, trying to sound gentle instead of horny. "Don't you have an island to drive to?"

She smiled slightly. "I already told you, I know I can't drive to Hawaii."

She looked at him. Despite being a grown woman, she obviously didn't know how to conceal what she was thinking. He could see every thought flashing through her big eyes. Hope, fear, excitement. He made her nervous, but he could see she still wanted him to say yes. For reasons that weren't clear to him, she wanted to spend time in his company.

Why? Did she see him as some knight who had come to her rescue?

"I'm not one of the good guys," he told her, angry at her for thinking the best of him and angry at himself for caring.

She frowned. "Of course you are. You're a U.S. Marshal. And last night—"

"Just forget about that. It doesn't count."

"It does to me."

Trouble, he thought again. She *was* trouble, he was *in* trouble and damn if it wasn't going to get worse.

He shouldn't say yes, but he couldn't say no. Somehow he'd been trapped.

Last night, she'd wanted him to kiss her. If she hadn't been drunk, he would have obliged. Then what would have happened? Stupid question. He already knew the answer.

If he wasn't strong enough to turn down her offer to drive him home, how was he going to resist anything else she might choose to throw his way?

"Be careful what you wish for," he told her. "You just might get it. And then where will you be?"

Haley blinked at him. "Was that a yes?"

He was slime. Actually, he was the single-celled creatures that aspired to be slime. He was going to hell for sure.

"Yes."

Chapter Four

The next day, despite several protests and some muttered grumbling, Kevin found himself being wheeled out of the hospital. The practice of forcing patients to leave via wheelchair didn't make sense to him. The second he was gone, he would be on his own and expected to walk, so why not now?

The drill-sergeant-looking nurse hadn't been impressed by his argument.

But his mild humiliation and annoyance were instantly forgotten when he was wheeled out in front of the main building and saw Haley waiting for him. Sure he noticed her—she had on yet another of her incredibly ugly shapeless dresses that fell nearly to her ankles and covered her arms down to the elbow. Somewhere underneath the faded-purple, floral-print fabric was a great body, not that anyone could tell by looking. Yet it wasn't Haley that captured his attention. Instead, it was her car.

He was a typical guy with some interest in cars. Faster

was always better than slower. Sleek was a nice bonus. Haley was a conservative young woman from a small town. He would have guessed she drove a sensible sedan of some kind. Nothing flashy. Nothing outrageous. He could never have put her with the massive pale yellow Cadillac convertible she stood next to.

It had stopped raining at some point between his being shot and now, which was a good thing because the top was down.

He shook his head to clear his vision—obviously this was an illusion—then wished he hadn't when pain exploded behind his eyes. When he could speak without wincing, he squinted slightly and told her, "This can't be your car."

She beamed. Really. It was like looking into the sun. "Isn't it fabulous? Don't you love it?" She opened the passenger door and stroked the buff-colored leather. Not exactly a practical color.

"I traded my car in for this. There's no way you would have fit in my old car. Not with your leg and all. I saw this on the lot and fell in love. I've never felt this way about a car before. It's spectacular."

He wasn't sure if she meant the vehicle or her feelings for it, then he decided he didn't want to know. "How much did you pay?"

"Oh, I got a great deal."

"Uh-huh." Somehow he wasn't convinced.

The nurse helped him to his feet. He shifted his weight, took a single step and slid onto the smooth leather. He had to admit it was certainly big enough. With the passenger seat all the way back, he could stretch out his injured leg and still have room to spare.

"Thanks," Haley said to the nurse, then took the paper sack holding Kevin's belongings from her and tossed it into the back seat. She shut his door and walked around to the driver's side.

"This is going to be so great," she said when she'd settled into her seat. "I stopped and got maps. I have our route all figured out. It took me a while to find Possum Landing, but then I did. A mechanic checked out the car for me and swears it won't be any trouble at all."

Kevin squinted against the sun and wished he had his sunglasses, or at least a hat to protect him from the glare. The late morning was warm. At least the heat felt good.

"You don't even know where we are. How did you find a mechanic?"

"I called a local church and asked the minister's secretary to recommend one. When I explained the problem, she said her brother was a mechanic and that he would be happy to help. He even came with me to the dealer."

Smart move, he conceded. Maybe she hadn't been robbed. "You've had a busy morning."

"I had fun." She started the engine. "We need to go by your motel and get your things. I'm all checked out and packed. Then we can head out. I figure it will take us four days to get to Possum Landing."

Kevin leaned his aching head against the headrest and closed his eyes. Three seconds later they popped open. "Four days? It can't be more than six or seven hundred miles." They could practically do that in a day.

"I know." Haley put the car in drive and headed out of the parking lot. "I like to go about two hundred miles a day. There are so many wonderful things to see."

He closed his eyes again. "Like what?" he asked, already sure he didn't want to know.

"Little out-of-the-way towns, museums, antique shops. I've had the best time exploring the country since I left Ohio. You meet the most interesting people."

How could he argue with that? He'd met her.

"Four days, huh?"

"It will be fun," she promised.

Maybe. Maybe not. He figured he could have stayed put, healed in a motel and been able to drive home in about the same amount of time it was going to take Haley to deliver him.

"Oh." She glanced at him, her smile fading. "I forgot. You need to get home quickly. You have that family thing going on."

She was wearing sunglasses, but he could imagine the light fading from her eyes. He remembered his mother's promise that everything was fine and what she had to discuss with him wouldn't go anywhere. She'd said it wasn't about anyone being sick or dying. As she'd never lied to him in the past, he had no reason to doubt her now.

"It's not an emergency," he said before he could stop himself. "We don't have to rush."

"Really?"

The smile returned and when it did, something inside him sparked to life. He didn't want to know what it was, or what it all meant. Just his luck, he was going to be trapped in a car with Haley for several days. While his injuries distracted him now, what would happen when he started to heal and found himself wanting her? Did he have enough self-control to do the right thing?

Hell of a way to find out, he thought as he closed his eyes again and tried to relax. Beside him, Haley turned on the radio. "Pink Cadillac" was playing. Wouldn't you just know it?

Haley drove to the row of motels by the bar where she and Kevin had first met. He directed her to the plain two-story building where he'd rented a room. She found a parking space right in front, turned off the engine, then circled around the car to help him to his feet.

"I'm fine," Kevin protested as she swung open the passenger door.

She reached into the back and handed him the cane he'd been given in the hospital. He used it to push himself slowly to his feet. Once there, he wobbled a bit. She moved close and started to put an arm around his waist.

"I'll be okay," he said, and took a step toward the motel door.

As Haley watched, some of the color seemed to drain from his face, leaving behind pale skin and multiple purple-and-red bruises. They'd removed the bandage from around his head. The bandage on his thigh was still in place. It was thick and very white against his skin where someone had cut the right leg of his jeans off just below the crotch to get them over the bandage.

"You look like you're going to fall over," she said, trying not to sound too worried. "I don't think I can pick you up on my own."

He glanced at her and almost smiled. "Thanks for the news flash. I'll keep it in mind."

He took small, halting steps toward the motel door, then fished the key out of his jeans' pocket. Haley grabbed the bag of his belongings from the back seat and followed him into the small room.

The space wasn't all that different from the room she'd had. Full-size bed, TV, a small dresser and a bathroom off to one side. Kevin sank onto the only chair in the room and sucked in a breath.

"Okay, maybe crutches would have been a better idea."

She studied the sweat on his face. "We could go back to the hospital and get them."

He shook his head. "By tomorrow I'll be fine."

She had her doubts, but didn't say anything. He was trying to act tough, but he wasn't doing a very good job of it. No doubt getting hit in the head and shot took a lot out of a man. If she'd been the one in his position, she would have refused to leave her hospital bed for a least a week.

He jerked his head toward the small closet. "My overnight bag is in there."

She crossed to the louvered door and pulled it open. A black duffel bag sat on the carpeted floor. "Is this it?" she asked.

"I was only planning to spend the night."

She thought about the three suitcases of her belongings that were currently in her trunk. Of course she hadn't had much of a plan when she'd decided to run for freedom, so she'd pretty much packed all her clothes.

She set the empty duffel on the bed and went into the bathroom first. An electric shaver, can of deodorant, toothbrush and toothpaste and a brush and comb sat on the small glass shelf. Haley put them into the black zip-up container sitting on the back of the toilet, then checked the shower for shampoo. There was only a small bottle provided by the motel.

She returned to the bedroom and tucked the shaving kit into the duffel, then turned her attention to the paper sack from the hospital.

His jacket was inside. The garment had been rolled up. When she shook it out, something hard, dark and scary fell onto the bed.

A gun.

Haley jumped back as if she'd been bitten by a snake.

Despite his battered appearance, Kevin managed a low chuckle. "Don't panic. The safety's on."

"How do you know?"

"I checked it myself. Bring it here and I'll show you."

Bring it? As in, pick it up and carry it? Haley sucked in a breath, then very carefully picked up the gun. It was cold and heavier than it looked. She crossed to where Kevin was sitting. He took it from her and pointed to a small lever.

"See how it's down?"

She nodded.

"That means the safety is on. It won't go off."

"Is it loaded?"

"Yes."

She'd never seen a gun before, not in the flesh, so to speak. And certainly not one that was loaded. She and Kevin were not from the same place at all, she thought.

She eyed the deadly weapon. "Have you ever killed anyone?" she asked without thinking.

The silence in the room grew, pushing against her until she wanted to drag the words back and never even think the question. Kevin tossed the gun onto the bed and rubbed the bridge of his nose.

"Don't ask questions unless you want the answer," he told her.

Haley sucked in a breath. He glanced at her and in that second she saw the truth in his eyes. He *had* killed someone. She saw the flicker of ghosts, the echo of pain.

"Rethinking your invitation to drive me home?" he asked wryly.

"Of course not. You'd never hurt me. Whoever you shot deserved it."

"You sound sure of yourself."

"I am."

"Does anyone deserve to die that way?"

"Did you have a choice?"

"No."

"That's good enough for me."

She walked to the dresser, but before she could pull out a drawer he spoke her name. She turned to him.

"Just like that?" he asked. "You're not curious, not worried?"

"You said you didn't have a choice. I believe you."

His dark eyes narrowed. "I could be lying."

"You're not."

"Maybe trusting me isn't such a good idea."

That made her smile. "The fact that you're trying to warn me about yourself only reinforces my point." She pulled out the dresser drawer and froze.

Logically she'd known she was helping him pack his clothes. That's why she was here. So it made sense that she would be seeing his clothes, even touching them as she put them into his duffel. But knowing and doing it were two different things.

She stared at the neatly folded pair of briefs—dark blue briefs—and the clean socks. But it was the underwear that caught her attention. She'd never seen a man's underwear before. Well, okay, she'd seen her father's on occasion, although the housekeeper usually did the laundry. Her father wore plain white boxer shorts. Not dark blue briefs.

"Everything all right?" Kevin asked.

She nodded without speaking, then scooped up the garments and tossed them into the bag. In the next drawer down was a clean T-shirt. There weren't any other clothes.

"I hadn't planned on an extended trip," he said when she straightened. "I guess we should stop somewhere and get me a few things. I remember there being a Wal-Mart store just off the highway. That should work."

"You don't have any pajamas."

He grinned. "Never bother with 'em."

"Oh."

So what did he sleep in? His clothes? No, that didn't make sense. His—

"Nothing."

She looked at him and blinked. "Excuse me?"

"You were wondering what I slept in. I told you. Nothing. I sleep naked."

The N-word. Heat flared instantly and she pressed her hands to her cheeks.

"You've got to get out more," he told her, chuckling.

She dropped her hands to her sides and nodded. "I guess so."

Naked. She didn't want to think about it. She didn't want to think about anything else. What would it be like to be so comfortable with herself and her body that she would be able to sleep without clothes? She couldn't imagine that happening.

It only took a few more minutes for her to double check the room, then help Kevin back to the car. She put his half-full duffel in the trunk, then returned the room key to the front desk.

He directed her toward the Wal-Mart. As she drove she couldn't help thinking about his colored briefs and the fact that he slept naked and that last night she'd wanted him to kiss her. He'd refused, but for a second, she'd wondered if he'd been tempted. Maybe if she hadn't thrown up he would have done it. And then what? Would things have progressed?

She glanced at him sitting next to her and knew that she wouldn't have protested. Even beat-up Kevin looked good. Last night he'd been...delicious.

She smiled slightly. No man had ever fit that description before, but he did. And she knew that he would never have pushed her too far. He wouldn't have made her feel uncomfortable and she would bet that he would have been a really good kisser. In fact, despite the bruises and the bullet wound, she still wanted to kiss him. Very much.

But she wouldn't say anything. Mostly because without the courage brought on by margaritas, thinking about it wasn't nearly as rough as actually convincing him to do it. Still, they were going to be together for several days. Who knew what could happen in all that time?

The sight of the Wal-Mart up ahead broke through her musings. She made a mental note to fantasize about Kevin another time and pulled into the parking lot.

She was lucky enough to find a spot up front, which meant Kevin didn't have to hobble very far. When she'd settled him into a seat at the snack bar, she sat across from him and pulled a piece of paper out of her purse.

"We'll need supplies for changing your bandage," she said, and started writing.

"New jeans," he said. "The bandage will be smaller in a couple of days and regular jeans will fit. Thirty-four waist, thirty-six inseam."

Haley scribbled the numbers down, not sure what they meant. But she hoped she would figure it out when she hit the men's department.

"Socks, briefs. Plain white is fine."

She glanced at him and saw humor brightening his eyes. So he *had* noticed her embarrassment when she'd seen his underwear.

"Maybe a couple of shirts?" she asked, trying to act as though this was no big deal.

"Yeah, but nothing fancy. T-shirts, polo shirts, whatever."

"Okay. I'll turn your pain-medicine prescription in first and pick it up when I'm done. You're going to want to stay here, right?"

He nodded. "I'm not feeling strong enough to walk the aisles and I'm too big to be pushed around in a cart."

She smiled. "Do you want something to eat or drink?"

"Maybe some water."

She got him a bottle of water and a pretzel from the attendant at the snack bar, then collected a cart for herself and headed out.

After turning in the prescription and collecting the medical supplies she would need, she walked back to the men's department. She went for easy first, and perused the jeans. Kevin's size information instantly made sense and she collected a pair to fit his specifications. They were new and a little stiff, so she made a mental note to do laundry tonight when they stopped.

Next up were shirts. She bought three, two short-sleeved T-shirts and a light blue polo shirt. Underwear was next. Haley felt her face flame as she pushed her cart into the rows of packaged briefs and boxer shorts. She grabbed two sets of three pairs, a bag of socks, and nearly ran toward the main aisle. A quick glance at her watch told her she had another fifteen minutes until the prescription would be ready.

She turned to go back to the snack bar, but slowed as she entered the women's department. It was June and the aisles were filled with light, pretty summer clothes. There were sleeveless shirts, floral print skirts, T-shirts and shorts.

She stopped at a rack of shorts and fingered the light cotton material. As if it had happened yesterday, she remembered her eleventh birthday. She'd had a great party with lots of friends, but when it was over, two of the mothers had stayed to talk to her. They'd carefully explained that she was going to be developing into a young woman soon, and young women dressed appropriately. It wouldn't do for the minister's daughter to be seen showing off her body.

At first, Haley hadn't understood, but eventually everything had been made clear. Shorts and shirts had been replaced by loose-fitting summer dresses that made her feel ugly. She'd been unable to climb trees or to even ride her bike. On her eleventh birthday she'd gone from being a kid to being a young lady, and she'd hated it.

Haley glanced down at her loose-fitting dress. It was sensible and not the least bit revealing. Allan had loved it. Then she turned her attention to cute summer clothes all around her. There were dozens of styles of shorts, with matching tops, and even cute little summer sweaters. She grabbed several of each in her size and moved toward the dressing room. On her way she picked up a sleeveless summer dress that would skim her curves, then came to stop in front of a display of feminine nighties and pj sets.

She picked out a light blue camisole with matching tap pants and a short nightgown with skinny straps and an appliqué declaring the wearer Queen of Everything.

Right in front of the dressing room was the lingerie. Haley stared at colored bras with matching bikini panties. There were bright colors and pastels, cotton, satin, nylon and—she gasped—animal prints. No plain white utilitarian undergarments in sight.

Instantly her conscience started telling her that she wasn't that kind of girl. Could she really see herself in a tiger print bra and matching panty?

"But I want to be that kind of girl," she murmured, and scooped up one of everything in her size.

After a flurry of activity in the dressing room, Haley settled on a week's worth of lingerie, three different styles of pj's, four pair of shorts with shirts for each, two sundresses that had nothing to do with the ugly garments she usually wore when it was warm, jeans and a denim skirt that didn't come close to touching her knees.

On her way to pick up Kevin's prescription she detoured through shoes and found a pair of strappy sandals and some white athletic shoes imprinted with rhinestones. She couldn't wait to get settled for the night to try on all her clothes again. Haley tried to remember the last time she'd been this happy, but no event came to mind. Maybe running away *had* been the right thing to do.

Kevin finished his bottle of water, ignored the pretzel and wished for a double dose of pain medicine. Every part of him hurt, even his hair. He couldn't tell how long Haley had been gone, but he sure as hell wished she would come back so they could leave.

Before he could figure out a way to have her paged, she appeared in front of him, pushing a cart overflowing with plastic bags.

"What did you buy?" he asked as he struggled to his feet.

"Just a few things." She was instantly at his side, helping him get upright, then supporting him.

"You look awful," she told him as they slowly made their way out of the store.

"Good. I feel awful. I like the two to match."

"Wait here."

She left him propped against the building and brought the car right up front, then eased him into the passenger seat. The world blurred a little as he leaned his head back.

He heard her putting away bags, then the driver's door slammed shut. The sound made his head ache more.

"You need to rest," she said as she placed her cool hand on his bruised cheek. "I'm going to get us a room for the night."

He thought about protesting. It wasn't even two in the afternoon and at her rate of travel, they couldn't afford to lose a day. But the thought of driving anywhere was impossible. Right now he just wanted something to take away the pain and he wanted to sleep.

"Here."

She pressed something into his hand. He opened one eye and saw a pill resting on his palm. She offered him a bottle of water. He downed the medicine and handed her back the bottle. She'd read his mind. He would have thought that was a bad quality in a woman, but in Haley's case, he was willing to make an exception.

"Don't worry," she said as she started the engine. "I'll take care of everything."

He thought about protesting that she couldn't take care of herself let alone someone else, but he couldn't form the words. Besides, there was a part of him that was willing to put his fate in Haley's small hands. Crazy, but true.

He might have dozed or just passed out. Sometime later, he felt Haley lightly touching his shoulder. He opened his eyes and saw that they were parked in front of a motel. At least it isn't pink, he thought, just coherent enough to be grateful.

Haley helped him to his feet, then led him into the room. She didn't look all that strong, but she didn't seem to be crumbling under his weight.

"You need to eat," she said as she opened the door and eased him inside. "But you should probably rest first."

She was taking care of him. Kevin tried to remember the last time that had happened. It had been years—maybe before he'd screwed up for the last time at home and had been sent to military school. If he remembered right, he'd stolen old man Miller's car. It had been a Caddy, too.

He chuckled at the similarity.

"What's so funny?" Haley asked.

"Just my past catching up with me."

"Let it catch up with you in bed. Here you go."

She stopped beside the bed and let him fall into a sitting position. Even as he collapsed back, she was shifting his legs so he was stretched out on the mattress.

Haley sat next to him and once again put her cool hand on his face. He liked her touching him. In any other circumstances, he would have asked her to touch a little lower. But things being as they were, he simply opened his eyes and gazed at her.

"I was afraid to leave you on your own for the night," she said, her blue-hazel eyes wide and serious-looking. "So we're sharing a room. I hope that's okay."

He turned his head just enough to see the other bed. "Fine by me," he rasped, feeling the pain medicine kick in. The edge came off his hurt and he was getting sleepy.

"I don't want you to think—" she began, then stopped.

"Right now, I'm not thinking at all. If you're expecting any action, kid, you're gonna have to come and get it because I'm not gonna be good for squat tonight."

He heard her suck in a breath and her cheeks might have been turning red, but things were starting to blur. He had one last coherent thought, and that was that she had a very kissable mouth. Then the room shifted once and everything went black.

Chapter Five

Kevin woke to a wonderful smell. He opened his eyes and saw Haley setting out a dinner of fried chicken, cole-slaw, corn and mashed potatoes on the small table by the window overlooking the parking lot. His stomach instantly cramped in anticipation of food. As he hadn't had much more than cereal in the hospital, he had a bad feeling that his last real meal had been the burger in the bar, nearly forty-eight hours before.

He pushed himself into a sitting position, was pleased that he only got a little dizzy, then lowered his feet to the floor. That movement sent a razor-sharp pain of protest through his thigh, but he ignored it.

"I hope you got plenty," he said, returning his attention to Haley. "Because I'm—"

Starved. That was the next word in the sentence. He knew it and he couldn't say it. He doubted he could say anything. Ever again.

She glanced over and smiled at him. "You look a lot

better than you did. You were out for nearly three hours. I guess you needed to rest. I broke my arm once, when I was little. It hurt a lot and I know I always felt better after sleeping. Not that a broken arm is anything like getting shot. Well, maybe it is. I don't know." She paused for breath and frowned. "Kevin? Are you all right?"

He was. At least he would be when consciousness returned. But until then he'd stepped into an alternative universe. Or hell. That was it. He'd died and this was hell. It couldn't be heaven because there was no way God would approve of what Haley was wearing.

Logically, Kevin knew that in warm weather women dressed in things like T-shirts and shorts. It was common. Expected even. He agreed, in theory. Just not Haley. She wore shapeless ugly dresses that covered her body like a shroud. She would never put on a tiny white T-shirt that barely came down to her waist and she would never be caught dead in tiny white shorts that settled low enough on her hips to expose her flat stomach and her delicate belly button. Would she?

"What the hell are you wearing?" he demanded, the words coming out a little more forcefully than he'd intended.

Haley jumped and set down the container of chicken. She glanced at herself, then back at him.

"Clothes."

He had a feeling she was doing her best to sound defiant. She didn't come close, but he gave her points for trying.

"What happened to your dress?"

"Nothing, except I hate it. I haven't worn shorts since I turned eleven. I figured it was long past time."

She pulled a quart of milk out of an ice bucket on the floor and poured them each a glass. As she bent to reach the far side of the small table, the T-shirt not only rode up a little, it gaped at her neckline and he could see down the front to the swell of her breasts and the white lace of her bra.

Desire and pain seemed to be battling it out. He was curious as to which would win.

She glanced at him out of the corner of her eye. Something about the set of her mouth and the tension in her shoulders told him she was expecting him not to approve. Kevin knew all about disappointing those who mattered most, and trying to balance between what was expected and what one really wanted. No way was he going to guilt Haley that way. Not on purpose anyway.

"You look nice," he said finally, and reached for his cane.

Haley was at his side in an instant and helped him to his feet. "Do you really think I look okay? This isn't too… brazen?"

Brazen? He held in a laugh. "If they sell it at Wal-Mart, it has to be all right."

"I hope so. I bought some other shorts and shirts, along with other things. While you were sleeping, I washed everything, including your jeans. They're not so stiff now."

As she spoke, she put her arm around his waist and led him to the table. He could feel her breast brushing again his side and he inhaled the sweet scent of her body. Speaking of stiff, he thought and sighed. In the battle of pain and desire, it seemed that baser instincts were going to win. He shouldn't even be surprised.

"I appreciate you doing the laundry," he said when he was at the table. "You got yourself into more than you bargained for by offering to drive me home."

She sat opposite him and picked up a napkin. "I don't mind. This is fun. If I were home I would be—" She stopped talking and pressed her full lips together.

"What would you be doing?"

"Nothing interesting."

"If you call driving me around and doing my laundry interesting, then you were right to run away."

She laughed. "You have a point. If nothing else, the motel has great cable."

"Aren't minister's daughters allowed to watch cable at home?"

"Sure, but there isn't much time for leisure activities."

"What sort of leisure activities *was* there time for?"

Haley took a bite of chicken and chewed slowly. Kevin couldn't help wondering if she was just being polite or stalling for an answer.

"I don't mean to make my life sound horrible," she said at last. "My father is a wonderful man who loves me very much."

"I don't doubt that. But sometimes it's hard living with a lot of expectations and rules."

Her eyebrows pulled together. "It is for me."

"Me, too." He shrugged. "My brother was always the perfect kid and I was always the one getting into trouble. I was forever getting grounded, then sneaking out, getting caught and being grounded again."

Haley nibbled on her coleslaw. "I never got in trouble at all. Sometimes I felt like I couldn't even think a bad thought without someone figuring it out."

"That would have been tough," he said. "I'm the kid who brought a box of cockroaches to school when I was seven and let 'em loose."

She stared at him. "You didn't."

He made an X over his chest. "Cross my heart."

"What happened?"

"There was a lot of screaming. I had detention for about six years. At least it felt that long."

She smiled. "I never had detention."

"It's not as fun as it sounds."

"I guess not. What else did you do?"

He wasn't sure if her curiosity about his checkered past was good or bad. "I got two of my friends drunk when we were nine, got caught shoplifting when I was fourteen. That was my first arrest. The first girl I kissed was fifteen and I was twelve and the first woman I ever—"

The self-editing switch kicked in just in time. Haley leaned forward. "Don't stop there."

He caught himself before he shook his head. There was no need to tempt fate with movements designed to leave him in agony. Besides, his loose lips had already gotten him into enough trouble.

"Let's just say she was an older woman."

"How old?"

"Nineteen."

"How old were you?"

He picked up an ear of corn. "This is a really great dinner."

"Kevin! How old?"

He sighed. "Fifteen."

She gasped. "You were fifteen the first time you ever…"

Her voice trailed off. Her expression hovered somewhere between horrified and impressed. He hoped she settled on the latter.

"I was a curious kid," he said.

"Obviously. And since then?"

He didn't catch the movement in time and shook his head. Instantly, pain exploded. He closed his eyes against it and when he opened them, he found her staring at him expectantly.

"No way," he told her. "I'm not getting into numbers."

"Can you give me a range?"

"Less than a hundred."

"More than ten?"

He sighed. "Yes."

"More than—"

"I'll tell you how many if you'll tell me what you're running away from."

As he suspected, that shut her up. She picked up another piece of chicken and took a bite. "It's not anything bad."

He grinned. "Haley, I doubt you've ever done anything wrong in your life."

"You're right. Which is why this is the perfect time to start."

Just what he needed. "Do me a favor," he said. "Wait to start a life of being bad until you've dropped me off home. I don't want to be responsible for leading you astray."

"But wouldn't you be really good at it?"

"Probably the best. But I'm already on shaky ground where my redemption is concerned. Taking you over to the dark side would push me over the edge. You wouldn't want that on your conscience, would you?"

"I don't know. I'll have to think about it."

Not exactly the answer he'd been hoping for.

Haley tried to concentrate on the cosmetics line being demonstrated on the television shopping channel. She'd never been one to wear much makeup and the skill required to line her upper lids had always eluded her, so the idea of a flat brush, almost like a mini paintbrush, to help with the application seemed sensible. Plus there were about a dozen color choices. She was leaning toward the dark purple, but then thought she might want to start with a more neutral brown or gray. Under other circumstances, she might have called and placed an order. Only two things stopped her.

The first was that she no longer had an actual address. She'd run away from home with no real destination in mind and she didn't plan on returning to her father's house anytime soon. The second problem was that she couldn't completely pay attention to the show. She was trying to, but at the same time she was listening intently for any sound coming from the bathroom.

Despite her protests, Kevin had insisted on taking a shower. She didn't think he should be standing for that long, nor was she sure he actually could. He'd sworn he would be fine and had even agreed to take his cane into the bathroom. At least there was a big bar in the shower, so he would have something to hold on to if he lost his balance. Still, she couldn't help worrying. If he fell, he could hurt himself even more than he already was. Plus, there was no way she was strong enough to lift him to safety.

So while the water ran, she tried to distract herself from her worry by watching TV. She'd already folded all the laundry she'd washed in the motel's machines. She'd put their new clothes away in the dresser drawers. The act had been oddly…intimate.

Funny how after all this time she was finally sharing a room with a man, and it was under circumstances she never could have imagined. She'd always assumed the first time she spent the night with a man, it would be after getting married. For the past several years, she'd pictured the man in question as Allan.

Kevin was about as different from Allan as it was possible for a man to be, which made the situation strange but not uncomfortable.

The water shut off. Haley half sat up, then flopped back down on the bed and watched the model on television apply lip liner. Her thoughts about which color she liked best were interrupted by a loud groan, then a grunt. She tensed, but didn't move. They'd agreed she would wait out here until Kevin called her in to change his bandage.

After a few minutes, water ran again, followed by silence and a couple more groans. Finally, when she could barely stand it, the bathroom door opened.

She was on her feet in an instant. "Are you all right?"

"I'm still standing. The bandage is soaking, so it needs changing. You sure you're up to that?"

"Absolutely." Haley had already collected the first-aid supplies. She scooped them up into her arms and headed toward the bathroom.

"Brace yourself," Kevin said, pushing the door open wide. "I managed to pull on a T-shirt, but I'm not wearing pants."

"No problem."

Haley spoke the words casually, even though her heart was pounding hard enough to bruise a rib. She told herself that seeing Kevin in briefs and a T-shirt was just like going to the beach. Not that she'd been since she was a kid. Actually he would be wearing more. She would be fine.

She stepped into the small, steamy room. The air was scented with soap and shampoo. After setting the fresh bandages and antiseptic cream on the narrow counter by the sink, she reluctantly turned her attention to the man sitting on the edge of the tub.

As promised he'd pulled on a loose-fitting T-shirt. He'd also draped a towel across his lap. She was both relieved and slightly curious about what he was covering up.

But this wasn't the time to deal with any of that. She sank to her knees and reached for scissors.

"Did you get dizzy? Does everything hurt?" she asked as she cut through the soaked bandage.

"Don't worry. The painkiller I took after dinner is kicking in."

"Which means you're dizzy but you don't care?"

He chuckled.

She glanced up and found herself getting lost in his brown eyes. He'd brushed his wet hair straight back. Two days' worth of stubble darkened his cheeks. He looked pretty darned good.

The bandage fell to the floor with a faint *thunk*. She pulled her attention from Kevin's face to his leg, then nearly fainted when she saw the raw wound from the gunshot.

"Haley? Are you going to pass out on me?"

Her stomach heaved once, but she ignored it. "I'm fine." It was only a white lie and shouldn't really count. She reached for the antiseptic cream and squeezed some on. Kevin's only reaction was to suck in his breath.

She worked quickly but gently. When the new bandage was secure, she rose and held out her arm.

"I'll help you into bed," she said.

He didn't protest, which told her how bad he was feeling. Together they made the short walk into the other room. She'd already pulled back the covers on his bed. He sat heavily, then shifted and stretched out on the mattress. Haley bent to grab the covers. But before she pulled them up she allowed herself one quick look.

Even with the bandage around his thigh, his legs looked powerful and long. His hips were narrow, his stomach flat. Broad shoulders pulled at the seams of his T-shirt. And his face—

When her gaze settled there, she realized he was watching her. Awareness brightened his eyes and turned up the corners of his mouth.

Horrified, she started to turn away, but he caught her wrist and held her in place.

"I don't mind you looking," he said, his voice low.

She kept her back to him. "I shouldn't have. You're injured."

"All the better to take advantage of me."

She spun back to face him. "I would never do that."

He chuckled. "I already figured that one out."

He released her and she pulled up the covers. When she would have stepped away, he patted the side of the bed.

"Have a seat."

She perched on the edge of the mattress, incredibly aware of her hip pressing against his body. He stunned her by taking her hand in his and lacing their fingers together. Heat filled her, making her breathing quicken. They were alone in a hotel room and he was holding her hand. How had she ever gotten so lucky?

"Tell me about the other men in your life," he said.

"What other men?"

"Yeah, that would be my point. Have you ever seen a man before?"

The question confused her. Of course she had. She could see him right now. Then she got it. Oh. "You mean—"

If he hadn't been holding her hand, she would have turned away.

"Naked, Haley. The word you're looking for is naked."

She stared at their fingers and at the way her wrist looked small and frail next to his. Instead of speaking an answer, she shook her head no.

"How did you get to the ripe old age of twenty-five without ever seeing a naked man?"

"They usually come to church with their clothes on." She risked glancing at him and saw him grin.

"Good point. Probably any boyfriends would worry

about what your father would have to say if they flashed the goods."

Flashed the goods? She was both shocked and amused. Would Allan have ever said anything like that to her? She couldn't imagine it.

"The other night you said you'd only kissed three guys. Is that true?"

She nodded, caught up in the fact that they'd only met a couple of days before. Somehow she felt as if she'd known Kevin forever.

"That's not very many," he said. "How can you compare technique and style with a sample of three?"

"It's been a problem. I never knew if I kissed okay and I didn't know how to ask."

When she'd gotten drunk, she'd been hoping Kevin would want to make it four and maybe give her some pointers, but he'd resisted her attempts to seduce him. It was just her luck to fall in with a gentleman.

"Haley, you don't have a clue as to what's going on, do you?"

"What are you talking about?"

"My point exactly."

He stared at her, his dark eyes seeming to see into her soul. His thumb brushed against the back of her hand in a way that left her more than a little breathless. The room seemed very quiet—she couldn't even hear the television.

"The thing is, with this painkiller, I'm pretty out of it."

"Sort of like me the other night."

"Exactly. So we're even."

She felt he was trying to tell her something, but she didn't know what.

"Do you want to kiss me?" he asked.

She would have thought she was done with her shocks

for the day, but no. Here was yet another one. Blood rushed from her head to her feet, which made the room spin, then hurried back in place. She tried to breathe and couldn't. Tried to stand, but not a single muscle so much as twitched.

"It's not like I'm in a position to protest," he told her.

She didn't understand. "But you said you weren't interested."

"I'm pretty damn sure I never said that. My point was that *I* wouldn't do anything about it. That point still stands."

"So you don't want to kiss me?" Hurt flared in her chest. Then why had he brought it up?

"I'm not going to take advantage of you. That doesn't mean you're under the same constraints."

She blinked. Her mind heard the words, processed them and sent the results back.

She could kiss him.

"Oh." She blinked again. "Oh!"

Kiss a man? Her? As in, initiate? As in, start it? As in—

"I can hear you thinking from here."

She looked at his face, then narrowed her gaze to his mouth. "I've never kissed a man before."

"Maybe you'll like doing it."

Maybe she would.

Slowly, carefully, she leaned forward. At some point Kevin's eyes closed, which was good because she couldn't remember ever being this nervous before in her life and the last thing she wanted was him watching her. When she was almost there, she closed her eyes, too, because she wanted to feel everything. Then her lips brushed against his.

Her breath caught at the sweet, hot pressure. His mouth was firm yet yielding and felt exactly right against hers.

She hovered there, not sure what to do. It had been years since she'd kissed anyone except Allan, and he'd always taken charge.

"Do whatever you want," Kevin murmured, once again reading her mind.

What did she want to do?

She pulled her hand free of his and gently touched his cheek. As she stroked his skin, she kissed him again, this time moving back and forth, pressing harder, then lighter, discovering possibilities. She found she liked being the one to kiss more, to pull back, to start again.

Tension swept through her body, making her legs tingle and her chest ache. The unfamiliar sensations forced her to lean closer. Kevin parted his lips in invitation and she didn't even hesitate before sweeping her tongue inside.

He tasted of minty toothpaste and something indescribably sweet. As they touched, fire seemed to leap between them. But the flames didn't burn. Instead, they pulled them closer together. He wrapped his arms around her, holding her against him. She could feel the pounding of his heart—somehow the rhythm matched her own.

She angled her head so they could kiss more deeply. They played and danced and circled and stroked. She wanted more. Funny how she wasn't clear on what that more might be, but she knew she wanted it. With Kevin. She trusted his strong hands to hold her and touch her. He would keep her safe on any journey.

She wasn't sure how long they kissed. Eventually the tingling in her thighs turned into something heavier and her breasts swelled uncomfortably in her new bra. Reluctantly, she sat up.

His eyes were dilated, his mouth swollen. They stared at each other without speaking. When he reached up and cupped her cheek with his palm, she turned her head to kiss his skin.

"You're full of surprises," he said, his voice low and husky.

She was a little surprised herself, but in a good way. She could feel her blood rushing through her body—reminding her of the pleasure of being alive. She'd just kissed a man for the first time ever. It had been great.

"Just for the record, you kiss fine."

"Maybe you should have kissed me last time I asked," she teased.

"No way. I wouldn't have stopped there."

"Really? You mean we would have—"

"Made love. A word of advice from someone who knows. Never do that when you're drunk."

His words made sense, but she would have to think about them another time. Right now she was too caught up in the concept of actually doing "it" with Kevin. Did that mean he wanted her? Was he aroused?

She didn't dare look and she couldn't ask. Did men get aroused just from kissing? What about making love? Did they—

He covered his ears. "Stop thinking so much."

He dropped his hands to his sides, then shifted and winced. She remembered his injuries.

"You'd better get some rest," she told him.

"Good idea. You going to be okay?"

"Uh-huh." Empowered by her recent experience, she bent and kissed his cheek. "Sleep well."

"I've created a monster," he muttered, closing his eyes. "You'd better not attack me in my sleep."

"I won't." But that didn't mean she wouldn't think about it.

* * *

Later that night, when Haley was sure that Kevin was asleep, she turned down the television and picked up the phone on the table between their beds. Using her newly purchased Wal-Mart calling card, she dialed the eight hundred number, entered her code, then the phone number for her father's office at the church. At this time of night the building would be deserted. She wouldn't have to worry about anyone picking up her call.

She listened to the four rings, followed by the answering machine message. When she heard the beep, she sucked in a breath and spoke quickly.

"Hi, Daddy. It's me. I wanted to call and let you know that I'm safe and well." She hesitated, not sure what else she should say. "I know you got my note, but that you'll still worry. I wish you wouldn't. I'm going to be okay. I just have to figure a few things out and I can't do that at home. I'm fine with Allan's decision. In fact I think he did the right thing. Please don't be too mad at him. I don't know how long I'll be gone. At least a few more weeks."

There was so much more she wanted to tell him, but not like this.

"I'll leave another message in a few days. I love you."

She hung up the phone. She didn't doubt that her father still cared about her. She was his daughter and nothing could make him stop loving her. But forgiving her was another matter entirely.

Chapter Six

They were on the road by ten the next morning. It was cooler and cloudy, so Haley had put the top up on the old Caddy, and rather than shorts, she'd dressed herself in jeans.

Kevin figured she should have been measurably less sexy with denim covering her legs, but she wasn't. He couldn't figure out if it was the cropped T-shirt that barely came to her waist or the confident bounce in her step. He'd noticed it as soon as she'd come out of the bathroom after her shower. She'd greeted him with a smile that had nearly sent him to his knees—fortunately he'd been lying down—and had sashayed across the room.

He tried to tell himself that her curves were no better than average. He'd always been partial to large-breasted women and while Haley didn't have anything to be ashamed of, she didn't qualify as busty. Nor was she as tall as he usually liked. And her—

He stopped himself in mid-thought because he knew

he was lying. Big breasts, small breasts, it didn't really matter. Something about Haley got to him. It had almost from the start. It didn't matter if she was covered in burlap and had a tail—he wanted her.

A night of sleep had left his leg slightly less painful and his head clear. Which meant he could remember every-thing that had happened the previous evening, including Haley's unexpectedly erotic kiss.

The whole thing had been a mistake. He shouldn't have made it clear that while he wouldn't kiss her she was free to kiss him. He should have kept his mouth shut—in more ways than one. Kissing her had taken things to the next level, and it was dangerous up there. After all, who was he kidding? A guy like him and a preacher's daughter? In what universe?

No. The right thing to do was to put the brakes on right now. There wouldn't be any more physical contact. No touching, no kissing. He wouldn't even tease her. They would have impersonal conversations. Maybe about the weather, or the scenery.

Not that there was much to look at right now. They were on the interstate, heading for Wichita. By his cal-culations they would be there by early afternoon. Haley said they would be lucky to make it by nightfall. She had several stops planned.

"I miss my hair," Haley said.

He turned to look at her. "What?"

She fingered her short blond hair and gave a quick shrug. "I cut my hair when I left home. It was an impulse. One I'm now regretting."

Regret was good. Haley was determined to take a walk on the wild side and someone needed to teach her consequences.

"Sometimes it's important to think things through," he said.

She nodded.

He knew he shouldn't ask. He really didn't want to know. But he couldn't help himself. "How long was it?"

"To my waist. I mostly wore it back in a braid."

She kept on talking, but he wasn't listening. Instead, he pictured her with long blond hair spilling down her back and over her shoulders. He pictured her naked, on top of him, moving lower, her hair tickling his thighs as she lowered her head and took him in her—

"Kevin?"

"Huh?"

"Are you all right? You seem tense."

He swallowed. "I'm great." And he would be right up until he slid into hell.

"You've mentioned your mother and your brother, but you haven't said anything about your dad. Is he still alive?"

He accepted the change in topic because the alternative was to be tortured by visions of what could never be. As his mind shifted gears, his body stopped heating, although it was going to be a long time until it cooled.

"I don't know where my biological father is," he said. "I don't know much about him. I know he was a lot older than my mom. She was seventeen when she got pregnant with Nash and me."

Haley sucked in a breath. "That's so young."

"She always says that he was a smooth talker who convinced her they were destined for each other. Before she knew what had happened, she was in his bed. That was in Dallas. He was in town for some kind of convention. After making promises to stay in touch, he went back to whatever rock he'd crawled out from under and she went home. Unfortunately for her, she turned up pregnant."

"He never contacted her again?"

"You got it." There was a time when even thinking

about his biological father made Kevin furious, but he'd learned to make peace with that which couldn't be changed. "Unfortunately my mom's parents weren't real supportive. They threw her out the day she turned eighteen. My brother and I were about three months old."

Haley glanced at him, her blue-hazel eyes dark with sympathy. "I don't understand that."

"Neither did she. A friend helped her out. That's when we moved to Possum Landing. For a while, Mom created a fake dead father to help us deal with not having a man around. I guess it was easier for her than answering a lot of questions. When Nash and I were twelve, her folks got in touch with us. They said they wanted to see us. At that point, Mom told us everything that had happened and said it was our decision. She refused to speak with them, but if we wanted a relationship with them, she wasn't going to stand in the way."

"Your mother sounds like a very special woman."

"She is. Nash and I talked it over and decided if they hadn't cared about us before, we didn't care about them now."

"You've never met them?"

"Nope."

"Any regrets?"

"Not about that."

"My father is an only child," Haley said. "I have a few aunts and cousins on my mother's side, but they all live in Washington state, so I've never had much to do with them. I always wanted a big family." Her voice sounded wistful.

"Then I guess you'll have to grow your own. Have a couple dozen kids."

"I'd settle for two or three. What about you?"

He shifted slightly and adjusted his seat belt. "I don't know. Maybe."

"You must have thought about it."

"Why?"

"Everyone does. It's part of growing up."

Maybe. "A couple would be okay, if they weren't like me."

"You told me some of the stuff you did when you were young and you weren't that bad."

"Right. Like you would know bad if it came up and bit you on the butt."

She laughed. "I probably would recognize it then."

"I doubt it. Your idea of a walk on the wild side is being five minutes late for choir practice or having two scoops of ice cream instead of one."

"So what's yours?"

Seducing an innocent woman like you.

"I did some things I'm not proud of," he said.

"Like what?"

"I stole a car."

"Yeah?" She sounded more impressed than shocked. Figures.

"It wasn't smart. I was arrested and as far as my mom and stepfather were concerned, it was the last straw. They sent me away to military school."

"If you went from being a car thief to being a U.S. Marshal, you must have done something right."

"I didn't like jail and I hated military school. For a couple of months I just felt sorry for myself, but eventually I figured out that I'd earned my place there and if I wanted another chance in the real world, I was going to have to earn that, too."

"Which you did."

"Yeah, but it's not as easy as it sounds. I'm only one mistake from being a screwup again."

She glanced at him. "Being bad sounds like fun."

"No way. Don't go there. There are consequences."

"Everyone always says that."

"Because it's true. Remember your haircut?"

She shook her head. "You have a point there, but maybe it was worth it. Maybe I needed to cut my hair as a symbol of my new life. Besides, just once I would like to be able to do something without worrying about what would happen later."

"Life doesn't work like that. Payback's a bitch."

The clouds had been moving steadily east. The sun broke through and Kevin reached for his sunglasses. Haley put hers on, as well.

"You say that so easily."

"Say what?"

"The B-word."

He stared at her. "Bitch?"

She gripped the steering wheel more tightly. "You just swear all the time. You don't even think about it."

"Should I? Are you offended?"

"No. Mostly just curious. I never swear."

"Like that's a surprise."

"I'd like to learn."

He had an instant flash of her saying very bad words, right in his ear. That fact that they were both naked only heightened the appeal of the moment.

"Swearing isn't required," he told her, forcing his mind to something safe like baseball.

"I'd like the option of trying." She glanced at the sky. "Do you mind if I put the top down?"

"No."

She pulled over onto the side of highway and lowered the roof. Kevin pulled on his cap and breathed in the fresh late morning air. Traveling with Haley might take a little longer but he had to admit this was a whole lot better than holing up in some motel waiting until he was well enough to drive.

"I'm thinking of practicing," she said when they were back on the highway. "You know, swearing."

"Go for it."

She looked shocked. "Right now?"

"Why not?"

"What if I get struck by lightning."

"Well, I haven't been struck yet. Although if you're going to do it, I'd start now because the weather report said storms were expected this afternoon."

Her mouth turned up slightly. "Wow. Just like that."

"You don't have to if you don't want to. It's not a big deal."

"It is for me." She sighed. "Why did you kiss me?"

He'd expected a whispered "damn" or "hell." Her question made him shift gears. "You kissed me." Which wasn't the point. He knew what she needed to know.

"Because I wanted to," he admitted.

"But you didn't that first night."

"We've been over this. You were drunk. You didn't know what you were doing."

"And I did last night?"

"At least you were sober. That gave you a fighting chance. You could have said no."

"Did you want to do anything else?" she asked.

He held up both hands. "No way. We're *not* having this conversation."

"Why not?"

"Because I'm not willing to be your first time. I'm not the right guy to have that responsibility."

She didn't say anything. He stared out the front window, knowing that if he looked at her he would see that he'd hurt her feelings. Fine. Better for her to be hurt now than seriously wounded by making love with the wrong man. Haley needed her first time to be after a wedding. Not in some motel with a screwup who knew better.

He leaned forward and flipped on the radio. After spinning the dial, he tuned in a country music station.

"What's it like?"

He almost didn't hear the question. When the words processed, he wished he hadn't. There was no doubt as to what she meant by "it."

"It's okay," he said cautiously, unable to believe they were talking about this.

"Can you be more specific? Is it as great as everyone says?"

He didn't want to be having this conversation. "Don't you have a girlfriend who can explain all this to you?"

"No, and I don't have a mother, either."

Ouch. That one hit below the belt. If he was the best confidant she had, she was in deep trouble.

"Kevin, I'm not trying to make you uncomfortable, I'm just looking for information. I'm too old to be this ignorant. I trust you to tell me the truth. Can we talk about it?"

He sighed. "Fine. We'll talk about it—on the condition that I get to refuse to answer anything that is too weird."

She shot him a grateful grin. "Perfect. So what is it like? Is it amazing?"

"Most of the time. If you care about the person you're with then sex becomes making love. Otherwise, it's just biology—like a sneeze."

"I don't understand. What's the difference?"

He wanted to change the subject. He wanted to get out of the car and start walking home, bum leg or not.

"Sex is the act without feelings. Without caring. It's just getting off. Think of a teenage boy desperate to do it with anybody. That's sex. Making love involves more than just the orgasm. It's about connecting." He leaned his head back and groaned. "I sound like a guest on 'Oprah.'"

"No. This is great. I understand what you're saying. But what about orgasms? I've read about them, but...well, you know." She cleared her throat. "How will I know if I'm having one?"

"If the guy you're with is doing it right, you'll know."

"That's not very helpful."

"If you're not sure, it didn't happen. When it does, you won't be wondering."

At least that was his personal experience with the women of his sexual acquaintance. Not that he was going to say that. Haley would have fifty more questions and he wouldn't want to answer at least forty-nine of them.

As it was, talking about the wild thing was making him think about it. Think about it with *her*—which he wasn't going to do. He stared out at the horizon and tried to disconnect from the conversation. He almost accomplished it, too, right up until her next question.

"What about being naked? Isn't that embarrassing?"

"No. It's fun."

"Not for me. I don't think I could ever be comfortable."

He was being punished. He got that now. His time with Haley was payback for all the stupid things he'd done when he was a kid.

"If you're caught up in the passion and with the right man, you won't mind taking your clothes off. It will feel natural and right. There's nothing more beautiful than a naked woman."

"I don't think so."

He glanced at her and grinned. "That would be a gender difference. For a guy, seeing the woman he's attracted to without her clothes is a peak experience. We want to touch her skin, see how she's put together, explore curves, hollows."

He stopped talking when he realized Haley was gripping the steering wheel just a little too tightly. Speaking of tight, parts of him were getting that way, too. He swore silently.

"Maybe we should talk about something else," he muttered.

Haley surprised him by agreeing.

But after exploring sex—verbally at least—there didn't seem to be much else to say. They drove in silence for nearly half an hour. As they headed toward the middle of Kansas, there were fewer and fewer cars on the road. While there were storm clouds in the distance, the sky overhead was a bright, clear blue.

"Would you mind if I went above the speed limit?" Haley asked. "This car has a lot more power than my old one did. I'd like to see what it can do."

Kevin figured she would freak out at eighty. "Go for it," he said, and pulled his hat down more securely.

She put her foot on the gas. The big car sped up.

She hit eighty and kept going. Eighty-five, ninety, ninety-five. The wind whipped past them. Haley laughed and he felt his own spirits lighten.

"I didn't think you had it in you," he said loudly.

"I want to go a hundred. I've never gone that fast."

He watched the speedometer hover just below a hundred, then the indicator crossed to one hundred and one, one hundred and two.

"You there. In the yellow Caddy. Pull over right now."

The loud voice came from above. Haley screamed and instantly lifted her foot from the gas. Kevin glanced up and saw the small plane above them.

"Don't panic," he said wryly. "It wasn't the voice of God. You were caught by the aerial patrol."

* * *

Haley absolutely could not believe this was happening. It seemed so unfair. She'd never gone above the speed limit before in her life. She'd never had a ticket, been in an accident or driven in an unsafe manner. So the very first time she actually cut loose, she got caught.

"Oh, this is bad," she whispered as she pulled off to the side of the highway. "This is so bad."

"There are always consequences," Kevin pointed out, which didn't make her feel better at all. He should be saying things such as this *wasn't* so bad.

"A spotless record up in flames."

"You're the one who wanted to walk on the wild side."

She glared at him, but he didn't seem intimidated. In fact, she would think he was almost *happy* about her getting caught.

"If I go to prison, you'd better come bail me out," she said.

He actually laughed. "I think the odds of you ending up in the slammer are pretty slim."

She noticed he hadn't actually promised to come rescue her. She covered her face with her hands. What if she did go to prison? She would be forced to call her father and tell him what had happened. He would be so disappointed. Plus he would probably tell Allan and they would come get her together. All her hopes and dreams for a life of her own would end. She would have a record and be trapped back in her old life.

Fifteen minutes later a state patrol car pulled up behind her. She had already dug out her driver's license. She didn't have any official registration for the car, just the paperwork from the car dealer where she'd purchased it.

She watched in her side mirror as the officer got out of

his car and walked toward her. She thrust the documents into his hands.

"I'm a worm," she said mournfully. "Really. I'm a horrible person and I know it. Being sorry doesn't help, so I won't even tell you I am. There's no excuse. Not even a medical emergency. I went fast because I wanted to. I've never had a car with a big engine before and I've never been one who speeds. I mean it's reckless and dangerous, and I'm never like that. I didn't mean to be today, but there was something about the open road and being in a convertible."

She paused for breath. "That's not an excuse. In fact it's worse than an excuse. I was immature and selfish. I did make sure there weren't other cars around because I'm not reckless enough to risk other people. I just love my new car so much. Not that it's really new, but it's new to me. But I was wrong. Really wrong. I deserve a ticket." She swallowed as tears burned in her eyes. "You probably want to take me to prison."

She held up her hands, fingers curled into her palms, wrists next to each other.

The officer slipped off his sunglasses and stared at her. "You don't actually need me here for this conversation, do you?"

Haley didn't know what to say. She blinked to hold back the tears.

"Wait right here," the man said. "I'm going to run your driver's license through the computer."

"Oh, I'm not wanted for anything."

"Uh-huh. You sit tight."

"Yes, sir."

Haley slumped back in her seat. She was afraid to close her eyes because she might see her whole life flash by.

Beside her, Kevin sighed. "A word of advice. Next time, wait to be charged with something before confessing."

"No. I was in the wrong. I shouldn't have been speeding."

"You sure seem anxious to try out prison food."

She sniffed. "I don't shy away from my responsibilities. As a citizen of this country, I need to abide by the laws of the land."

The officer returned with her paperwork, her license and an ominous-looking pad.

She tucked her license back into her wallet and handed the paperwork to Kevin to put in the glove box.

"You know you were going over a hundred," the man said.

Haley nodded and hung her head. Would they let her make a phone call from jail? Would she have one of those horrible mug shots that made everyone look drawn and guilty?

"What's your story?" the man asked Kevin, pointing to the bandage on his leg.

"Work-related injury," Kevin said.

"He was shot," Haley offered, which earned her a disgusted look from Kevin.

"What?" she asked, confused by his reaction. "It's what happened."

"You have some ID?" the officer asked.

Kevin nodded and pulled out his wallet. He flipped it to an official-looking document and passed it to Haley who handed it out the open window.

"U.S. Marshal?" the man asked.

Kevin nodded. "I got caught up in the prison riot."

"He'd been delivering a prisoner," Haley offered helpfully. "When there was trouble, they called him to come back. He was hit in the head and shot which is why I'm driving him home. He's not allowed to fly."

"Your wife?" the man asked, pointing at Haley.

Haley felt herself blushing.

Kevin sighed heavily. "No. Just a friend."

"A friend with a lead foot." The officer handed Kevin back his ID, then turned to Haley. "Keep it at the speed limit, miss."

She blinked at him. "What?"

"I'm letting you off with a warning. If this happens again, I'm hauling you in for reckless driving. You understand?"

He was letting her go? For real? She couldn't believe it.

"I—sure. Yes, I understand. The speed limit. I can do that."

"Have a nice day."

The man flipped his pad closed and returned to his patrol car. Haley sat there until he'd pulled out onto the highway. Then she leaned her head back, raised her arms and yelled out a big "Thank you" to the universe.

"I didn't get a ticket," she told Kevin.

He didn't seem as excited. "I know."

"Isn't it amazing."

"You were lucky. He felt bad because I was shot." His gaze narrowed. "You *deserved* a ticket."

She refused to be anything but thrilled by the change in circumstances.

"I'm not going to prison. I don't have to call my father or—" She hesitated. "Or anyone else. No one is going to know. Isn't this wonderful?"

"No, it's not. You need to learn a lesson in consequences."

As she started her engine, a delightful thought occurred to her. "Maybe there aren't any. Maybe that's just a line made up by worried parents."

Kevin groaned. "Why did I know you were going to say that?"

She checked her mirror, then pulled back onto the

highway. "Isn't this the best day? Aren't we having a wonderful time? Isn't life terrific?"

Kevin leaned back and closed his eyes. "You're giving me a headache."

"You need to lighten up."

"What I need is a drink."

Chapter Seven

Shortly after four that afternoon, they stopped at a seamy antique store outside of Wichita. Kevin watched as Haley pounced on various "treasures." Her squeals of delight brightened the eyes of the owner, as the sixty-something woman calculated profits. Kevin didn't have the heart to warn her that Haley's idea of a magical find didn't match most people's and was rarely over three dollars.

In almost seven hours he and his traveling companion had barely gone two hundred miles. It turned out that Haley not only had a burning desire to explore every shop, out-of-the-way museum and monument within twenty miles of the highway, she had the attention span of a gnat once they got there. She bounced from exhibit to exhibit, item to item, barely pausing long enough to see anything, which made him question why she'd wanted to stop in the first place. She also had a bladder the size of a thimble and yet insisted on drinking quart-size bottles of water, which meant there were pit stops every twenty or thirty miles.

She should have been making him crazy—instead, he found himself completely charmed. Shortly after lunch—where they'd stopped at Mom's Café and Home Cooking Emporium—he'd realized that with Haley, it was all about the journey. After being cooped up for years in a small town and never going anywhere, she wanted the adventure of exploring life. And if that meant examining a stuffed armadillo, then that's what she did.

"Kevin, look!"

He followed the sound of her voice and found her crouched over a bucket of arrowheads. She held two in her hand and was digging through the rest, apparently looking for a matched set.

"Aren't they cool?" she asked, holding out her finds to him.

"They're great."

Arrowheads? She was so happy to have found them that he didn't have the heart to point out they were so plentiful that she could practically pick them up on the side of the road.

"How many are you looking for?" he asked, thinking that if it was too many, he should plan on them spending the night here.

"Three. And they have to be exactly the same. What about this one?"

She handed him an arrowhead. He compared it with the others and reluctantly gave it back. "Too round. You want one that's more pointy."

"Okay."

She happily dug away, finally producing the triplet to the two she'd already chosen. When she stood, she offered one of those generous, beaming smiles that always made him think that the men in her hometown were idiots for not snapping her up the second she turned eighteen.

"Let's go inside," she said, pointing to the rickety building that could almost pass for a store.

Kevin leaned on his cane and mentally braced himself for more stuffed dead animals and maybe some old clothes. She seemed real fond of them, although she'd yet to buy either.

Heavy clouds had obscured the sun, so it was dark inside. Haley walked down crooked rows, pausing to admire an old cookie jar and a set of mismatched spoons. When she reached the back, she called his name.

"It's Depression glass," she said when he joined her in front of an old glass case. "My mom used to collect it. We have it back at the house. My father always told me it was mine when I married."

She pressed her fingers against the case. Her full mouth pulled into a straight line and her eyes turned sad.

Kevin didn't know if she was missing her mother, her father, her old life or just the promise of whatever future she'd run away from. He'd been putting bits and pieces of the puzzle of her life together since he'd met her and decided to take one of his theories for a test drive.

"You didn't want it enough to get married?" he asked.

She looked at him and rolled her eyes. "No one gets married to inherit a collection."

"Depends on what's in it. I could be had for the right price."

She laughed. "You are so lying. Aren't you the man who explained the difference between having sex and making love? Men who make love cannot be bought."

"You're wrong. I like to think of myself as a potential gigolo."

"Really?"

He'd dug the pit himself, then had pretty much fallen into it all on his own. He took a single step back. "Ah, no. Not really."

She was still chuckling as she headed up the next aisle. An old tintype caught her attention. It showed several lawmen standing next to their horses.

"Your ancestors," she said, holding it out to him. "They were good guys, just like you."

He knew he couldn't describe himself that way, but it wasn't for lack of trying. He put the picture back on the shelf.

"I'd like to get to Texas before Christmas," he said, pushing lightly on the small of her back. "Unless you see another armadillo that tempts you, I suggest we pay for your treasures and hit the road."

"You're so pushy."

"And you could happily shop in a used sock store."

She shook her head and walked to the counter where she paid for her three arrowheads. "You underestimate the value of treasure," she told him.

"No, I don't share your definition of the word."

"These are a part of our country's heritage."

Haley collected her change and thanked the woman, then headed toward her car. Kevin didn't understand that little things like arrowheads and the glass vase she'd purchased after lunch were all symbols. Sure, a lot of people would think they were junk, but to her they were the talismans of her journey to freedom. She tucked the arrowheads into a small paper bag with an old leather bookmark.

Kevin came up beside her. "I'll call them treasures as long as I don't have to claim any of them."

"Fair enough."

He jerked his head toward the back seat. "What's your

dad going to say when he sees all that? Will it fit in with the family decor?"

"I'm not going to be living with him anymore. I'm going to get my own place."

Haley spoke the words with more bravado than she felt. When she was done, she hunched her shoulders, half expecting lightning to strike her. But nothing happened.

She straightened and glanced at the gathering clouds. Was it possible that moving out on her own wasn't as completely horrible and selfish as she'd first thought?

She almost asked Kevin, but she knew he wouldn't understand the question. For him, life was simple. He was a man who knew what he wanted and either went after it or did it. He didn't fret about other people's opinions or expectations. He wasn't afraid of anything. If only she could be more like that.

"So where are you moving to?" he asked as he opened the passenger door and slid onto the seat.

"I don't know. Once I know where I'm working, I'll find a place close by. It doesn't have to be big or anything." As long as it was hers and no one else's.

"Do you have any specific places in mind?"

"No. I want to teach, and I can do that anywhere. It's what I've wanted since I was a little girl."

"What do you teach?"

She sat next to him and smiled. "Middle school math."

"You're kidding?" He looked her over. "If my middle school math teacher had looked like you I would have been a whole lot more interested in algebra."

His compliment pleased her. Kevin had made it clear that he was attracted to her, at least a little. She still thought he was good-looking and very sexy, but the more they were together, the more she liked who he was.

A rumbling in the distance caught her attention. She

turned toward the horizon and studied the dark clouds. "That looks like a bad storm."

Kevin nodded. "I hate to say this, but we should probably find a place for the night."

"Okay."

She spoke casually, but her heart was pounding hard. They were going to have another night together. Last night they'd kissed. Would they again tonight? Would they do more?

She started the engine, then put up the convertible top. As they drove down the narrow road that led back to the highway, the first drops of rain hit the windshield.

"Let's look for a place close to a decent restaurant," he said. "I'm up to going out for dinner. What about you?"

She thought of the pretty summer dresses she'd bought. This would be her first chance to wear one. "That sounds like fun."

He shifted in his seat and stretched out his leg.

"Do you want another pain pill?" she asked.

"I'll wait until bedtime. If we talk it will distract me. I'll even let you go first. Why do you have to run away to become a teacher?"

The question shouldn't have surprised her, but it still made her tense. She tightened her hold on the steering wheel and tried to figure out how much to tell him.

"I don't know how to explain my life without sounding like a spineless idiot," she admitted.

"I don't think you're either."

She gave him a quick smile, then turned her attention back to the road. The highway was up ahead. She put on her blinker, then merged with the traffic.

"You're nice to say that, but running away, as you put it, has shown me that I've been both for a long time. I guess it became a habit. I remember being a little girl. Nice ladies from the congregation would come over and help me pick out clothes for church. They would brush my hair and put ribbons at the end of my braid. They always told me that I had to be a good girl and make my daddy proud. They said that I was the minister's daughter and that meant I was held to a higher standard. For a long time I thought that meant I had to be tall."

Kevin didn't laugh. "That's a lot for a kid to have to deal with."

"Some of it wasn't so bad. I liked that someone was always around to help with homework or take me shopping. But they never stayed. Eventually they went home to their own families, their own children, and I was left alone with my dad."

"He never remarried, right?"

She shook her head. "A lot of people said that he would, but he never even dated. I hoped he would. I wanted a mother of my own. I wanted to feel that I belonged. To someone. To a family. But that never happened. And then I grew up and I stopped waiting to belong."

"I don't believe that."

She didn't look at him—she didn't dare. Was Kevin right? Did she still want to be a part of something? She supposed that everyone did in one way or the other.

"Maybe you're right," she admitted. "I found myself not wanting to disappoint anyone. Doing what was expected wasn't all that hard, so I did it. I made the right choices."

"Which meant not moving away?"

"Yeah." She sighed. "I don't want you to think my father was a difficult man, because he wasn't. He's wonderful. So loving and giving. We're all lucky to have him."

"You and the congregation?"

"Right. He never punished me or yelled at me, but I knew when he was unhappy with me. I could see it in his eyes. So I did what I was told. Like the summer I turned eleven and the ladies in the church didn't think I should be running around in shorts anymore. So I wore dresses. And when I went to high school, three different women talked to me about the perils of having a bad reputation and how easy it was to take the wrong road. So I was always careful never to do that."

"In the end you worried so much, you didn't date at all."

She nodded. The rain came down a little heavier and she turned on the windshield wipers.

"My father always hoped I'd marry a minister. I wanted to study to be a teacher, but everyone knows that ministers' wives have to play the piano, so I studied music instead."

"I thought you said you had your teaching credentials."

"I do." She shrugged. "It was a small act of rebellion, but when I went back to college and got my master's of fine arts in music, I completed the rest of the courses I need for my teaching certificate."

"A quiet rebellion?"

"One I never confessed to." She bit her lower lip. "I'm not very proud of that. I should have told my father the truth."

"Maybe he shouldn't have put you in the position of having to hide your heart's desire."

She'd never thought of it that way. Could her father have made things easier for her?

"We're about as different as it's possible to be," Kevin told her. "When I was growing up I never met a rule I didn't want to break."

"Sounds like fun. I would have liked that, but breaking the rules is more difficult, coming to it this late in life."

"You're making progress. Look at your car."

"Good point." Her father would never have approved

of the car. Allan would have gone one step further and forced her to return it.

"What about that place?"

Kevin pointed across the highway to a small motel sharing a parking lot with a steak house. It was still early but there were several cars parked outside the restaurant. Always a good sign.

"Works for me," she said. "I'll take the next off-ramp and circle back."

When she pulled in front of the motel, the rain seemed to let up a little. They climbed out and started toward the front office. Kevin was limping pretty badly.

"Does it hurt?" she asked as she walked next to him.

"I'm stiff from sitting so long. I just need to stretch my muscles out."

She eyed his drawn features and the tightness around his mouth. She would guess he needed another dose of pain medicine, but he was being stubborn about taking as many as he was allowed.

"Suffering isn't macho," she muttered.

He grinned. "Sure it is. You're fussing over me. If nothing hurt, you wouldn't give me the time of day."

They both knew that wasn't true, but she liked his teasing her, so she didn't say anything.

They approached the front desk, where an old man gave them a toothy grin. "What can I get you folks?"

Haley's mind hiccuped. What did they need? One room? Last night she hadn't thought twice about sharing quarters with him. He'd been injured and completely out of it. But tonight was different. He was certainly alert. Plus, they'd spent a whole day together, which somehow made sharing a room more intimate than it had been the previous evening. Yet he was still hurt and what if he needed her help? She didn't want to be too far away. Was she being overly cautious about something that didn't really matter?

Before she could find the answer to any of her questions, Kevin spoke. "We'd like adjoining rooms, please."

"Sure thing."

The old man collected two keys, then handed them each a registration card. As Haley filled hers out, she tried to figure out if she was relieved or disappointed. Probably a bit of both. While she'd *wanted* to stay in the same room as Kevin, she was also terrified to do so.

"How's the steak place next door?" Kevin asked as he handed over his completed card.

"Best steaks in three counties," the manager said. "I suggest you go early. The wait'll be shorter and we're expectin' some pretty bad storms tonight. Might even have a twister come on through."

"Beats cable," Kevin said. "You finished?"

Haley nodded and gave the man her card. He swiped Kevin's credit card, accepted her cash, then gave them each a key.

"Ground floor at the end. Should be plenty quiet. Enjoy your stay."

"Thanks."

Kevin headed for the door. Haley trailed after him.

"Was he saying we could have a tornado tonight?"

"Looks that way."

Except for *The Wizard of Oz,* she'd never had any personal experience with that kind of storm.

"What do we do?" she asked.

He glanced at her. "We go have a steak dinner."

"I meant about the storm."

"There's nothing *to* do. If one comes through, it comes through."

"But where do we go? Is there a storm cellar or some-thing? What about my car?"

He put an arm around her. "For a minister's daughter, you don't have very much faith."

"I have plenty of faith. What I don't have is an escape plan if a tornado comes."

"If we hear the sirens, we'll get in the bathtub and pull a mattress over ourselves."

Did people really do that sort of thing? "It doesn't sound very comfortable."

"It beats getting hit on the head by a dresser."

They got back into her car and she drove down to the end of the building. After collecting their luggage, they each went into their own rooms.

Haley stood in the middle of a bedroom that looked a lot like the other motel rooms she'd stayed in over the past few days. But instead of flipping on the television to check out the cable channels, she stared at the closed and locked door separating her room from Kevin's.

Should she open it? Were they semi-sharing quarters? If they weren't going to open it, why had he asked for adjoining rooms? And why was her stomach getting all tight and knotted from thinking about this?

She was rescued by a knock on the door. Haley unfas-tened the bolt and pulled it open. Kevin smiled.

"Want to keep these open?" he asked.

"Sure."

He stepped into her room. "Have you noticed these places all look the same?"

"Pretty much. I hope the cable's good."

"So you can shop on that home shopping program you like so much?"

"I haven't actually bought anything yet."

"Give it time." He glanced at his watch. "When do you want to go to dinner?"

"I'm hungry now."

"Me, too."

Haley glanced down at her jeans. "I'd like to get changed."

His gaze narrowed. "You're not putting on shorts, are you?"

"To go to a restaurant?" She was shocked. "I'll wear a dress."

"Uh-huh. Is that going to be better or worse for me?"

"I don't understand the question."

Kevin sighed. "I know. See you in twenty minutes."

He retreated to his room, half closing his adjoining door, but leaving hers open.

She hesitated, wondering what on earth he'd meant, then she realized she didn't have much time and hurried toward the suitcase she'd brought in. After collecting a dress and the small bag of cosmetics she'd purchased at Wal-Mart, she ducked into the bathroom.

Haley washed her face and applied moisturizer, then studied the contents of her makeup bag. The basics were easy. She'd applied mascara a few times and lip gloss was self-explanatory, but what about eye shadow and base?

She shook the flesh-colored bottle, but chickened out at the thought of putting that goopy liquid all over her face. There was a little diagram on the back of the eye shadow compact, showing where each of the three colors should go. She followed the instructions, using a minimal amount of color, then smudging everything with her finger.

Huh. Maybe it was just the light in here, but she thought her eyes looked bigger and more blue. Was it possible that shading her eyelids had really worked?

Mascara went on next, then lip gloss. She studied her hair, but there wasn't much she could do with the short, flyaway style. Unfortunately.

Next was her outfit for the evening. She pulled off her jeans and T-shirt and stood in her underwear while she studied her choice. The breezy summer dress she'd bought had skinny straps. Very skinny straps. Straps that were much, much skinnier than her bra straps. She hadn't noticed that before.

Okay, so what exactly did she do about that? She didn't want her bra showing, but the alternative was unthinkable. She would be punished for sure. After all, wearing shorts was one thing, but going without a bra? A tornado would suck her up in a heartbeat.

Still, showing her bra straps was just plain tacky. A lot of people seemed to do it, but to her it was like going out with her slip hanging two inches below her dress. Yuck. Which meant she could either pick another dress, wear this one with a bra or wear it without and risk potentially cosmic consequences.

Haley squeezed her eyes tightly shut and turned away from the mirror. Without even daring to breathe, she undid her bra and let it fall to the floor. Then she pulled the dress over her head and tugged it into place. Only then did she dare to open her eyes and face her reflection.

The first thing she noticed was the big old tag hanging down nearly to her waist. She pulled that off, then held out her arms to try to see if anyone could really tell she wasn't wearing a bra. It wasn't as if her chest was huge; if she didn't move too much, neither did her breasts. The fabric was lined, so nothing physically showed through. Still, Haley felt more than a little naked.

Reminding herself that she was supposed to be living life on the wild side now, and determined to ignore the sensation of being unclothed, she went in search of her strappy sandals. She'd barely finished fastening them when Kevin knocked on the adjoining door.

"Are you ready?" he asked.

"Um, I think so."

She stood and grabbed for her purse as he walked into her room.

"I'm looking forward to having a steak tonight," he said. "There's nothing like a bullet wound to make a man want red—"

He came to a stop about three steps into her room. His mouth stayed open, but he wasn't talking. His gaze moved over her, starting at the top of her head and slowly moving down to her bare toes, then making the return trip. She couldn't tell if he'd hesitated on her chest or not and she didn't really want to know. Instead, she stared slightly over his left shoulder and waited for him to say something. Anything.

"You look amazing."

She blinked, then smiled at him. "Really?"

"Absolutely. Apparently preachers' daughters from Ohio clean up real good."

His compliment made her beam. "You don't think it's too much? I mean I was worried that the dress was a little too..." She shrugged. "Racy."

She wasn't sure but she thought he might have swallowed.

"It's perfect. I'm going to be fighting guys off all evening. Maybe I should bring my gun."

She knew he was teasing, but his words still made her feel good. No one had ever even hinted that she might be attractive enough to capture the attention of more than one man at a time.

She studied his new jeans pulled on over his bandage and the tucked-in polo shirt that revealed his broad chest and narrow waist. "You look nice, too."

"Thanks. Let's go eat. I'm starved."

They made their way out of the motel room and across the parking lot to the restaurant. The hostess showed them to a booth right away. Haley slid in across from Kevin. He settled himself in place and hooked his cane over the edge of the table. She picked up the menu the hostess had left, but instead of opening it, she studied the restaurant.

Booths lined the walls of the open room. There were votive candles on the tables and sawdust swirls on the floor. A bar filled the left side of the building and she could just catch the faint sound of a country music song.

This was the kind of place people came to have fun and Haley found herself wanting to join in. Her foot tapped in time with the music and she couldn't help smiling as she turned her attention back to Kevin.

"This is great," she said.

"Your kind of place?"

She'd never thought of herself as having a "place." A type of establishment that appealed to her. She'd never been the one making the decisions about where to go to eat at a restaurant. But if it were up to her...

She nodded. "Absolutely. What about you?"

"Show me a good steak and I'm a happy man."

"Hi, there. Can I get you a drink?"

Haley turned her attention to the woman standing by their table. She was tall, busty and blond. Her low-cut spandex top clung to curves impressive enough to make a rock star look twice. Haley suddenly felt as if she were playing dress-up and not doing a very good job of things.

Kevin shrugged. "I'm off liquor because of the pain-killers. What would you like?"

Haley couldn't think that fast. She didn't know the names of drinks and she didn't want to appear stupid in front of the centerfold-material blonde. She was about to ask the woman to give her a minute when Kevin came to her rescue.

"Maybe you'd allow me to pick a glass of wine for you," he said.

"I'd like that."

He glanced at the wine list on the back of the menu. "The lady will have a glass of Pinot Noir."

The waitress scribbled the order, flashed a smile and left. Haley was too caught up in the words "the lady will have" to much notice. She knew it was just good manners and all that, but no one had ever called her a lady before. Not like that. She'd been instructed to *act* like a lady for most of her life, which wasn't the same thing at all.

A young man brought them water and bread, then their waiter took their order. She and Kevin both picked steaks, although she chose a petite fillet and he went for the large New York cut. Seconds later, her wine appeared.

She eyed the purplish-red wine. If she hadn't liked white, which everyone said was easier to drink, she had a bad feeling she wasn't going to like this one, either.

Kevin picked up his water glass. "Try it," he urged. "You'll be surprised."

As nearly everything about being with him was surprising, that wasn't a stretch. She took a cautious sip and blinked.

"It's nice," she told him. "Sort of sweet and fruity. Not bitter at all."

He grinned. "Trust is an important part of our relationship. I figure you'll be safe with two glasses. That way you'll have the fun of getting buzzed without feeling bad like last time."

She grimaced. "I don't want to get that sick again ever."

"Good for you. Smart people figure that out the first time. The rest of the world keeps getting sick."

That didn't make sense to her. Who would want to go

through that kind of near-death experience more than once? She would have to—

"Stop fidgeting," Kevin growled.

Haley stared at him. "What?"

He jerked his chin toward her left shoulder. She realized she'd been playing with the skinny straps of her dress.

"You're making me crazy," he told her. "It's bad enough that you're showing more skin than should be legal, but I don't need you reminding me that you're not wearing a bra."

Heat flared on her cheeks with the speed of a rocket heading for outer space. Her mouth opened then closed. Instinctively she crossed her arms over her chest and ducked her head. She felt like an idiot.

Kevin sighed. "Dammit, Haley, I'm not trying to hurt your feelings. But I would like to get through dinner without thinking about sex more than fifty or sixty times."

She remembered the blond waitress who had made her own modest "charms" seem positively concave by comparison. "Sex with me?" she whispered.

"Yes, with you."

Wow! Kevin had thought about them…well, doing it? Being naked and…

She blushed harder. "Wow," she said, then took a sip of her wine.

He sighed heavily. "Are you okay?"

She nodded. Her shame had faded, leaving only delight.

"Then let's change the subject." He leaned toward her. "Why don't you tell me about the guy you're running from?"

Chapter Eight

Haley was glad she'd already put her wineglass down because her whole body lurched when Kevin spoke. She didn't know what to say, what to think. Had she mentioned Allan? In the past couple of days had she inadvertently explained why she'd left town?

She searched her memory and couldn't come up with a single instance, which meant Kevin had somehow figured out the truth.

"How did you know?" she asked.

"I put the pieces together. It wasn't that hard. Why else would you leave a town filled with people who care about you?"

She hated to think she'd been so obvious. "They care, but they also stifle me. One of the reasons I left was to figure out how to be my own person."

"A reason to move," he told her, "but not to run. So who's the jerk? Did he break your heart?"

There was something about the way he asked the

question—as if the answer mattered. As if Allan being mean to her would make Kevin angry. A little thrill shot through her. Until Kevin, no man had ever offered to defend her before. Not that he had come and said he would, but she guessed if this was her private fantasy, she could imagine him riding to the rescue and drawing his sword on her behalf.

She allowed herself a half-second vision of Allan stretched out on the ground, a large sword pointing at his throat, then pushed it away. He'd done a lot of things she didn't agree with but she couldn't exactly say he'd been horrible to her. Was not listening an offense worthy of death? She didn't think so.

She glanced at Kevin and shrugged. "I'm not sure where to begin."

"Why don't you tell me his name and how you met?"

She considered the question, then realized the problem had started long before Allan had showed up in her life.

"I told you about how I grew up," she said. "Not with one mother but with fifty. How everyone always had an opinion about what I should be doing and wearing and where I should be going."

He nodded.

"So I was used to be pushed around. I know they all did it out of love, but somehow what started out as a gesture of affection somehow became a community hobby. Everyone had a piece of my life but me."

She rested her fingertips on the base of her wineglass. "I've already explained that I didn't date much in high school or college. I really wanted to find someone, though. I'd always imagined myself as a wife and a mother. I love kids."

"Then you picked the right profession."

She brightened at the thought. "Yes, I did. I think I

would be a very good teacher. Not that anyone else agreed with me."

"What about the guy?"

"I met Allan the summer I turned twenty. I was home from college and he'd just been hired as the associate pastor. He's a few years older than me."

Kevin didn't say anything. He just watched her with his dark eyes and kept his expression unreadable. She would guess that none of this made sense to him. Kevin had never let anyone run his life. He'd been in charge of his own destiny for years. Why couldn't she be more like that?

"So you were instantly attracted to him?" he asked.

"No. Not really. I mean, he was nice and everything, but I didn't even see him as a guy until my father's secretary said something about him being good-looking. Then someone else mentioned he was single and a third person told me he'd said he thought I was pretty. After a while I got the message that the congregation thought it would be wonderful if we started dating, so we did."

"How did Allan feel about the decision being made for him?"

"I don't know. At the time I would have said it was his idea, too, but now…" She sighed. "I'm not sure."

"So you dated?"

"Yeah. He was fun and interesting, but he had some really specific ideas about the woman in his life. He didn't want me wearing jeans, not even at home. I think if I'd put on shorts, he would have had a heart attack. When I told him about wanting to be a teacher, he talked about how beautifully I played the piano, and how important that was for a preacher's wife. He encouraged me to volunteer, to not have any friends of my own or any opinions."

She took a sip of her wine. "I didn't get that all at once. Over the past few years I've figured out that his 'suggestions' were really instructions. I'd never felt in control of my life and suddenly I had less control than before. I was sneaking around at college, secretly taking courses for my teaching credentials while getting a masters in music."

"So why did you stay with him?"

"Because it was expected. Because I didn't know what love was and everyone told me I was in love with him. After a while, I thought I was. So when he proposed, I said yes."

She waited for a reaction, but except for the faint twitch of a muscle in his jaw, Kevin didn't react.

"Did you marry him?" he asked.

Her eyes widened. "No! I wouldn't be here with you if I was married. I wouldn't have…have…" If there was a time to swear, this was it. She could feel her face getting hot.

She glanced around to make sure no one was paying attention to them, then leaned forward and lowered her voice. "I would never have kissed you if I'd been married."

"Fair enough. So what happened to the engagement?"

"We were supposed to be married at the end of the month."

Finally Kevin looked surprised. "This month."

"Uh-huh. Things hadn't been going well between us, but the wedding plans were a runaway train and I didn't know how to stop them. Everyone was involved. Over three hundred invitations went out." She briefly closed her eyes against the memory of addressing all those envelopes. It had taken her weeks. She'd wanted to ask for help, but Allan had believed it was the bride's responsibility to do it herself, that it showed respect for the guests.

"I couldn't talk to anyone and even if I could, what

could I have complained about? That Allan didn't listen? That sometimes I felt I wasn't a person to him?" She shook her head. "They would have said I was ungrateful."

"How didn't he listen?"

"Oh, in different ways. I wanted kids right away but he didn't, so three months ago he made an appointment and took me to my doctor to get me on the Pill. I wanted to go to Hawaii for our honeymoon, but he wanted to go to Branson, so that's where we were going. Silly stuff."

Kevin reached across the table and put his hand on top of hers. His dark gaze seemed to see down to the depths of her being.

"None of that is silly," he said quietly. "Marriage is supposed to be a partnership, not a dictatorship. Allan was wrong not to pay attention to what would make you happy."

No one had ever said that to her before. A lightness filled Haley and made her want to float up to the ceiling like an escaped balloon.

"Yeah?"

He nodded. "The guy sounds like a jerk. So what happened? You finally couldn't stand it anymore and took off?"

Suddenly ashamed, she withdrew her hand and ducked her head. "No," she whispered. "I didn't have the backbone for that. I was having a lot of second thoughts, but I was afraid to say anything. Then Allan came to me and told me he wasn't sure he was in love with me. He wanted to postpone the wedding."

Kevin muttered something that sounded like a string of really bad words. She tried not to listen.

"I got mad," she admitted, looking at him again. "I wasn't hurt, I was furious. I couldn't believe that I'd given up my entire life and everything I wanted for a man who wasn't even sure he was in love with me."

"So you ran."

"I escaped," she corrected. "Right then and there I vowed I would never again, as long as I lived, do what other people thought was right. I would only do what *I* thought was right for me. So I left home and started driving to Hawaii." She thought about the beautiful pictures she'd seen over the years. "I've always wanted to visit the islands."

Kevin watched Haley's expression turn wistful. His gut twisted in a rage he hadn't felt in years. He wanted to go find the jerk who'd treated her so badly and pound his self-centered, egotistic self into dust. He didn't have time for bullies and that's just what Allan had been. He sensed right away that the guy was stronger than Haley so he'd assumed that had given him the right to run her life and dictate terms.

Somewhere along the way Allan had decided it was all right for him to be in charge, to know best.

"I'm impressed you managed to get your teaching degree, despite everything," he said.

"I can be patient." A smile curved up the corners of her mouth. "And maybe a little bit sneaky. Honestly, I hated lying to everyone but getting that degree was really important to me and I didn't think it was such a horrible thing. It's not like I wanted to be a stripper. Besides, we need more teachers."

The waitress appeared with their salads. Haley reached for the bread basket and offered it to him. When he'd taken a roll, she picked one for herself.

"You're better off without Allan," he said. "Do you believe that?"

She nodded, then paused and shook her head. "I tell myself that. I want to believe it, and most of the time I do. I just wish I didn't feel so guilty. It's complicated."

"Life often is."

"Mine wasn't before." She took a sip of the wine. "I really like this. You made a great choice."

He grinned. "Stick with me, kid, and I'll show you the good life."

As soon as the words were out of his mouth he wanted to call them back. Haley's face brightened and she beamed at him. He felt both ten feet tall and as small as the biggest lowlife on the planet. While he knew she was perfectly safe in his company, he also knew how much he wanted her. Liking her was fine—Haley was a likable sort of person. But sex?

He'd reformed his ways, become one of the good guys. He had a bad feeling that giving in to Haley's particular brand of temptation was a slick, steep road back to hell.

"Let me rephrase that," he said. "I'm not someone to stick with."

"Of course you are. You're one of the best people I've ever met."

"Not even by half. My mother used to drag me to church every week, but it sure as hell didn't take. I stopped going as soon as I could."

"What does church have to do with anything?" She speared several lettuce pieces but didn't eat. "Allan and I used to argue about that all the time. I've always believed that God is so much more than a building. People find Him wherever they need Him. But for Allan, church was everything.

"I'll agree that belonging to a church provides a sense of community and structure. A good pastor or rabbi or whatever can encourage people and teach them to be their best selves, but God is the point. Do you believe in God?"

He'd been so caught up in her words, in her beliefs, which were a bit of a surprise, that he almost didn't catch the question.

"Yes," he answered without thinking.

She shrugged. "So if you believe, then how can you keep from worshiping and giving thanks, in whatever form that takes? Appreciating the beauty of a morning, or being grateful for being alive. Isn't that praise?"

"I've never thought of it like that," he admitted.

"I think about it a lot. Like I said, Allan didn't agree with me. For him if someone didn't belong to the church, they weren't of value. Sometimes I was afraid that for him it was all about how things looked, not how they were inside."

He shook his head. "You were wrong before when you said you didn't have any backbone. You're pure steel. I admire that."

Her eyes lit up. "Really?"

"Allan was an idiot for not seeing it." He tore open his roll. "So did you love him?"

He asked the question for a couple of reasons. First, because he needed to change the subject. His compliments had a way of making her see him as something of a prize. For another, as much as he didn't want to know the answer, he figured that if she was still in love with the guy, the information would be enough to crank down his desire to escort Haley right into his bed. He might be a bit of a bastard, but he didn't poach.

"I don't know," she admitted. "I thought I did, but now things are all muddled. Maybe I don't know what romantic love is. What about you? Have you been in love?"

"Once. A long time ago."

"Did you marry her?"

"She was already married. I didn't know. I was looking for forever and she just wanted a good time."

"I'm sorry."

"Hey, it happens." He could tell the story now without feeling the pain, but when it had happened... He didn't want to think about that. "I got over it. Maybe I wasn't as in love as I thought."

"I want to be swept away," she said. "I want love to crash over me like a wave and carry me out into the ocean."

"Sounds dangerous."

"It sounds exciting."

He looked at her and their eyes locked. Kevin felt a rushing sensation deep in his chest. He didn't know what it was and he didn't want to know. He could smell the danger all around. But he wouldn't go there. Not with Haley. She wasn't for him. He'd known that from the beginning. But that didn't mean he had to like it.

Kevin knew he was being punished. Or tested. Or maybe both. He probably deserved the former and was going to fail the latter, which was interesting but not particularly helpful in his current situation.

He was in pain. He told himself that over and over again, as if it would make a damn bit of difference. Nothing about the situation was sexy or erotic. He rubbed his hand over his face and figured there was no point in lying to himself. Once Haley was in the room, everything became sexually charged—at least for him. Sitting on the bed in nothing but his shirt and briefs while she changed his bandage was about the most *physically* interesting thing to happen to him in months. Maybe years.

Damn depressing, he thought, leaning his head back on the pillow he'd propped up against the headboard and tried to concentrate on the game on TV. He'd ended a relationship going nowhere about four months ago. He and Millie had been on-and-off lovers for nearly six months. What did it say about his life when having a bandage changed on his gunshot leg was sexier than having sex with someone else?

He heard a soft sound and opened his eyes. Haley had walked into his bedroom, her hands filled with tubes, bandages and tape. She dropped her supplies next to him and settled on the edge of the bed.

"How does it feel?" she asked.

Hard.

He clenched his teeth and tried to think about carburetor parts, but it didn't help. Just knowing she was wearing that damn dress without a bra killed him. He didn't even have to look at her breasts, either. He was hard and getting harder by the heartbeat.

"Kevin?"

He stared at her. "I'm fine," he muttered.

"Are you sure? You look kind of…" Her voice trailed off. "Uncomfortable."

Good a word as any, he thought with a laugh. "I'm okay. Just change the bandage."

He stared at the ceiling as she messed with her supplies and reached for the scissors, then knew the exact moment she'd caught sight of his "problem." Her breath caught and he felt her gaze shift to his face.

"Ignore it," he said, still looking upward and wondering what he'd done to deserve this in his life.

She didn't speak, didn't move. As far as he could tell, she wasn't even breathing. Finally he looked at her.

Her eyes were the size of baseballs, her mouth was parted and color stained her cheeks.

"It doesn't mean anything," he told her. "I'm a man, you're a woman. I find you attractive and we're alone in a bedroom. It happens."

She swallowed. "I've never seen a man before—you know. That."

The "that" in question pulsed slightly.

"C-can I ask you some questions?"

He would rather she hacked off his arm. He sighed. "Sure. What do you want to know?"

More color flooded her face. "So you're, um, aroused?"

"Isn't that obvious?"

She turned away. "Not to me."

Damn. He'd inadvertently sucker punched her, which only proved he was the wrong guy for the job. Knowing he was courting twenty-seven kinds of trouble, he touched her arm.

"Sorry, Haley. I'm not handling this well. I'm a little uncomfortable with the situation. At thirty-one I should be able to control myself better. Go ahead and ask your questions."

He was talking about his erection, but he didn't know if she would understand that. Either way, she seemed to accept his apology. She turned her attention back to his face.

She bit her lower lip. He watched as curiosity battled with modesty. Curiosity won.

"I've heard that blood fills, um, it and it gets bigger. Does that hurt? I'm asking because I broke my arm once and it really swelled up and it hurt more than anything."

Despite the strange situation, he couldn't help laughing. "No, it doesn't feel like a broken arm. There's tension and an aching when I get hard, but no physical pain. Blood flows in and eventually flows out."

She glanced down at his lap, then back at his face. "I thought it would stick out more."

He held in a grin. "It does. If I were to take off my underwear, it would stick straight out."

Her expression turned intrigued.

"No way," he said before she could ask. "That's not

going to happen. Looking would lead to other things and I'm not into defiling virgins."

"You'd probably be very good at it."

"We're not going to find out."

She sighed heavily. "And you say you're not a good guy. Someone bad would have already taken advantage of me."

A good guy wouldn't want her so much, he thought, but didn't share that with her. Instead, he shifted his leg.

"Go ahead and torture me," he said. "I'll watch the Braves kick butt."

He focused on the third inning, then groaned when the team left two men on. Haley worked efficiently, peeling off the old bandage, applying the ointment and putting on the new dressing. He'd only had one pain pill that morning and wouldn't take another until bedtime. He was already improving, which was a good thing. He had a feeling he was going to need all his strength to resist Haley.

When she finished, she stood and carried her supplies back into her room. He relaxed. At least that hurdle had been passed. Maybe tomorrow he should change his own bandage. It would be a whole lot easier if he—

She reappeared in the doorway. "Would you want me if I wasn't a virgin?"

Had he been standing the question would have knocked him on his ass. There were a thousand safe ways to answer that question. A thousand games he could play with her. Instead, he stared into her eyes and knew he could only tell her the truth. After the hell that bastard Allan had put her through, she deserved that.

"I want you now. The difference is, if you weren't a virgin, I'd act on it."

He'd hoped that would send her running, but Haley being Haley crossed to the bed and sat next to him. Before he could gather his defenses, she leaned forward and kissed him.

In seconds he was drowning in her softness, in the taste of her and the quick, eager strokes of her hot tongue. She was innocent, tempting and a damn fine kisser all in one package. Was it his fault that his arms came around her and he pulled her close? He was a man, not a statue.

He was used to lush women with curves to spare. Haley was slight in his arms, but still appealing. He angled his head so he could kiss her more deeply, following her back into her mouth, tracing the sweetness of the inside of her lower lip, then circling her tongue with his. He tasted her, teased her, stroked her. They established a dance that sent fire to points south. Hard became harder and the ache made the pain in his leg feel like a mosquito bite.

He cupped her face, his fingers stroking her soft skin. She smelled like flowers and candy. She tasted like heaven. When her hands settled on his shoulders, he wanted to pull free and rip off his shirt. He wanted her hands on his chest, his back, his groin. He wanted her to rub him until he exploded. No, he wanted to bury himself inside her and then explode.

Haley nearly lost her breath when Kevin bit down on her lower lip. He nibbled her there, then soothed the sensitive skin with a quick lick. From there he moved to her jaw, biting, kissing, making her feel things she'd never felt before. The world was spinning and she was caught up in the vortex, tossed first one way, then the other. She couldn't think. She didn't want it ever to stop.

But while her brain wasn't working, her body seemed to be doing just great. Every touch, every point of contact, was exquisite pleasure. Yes, of course Allan had kissed her, but it hadn't been with this fire or passion. She'd never felt a trembling in her chest before. Her breasts had never seemed too tight and uncomfortable for her clothes. She wasn't even wearing a bra and yet she felt confined. Between her legs little jolts of heavy, throbbing electricity made her press her knees together as if to hold in something she couldn't really contain.

Kevin kissed his way down her neck. He shifted and reached for the strap on her dress, then pushed it off her shoulder. When his mouth settled just over her collarbone, she caught her breath. How could that be such a sensitive place on her body? Was he as sensitive?

Caught up in the feel of his mouth and lips and tongue, she had trouble forcing herself to move but eventually she slid her hands down to the front of his chest. His muscles moved, tightening and released as she slid over them. His body was so different from hers. Angled, strong, unyielding.

He licked the hollow of her throat and her head fell back. Yield. Yes, that was what she wanted to do. She still kept her knees tightly pressed together but now she did it because part of her wanted to let them fall open.

"Haley," he breathed, the word hot against her skin.

The sound of his voice made her shiver. He lifted his head and found her mouth. She wrapped her arms around him and clung as their passionate kiss swept her away.

She couldn't breathe, but then what did breath matter? She couldn't think, she could only feel the deep kisses. One of his hands settled on her waist. She felt the pressure, the heat, and when it began to move upward, she understood the destination.

Anticipation flooded her. Anticipation and need. Higher and higher he moved until finally he cupped her breast in his hand.

Time stood still. Haley didn't have the words or even the images to describe that feeling. His warm fingers, his palm holding her so delicately yet firmly. Then he brushed against her nipple. The sensation was so incredible, so unexpected, that she gasped a sound. Not a word but an unintelligible expression of her satisfaction.

He brushed her nipple again. She had to stop kissing so she could concentrate on the delight that coiled through her. She ached. She wanted more. She wanted everything.

Over and over he stroked, then he pinched the tight peak and she thought she might die from the wonder of it all. Again and again until the rhythm became the universe.

His other hand joined the first. They moved together. It was too much. It was wonderful. Unable to stop herself, she took his face in her hands and kissed him. She wanted all of him and when he entered her mouth, she sucked on his tongue, matching the movements of his fingers on her breasts.

Tension spiraled through her. It began in the center of her body and moved lower to settle between her legs. She felt full, yet oddly empty.

Kevin broke the kiss. With his hands still on her breasts, he rested his forehead against hers.

"Okay, now it hurts," he said.

She opened her eyes and glanced down at his lap. His…maleness…seemed even larger than before. He looked very, very ready.

She raised her gaze to his face.

"Don't even think about it," he said, straightening and dropping his hands to his sides.

She hadn't decided if this was what she wanted or not, but having him tell her no before she could make up her own mind was a little annoying.

"Why do you get to decide?"

"Because both of us have to be willing."

"But you *are* willing."

"Physically, yes. But otherwise, no." He touched her cheek. "Not like this, Haley. Not in a motel on the highway with a guy you've only known a couple of days. The first time should be with someone you care about."

He spoke tenderly and his words brought tears to her eyes. He was right about all of it. Everyone had thought that Allan was a prince among men, but they'd been wrong. The injured man in front of her had turned out to be the most honorable person she'd ever met.

"I thought I loved Allan and I was wrong," she said. "How will I know when it's right?"

"You're asking the wrong guy. My track record stinks." He traced her lower lip with his thumb. "My mom always said I'd just know. Not very helpful, huh?"

Before she could respond, there was a loud beeping from the television. She turned and saw a red band at the bottom of the screen. The picture had switched from the ball game to a man standing in front of a weather chart. Kevin grabbed the remote and turned up the sound.

"Tornados have been seen in several counties," the man was saying, then he began listing them.

"I have no idea what county we're in," she said.

"Me, either." Kevin frowned at the map on the screen. "Isn't that the town we drove through earlier?"

"I think so." She glanced toward the window. "Are we going to be okay? Should we go to a shelter?"

Kevin wrapped his arm around her. "We'll be fine."

"I've never been in a tornado." And she wasn't much interested in experiencing one now.

Kevin sighed heavily. "Go put on your pj's, then come back here. You can stay with me. We'll leave the TV on and monitor things."

"You won't mind?" She knew she would feel much better being in the same room with him.

"I'll take care of you," he promised.

She liked the sound of that because she wanted to take care of him, too. They could take care of each other. With Kevin that felt exactly right.

Chapter Nine

The next morning Haley found herself singing along with the car radio. She felt happy, light and in her best mood in days. The tornados had decided *not* to pay them a visit in the night, so she hadn't had to wrestle a mattress into the bathroom and fling herself and Kevin into the tub for safety. But she had spent the night in his arms.

Yes, it was true. Two nights out of the past four she'd slept with a man. And while he had made her drag in a sheet from her own bed so they didn't actually touch skin-to-skin, they'd been close enough for her to feel the heat of his body and to wake up with his arms around her and her head on his chest. It had been the absolute best morning ever.

She glanced at him out of the corner of her eye. He was sitting beside her in the passenger seat with his injured leg out straight, tapping his fingers in time with the upbeat country song. When he saw her looking at him, he gave her a slow, sexy smile that made her entire body shiver with delight. In a word—cool.

Kevin was something special. She'd started to figure that out the very first night when he'd refused to take advantage of her drunken invitations to kiss her and more. He'd been funny, gentle, kind, respectful and last night he'd managed to make her feel like a princess, even as he'd once again refused to take her to his bed. Well, he *had* taken her to his bed, but once the lights were out their activities had been strictly rated G.

Part of her understood his reluctance, even if she would never admit it. She supposed that making love with a twenty-five-year-old virgin was something of a responsibility. But what she couldn't seem to make Kevin understand was that she trusted him completely. His comment that she should care about the man before giving herself to him only made her trust him more. That bit about not doing it in a roadside motel hadn't made any sense. Location wasn't the point. But caring about the man—he was right with that.

What he didn't seem to get was that she cared about *him*. How could she not? He'd seen the truth about Allan in forty seconds and it had taken her nearly five years. He'd called Allan a jerk and had defended her. Kevin was the most amazing man she'd ever met. How was she supposed to resist him?

He thought she wanted to have sex just for the experience, but he was wrong. Okay, maybe things had started out that way. When she'd first hit the road, she'd been determined to be as bad as possible and part of that had been to find the right guy to show her what was what between a man and a woman. But somehow Haley didn't think she could have been with just anyone. And Kevin wasn't just anyone.

She found herself wanting to tell him things she'd never

told another person. She wanted to hear all about his life and to be the keeper of his secrets. She wanted to spend time with him. She wanted to make love with him.

Just thinking about it made various body parts tingle. Somehow she was going to have to get him to see that she was more than just an innocent on the lookout for a life-altering experience. She and Kevin had a connection—one she couldn't explain. For all those years she'd thought she was in love with Allan, she'd never once felt the same bond.

Beside her, Kevin pulled out his cell phone. "When we get closer to Oklahoma City I should be able to get a stronger connection. I need to check in with my office. And I want to call my mom and let her know when to expect me." He glanced at her. "Anyone you need to call?"

"Not until tonight," she said, trying not to feel guilty.

When she knew everyone had left the church she would leave another message for her father, telling him that she was fine. She'd been gone a week—no doubt he was worried about her. As for what Allan might be feeling, she didn't want to know. She was still angry with him. To be honest, she was also angry with herself for not canceling the wedding months ago when she'd known she didn't love him and that getting married would be a mistake.

"Your father?" Kevin asked.

She tightened her hold on the steering wheel as she nodded.

"Where's your office?" she asked before he could question her further.

"D.C."

"What do you do there?"

"Not deliver prisoners." He shifted his leg a little to the left. "I picked the short straw this time."

"Is it usually dangerous?"

"Depends on who is being transported. This is the first time I got called back for a riot."

"When did you decide to go into law enforcement?"

Kevin considered the question. There hadn't been any one event that had sent him in that direction. "Sometimes I think I did it as a joke," he admitted. "I've told you that I was a screwup as a kid. My days in military school showed me a life I didn't want to be living. So I cleaned up my act. When I got to college, I looked around for a major. Criminal justice appealed to me. I figured I knew the bad guy's side of things, maybe it would be interesting to check out the other half."

"You must have liked it."

"I did. When I graduated, I knew I didn't want to go to law school. The Dallas police department had done some recruiting. I applied and they took me." He remembered his surprise when he'd been notified. "I kept waiting for them to realize they'd made a mistake."

She glanced at him. "They didn't make a mistake. You were a good cop."

Typical Haley—always believing the best of him. "You don't know that."

She smiled. "Of course I do. You wouldn't have moved up to the Marshals if you'd been bad at law enforcement."

"Good point," he said wryly. "I did okay. Got a couple of promotions, then heard about the Marshals. I applied and they accepted me."

He'd spent the past several years waiting for *them* to find out the truth, but so far he had them all fooled. They still thought he was one of the good guys.

"My boss keeps offering me a promotion," he said without thinking.

"You say that like you've turned it down before."

"Yeah. Twice." Kevin rubbed his sore leg. "It's more

of a desk job, coordinating fieldwork. I took the test for it, which was stupid. Or maybe passing was stupid." He didn't tell her that he'd aced it, coming in on top.

"Aren't you interested in a new challenge?"

He chuckled. That's exactly how Haley would view change—as a challenge. She was a lemons-to-lemonade, the glass-is-half-full kind of gal.

"I thought I was interested."

"So what's the problem? Are you afraid you'll miss being in the field all the time?"

"Maybe."

He felt uncomfortable and wished he hadn't brought up the subject. When he had problems, he didn't like to talk about them with anyone. Instead, he worked them through on his own.

"That happens in the church," she said, and pulled on her sunglasses as the sun broke through the clouds and flooded the car with light.

Kevin put on his own glasses and tugged down the brim of his hat.

"Some missionaries head out into the world, do their three- or five-year tour, then come back. But others love what they do so much they make it their life's work. They can't adjust back to the 'regular' world, or they don't want to."

He understood the analogy, but knew that wasn't the problem. Sure fieldwork could be exciting, but mostly it was tedious and detail-oriented. TV cop dramas never showed all the grunt work that went into cracking a case.

"It's not that," he admitted slowly. The truth formed in his mind and he wondered if he could tell her. With anyone else, he would say no. But his gut said she would understand. Crazy, considering she was about the least sophisticated person he knew.

"I know what I am on the inside. One day they're going to find out, too, and then all this will be over."

He couldn't see her eyes, but the corner of her mouth twitched. "You think you're just a bad seed waiting to sprout again?"

"Sort of. I don't like the seed reference."

The twitch turned into a smile. "Would something more macho be preferable?"

"Yeah. Macho and dangerous. A seed? Come on."

"I can't think of anything better, sorry." Her smile faded a little. She glanced at him. "How long has it been since your last legal infraction or whatever you want to call it?"

He shrugged. "Fifteen, sixteen years."

"That's about half your life. If you were going to suddenly transform back into a menace to society, don't you think it would have happened by now? No one can avoid his real nature for very long. So either that isn't your nature or you have extraordinary skills in subjugating your evil side."

The simple truth of her words slammed into him like a speeding bullet. He turned the idea over in his mind, then mentally groaned. Well, hell.

He felt foolish, sheepish and relieved all at once. Damn if he hadn't been hiding from ghosts all these years. He'd been so caught up in his past, in the fear of what he *could* have been that he hadn't once thought about what he was. What he'd become.

"Pretty smart for a girl," he mumbled.

"Thank you." She wiggled in her seat. "Brains and beauty. However will you resist me?"

He was not going there. Resistance was hard enough without her bringing it up. "How'd you figure me out so easily?" he asked by way of shifting the subject.

Most women told him he was emotionally inaccessible. Obviously, Haley didn't agree.

"I just saw who you were. From the first second we met, you've been nothing but kind and gentlemanly. How could I keep from believing in you?"

Her words make him both proud and apprehensive. He'd seen the light in her eyes when she looked at him and he didn't want to do anything to make it fade. But despite finally figuring out he was unlikely to start a life of crime at any second, he still wasn't the right guy for her. Reformed bad boys weren't known to be good relationship material.

"Don't make me into a hero," he warned.

"Too late. You became that the first night we met when you rescued me from those men and didn't take advantage of me. You cemented my opinion last night when you once again chose honor over, um, you know."

"'You know'?"

She sighed. "You're trying to get me to say the S-word and that isn't going to happen."

He chuckled, then turned serious. "I wouldn't take advantage of you, Haley. I couldn't."

She pulled off her sunglasses and glanced at him. The light was burning on high.

"I know," she said. "That's why you're one of the good guys."

As he looked at her, he felt something tugging in the center of his chest. A connection he'd only ever felt once before, with his twin brother. For years he and Nash had been close enough to be halves of the same whole. But as they'd grown up, that had changed. They'd separated, becoming their own persons. Kevin never thought he would feel that bond again.

Only this time it was different. His relationship with

Haley wasn't brotherly. It was far more dangerous. Maybe for both of them.

Hands off, he told himself as she returned her attention to the road. If he was going to live up to her expectations of him, he would have to remember the rules. Rule number one: he would leave her as he'd found her.

Kevin checked his watch. It was just after three. "We can drive through, Mom," he said into his cell phone. "I'd be home late tonight."

"Don't even think about it," his mother told him firmly. "You've been shot. Your stepfather and I want to see you, but we'll wait until you arrive. Take it easy. You probably shouldn't be traveling in the first place, so I don't want you to push things."

Kevin thought about Haley's leisurely pace and the way she watched after him. "I'm in good hands. You don't need to worry."

He heard the smile in his mother's voice as she spoke. "I'm allowed to worry. It comes with having children. But I'll admit I worry a lot less than I used to."

After all he'd put her through in the years he'd spent growing up, she deserved a little peace of mind. "Then I'll see you in a couple of days. I love you, Mom."

"I love you, too. See you soon."

They said goodbye and hung up. Kevin tucked the cell phone back into his pocket and watched Haley walk out of the bathroom and head for their table. As she slid in across from him, she glanced at his empty plate.

"See. I told you it would be good."

She'd insisted they stop for afternoon dessert when she'd seen the sign for homemade berry pie. For a skinny thing, she sure packed away the food. She'd ordered her pie with ice cream on the side and had polished off every bite. Not that he was in a position to cast stones, he'd done the same thing.

"You were right," he said. "It was homemade and delicious."

The café was straight out of the fifties, with red-vinyl bench seats in the booths along the front window and several counter seats up front. The waitresses wore pink uniforms with starched white aprons and the jukebox held real forty-fives. Currently Elvis was asking for someone to "Love Me Tender." The scratchy music made Kevin feel as though he was back in high school. Had that been the case, he would have slipped his letter jacket over Haley's shoulders so the whole world would know she was with him.

"Did you call your boss?" Haley asked, rearranging the condiments by the window.

"Uh-huh."

"And?"

She looked at him, her hazel-blue eyes wide with anticipation. So that was why she'd been gone for so long. She'd been giving him privacy.

He shrugged. "I told him I should be back at work in a couple of weeks."

Haley rolled her eyes. "I don't care about that. What did you say about the promotion?"

"I said I was interested."

She straightened and beamed at him, then thrust her hands across the table to clutch his. "Oh, Kevin, I'm so glad. You're going be terrific."

High praise considering she didn't even know what the promotion entailed. But that was Haley. For reasons he couldn't understand, she had total faith in him.

Her fingers pressed against his and she squeezed. The contact warmed him from the inside. Funny how after such a short period of time she could get to him. He found himself wanting to pull her close and hold her against him. Not for sex, although he still wanted her in his bed, but just to feel the beat of her heart. Being around Haley felt…right.

That thought scared the hell out of him so he released her hands and tossed a couple of bills onto the table to cover their check.

"Where do you want to spend the night?" he asked. "We could probably go another eighty miles before stopping."

Haley shook her head. "We have to stay here."

He glanced around at the café. The pie had been good, but not that good. "Why?"

She pointed out the window. He looked across the street, saw the sign and groaned.

"You're kidding," he said, even though he already knew she wasn't.

The large, sprawling wooden building looked like what it claimed to be—a country-western bar. The big marquee up front proclaimed Talent Night At Honky-Tonk Blues. The winner is promised fame and fortune. Or at least a hundred bucks in prize money.

He returned his attention to her. "You're not serious."

She nodded vigorously. "Absolutely. I play a mean piano. I could win."

Kevin slumped down in his seat. Hell. Just what he needed. Haley back in a bar and playing church tunes for a rowdy crowd.

The whole situation was worse than he'd thought, Kevin realized five hours later as he and Haley crossed from the motel they'd checked into and headed for Honky-Tonk Blues. Not only had the parking lot filled up with pickups and SUVs, but the sounds coming from the bar warned him the place was anything but quiet.

"Are you sure about this?" he asked Haley as he held open the wooden door.

She answered, but the words were pulverized by the wall of noise that slammed into them when he opened the second door.

They stepped into a pounding beat of music punctuated by loud conversation, rowdy laughter and plenty of cowboys who instantly gave Haley the once-over.

Kevin didn't have to glance back at her to remember she was dressed in a denim skirt that barely fell to mid-thigh, another of those damned tight T-shirts and high-heeled strappy sandals that made her legs look endless. She was walking, breathing temptation.

But while she was in his company, she was his responsibility. So when a tall, skinny guy in a cowboy hat headed in their direction, Kevin grabbed Haley's hand and pulled her toward a table that had just been vacated by three women with big hair.

"You can still change your mind," he said when they were seated. He had to yell to be heard over the throbbing music.

Haley shook her head as she glanced around at the oversize room. He followed her gaze and saw couples moving together on a crowded dance floor. Behind them was the stage where a pretty decent band provided the noise and the rhythm. A bar lined the far wall. People were six deep waiting to be served. Banners hung down from the ceiling proclaiming tonight to be Talent Night.

"You ever play in a place like this?" he asked, even though he knew the answer.

"Not really. I've played in church, of course. And did recitals at school."

Figures. "So you didn't moonlight in a rock-and-roll band in high school?"

She looked at him and laughed. Her eyes lit up with humor and her soft mouth parted slightly. At that moment he wanted to kiss her more than he had wanted anything. He also wanted to whisk her away because there was no way she was going to be able to tame this crowd. He winced when he thought of the potential disaster.

"You don't have to do this," he said.

Her gaze narrowed. "You're right. I don't have to do anything. But I've spent the past twenty-five years doing what everyone else has told me to do. I think I'll spend the next twenty-five years doing just what I want."

He wasn't about to force her, so all he could do was flag a passing waitress and ask who they talked to about entering the contest.

Fifteen minutes later he'd finished a beer and was thinking that maybe he should have ordered something with more alcohol. Being drunk would take the edge off his tension, not to mention douse the ache in his leg. If he was drinking tonight, he wouldn't be taking any painkillers, which meant getting drunk had a lot of appeal.

Haley signed her name on the bottom of the release form and stood, prepared to head for the stage. There were going to be six acts tonight—she would be the last.

Kevin grabbed her wrist. "You okay?" he asked.

"No, but I'll survive."

"Don't go picking up any strange guys."

"As if," she said with a grin. "Besides, I don't want anyone but you."

Then, while he was still immobilized by her simple, honest and unexpected confession, she leaned forward and planted a quick kiss on his lips, turned and sashayed her way to the side entrance to the stage.

She'd managed to hit him right where he lived, and

with just one sentence. He'd be laid low for a week if she ever worked up to full paragraphs.

Kevin noticed he wasn't the only male to catch the sway of her hips or the way her short blond hair bounced with each step. There was going to be trouble, he thought grimly, and he'd left his gun back in the room.

The first talent-show contestant seemed to be a regular. Several in the crowd called out greetings to the buxom redhead who carried a guitar onto the stage. When she was seated, the room went relatively quiet as she sang a couple of ballads.

Kevin ordered a second beer, then decided he'd better not drink it. He nursed a glass of water instead and sat through a lousy band, a magician who looked young enough to still be in grade school and two more singers who didn't have enough talent between them to fill up a shot glass. Then it was Haley's turn.

By this point, his nerves were stretched tight enough to *be* guitar strings. While the crowd had gone easy on the underaged magician, they'd hooted the band and both lousy singers off the stage without even letting them finish their two numbers. Haley was pretty enough to get the sympathy vote, but was that going to save her?

His muscles clenched tight the second she appeared on the stage. There were several whistles and catcalls as she walked to the piano that had been rolled out onto the middle of the stage. The man in charge adjusted a microphone so that it was level with her mouth. The house lights went down and a spotlight appeared on her.

"Hey, baby, why don't you show me another kind of talent?" one of the guys up front yelled.

Haley shaded her eyes against the glare of the spotlight, glanced at the man, then shook her head. "Thanks, but I'd rather play the piano."

The room exploded into laughter. Kevin relaxed a little. He didn't think Haley had understood what the guy had been talking about but she'd handled him perfectly.

"I haven't played in a while," she said, resting her hands on the keys. "Can I have a second to warm up?"

"I'm hot already, baby!"

Haley frowned slightly, then ran her fingers up and down in a quick series of scales. Kevin sensed people getting restless. She moved into a piece he didn't recognize but that sounded classical. He groaned. This wasn't the place for Bach.

A couple of people booed. Somebody yelled at her to get off the stage. Haley paused uncertainly. Kevin started to stand. If she needed rescuing, he wasn't going to let her down.

"Not your style, huh," she said, then shrugged. "I was trying to provide a little culture, but I guess not. Then how about this?"

At the first tinkle of the keys, Kevin froze. He didn't recognize that song, either, but it sounded like an intriguing combination of jazz and bluegrass. As people began clapping, he sank back into his seat. He raised his beer in a silent salute. Looked as though Haley wasn't going to need rescuing at all. She was doing just fine on her own.

Haley lifted her hands from the keyboard and set them in her lap. There was a second of silence, followed by an explosion of applause. People yelled for her to keep on playing. She was about to shake her head no when she saw the nice man who had moved the piano onstage for her nodding at her to continue.

She started on another piece by a friend of hers from college, speeding it up a little and throwing in some country-sounding bass notes. If the dance floor had been crowded before, it was positively jammed now. She looked at the men and women moving together and started to smile. This was a lot more fun than playing at choir practice.

She stretched out the song, repeating the middle section. It had been so long since she'd played for pleasure that she'd nearly forgotten how much she really did like music. Somehow the piano had become part of the world she'd been trying to escape and she'd lost her joy in it.

Yet tonight she'd found it again. Her fingers moved with a lightness and confidence she'd never experienced before. It was almost as if she didn't have to think about the notes—they simply flowed from inside of her. She could have played for hours.

When the song ended, the nice man returned to stand next to her. He motioned for her to rise, then he took her hand and raised it in the air.

"We have a new winner!"

Everyone applauded. Haley couldn't believe it. "I won?"

"Sure thing, honey. Here." He handed her a hundred-dollar bill. "Feel free to spend it all here."

Haley laughed, then gave him an impulsive hug. She'd won!

After hurrying off the stage, she wove her way through the crowd, searching for Kevin. She wanted to show him the money. She also wanted to hear what he thought of her playing. Mostly she just wanted to be with him.

"Hey, not so fast."

Someone grabbed her wrist and swung her around. She found herself facing a dark-eyed man with a moustache.

"How 'bout I buy you a drink."

Haley smiled as she shook her head. "No thanks. I'm with somebody."

The man released her. "Then he's a lucky man."

Haley nodded and headed for the center of the room. She saw Kevin and waved. At that moment, her heart thudded against her rib cage in an unfamiliar rhythm. *I'm with somebody.* Weren't those the best words ever?

"You were terrific," Kevin said as she approached.

She hurried toward him, rushing the last few feet when he stood and opened his arms.

His embrace felt like coming home. The heat of him, the feel of his body, his scent, it all felt exactly right. She belonged here. Maybe it had only been a few days, but she was more comfortable with Kevin now than she'd ever been with Allan, or anyone else she'd met.

"You scared ten years off of me when you started with that classical music," he told her. "Then you blew my socks off. Pretty sneaky."

She waved the money in front of him. "And now I'm rich. Dinner's on me. Where do you want to go?"

His dark gaze settled on her face. At that moment something dangerous and fiery flashed in his eyes. Something that made her stomach clench and her legs tremble. Something that reminded her of them kissing the previous night.

Even with her limited experience, she recognized the look of a man who wanted a woman. But instead of saying anything about that, he wrapped his arm around her and said, "I think I have a taste for a burger. What about you?"

Haley didn't mind that he wouldn't admit his feelings. She agreed to a burger all the while knowing that they were in adjoining rooms and that it was the kind of night where anything could happen.

Chapter Ten

"You should have let me pay for dinner," Haley said as they walked toward their motel. "I wanted to."

"No way. Contest winnings are play money. Find something you would never let yourself buy and get it." He grinned. "Maybe one of those stuffed armadillos you're so fond of."

She wrinkled her nose. "I think they're interesting but I would never want one in my house. I'd always feel bad about it being dead."

"You wouldn't want a live one in the living room."

"Probably not."

Haley paused while Kevin pulled his room key out of his pocket. They were in adjoining rooms as they had been the previous night, but Haley was hoping that she wouldn't be sleeping alone. She'd liked sharing a bed with Kevin, even if he had kept his hands to himself.

He pushed open the door and motioned for her to go in

first. She walked into the room and flipped on the light switch, then spun around in a circle.

"I still can't believe I won."

He smiled. "You did great. When you said you'd studied music for years, I didn't know it was anything like that."

"Oh, there were plenty of days spent on the classics, but sometimes we had fun. I'd nearly forgotten how much I enjoy music. I'm going to put playing just for pleasure on my to-do list."

He closed the door and tossed the key on the dresser. "You have a to-do list?"

"Uh-huh. It's all the things I want to do now that I'm free to follow my dreams." She began ticking items off on her fingers. "I'm going to play what I like on the piano. I'm going to visit Hawaii, and become a schoolteacher."

"What about winning a talent contest? Was that on the list?"

"Nope, just a bonus."

He sat on the bed and rubbed his thigh.

"Is it hurting?" she asked.

"Some. I had a beer, so I won't be taking a painkiller tonight."

"I have some over-the-counter stuff in my suitcase," she said. "You can take that."

He nodded gratefully. She studied the lines of pain around his eyes and mouth, the fading bruises on his face. If only she could do something to make him feel better.

"Okay. Let me go get the bottle and also the stuff to change your bandage. I'll be right back."

She hurried through the open adjoining door and into her room. After turning on a light, she unzipped her suitcase and fished out the bandages and antiseptic cream, along with a bottle of aspirin. Before returning to his room, she kicked off her sandals, then walked barefoot across the carpet.

Kevin was where she'd left him, still sitting on the side of the bed. She handed him the aspirin first, which he swallowed without water. She grimaced.

"How can you do that?"

"Practice."

The thought of that taste in her mouth made her shudder.

"Do you want me to change your bandage now or do you want to let the pain ease a bit first?"

"I can do it," he said, taking the supplies from her.

Haley blinked at him. "What do you mean?"

"I appreciate all you've done, but I don't need your help tonight."

He didn't sound angry as he spoke, and the words were polite enough, but she still felt as if he'd slapped her. Not need her help? But she'd always changed his bandage. Some of her fondest memories were of what had happened after.

Heat flared suddenly. Was that the problem? She'd made her interest in him very plain. Maybe he didn't like it. Maybe he didn't like her. After all, he'd turned her down enough times.

"I'm sorry," she said quickly. Her eyes burned with tears, although she didn't know why she would want to cry. She felt both hot and cold and very, very small. "I'll just—"

She motioned vaguely, then hurried back to her room.

"Haley, wait."

She didn't listen. Instead, she pushed the door between their rooms closed and looked for a place to hide.

There wasn't one. She was in a strange motel just outside Oklahoma City. All the pleasure of her win earlier that evening dissipated as if it had never been. Her stomach lurched, protesting what she'd had for dinner.

She should leave. She could get in her car and drive far, far away. Except then she would strand Kevin and she couldn't do that. She was supposed to take him home. All right—she would get him in the car and they could make it to Texas tonight.

She sank onto the bed and covered her face with her hands. She couldn't do that, either. He was injured and in pain. She couldn't ask him to sit in the car all night just because she'd realized she'd made a fool of herself by throwing herself at a man who wasn't interested.

She swallowed hard, still fighting the tears, but eventually they won. She was cold and lost and humiliated. All she could think of was how much she liked Kevin and how he didn't like her and how all of this was so much worse than Allan telling her he didn't want to marry her.

"Haley."

She looked up, then quickly wiped her cheeks when she saw Kevin standing just inside the adjoining door.

"How did you get in here?"

He held up the credit card he'd used to pop the door open. Her gaze flew to the dead bolt she hadn't bothered to latch, then back to him.

"Don't cry," he said, limping toward her.

"I'm not," she said automatically, even as fresh tears spilled down her cheeks. "I'm fine. Don't worry about me."

"I can't help doing that."

He sat next to her. She wanted to move away, but that seemed kind of childish. Worse, when he put his arm around her, she found she *couldn't* move because having him hold her felt too good. But wasn't he her problem to begin with? How could he be the solution?

He pulled her close. She resisted, determined to stay upright. He sighed and shifted back so he could face her.

"You don't understand," he said quietly. "I'm trying to be the good guy here and you're making it damned hard." He frowned. "What happened to your swearing lessons? I thought you were going to practice."

She sniffed. "I don't think I'm the swearing kind of person."

"Probably not." He took her hand in his and turned it over so he could study her palm. "But I am. I'm a lot of things that you're not used to."

He turned her hand back and laced their fingers together, then looked at her face. "Women are easy for me. They always have been. They find me attractive and enjoy my company in bed."

She stiffened. Great. So not only was he not interested, she was one of a crowd. Her face burned even hotter. She tried to pull her hand away, but he didn't release her.

"Getting laid has never been the issue," he said.

She didn't know what to do with that information. "What's your point?"

"I told you the difference between making love and sex. Do you remember?"

She nodded.

He stared into her eyes. "I can find plenty of women for sex, but finding women to make love with—women who matter—well, that's a different story." He stroked the back of her hand with his thumb. "Maybe it's me. Maybe I'm shallow. Or maybe I just have bad luck. I can't seem to find women I really care about. After a while, just having sex isn't enough. I want to be with someone I respect and care about."

This time she jerked her hand free and clenched it against her stomach. Pain sliced through her. It was worse than she thought. Not only didn't he want her, he didn't even like or respect her.

"I see," she said, although the words hurt. It was as if her throat had been rubbed raw by the pain.

"No, you don't." He cupped her face in his hands. "Dammit, Haley, I'm trying to tell you that I like and respect you *too much* to just have sex with you."

Now she was really confused. "But I like you, too. You said I should wait until I cared about someone, and I care about you. I don't understand. If you don't want me, then just tell me. I'm sorry I've been throwing myself at you. I never meant to make you uncomfortable. I thought—"

Her insides got all tight and she was afraid she was going to cry again. "I thought you wanted me, too."

Kevin let loose a string of swearwords he was pretty sure that Haley had never heard. She looked startled but didn't run for cover, which he guessed was something.

"I'm saying this all wrong," he told her.

The problem was, he didn't know how to say it right. His goal from the beginning had been to not hurt her. Yet he had. He could see it in her eyes, in the set of her mouth. He'd wounded her and all he'd been trying to do was be a good guy.

He sucked in a breath. "This is all new to you," he said. "You're on an adventure for the first time in your life. You're experiencing new things and that's great. I'm having a good time with you. I can't remember enjoying anything more. You're sweet and funny and you experience everything with your whole heart. There's no holding back. I admire that."

Some of the pain faded from her eyes, but she still looked wary. "And?"

"And I wonder how much of what you're feeling is about this being a new and exciting situation. I don't want you reacting without thinking of the consequences."

He couldn't believe that a beautiful woman was throwing herself at him and he was trying to talk her out of it. He deserved the Moron of the Year award.

Haley stared at him for a long time, then nodded slowly. "You're afraid I'm more caught up in the moment than in you. That this is about the new experience, not who you are as a person."

Kevin didn't like the sound of that. It made him feel like a touchy-feely New Age tofu eater.

"I have enough regrets for two lifetimes," he said, sidestepping her comment. "I don't want you to have the same."

"I want to say that I won't, but things are happening so fast. Sometimes it's hard to catch my breath." She ducked her head. "I'm sorry I've been throwing myself at you. Guys get the 'no means no' lecture all the time and I've been guilty of ignoring what you were saying."

She was apologizing for coming on to him? Okay, now he *knew* they were in an alternate universe.

He brushed her cheek with the back of his hand. "No matter what happens or doesn't happen, never doubt that I've wanted you from the beginning."

She glanced at him from under her lashes. "Really? So it's okay for me to suggest stuff?"

He had a feeling he was going to regret agreeing to anything but he would rather walk on hot coals than hurt her again. "You can suggest all you want as long as I'm free to say no."

Was he really saying that? What the hell was wrong with this picture?

She straightened and smiled at him. "Okay. I won't ask for sex or anything, but can we sleep together tonight?"

* * *

They might be sharing a bed but Kevin knew he wasn't going to be sleeping. Not while he was hard enough to hammer nails into concrete.

He groaned softly and rested his forearm over his eyes. Why had he agreed to this? Sleeping, or not sleeping, with Haley was going to be pure torture. Maybe if he asked her nicely she would hit him on the head with a lamp and he could pass out. Even the headache that would follow would be better than the low and steady throbbing ache in his groin.

The pain cranked up about twenty percent when the adjoining door opened and she stepped into his bedroom. Her face was washed, her hair brushed and she'd replaced her sexy denim skirt and cropped T-shirt with a camisole and matching panties.

As she crossed the room, her small, perfect breasts moved in a way designed to make a dead man hot. His gaze slipped to her long, bare legs, then back to her face where happiness radiated with a light bright enough to blind.

"How's your leg?" she asked as she pulled back the covers and slid in next to him.

Instantly her sweet scent surrounded him. In a second he would feel her heat and he would be lucky if he didn't just explode right there.

"Kevin?"

Oh, yeah. "The leg's fine."

She eased next to him and rested her head on his shoulder. Her hand settled on his bare chest, burning his skin and making rational thought impossible. Every fiber of his being focused on mentally forcing her hand down and down and down. As if that was going to happen.

He glanced at her and found her looking at him. She

smiled. His chest clenched in response as he realized he could look at her forever.

"Never settle," he told her. "Whatever you do, Haley, don't accept second best. If the guy you're seeing isn't interested in what you want, then dump him and find someone who is. Only accept the best. That's what you deserve."

"You mean, like Allan not wanting to go to Hawaii on our honeymoon?"

"Right."

"Or the kid thing."

He nodded, not wanting to think about the fact that she was on the Pill. Birth control wasn't going to be an issue for them because—

His brain froze. It wasn't his fault. Considering more than half his blood supply was otherwise occupied, he figured he'd been doing a fine job of communicating. But then she started moving her hand against his skin, rubbing her fingers against his chest, slipping back and forth…back and forth. He held in a groan. Why didn't she just shoot him?

Haley liked the feel of Kevin's warm skin and the way the hair on his chest tickled her fingers. He was so much more muscular than she was. She liked his scent, too, and the way he was warm and made her feel safe. He was really nice and good-looking. He had a good job.

"Why aren't you married?" she asked. "Why didn't you try again after that one time went wrong?"

"I never fell in love."

"Huh. I guess that's the same as wanting to be swept away. That's what I want."

He chuckled. "Guys don't want to be swept away. That's a chick thing."

She'd never thought of herself as a chick, but it was

still kind of cool to be called one. "But it's still true. We want the same thing."

"Yeah. But don't tell anyone I said that."

She smiled, then closed her eyes and lost herself in the feel of his body next to hers. Certain body parts were tingling and aching in a way she now recognized. She was getting turned on.

The feelings made her both tense and completely relaxed. She liked knowing that being around Kevin made her hot, even as the realization made her blush.

She trailed her fingers from his chest to his stomach until she reached his belly button. She was so startled to come in contact with something that intimate that she momentarily froze. Which meant she didn't fight when Kevin shifted suddenly and flipped her onto her back.

She opened her eyes and looked up at him. His face was chiseled and strained. Tension pulled his mouth straight.

"What's wrong?" she asked. "Did I hurt you?"

"How far did you and Allan go? I know you're a virgin, but what did he do? Touching, petting? First base? Third?"

His voice was low and hoarse. Haley didn't understand what was going on. "We kissed, nothing more. And I don't really know about the bases. I mean, I know what people mean when they talk about them, but I don't know what happens at each base."

In high school she'd overheard girls talking about what they let their boyfriends do, but she'd never been a part of a crowd that went further than chaste kisses.

Kevin squeezed his eyes shut. "I'm going to hell," he muttered.

"No, you're not. You're a very good person."

He opened his eyes. "Honey, you don't have a clue what I'm thinking right now."

Whatever it was, she wanted him to do it. The ache inside of her increased, as did the anticipation. She shifted to get closer. "You could tell me."

He groaned. "You have no idea how much I want you."

She nearly bounced with excitement. "I want you, too. This isn't just about sex. I swear. I couldn't imagine doing this with someone else."

"You were supposed to tell me no."

"Oh. But I don't want to say no."

"And I'm not ready to deal with you being a virgin."

Which put them at an impasse. She didn't know what to say to that.

"I want to touch you," he said, "but I won't make love with you. I plan to stop just short of that, even if it kills me. You can agree or if you've changed your mind, we can just go to sleep."

Sleep? When the alternative was being touched by him? She didn't think so.

"Go for it," she whispered, and raised her head to kiss him.

The touch of his lips was as soft and perfect as she remembered. He leaned over her, his arm braced by her head, his body pressing against hers. As he moved back and forth against her mouth, she parted and his tongue slipped inside.

He tasted of toothpaste and heat. They came together in a dance that took her breath away. Everything was familiar yet new.

He explored her mouth, circling her, teasing her, making her squirm, then he broke the kiss and pressed his mouth to her jaw. She reached up and rubbed her hands along his bare back as he kissed his way to her ear, then took the lobe in his mouth and sucked. Tingles exploded like fireworks, arcing across the darkness of her passion.

He settled his hand on her stomach. The warm weight filled her with anticipation. But he didn't move, which made her want to grab his wrist and pull him up to her breasts.

He kissed her neck, licked the hollow of her throat, then blew on the damp spot and made her break out in goose bumps. But still that hand just sat there.

He raised his head. "I'd like to take off your top."

Embarrassment battled with desire. It wasn't much of a fight. Making love meant getting naked. While the thought of taking off her clothes even at the doctor's office made her want to hide under a desk, she didn't mind if Kevin saw her. Not when he looked at her with such tenderness and fire.

She scooted into a sitting position and reached for the hem of her camisole. With one quick move, she pulled it over her head and let it fall to the ground.

In case she managed to forget what she'd done, the cool night air was an instant reminder. She waited for him to look at her, to say something, but his gaze didn't leave her face. Instead, he tugged her back onto the mattress and kissed her again. His tongue swept into her mouth with all the power of a man on the prowl. She felt both feminine and vulnerable, but in a good way. In a jungle fantasy sort of way. And when his hand settled on her again, she had a feeling that this time he meant business.

She wasn't wrong. She felt the instant his hand slipped from the silky fabric of her tap pants to her bare stomach. Every cell went on alert. He moved higher and higher until he settled over her left breast.

He'd touched her there before, but she'd been wearing her dress and nothing about that experience had prepared her for the liquid pleasure of having bare skin against bare skin. When he cupped her curves she couldn't breathe. When he brushed his thumb against her tight nipple, she thought she might pass out. When he broke their kiss to lean down and take her nipple in his mouth, she knew that she had in fact left gravity behind and was now floating in the cosmos.

Warm, wet, sucking heat surrounded her. She hadn't known it could be like that, that she could be so sensitive, that she could feel this good. Ever. She gasped for breath and clutched at his head, never wanting him to stop.

He shifted to her other breast and used his fingers to mimic the movement of his tongue. It was too much. It would never be enough. It was endless…it was the most perfect moment in time.

She gave herself up to him then, not able to speak as he sat up and reached for her tap pants. Suddenly she wanted them off, too, because if he could make her breasts feel that good, imagine what would happen when he touched her there!

Then she was naked. Somehow Haley had thought the moment would be notable. That she would remember getting naked and feel that it was significant. But all it felt was right. When Kevin settled next to her again, he smiled.

"Have I told you how pretty you are?"

She shook her head.

"You are. Very pretty. Everything about you is lovely."

As he spoke, he rested his finger in the valley between her breasts, then moved it over one and then the other. He brushed against her nipple and when she gasped, he smiled again.

Those magic fingers trailed down her chest, then across her belly.

"I'll stop if you want," he said as he circled her belly button.

She still couldn't speak so she shook her head and even parted her legs a little, although that was kind of embarrassing. He moved lower, tickling as much as he excited. Heat flared ahead of his touch, making her feel as though she was melting from the inside out. When he slipped between her legs she felt several powerful jolts. She also realized she was slick and swollen. She glanced at Kevin to see if that was okay, but his eyes were closed. He went deeper, then groaned.

Questions filled her mind but before she could speak, he started kissing her again. Everything got very intense as he swept inside of her mouth, claiming her.

At the same time he moved his fingers as if he wanted to discover all of her. She liked the feel of him rubbing against her. It was just as nice as when he'd touched her breasts. Maybe nicer. Maybe—

Lightning shot through her. Haley wasn't sure what had happened but she wanted it to happen again. And then it did. He'd found this one incredible spot—this place that was so...

She gasped. Her legs fell open completely. Now she was the one to deepen their kisses. She wanted more. She wanted it all. Harder. Softer. Faster. Slower. She didn't care. Just as long as he was there, touching her like that.

It was like climbing and falling and floating all at the same time. When she realized her hips were pulsing in time with his movements, she didn't know how to make it stop. Then she didn't care. More. There had to be more.

He circled her sweet spot, brushed across it, then rubbed it again. The movements got faster. She couldn't breathe, but she didn't care. Breath wasn't required. There was so much to feel, to experience, and then suddenly it all rose so high that the world disappeared and there was only the sensation of rushing pleasure sweeping through her body over and over again until she returned to Kevin's arms.

She opened her eyes and found him watching her. "How was it?" he asked.

She couldn't believe it. She'd had an orgasm. Her first ever. Who had thought that up? "Amazing. Can we do it again?"

He laughed. "Sure, but if we do it right away, you'll be sore in the morning."

"Okay. We can wait."

He shifted onto his back and she cuddled next to him.

"Wow," she said, energized and ready to conquer new worlds. "I just had no idea I was capable of that. No wonder people run around doing it all the time."

"I've created a monster," he said.

"No, but you have unleashed my carnal nature." She snuggled closer, liking the way her bare breasts nestled against his arm. Then she shot up into a sitting position. "What about you?"

"I'm fine."

She narrowed her gaze, then flipped back the covers he'd kept over his lower half. The size of his arousal made her mouth drop open.

"Tell me what to do," she said.

"Don't worry about it." He reached for the covers.

She stopped him. "Why can't I make you feel good? Do you think I'll do it wrong?"

"No." He hesitated. "It's okay that this is just about you."

"But I want it to be about both of us."

"So much for being noble," he muttered, and reached for his briefs.

She watched as he pulled them off. He was careful as he slid them over his bandage. When he stretched out on the bed, she stared at him, at how big he was and, golly, if he didn't stick straight out, the way he'd promised.

She wanted to study his body, to explore their differences, but the strained look around his eyes told her that he was a man on the edge. She would explore later, right now it was time for his orgasm.

"Okay, what do I do?"

He had her kneel next to him, then took her hand in his and wrapped it around him. He was hot, hard, yet the skin was so soft.

"Up and down," he said through slightly clenched teeth. "It's not going to take long." He looked at her. "You know what happens to men when they—"

She nodded. That much was clear to her.

He taught her the rhythm, then dropped his hand to his side. His eyes closed and as she moved she could see the tension tightening his body.

She liked how he filled her hand and the way he groaned as she quickened the pace. It felt as if she'd just gotten the hang of things when he stiffened and climaxed. Haley watched all of it, amazed at what she'd been able to do. Winning a talent contest, having her first orgasm and pleasuring Kevin all in one night. Life had just gotten very good.

Chapter Eleven

As Haley finished dressing she tried not to notice the look of apprehension in her eyes every time she glanced in the bathroom mirror. She wasn't nervous exactly, she just didn't know what was going to happen next.

Last night had been…spectacular. The things Kevin had done to her and that she had done to him had made her feel happy and alive and very connected to him. They'd fallen asleep holding each other and had awakened the same way. But he was still sleeping when she'd slipped out of bed to duck into her own room for a shower and she wasn't exactly sure about morning-after protocol. Did they talk about it? Did they not talk about it? Would things be awkward and icky?

She didn't want that. However wonderful things had been in bed, she didn't want what they had the rest of the time to change. In the past few days Kevin had become very important to her. She liked being around him and talking to him. They were good together.

Haley pulled on her socks and shoes, then turned her attention to her short hair. As there wasn't much she could do with the mussed style, she ran a comb through the damp strands, then put on mascara and lip gloss.

Somehow she and Kevin had become a team, she thought as she packed her shampoo into a clear plastic bag. Had her eagerness to experience life on the wild side ruined that?

She stepped out into her room and came to a stop when she saw Kevin sitting on her bed. He was dressed and obviously ready to go, but she couldn't read his expression. Before she could ask how he was—how *they* were—he rose and crossed to her, then pulled her into his arms.

He felt as warm and strong as she remembered and when he kissed her, all her fears melted away.

"Morning," he said when he pulled back a little and gazed into her eyes. "How are you feeling?"

"Good."

He grinned. "Just good? Not amazing?"

"That, too."

"I'm glad." He studied her. "No second thoughts?"

"No."

He picked up her free hand and kissed her knuckles, then led her to the bed. When she was settled next to him, he turned serious.

"I want to push through to Possum Landing today," he said. "I know we talked about spending the night in Dallas, but I can't stay in a hotel with you, Haley. We both know what will happen."

She didn't know what to think. While part of her knew he was right, another part of her wanted to scream in protest. She wasn't ready to let him go. It was too soon. She hadn't prepared. Kevin had become so important to her. Was she just supposed to walk away without any warning?

He squeezed her free hand. "This may sound a little strange, but I'd like you to stay with me at my folks' house. Just for a couple of days. I don't want to get in the way of your travel plans, but…" He shrugged. "I guess what I'm trying to say is that I'd like to spend some more time with you."

Her panic faded, replaced with a contentment so powerful she practically purred. "I'd like that, too."

"I won't be keeping you from your drive to Hawaii?"

"The islands will still be there when I head out."

"Good." He rose. "I'm starved. Let's go get some breakfast before we hit the road."

She nodded and dropped her makeup bag onto the bed, then took the hand he offered and followed him out of the room. As they stepped into the clear, warm morning, Haley suddenly remembered something her father had said a long time ago.

She'd probably been ten or eleven and had been talking to him about why he'd never remarried. He'd explained that he'd loved her mother so much that just being in the same room with her, not doing anything special, was better than the most exciting party with anyone else. At the time she hadn't understood his point, but suddenly it all made sense. She would rather have breakfast at a diner on the highway with Kevin than tour Europe with another man. Given the choice—

Haley's thoughts shifted as she felt an unexpected stab of longing. For the first time since running away, she missed her father. She wanted to see him and to talk to him, to tell him about her adventures—okay, maybe not *all* of them. She wanted to hear his voice and to have him meet Kevin. She wanted him to say that he still loved her.

"You all right?" Kevin asked.

She glanced at him. "I'm fine. Just thinking about my dad."

"Want to use my cell phone to call him?"

She shook her head. "Maybe later." When she'd figured out what she was going to say.

"Are you sure this is okay?" Haley asked for about the four thousandth time.

"How often do I have to say yes?" Kevin asked.

"I don't know. I'll let you know when I stop being nervous."

They'd left the interstate about an hour ago and were now on the outskirts of Possum Landing. Haley glanced around at the well-maintained houses and tidy lawns and tried not to notice the rock sitting in her stomach.

This was crazy. "I should check into a motel," she said. "I can't stay at your house."

Kevin grinned at her. "Technically, it's not my house. It belongs to my mom and Howard."

She tightened her grip on the steering wheel. "And that makes it better?"

"It doesn't make it worse." He touched her arm. "Relax. I talked to my mom and she's happy to have you stay with us. You heard my half of the conversation. Did it sound like anything bad?"

"No, but…"

But wasn't it weird that he was taking her home with him? It wasn't as if she were an old college friend, or even a lost dog he'd picked up somewhere.

"Turn here," he said, directing her.

She came to a stop at the light, then turned right. Possum Landing reminded her a lot of her hometown, she thought, feeling more miserable by the minute. She half expected to start recognizing people. Which made her feel really guilty about having run away in the first place, and not having called and actually spoken with her dad.

Kevin led her into the homey-looking neighborhood. Guilt and nerves grew by the second. When they finally came to a stop in front of a large, two-story house, Haley didn't know if she was going to throw up or simply expire from the stress.

"Ready?" Kevin asked as he pushed open the passenger door.

She wanted to say no, but before she could speak, the front door of the house opened and two people stepped out onto the wide front porch.

Haley didn't remember getting out of the car, yet suddenly she was standing on the sidewalk being introduced to Kevin's parents. She thought she might have spoken, smiled and shaken hands, but the moment was just a blur of impressions and terror.

Kevin's mother, Vivian, looked far too young to have thirty-one-year-old twins. Even knowing she'd given birth to them when she'd been seventeen, Haley thought she looked fabulous. Tall and slender, with thick dark hair and cat-green eyes, she was as attractive as her son was handsome. Howard was a few years older, balding, with a friendly face and an air of a man who is comfortable with himself in the world.

After greeting her, Vivian and Howard turned to Kevin and hugged him. His mother cupped his face and looked more than a little worried, while Howard fussed over his cane.

"I can't believe you were shot," Vivian said as she led them to the house.

"Me, either." Kevin could walk without his cane, but when Howard handed it to him, he took it and used it without saying anything.

"Any side effects from that blow to the head?" Howard

asked. He got to the front door first and held it open. "Should we call Doc Williams?"

"I'm fine," Kevin insisted with a grin. "We'll all go square dancing tonight and I'll prove it."

He waited for Haley to go in front of him. As she passed him, he winked at her.

Inside, the house was tastefully decorated in earth tones. Family pictures were scattered around on tables and shelves. Haley saw a much younger Kevin with a boy about the same age. His fraternal twin, she thought, liking Nash's broad smile and the glint in his eye.

"You tired?" Howard asked Kevin. "You can lie down before dinner if you like."

"Thanks, but all I did today was sit. Haley did the driving."

"Then I'll go get the suitcases." Howard headed for the front door.

"Oh, I'm only using the brown one," Haley said, re-membering the several large suitcases in her trunk. "Kev-in's is the duffel bag."

Kevin eyed the stairs. "I'm not looking forward to climbing those."

"Do you want to sleep on the pullout sofa?" his mother asked.

"No. I can make it. Just ignore the groaning."

Vivian looked more than a little worried as she studied her son. He wrapped an arm around her and squeezed.

"I'm fine," he insisted. "Stop fretting. I'm here, I'm upright and I'm not bleeding. Didn't you always say that was the best you could hope for with me?"

"In the past few years, I've raised my expectations."

He grinned. "Big mistake." He released her and gave her a little nudge. "Why don't you show Haley her room? I'm sure she'll appreciate that handmade quilt you bought a whole lot more than Nash and I did."

Vivian touched his cheek. "It's good to have you home."

"I'm happy to be here."

Haley watched the two of them together and felt the love that flowed between them. She hadn't much thought about Kevin's relationship with his family, but if someone had asked, she would have assumed it was strong. Having that confirmed made her feel warm inside.

"You must make yourself at home," Vivian said as she turned her attention to Haley and motioned to the stairs. "The guest room was redone a couple of years ago, so I hope you'll be comfortable."

"I'm sure it's lovely," Haley said. She quickly glanced at Kevin over her shoulder before following her hostess upstairs. He gave her a thumbs-up.

"You've been so kind to take me in," Haley said when she figured she was out of earshot. "I would really be fine at a motel."

"Nonsense." Vivian turned left at the top of the landing. "Howard and I rattle around this old place. If the spare room didn't have the television in it, we wouldn't even get up here very often. Our bedroom is downstairs."

She paused in front of an open door. "Here you go."

Haley moved into a bright, cheery room filled with a queen-size bed, a white desk and double dresser. The quilt was done in yellows and blues and matching curtains hung at the wide window that faced the rear of the property.

"The bathroom is across the hall," Vivian said, "but you won't have to share. Nash and Kevin each have their own room with a bathroom in between."

"It's very nice," Haley said sincerely. She heard voices downstairs and assumed Howard had returned with the luggage. She expected Vivian to go to the top of the stairs and call him, but Kevin's mother only leaned against the door frame and studied her.

"Thank you for bringing Kevin home," she said. "Knowing him, he would have started driving before he should have and probably made his injuries worse."

"I was happy to help."

More than happy. The past few days had been the most incredible of her life.

Vivian's green eyes darkened slightly. "I don't mean to pry, except I'm going to." She smiled. "I'm curious about your relationship with my son."

Haley felt heat on her cheeks and had a bad feeling she was blushing. Oh, no. "Um, what do you mean?"

Vivian shrugged. "He was never one to bring a girl home. I suppose he was always too much of a trouble-maker for that. He would rather have been out racing cars or cutting school than court a girl. Of course, he's grown up. Women have become more interesting and cars less so. Are you two just friends or can we hope for something more?"

Haley had no idea how to answer that question. She desperately willed Howard to appear with the luggage, but he didn't, which left her with an empty silence to fill.

"We, ah…" She cleared her throat. "I guess we're friends." Did friends do what they'd done last night? "I like Kevin very much. He's a wonderful man."

"I think so, but then, I'm his mother. What else would I say?" She straightened. "I won't grill you any more. Just know that we're very happy to have you here. Dinner is at six." She glanced at her watch. "Which means I need to get cooking."

"May I help?"

"We're just having a lasagna I took out of the freezer and salad. Unfortunately, Howard and I have to go out tonight." She wrinkled her nose. "I hate to be gone on

Kevin's first night back, but our bowling team is in the county championships and we can't miss."

"He'll understand," Haley told her.

Vivian smiled. "Plus he'll have you for company."

She turned and walked down the hall. Haley watched her go. At least Kevin's mother didn't seem to mind that he'd brought her home with him. And she liked knowing that he hadn't brought other women to the house. It made her feel special—which happened pretty much any time she and Kevin were together.

"You wouldn't believe how much trouble one dog could cause," Vivian was saying. "Still, with freshly planted shrubs, a good rain and sharp claws, he created a disaster. Mrs. Wilbur went after him with a rake. Chased him right down the center of the street."

Kevin chuckled. "Tell me the dog got away."

"Of course he did," Howard said, taking a second serving of salad. "She was spitting mad for weeks."

Haley listened to them talk over dinner. They'd brought Kevin up to date on the goings-on around town while he'd been gone. As everyone seemed to know everyone else's business, she was reminded of home again. It was that way for her and her father. They often spent dinners talking about what dog got loose and what ten-year-old had fallen out of a tree and broken his arm.

Kevin stretched back in his chair and patted his stomach. "Haley and I have had some fine meals on the road, but nobody beats your lasagna, Mom."

She smiled her thanks. "You'd think it would be good enough to tempt you home more often."

He held up his hands. "Give me another twenty-four hours before you light into me about that."

"Fair enough." She sighed. "It's just good to have you here now."

Howard nodded his agreement.

"So what's the big news you didn't want to tell me by phone?" Kevin asked.

Vivian and Howard glanced at each other. In the look that flashed between them, Haley saw silent communication that spoke of love and trust and many wonderful years together. She turned away, as if she'd glimpsed something intimate and private. But married people shared looks like that all the time. Even couples who were just dating connected like that.

But not her and Allan, she thought. They'd never connected at all. She sat up a little straighter as she realized that in all the time she'd been gone, she hadn't once missed him. She'd thought about him but only as someone she'd managed to escape. Despite the small diamond ring she'd left on her dresser when she'd fled, she'd never loved him. Not even a little.

"Let's talk in the morning," Vivian said, interrupting Haley's thoughts. "After that, we'll go visit with Edie."

Kevin hesitated, then nodded. He turned to Haley. "Edie Reynolds has been a friend of the family since before Nash and I were born. Her oldest, Gage, is the same age as Nash and me. Quinn is just a year younger. The four of us grew up together, more like brothers than friends."

Howard glanced at his watch. "We need to get going."

Vivian motioned to the table. "You have to give me a minute."

"I'll clean up," Haley said quickly. "It's the least I can do."

Vivian looked as if she was going to protest, but Kevin told her to head on out. "I'll supervise Haley so she does the job right," he promised.

His mother laughed, then kissed his cheek. The couple

waved as they picked up matching bowling bags and hurried out the back door.

Kevin watched them go. "Why didn't she tell me tonight?" he asked when they were alone.

Haley didn't have a good answer. "Maybe because they were rushed. Maybe she didn't want to say whatever it was and then have to leave." She looked at him. "Are you worried?"

"No, but I could be." He shook his head. "Whatever it is, she'll tell me in the morning. In the meantime, let's get the dishes done, then we can head upstairs and you can flip through the cable channels. Or we can watch a movie."

"Either," she said, just happy to be with him.

He rose, but instead of picking up a plate, he helped her to her feet and pulled her close. "You doing okay with my folks?"

She nodded. "They're great."

He brushed his mouth against hers. "What about me?"

"You're great, too."

He winked at her. "I know."

Kevin tried to sleep, but he couldn't. Maybe it was because he was by himself instead of with Haley. After cleaning up, they'd watched a movie, then he'd sent her off to bed before their occasional kisses turned into something more dangerous.

He sat up, reached for his jeans and pulled them on, along with a T-shirt. Then he quietly limped down the hall to the stairs.

When he reached the main floor, he headed for the kitchen. His mom always kept cookies in the teapot-shaped cookie jar he and Nash had bought her for Mother's Day about twenty years ago. He smiled as he remembered pooling resources with his brother and then arguing about what to buy.

Headlights swept across the kitchen window as he poured himself a glass of milk and settled at the table. A couple of minutes later, his mom and Howard stepped inside.

"You're up late," his mother said when she caught sight of him. "Is your leg hurting?"

He shrugged. "No more than usual. How did it go?"

Howard held up a gaudy trophy. "Second place. Not bad for a couple of old folks."

"Congratulations."

His mother set her bowling bag on the floor. "Want some company for your snack?"

"Sure." He passed her the plate of cookies.

She took one but didn't eat it. Instead, she set it on the table and stared at him. "You want to talk about it now, don't you?"

Kevin shrugged. "I'm not doing anything else."

Howard patted his wife's arm. "I'll be in our bedroom when you're done."

Kevin was surprised that he left, but his mother's expression told him that they'd already discussed this and had decided she would be the one to tell him whatever she had to say.

He tried to shake off the uneasy feeling, but it wouldn't budge. The cookies stopped tasting so good.

"You said you weren't sick," he reminded her.

"I'm not. It's nothing like that." Vivian laced her fingers together. "Actually this is about your biological father."

Kevin had been braced for a number of different topics, but not that one. "What about him? He's a jerk."

He was a whole lot worse than that, but Kevin knew how his mother felt about swearing. Besides, there weren't enough bad words around to describe a man seducing a seventeen-year-old, getting her pregnant and then abandoning her.

His mother smiled. "I've always appreciated your support. Nash's, too. You boys never blamed me for what happened."

"That's because it's not your fault. You were a kid. He's the one to blame."

"I know. I tell myself that. I thought I was so in love with Earl Haynes. He was handsome and funny."

Kevin thought he was more of a bastard, but he didn't say that.

His mother sighed. "What I never told you was I went to see him again. The following year. I found out he was returning to Dallas for the convention. My parents had just thrown me out and I didn't know what else to do. I thought if I explained what had happened he would help."

Kevin leaned back in his chair. His muscles tensed as he prepared to hear something that would make him want to send the guy through the windshield of a car.

"Let me guess," he said. "He blew you off."

"Sort of. When I knocked on his hotel room, I interrupted him entertaining another woman. I was crushed. I'd thought it was love and I found out it wasn't. Worse, he claimed you boys weren't his and he said I hadn't been interesting enough to stay in touch with."

His mother shook her head. "I still remember how much it all hurt. I found my way to the lobby, but I was crying too hard to leave. I could feel people looking at me. I had nowhere to go, no money. I didn't know anything about social services or getting help. Then someone spoke to me. When I looked up, I saw the woman who had been in Earl's hotel room. I'd never seen her before, but she took me under her wing. We spent the morning together, sharing sad stories about Earl."

"He'd seduced her, too?"

"Sort of. She was a little older and married. It seems her husband couldn't have children. They couldn't afford cutting-edge reproductive treatment. Don't forget this was over thirty years ago. Things weren't as advanced as they are today. Her husband wanted her to find someone who looked like him and get pregnant."

Kevin flinched. "That's barbaric."

"She wasn't too happy about it, either. Eventually she agreed and headed up to Dallas where she met Earl the same weekend I did, the year before. He was real busy. We both got pregnant. The problem started when she realized she'd fallen in love with him. She came back to him, much as I had. They fell into bed again. That's where I found them."

She shrugged. "I would have been lost without her. She brought me here and helped me get a job and an apartment. It was her idea to create a fake dead husband so people wouldn't look down on me or you and your brother. When she found out she was pregnant a second time, her husband wasn't happy. They almost split up over it."

Kevin's bad feeling had been growing with the telling. There was one piece of information his mother hadn't told him and he was starting to think it was damned significant.

"Who's the woman?" he asked.

"Edie Reynolds."

The name slammed into him with all the force the bullet had used. Edie Reynolds? The woman he'd known all of his life and thought of as a member of the family? Her sons—Gage and Quinn... The four of them had been inseparable.

"Your brothers," his mother said, just in case he hadn't

figured it out. "Actually, your half brothers. I never told you before because Edie didn't want her boys to know. Don't forget she was passing them off as Ralph's children. You knew your biological father had abandoned us and that was all that mattered."

He was having trouble absorbing all this. "What changed?"

"Gage found out the truth, so I knew it was time to tell you who your father really was and that your two best friends were really your half brothers."

Chapter Twelve

Kevin sat up well past midnight. His mother had long since gone to bed, although he doubted she would get much sleep. Telling him would have upset her almost as much as hearing the news had bothered him.

He tried to convince himself that nothing much had changed. He was who he had always been. His biological father was the same bastard he'd been two hours ago. Yet everything felt different. Gage and Quinn were his half brothers. They always had been. Why hadn't he seen it?

A soft creaking on the stairs broke into his thoughts. He turned toward the doorway and saw Haley tiptoe into the kitchen.

He took in her mussed hair and wide eyes. At least she'd stopped to pull on jeans and a T-shirt. He didn't think he could have resisted her in one of her sexy pj outfits. Despite the confusion he felt about a lot of things, he still wanted her.

"Couldn't sleep?" he asked.

She took the seat next to his and shrugged. "I was worried about you. I heard you go downstairs, and then your parents came home. I thought maybe you were talking about whatever your mom had to tell you and when you didn't come up to bed, I wondered if you were okay."

Her pale face was beautiful, her expression so damned earnest that it made him ache inside. Haley didn't have the life experience of a gnat, but still she worried about him and wanted to help.

"I'm fine," he said, taking her hand in his. "Confused, but fine."

"Do you want to talk about it?"

"Sure." He didn't mind her knowing. He'd already told her the worst about his past and had yet to shake her good opinion of him.

"My mom wanted to talk about the guy who got her pregnant with Nash and me. It seems he was more of a jerk than I'd realized."

He outlined what his mother had said, explaining how Edie Reynolds had been the one responsible for bringing his teenage mother to Possum Landing and helping her start over.

"I've known Gage and Quinn all my life," he said. "We played together, fought together, grew up and never guessed we were brothers."

"You must be happy having them as a part of your family."

"Why do you say that?"

She smiled. "Because family is so important. More is always better. Having people around who care about you and want you to do well. I would think that after being good friends all your lives, you would be happy to know there was an even deeper connection."

"Do you ever *not* see the bright side of things? I swear

you could look at a pile of trash on the highway and claim it was modern art."

Her mouth trembled at the corners. "Is that bad?"

"No." He squeezed her fingers. "It's exactly as it should be."

He didn't want to figure out the reasons why, but he liked Haley seeing the world as a good and honest place. Maybe her thinking the best of people allowed him to believe that she saw the best in him. Maybe it wasn't all a crock.

"What happens now?" Haley asked.

"I'm going to talk to Gage tomorrow, and his mother. I guess I should get in touch with Nash, too."

She leaned toward him. "Are you sad about your dad? About what he did?"

He shrugged. "I made peace with what he did a long time ago. As far as I'm concerned, he was simply the DNA provider. When Nash and I were young, we didn't think much about having a dad. By the time my mom met Howard, we were old enough to appreciate having another guy in the house. He's the only father either of us has ever known. He's a great guy. He was always there for me when I was screwing up."

The grandfather clock in the living room chimed the hour. Kevin released Haley's hand. "It's late. We should be in bed."

Her eyes widened but before she could say anything, he shook his head. "Alone, Haley. You're going to your room and I'm going to mine."

"I knew that."

"Right."

He rose and pulled her to her feet. When she was standing, he kissed her. "For a good girl, you're sure doing your best to lead me down the path of being bad."

"For a reformed bad boy, you're certainly resisting."

He kissed her again, enjoying both the taste of her and the fire that flared to life in his groin. Wanting her felt good, even though he knew he wasn't going to have her.

They walked to the stairs together, then he followed her up to the landing. Once there, he gave her a push in the right direction and watched as she entered the guest room. He thought about following her inside and what would happen. Funny that as much as he wanted to make love with her, he also enjoyed just being with her. Haley might be ten kinds of trouble, but she was also one of the best things that had ever happened to him. In a short period of time, she'd become a part of his world and he didn't want to think about how much he was going to miss her when it came time to let her go.

"What do you think about all this?" Kevin asked Gage the following morning. Edie and Vivian were still talking in the living room while he and Gage had gone out onto the porch.

"It took some getting used to," Gage admitted. He leaned one foot against the railing. "You always had an idea of who your real father was, but until a few weeks ago, I'd never heard of Earl Haynes."

Kevin studied the man he'd known all his life. Last night Gage had been a good friend, but now he was his brother. The information made him realize that he and Gage were about the same height, with similar coloring. In fact all four of them were tall, with dark hair, dark eyes. Gage's khaki sheriff's uniform emphasized broad shoulders similar to Kevin's. Hell, the proof had been there all along. None of them had ever thought to look for it.

"What happens now?" Kevin asked. "Did you tell Quinn?"

"I have a message out for him to call me. It could be

weeks before I hear back from him. You getting in touch with Nash?"

"Yeah."

Gage looked out toward the yard. "Kari and I are heading to California. From what I could find out, Earl Haynes has several sons living out there. I guess they're our half brothers."

Kevin hadn't thought of other family, but it made sense. "Want some company?"

His friend grinned. "Sure thing. As long as you don't mind the mushy stuff. Kari and I are still at the crazy-in-love stage."

"I won't watch."

Kevin meant the comment as a joke, but as he spoke the words he realized something inside his chest ached. Gage was engaged and while he was happy for his friend, he also felt a little envious.

No way, Kevin thought, shaking off the feeling. He wasn't the kind of guy who wanted to get tied down. He'd considered it once and it had been a disaster. Long-term relationships weren't for him.

"Are you going to warn the California Haynes family that we're coming?" Kevin asked.

"I haven't decided. I don't know what kind of reception we'll get there. Maybe I'll try to contact them through email. I was thinking we'd head out at the end of next month. I can get some time off then."

Kevin had more than enough vacation time due him. "That works for me."

The front door opened and his mother walked out. "Are you two about finished?"

Kevin and Gage looked at each other, then nodded. "I'll be in touch," Kevin said. They shook hands.

Gage studied him. "I can't help thinking we should have known."

"Me, too."

"We know now."

Kevin nodded. He thought about what Haley had said about being happy to have more relatives. At the time he hadn't understood, but now he did. He was glad to know that Gage and Quinn were members of his family.

"Are you all right?" his mother asked as they drove back to the house. "I know this has been a lot to take in."

"It's been a lot easier for me than for Gage. I've always known about my biological father."

"At least he has Kari to help him. You know they're engaged."

"I heard."

Kevin figured his mother was trying to be subtle, but he could see her coming a mile down the road. He braced himself for the inevitable questions.

"Haley seems very nice," she said right on cue.

"She is."

Vivian glanced at him and smiled. "Want to talk about it? It wouldn't kill you to tell me what's going on between the two of you."

"If I had a clue, I'd tell you everything." At least that was honest. He sighed. "Haley's very special, but she's not like anyone I've ever met. She's lived a sheltered life and until now, she hasn't seen much of the world."

"Are you concerned that the two of you are too different in that respect?"

"It's crossed my mind."

"Is it possible that you're thinking of settling down?"

Trust his mom to cut right to the chase. He opened his mouth to give his standard response, which was that he would get married when hell froze over, then reconsidered. There was no way that he and Haley could ever have anything permanent. He was a hundred percent the wrong man for her. But was she the right woman for him?

"I can't say how things are going with the two of us," he told his mother.

She smiled. "Can't or won't say?"

"You make me crazy."

She laughed. "I know. It's one of my favorite ways to spend an afternoon—paying you back for all the gray hairs I'm going to get."

Haley paced through the empty house. Kevin and his mother had left to visit with Edie and Gage Reynolds, and Howard was at work. She was alone and she knew exactly what she should be doing. The thing was, she didn't want to.

"He's my father," she whispered as she paused by the phone in the kitchen. "I shouldn't be afraid to call him."

She wasn't…not exactly.

She reached for the phone, then dropped her hand to her side. "This is stupid," she muttered, and picked up the receiver.

The connection went through quickly and before she was ready, she head a familiar voice say, "Pastor Foster's office. This is Marie."

Haley sucked in a breath and did her best to ignore the sudden burning in her eyes.

"Hi, Marie."

The woman on the phone gasped. "Haley? Is that you? Child, we've all be frantic with worry. Where are you? Are you all right?"

"I'm fine." Haley pulled out a kitchen chair and sank onto the seat. "I've left my dad a few messages saying everything was okay."

"Even so. Oh, Haley, he's going to be so happy to

hear from you. Hold on one second. Don't you go any-where."

There was a brief silence, then she heard her father's deep voice. "Haley? Is that really you?"

Tears filled her eyes. "Yes, Daddy. I wanted to let you know that I'm alive and well. I'm sorry I worried you."

He sighed. "Worry doesn't begin to describe it."

He hadn't said anything mean or judgmental, but still she felt guilty. "I just needed to get away for a while so I could think things through."

"Where are you? When are you coming home? You should be here, Haley, with the people who love you."

"I can't," she said as the tears spilled down her cheeks. "Not yet, Daddy. Things happened."

He sighed. "I know all about 'things.' Allan told me everything."

Somehow she doubted that.

"You need to understand," her father continued. "Ev-eryone gets last-minute jitters. I was surprised when Allan admitted to them, but his honesty impressed me. We've had a lot of talks and his mind is clear. He loves you and very much wants to marry you."

Somehow that didn't make Haley feel any better. If she hadn't already figured out that she'd never been in love with Allan her lack of relief would have been a big clue. She didn't want to know that he was now willing to marry her. She didn't want anything to do with him.

"The problem is a lot bigger than last-minute jitters," she said. "I don't love him, Daddy. I went out with him because it's what everyone wanted. I think I got engaged for the same reason. He's a very nice man but he's not the one for me."

He wasn't Kevin, she realized. Kevin who made her heart beat faster just by walking in the room. Kevin who treated her as if she were the most precious woman in the world. Kevin who made her laugh and listened to her opinion and believed she could do anything she wanted.

"You don't know what you're saying," her father told her. "Haley, you've never been very good at making your own choices. Hold on a minute."

Outrage erupted inside of her but before she could vent, there was a click and the sound of a voice she didn't want to hear.

"Hello, Haley."

This is why she hadn't wanted to talk to her father. He loved her, but he didn't listen. He'd never listened.

"Allan."

Her ex-fiancé cleared his throat. "I know you're angry with me. No bride wants to hear her prospective bride-groom is having second thoughts. Although I would think you would appreciate my honesty."

Haley frowned. Allan was saying almost the same thing her father had. It was creepy.

"I do appreciate your honesty," she said. "As I hope you'll appreciate mine. Being away has allowed me to think about my life, what I want and what I don't want. I don't want to be engaged to you anymore."

"Haley, you're not being reasonable. Of course you want to punish me, but don't you think you're taking this a little too far?"

She could hear the temper in his voice. "I'm not trying to do anything but tell you our relationship is over."

"Where are you?"

"Why does that matter?"

"Because you don't know what you're saying. Tell me where you are and I'll come get you and take you home. I made a mistake and I'm sorry. You need to forgive me so we can go on with our lives."

"Why won't you listen to me? There is no 'us,' no 'we.'"

"But you love me. We belong together."

She held the phone out in front of her and stared at it. Was there some kind of technical malfunction that prevented her words from getting through?

"I don't love you," she said slowly and clearly. "I don't believe you love me."

"We have a wedding in less than two weeks. Are you telling me you want to break things off now?"

"Yes, I am." She closed her eyes. "Allan, we both got caught up in what other people thought. I'm not sure we ever saw each other for who we are. I accept my share of the blame for that. I never did a good job of going against other's expectations. But that's changing. I want my life back. I want to make my own choices. I want to be in love the way my parents were and I know I could never love you like that. I'm sorry. I hope you can find someone to make you really happy."

She opened her eyes and hung up the phone. As she turned, she saw Kevin standing in the doorway.

He shrugged when she looked at him. "My mom had to go to the grocery store, so she dropped me off first." His dark eyes softened with concern. "Allan?"

She nodded.

"You okay?"

She nodded again, but she was lying. Talking to her ex-fiancé had shaken her and the only place she wanted to be was in Kevin's arms.

"How did your parents love each other?" he asked.

"With their whole hearts. My father never remarried because he couldn't find someone else to love as much and anything less wasn't worth having. I don't think Allan understands that we never cared about each other. I shouldn't have let myself be swayed by what other people think. I shouldn't have ever dated him, let alone gotten engaged."

"You figured it out in time."

She nodded. "So, how was your morning?"

"Better than yours. Gage and I talked about the next step. We're going to California in a few weeks to find the rest of the Haynes clan. It turns out there are several other brothers."

He looked both happy and nervous about the prospect. Haley wasn't sure who moved first, but suddenly he was holding her and she was hugging him as hard as she could. Everything might be spinning out of control but with Kevin nearby she felt as if she could withstand even a tornado.

"It's all right," he murmured, kissing her cheek, then her nose.

She tried to smile but couldn't. "I wish we were still on the road," she told him. "I wish it was just the two of us and that we never had to come back to the real world."

"I wish that, too."

Her heart swelled. "Really?"

He nodded.

The phone rang. He gave her a quick kiss on the mouth, then reached past her to grab it. "Hello?"

Haley walked to the cupboard for a glass, but an odd premonition made her turn around. Kevin stood listening. His face was unreadable but she knew something was wrong.

"Yes, this is the Harmon residence," he said coolly. "Yes. She's here."

He covered the mouthpiece with his hand and looked at her. "It's Allan."

She shouldn't have been surprised. The church had caller ID. Obviously Vivian and Howard didn't have their calls blocked.

She moved next to Kevin and took the phone from him. "There's no point to this, Allan," she said.

"You're making a mistake and we both know it," he said. "I've looked up the address for this number. I'll be there in the morning to pick you up. Try to be mature this time, Haley. It wouldn't look good for you to run away again."

She felt cold and angry. "That's what matters, isn't it? How things look, not how they are. I'm not going back with you."

"Of course you are, but we'll discuss it when I get there. By the way, who are these people you're staying with? You aren't alone with a man are you?"

She hung up the phone without saying anything else. Kevin watched her. "He's coming for you."

He made the sentence a statement, not a question. Haley nodded slowly. "He said he would be here in the morning. I guess he'll fly into Dallas and drive the rest of the way."

"What do you want to do? If you need to go, I'll understand."

His gaze was steady. She saw understanding in his eyes. He wouldn't judge her for running. He knew how precious her freedom was.

But she wasn't the same person she'd been a couple of weeks ago. She'd changed, maybe she'd grown up.

"I'm staying," she told him. "I'm a fighter. I think I always have been, I just never bothered to stand up for myself before."

"I won't let him hurt you."

Haley smiled. How had she ever gotten so lucky as to find Kevin? "I know you won't."

He held out his arms and she stepped into his embrace. This was where she belonged. But how long would she be allowed to stay?

Chapter Thirteen

While Howard and Vivian went to bed shortly before ten, Haley and Kevin stayed up to finish the movie they were watching. At least, Kevin was watching it. Haley couldn't concentrate. Not when she was worried about Allan showing up in the morning. While she didn't doubt her resolve to do as she wanted and not as he insisted, she was fighting against twenty-five years of doing what everyone else thought was best for her. What if she wasn't strong enough to stand up to him?

Kevin reached for the remote and clicked off the television. "You don't need to be worried," he told her.

She smiled at him. "Thanks for the vote of confidence. I just wish I had a little more experience standing up to people and telling them no."

"Are you concerned about your feelings for Allan?"

He asked the question casually, as if the answer didn't matter. Haley hoped that was an act and not the truth.

"No. Whatever I felt for Allan, it was never love and it died a long time ago. It's the whole expectation thing."

"Just say no."

She laughed. "I'll do my best."

"We can practice tonight."

"I don't want to say no to you."

She'd spoken the words without thinking but as soon as she said them, she realized how true they were. She never wanted to say no to Kevin. She only wanted to say yes. Yes, she loved him. Yes, she wanted to be with him always. Yes, he was her heart's desire.

Of course. Why hadn't she figured this out before? She'd been falling in love with him from the first night they'd met. He was everything she could ever want in a man. She could imagine being with him for the rest of her life. Knowing that there would only be him made her want them both to live forever.

"Haley, what's wrong?"

She turned to look at him. His face had grown familiar to her. She knew his voice, his smile, his sense of humor. She admired his need to do the right thing. She trusted him. She wanted him.

"Make love with me," she whispered.

He stared at her. "Haley, we've been over this before."

She shook her head. "I'm sure. I'm more sure than I've ever been about anything. I want you to be my first." *My only.* But she didn't say that. She wouldn't play love like a card in a game. This was too important.

She watched the desire ignite in his eyes, but there was caution, as well.

"I don't want you to have regrets," he said.

How like him, she thought happily. To want her to be sure. "If you don't want me, I won't ask again." She took his hands in hers. "The only regret I'm going to have is if we don't make love. I know I'll spend the rest of my life being sorry."

He stared at her for a long time. She didn't move because as much as he needed her to be sure, she needed the same thing.

Silence stretched until it nearly snapped. Haley stopped breathing. Finally, when she was sure he was going to tell her no, he leaned forward and brushed her mouth with his.

"There aren't any words to tell you how much I want you," he said. "But not here, on the sofa. I want to make love with you in bed." He smiled. "At least my folks sleep downstairs. We don't have to worry about them."

She wasn't worried about anything. When he rose and held out his hand, she placed her fingers on his palm. They made the short walk to his bedroom at the far end of the house.

As she entered, Haley had a brief impression of light blue walls and shelves filled with mementos from a busy childhood. There were baseballs and sports posters, part of an engine on a desk and a stack of books. A dark blue comforter covered the full-size bed. Kevin walked to the nightstand and clicked on the lamp, then returned to stand in front of her. He cupped her face in his hands and studied her.

"I thought you were pretty the first time I saw you," he said. "But I was wrong. You're beautiful."

His compliment both pleased and embarrassed her. "I'm not so special."

"You are." His dark eyes glowed with intensity. "You're sweet and funny and smart. You care about other people, yet you're willing to stand up for what you think is right."

Her heart beat faster with every word. Knowing that Kevin cared about her, that he thought she was more than ordinary, made her want to burst free of the room and soar toward the heavens. Then he bent his head and pressed his mouth to hers. As the heat of his kiss spiraled through her body, she decided that staying right here on solid ground might be a better plan.

They'd kissed enough times that the contact was familiar. Soft, tempting brushes of sensitive skin against sensitive skin. As her arms came around to hold him close, her lips parted to admit him. He swept inside, touching her tongue with his, making her blood race and her body heat. Her breasts swelled and a sweet pressure built low in her belly.

He aroused her. With just a kiss, and sometimes with just a look. Knowing they were going to really make love sent a tingling sensation through her midsection. She wasn't afraid. Not with Kevin. He'd never done anything but make her world a perfect place to be. Tonight would be no different.

As he deepened the kiss, he rubbed his hands up and down her back. When he cupped her rear, she instinctively arched toward him. Her stomach brushed against him and she felt that he was already hard.

He wanted her. He'd said as much, but the physical proof delighted her. She remembered the last time they'd been together, when she'd seen him naked and touched him until he'd experienced the same release she had. She wanted that again, only this time she wanted him inside her. She wanted them to be one.

She felt his fingers on the back zipper of the summer dress she'd slipped on for dinner. As he pulled the tab, warm air brushed against her bare skin. She pulled back enough to drop her arms to her sides and shimmy out of the dress. At the same time, she kicked off her sandals. Kevin pulled off his shoes and socks, then shrugged out of his shirt. He moved to the bed and sat on the edge. Wearing only a bra and panties, she slipped between his parted legs.

With him sitting and her standing, she was taller. She bent her head and kissed him. He rested his hands on her bare waist. She could feel the imprint of each finger. He was warm and strong and, even undressed, she felt safe.

His hands moved higher. She braced herself for the first sweep of his hands on her breasts. Her breath caught in anticipation, then she sighed her pleasure as he cupped her curves. Even through the fabric of her bra, she felt his gentle caress. When his thumbs brushed over her tight nipples, she gasped as fire blazed through her.

She fumbled for the hooks of her bra and tugged it off. When the garment fell to the ground, Kevin looked at her bare chest. His breath caught audibly, which made her thighs tremble with excitement.

"So perfect," he murmured before leaning close and taking her left nipple in his mouth.

Gentle sucking sent ribbons of need curling through her. Between her legs, her body swelled and dampened in anticipation. His fingers teased her right breast, mimicking what he was doing with his tongue. It felt so right, so amazing. She could barely stand. Her head fell back and she wanted to surrender right this minute. Kevin could take her any way he wanted. As long as he touched her like that, as long as the tension built and the pleasure grew, she was his to command.

He moved his mouth to her right breast. More. She wanted more. She wanted this moment to never end. She wanted—

A single finger stroked her between her thighs. The unexpected touch chased away her last coherent thought. Breathing was impossible. She could only feel the light, teasing whisper of movement. It wasn't enough. She tried to part her legs, but she was standing between his and there wasn't room. She clutched at him, pulling him closer, wanting, needing bare skin against bare skin.

He straightened and tugged at her panties. The air tingled against her damp nipple. There were so many sensations. His hands against her legs, the sheets when he pulled back the comforter and eased her onto the bed. The sound of the zipper on his jeans being pulled downward seemed loud in the night.

She wasn't afraid. Not even a little. All of this felt right. This was the man she was meant to love. There would only ever be him, so how could joining with him be anything but her destiny?

He pulled off the rest of his clothing with one quick movement. She had a brief glimpse of his heavy arousal, then he knelt between her legs and bent low to kiss her right knee.

The sweep of his tongue tickled. She giggled softly.

"So you're ticklish," he said, raising his head and looking at her.

She nodded. "Pretty much everywhere."

"I know one place you're not."

"I'm not sure there is one. I remember—"

Whatever she'd been planning to say was lost when he bent low and pressed an openmouthed kiss on the top of her thigh. She would have sworn she was ticklish there, too, but the intimate contact surprised her so much she couldn't react. Just as well, because his next move was to reach between her legs and gently part her, exposing her most intimate self to his gaze.

She barely had time to register shock when he kissed her *there*. Right there. Just like that. With his lips and his tongue and—

The pleasure slammed into her. It ripped through her, sucking away air and the ability to move. She could only feel the stroke of his tongue, the gentle circling, the heat, the need. Every muscle tensed harder and tighter. Her body ached and burned. He moved slowly, deliberately, setting a pace that made her hips pulse in time with each flick of paradise.

The wanting crested, then went higher and higher until it was impossible to reach so far and still want more. Tiny spasms rippled through her fingers. She pulled her knees back and gasped, then found herself reaching again and again. There was a single heartbeat during which she balanced on the edge of the universe before the sweep of his tongue sent an explosion of intense pleasure flying through every cell in her body.

It was like coming apart, while staying together. The climax shook her down to her soul and left her gasping. Nothing, not even what they'd done before, had prepared her for the intensity that seemed to go on forever before finally fading into aftershocks.

Kevin moved next to her and pulled her into his arms. She clung to him until she could think again, until the world stopped spinning. When she was finally back, she felt his soft kisses on her face.

"Wow," she said, opening her eyes and trying not to grin too broadly. "That was really great."

"I'm glad you liked it."

"No, it was really amazing."

He smiled. "I guess you'd been saving up for a while."

"Too long."

She thought about asking him to do that again when she felt the brush of something hard and insistent on her thigh. She reached between them and closed her fingers around his arousal.

"Can I do that to you?"

His expression turned rueful. "Sure. It would take all of thirty seconds."

She considered her options. "Maybe later," she said. "I want us to make love the traditional way."

His expression tightened. "Haley, we don't have to—"

She pressed a finger to his mouth. "I want to. I want you inside of me. I want to know how that feels, and I want you to be my first time." She cleared her throat. "In case you're worried, there isn't any, you know, *physical* proof that I'm a virgin. My doctor told me that a while ago."

One corner of his mouth turned up. "Good. Then it won't hurt."

She didn't expect it to. Not with Kevin.

He pushed on her hip until she rolled onto her back. He propped his hand on one of her hands and rested the other on her stomach.

"You understand what happens when couples make love," he said.

She wasn't sure if he was asking a question or not, so she nodded anyway. "You, ah, are inside of me."

"Right." He slid his hand between her legs. "This is where I was touching you before."

He rubbed his fingertips against her swollen center. Instantly her toes curled.

"It was very nice," she said, barely able to speak as he continued to touch that one amazing spot.

"This is where I go inside."

He slipped a finger into her, all the while keeping his thumb moving back and forth.

The combination of sensations caught her off guard. Finger and thumb moved together. The wanting began, as did the tension. He bent low and licked her breasts. It was a pretty unbeatable combination, she thought as her eyes fluttered closed. Why hadn't anyone told her she could feel this good?

He slipped out of her, then moved back inside, but this time there was more pressure. Two fingers, maybe? She liked how the stroking brushed the sides. As he pushed in, he reached up and she groaned as her body contracted in delight. He began to move faster. His lips closed over her nipple and he sucked, taking the tight point into his mouth. It was too much. It was everything. Tension built. She could feel it. She was getting closer and closer. She was right there. She was—

He stopped. Haley opened her eyes.

Kevin shrugged. "Sorry. We have a logistical issue."

He rolled away and opened a drawer in his nightstand. She caught a glimpse of a small box, then realized he'd reached for a condom.

But she was on the Pill. Her brain clicked into gear. Oh. There was more to worry about than just getting pregnant. Even humming with unreleased need, she appreciated that he was trying to protect her. The tender gesture made her eyes burn.

He pulled on the protection then knelt between her legs.

"Where were we?" he asked with a smile as he found her center with his fingers and began to rub.

In less than fifteen seconds, she was right back on the edge. Her breathing came in short pants and she arched her back as her release approached. Then she felt something thick and hard pressing into her. It was bigger than two fingers.

He moved slowly, filling her. Her body stretched to accommodate the unfamiliar presence. Some of her tension faded, but he kept moving his fingers and she soon found herself reaching for her release. Then he began to move.

This was it! Haley couldn't believe they were actually doing it. She opened her eyes and saw Kevin watching her.

"You all right?" he asked. His voice sounded low and hoarse.

She nodded, then raised herself up on one elbow. He was kneeling close to her. She could see him entering her and pulling out. The hand against her center continued to rub her. She could see and feel him touching her at the same time. It was the most incredible experience ever.

The slow, steady in and out became less unfamiliar. Then it started to feel kind of nice. Suddenly the combination of his fingers and his...well, you know, were too much. She fell back on the bed and closed her eyes. Need grew. Her body tensed.

He shifted and then he was on top of her, holding her close, kissing her. She wrapped her arms around him, savoring the weight of his body and how they were really joined together. It was everything she'd ever wanted.

He started to move a little faster. Suddenly she was aware that the tension hadn't faded. If anything it seemed to be building. In and out, in and out. She clutched at his hips. More, she thought frantically.

Somehow he knew. He read her mind, or maybe it was her nails digging into his rear. Whatever the cause, he filled her again and again until something inside her snapped and she lost herself in a release unlike the others she'd experienced. Even as she climaxed, she seemed to be building and releasing at the same time until there was nothing but the feel of him inside of her and the rush of pleasure.

Kevin felt the first spasm deep inside Haley. She'd been so close before that he'd hoped he could take her over the edge, but he hadn't been sure. He felt the powerful contractions that ripped through her. She clung to him, writhing, gasping, calling out his name. Her legs wrapped around his hips as she opened herself even wider.

He'd been holding back but now he plunged into her harder and harder. The dull ache in his leg didn't diminish the building pressure. Pressure that threatened his ability to hold back. He sucked in his breath, holding on until her contractions exploded into one long powerful convulsion that destroyed his last shred of control. He lost himself in her, as his body shuddered with release.

When he could breathe again, he opened his eyes and looked at her. Haley's expression was one of blissful contentment. She smiled.

"You're really good at that," she murmured.

"Not bad for our first time together."

She nodded.

Her cheeks were flushed, as was her chest. Her hair was mussed and her lips were swollen. She looked like a woman who had been thoroughly pleasured. She looked like a woman in love.

Wishful thinking, he told himself. With his defenses down, he could no longer ignore the obvious. That he'd fallen for her. He didn't know when it had happened. Maybe that first night when she offered to be forbidden fruit. Or had it been later, when she'd charmed him and made him believe that he wasn't always a screwup? Regardless, he loved her now.

"Thank you, Kevin," she said, and kissed him. "I'll remember this night forever."

He thought of how empty his world was going to be when she was gone. "I'll remember it just as long," he promised. "No matter what."

Haley tried to hold on to the glow as long as possible, but by noon, it had faded. She kept glancing at the clock, then wishing she hadn't.

Kevin sat across from her at the kitchen table. Vivian and Howard were both at work, so they had the house to themselves. She was glad. She didn't want Kevin's parents to witness whatever was going to happen.

"Do you know what you're going to say?" Kevin asked.

"No. I'm going to try to be mature and not to call him names."

"He probably deserves them."

She tried to smile. "I wish I'd practiced my swearing more."

He took her hand and squeezed. "You never swore at all. Do you want me to hang around or would you rather be alone with him?"

Her breath caught. "Don't go. Please. If you can stand to stay, I would really appreciate you being here."

"I'm not going anywhere."

His dark eyes promised. She studied his handsome face, the wave in his black hair, the way his shoulders seemed so broad. Her heart ached with her love for him. Last night had been the most wonderful experience of her life, and all because of him.

Impulsively she rose to her feet and crossed to his chair. He shifted back so she could settle on his lap. He wrapped his arms around her as she clung to him. If only he would never let her go.

"I'm not going to say anything," he told her, "but if he uses physical force, I'm going to beat the crap out of him."

Despite her apprehension, she laughed. "Allan isn't the physical-force type."

"Can I beat him up anyway?"

She looked at him. "You'd do that for me?"

"Sure."

"No one has ever offered to beat someone up for me before."

"I'm a rough, tough kinda guy."

He was that and so much more. He was—

A car pulled up in front of the house. Haley stiffened, then slid to her feet. "He's here."

She walked toward the front door. Kevin followed partway and stopped in the hallway. She thought about asking him to stand next to her, then changed her mind. This was her problem and she would solve it herself. Knowing Kevin was close gave her strength.

She waited for the knock before opening the door. Allan stood on the wide porch. She blinked in surprise as she took in his close-cropped blond hair and light eyes. In her mind, he'd always been fairly good-looking, but now he seemed pale and cold.

"Hello, Allan," she said, stepping back to allow him into the house.

"What is this place?" he asked by way of greeting. "Whose house is this? How do you know these people?"

"They're friends."

He looked around the living room, then turned his attention to her. "Are you packed?"

"No."

He frowned. "You're going to make this difficult, aren't you?"

"If by difficult you mean I'm not going to do what you tell me, then yes. I already explained everything on the phone. I told you not to come. There was a reason for that. I'm not coming back with you."

His gaze narrowed. "You cut your hair."

The statement sounded more like an accusation. Haley reached up and fingered the shorn locks. She'd nearly forgotten about her hair-based rebellion the first day she left. In the time she'd been gone, she'd gotten used to short hair.

"I like it this way," she said.

"At least it will grow back." He reached for her wrist. "Show me your room. We'll pack your things and get out of here."

Haley shook free of his grip and stepped back. She looked at the man she'd dated for nearly five years. His eyes were too close together and his expression was pinched. Why hadn't she noticed that before? He never listened to her. They'd never done anything she wanted. Their relationship had never been a partnership—instead Allan had been in charge and she had done his bidding.

She closed her eyes and tried to picture Allan naked, touching her, making love with her. Her imagination wasn't up to the task. She didn't want his hands on her body. She didn't want anything to do with him.

"I don't love you, Allan," she said firmly. "I'm not sure I even like you. You want a woman to do what you say, and I want a man who is interested in my opinions. You want to be in charge, I want a partner."

"You don't know what you want."

"Yes, I do. I want to love someone the way my father

loved my mother. I want to love with a deep honesty that touches my soul. I want to be a teacher and go to Hawaii on my honeymoon. I want to have children right away. I want a big old house that looks lived in, not designer perfect. I want a man who believes in me, and who I can believe in. I don't want you, Allan. I don't want to marry you, and I don't want anything to do with you."

He flushed. "You don't know what you're saying. Your father wants this marriage."

"Maybe he wanted it once, when he thought I loved you, but as soon as I tell him the truth, he'll back me up." She sighed. "Let me go. You don't really love me. You haven't for a long time. In fact you were the one questioning whether or not we should get married. Obviously something inside you told you it was wrong."

"Last-minute jitters," he told her. "Nothing more."

She moved close to him. "Tell me you love me with all your heart. Tell me you didn't feel even a little relief when I ran away."

"Haley, you're—" He broke off. His mouth twisted. "You're on drugs."

She burst out laughing. "It has to be that, right? Because I couldn't possibly have figured out how to be my own person."

He glared at her. "If you don't come back with me right this minute, it's over between us."

She walked to the door. "Goodbye, Allan. I hope you find someone to make you happy."

He stalked toward her. "You'll regret this. I won't take you back."

"You shouldn't. I'm the wrong woman for you."

He stepped onto the porch, then swung to face her. "You're disappointing a lot of people with your behavior."

Magic words designed to make her feel small. She ignored the automatic guilt. "Those who care about me will understand and support my decision. Those who don't will judge me. I can live with that."

"You're making a mistake."

She watched him walk to his rental car. He paused before climbing inside. "This is your last chance."

He waited and when she didn't say anything, he got inside and drove away. Haley watched him go and felt only relief.

Chapter Fourteen

Kevin listened to the sound of the front door closing. Haley had done it—she'd stood up to Allan and reclaimed her life. She'd come a long way from the young woman who had walked into a bar, looking for trouble. While he'd never doubted her ability to do whatever she wanted, he knew she'd been afraid. Until recently, she'd always let others' opinions dictate her actions. That wasn't likely to happen again.

"Did you hear?" Haley called as she burst into the hallway where he leaned against the wall. "Wasn't that something? I couldn't believe he expected me to come back with him. I mean, I told him and told him I wouldn't. Why on earth did I go out with him? I was crazy."

"You were doing what your family wanted."

She considered that. "By family you mean everyone at church." She sighed. "You're right. They seemed so happy to see me with Allan and I didn't care. I wasn't crazy about him, but he wasn't too awful. I guess over time I thought I was in love with him because that seemed to be the next logical step. Just think, if he hadn't had second thoughts, I might never have run away. I could have ended up married to him."

Kevin walked into the kitchen, with Haley on his heels. "You wouldn't have gone through with it."

He took a seat at the table. She plopped down next to him. "I hope you're right. I want to think that I would have balked at the last second, but I'll never know for sure." She shook her head. "I couldn't believe he accused me of being on drugs. Oh, like that's the only possible explanation for me turning him down. What a creep."

"You didn't even let me beat him up."

She leaned toward him and rested her hand on his arms. "I love that you offered to do that for me. It was so sweet."

Her face was bright with happiness. Humor flashed in her eyes. She looked young and alive, and filled with possibilities. There was a whole world waiting for her out there. One she'd never experienced. Haley had dreams.

He knew then what he'd always known but had never wanted to admit out loud. That she deserved to be free to find whatever her heart desired. He loved her too much to tie her down when she'd just found her freedom.

He cupped her face. "You did good today. You proved something to Allan, but more importantly, you proved something to yourself. No matter what happens, you'll always remember that you have the strength and determination to do whatever you want. You spread your wings."

She smiled. "I like that analogy."

"It's time to take them out for a test drive."

Her smile faded. "Kevin?"

He could still remember the way the bullet had slammed into his leg. The pain had come as a surprise. This time he was expecting it, but the intensity still stunned him. It was as if he was being ripped apart from the inside.

He swallowed. "You need to go live your life. It's all out there. Everything you could ever want."

"But what if everything I want is right here?" She blinked several times and her lips trembled. "Do you want me to leave?"

"This is about you."

Tears filled her eyes. "I understand what you're saying and I even know why, but I want to stay."

He wanted that, too. More than he'd wanted anything. For the first time in his life, he'd finally found a woman he could love forever. Unfortunately she was the one woman he couldn't be with. Fate sure had a twisted sense of humor.

"I'm heading back to Washington. I have a job waiting there."

"And the promotion?" she asked.

He shrugged. "If they still want me."

"For real?"

He kissed her. "Because of you, Haley. I'm willing to take the chance. You have to do the same."

Tears spilled down her cheeks. "I love you. I want to marry you."

He felt that blow down to his soul. "I love you, too. I want…" He wanted so many things. "I want what's right. I told you from the beginning I wasn't going to screw up with you and I meant it."

He brushed away her tears. "All your life people have told you what to do and you've listened. I'm not going to be like them. I want us to be together, but not like this. You need time to figure out what's right for you, to find your own life. Once that's straight, you come find me. I'll be waiting."

She bit back a sob. "F-for how long?"

"For always. You're the first woman I've ever loved. What I felt before doesn't begin to compare. There's just you, Haley. I'll be waiting."

Telling herself that Kevin was right and actually leaving were two different things. Haley had to pull over twice in the first twenty miles because she was crying too hard to see the road. She loved him and he loved her, so why was she leaving?

She brushed away the moisture and checked her mirrors before easing back into traffic. The answer was simple. She was leaving because as much as she loved him, she needed time to think things through. She'd fallen for him so fast that she could barely keep up. She needed to calm down and to take a look at her life. She needed to go home, to make peace with her father and to reevaluate her world.

The childish part of her demanded that she turn around and drive back to Possum Landing. She loved Kevin; she wanted to be with him right now. But the sensible part of her knew that getting closure was more important.

She reached into her shirt pocket and felt the card he'd given her. On it was his home number, his work number and his cell number. When she was ready, she was to call. But until then, they would be apart.

He wanted her to be sure. She suspected he had considered the possibility that this was just a vacation fling for her. That time and distance would cause a change in heart.

"I'm my father's daughter," she whispered as she drove. "He's loved the same woman all his life. You'd better be waiting, because I'll be coming to find you."

Haley walked into the church office late the following afternoon. Her trip home had been much faster than her aborted journey to Hawaii. She'd ignored all the tempting roadside shops and museums, instead driving until she was exhausted, then getting a room for a few hours before continuing north.

She looked around at the familiar office with its big windows and glass-enclosed bookcases. Marie's desk sat in the center of the room. Her chair was empty, but Haley could hear her talking in the other room.

In some ways Haley felt as if she'd been gone a lifetime. In other ways it seemed she'd only left a few minutes before. So much had changed and yet so much remained the same.

The door to her father's office opened. Marie stepped out, saw her and screamed.

"Haley! It's Haley!"

The petite fifty-something brunette rushed forward. Papers went flying as she wrapped her arms around Haley in a bear hug strong enough to snap ribs.

"We were so worried. You should have called more. You look fine. Are you all right? Allan came back and said some horrible things. He and your father had words. I tried not to listen, but I couldn't help it. Now Allan is going to be looking for another position. Oh, and you cut your hair!"

Marie paused for breath. Haley hugged her back, then kissed her cheek.

"I missed you, too," she said. "I'm sorry I worried you."

She didn't know what to think about her father and Allan, but she would find out what had happened soon enough.

"Hello, Haley."

She looked up and saw her father standing in the doorway. He was tall and as handsome as ever. When he smiled at her, she felt all her concerns fade. Whatever she'd done, he still loved her, would always love her. Of course, she thought as she hurried to his side. Why had she been so afraid to tell him what she was feeling?

"Oh, Daddy."

She hugged him close, feeling the familiar combination of strength and love radiating from him. He pulled her into his office and shut the door, then rested his hands on her shoulders and studied her.

"It seems you survived your adventure," he said, his low voice rumbling in the small room.

She nodded. "I did just fine. I'm all grown up now."

"You've been that for a while, although no one around here noticed. Not even me." He sighed. "Things have been very interesting since Allan returned from Texas. Why don't you tell me your version of things?"

He motioned to one of the leather chairs in front of his desk, then settled himself in the other.

She didn't know where to begin. "What did Allan say about me?"

"That you'd cut your hair and were probably on drugs." Her father sighed. "It was his only explanation for your refusal to come back and marry him."

"What did you think?"

"That you didn't love him. Was I right?"

She nodded. "I didn't realize it for a long time. I knew something was wrong, but I couldn't figure out what. When he said he was having second thoughts, I got so angry. I felt that I'd given up everything I wanted to make him happy and then *he* had second thoughts? It was so unfair. That's why I took off. I couldn't stand it anymore."

"I pushed you into a relationship with him," her father said. When she started to protest, he cut her off with a wave. "We both know it, Haley. You've always been so eager to please and do the right thing. I convinced myself you were in love with him, but I think deep in my heart

I knew you were with Allan because I wanted it and the congregation wanted it. I'm sorry. I should have seen what was happening and told you not to get married unless you were absolutely sure you were in love with him."

"Thank you, Daddy," she whispered.

She'd only been gone for a short time, yet her father seemed to have changed. There was more gray in his dark blond hair, or maybe she'd just never noticed it before. He was a good man. Wise and kind and giving. But every memory she had was of him by himself.

"Mom would never have wanted you to live so alone," she said.

He raised his eyebrows. "What brought that on?"

"I don't know, but it's true. She's been gone twenty-five years. Wasn't there even one woman who touched your heart?"

"Maybe." He shrugged. "I loved her so much. Losing her was the worst thing that ever happened to me. I didn't want to risk that again. Besides, I wasn't lonely. I had you, my work. Friends. God."

"During the day, but what about at night?"

"God is with us always."

She smiled. "You know what I mean."

"I do. I've thought about it from time to time."

"Is there someone?"

His gaze narrowed. "We're supposed to be talking about you, young lady."

She laughed. "All right. Keep your secrets. But if there's a spark, I think you should pursue it." She twisted her fingers together. "I know what you meant when you used to talk to me about loving Mom."

"You've found someone?"

She nodded. She could feel the smile curving her lips and wouldn't have been surprised if her entire body started to glow. "His name is Kevin and he's a U.S. Marshal. He's so wonderful, Daddy. He's strong and caring and generous. He loves me and wants only the best for me. He's a good man."

"So where is this paragon of virtue? As your father, it's my duty to terrify him into taking good care of you."

She laughed. "That won't be necessary. He already does." Her humor faded. "He's in Texas and will soon be flying to Washington, D.C. That's where he works. That's where I want to be."

Her father frowned. "What's standing in your way? Is he married?"

"Oh, Daddy. He's not married. He wants me to be sure." How exactly was she supposed to explain the complexity of her relationship with Kevin? Did her father really want to know she'd spent their entire time together trying to get him to sleep with her? She thought not.

"He knows about Allan and how I've been doing what everyone wanted me to do and not what I wanted. He loves me and wants me to come back to him, but first he wants me to figure out what I want. He says I need to be doing for myself now."

Her father winced. "I didn't mean not to listen."

"I know. It just sort of happened. I was willing to do what everyone thought was right. I should have stood up to people, but I didn't know how."

"Do you now?"

"Yes. I love you, Daddy, but I'm not going to be able to live here anymore. I want to be a schoolteacher. I want to marry Kevin and have a life with him."

"It sounds to me as if you've got everything planned."

"Pretty much."

"Then what are you doing here? I thought you said your young man was in Washington."

Haley caught her breath. Her father's love and acceptance filled her heart with a joy and peace that nearly gave her wings. She threw herself at him.

"I love you, Daddy."

He hugged her tightly. "I love you, too. I always have. You're a wonderful daughter and one of the most special people it has been my privilege to know. God blessed me when he brought you into my life. But it seems to me, it's long past time for you to be moving on. Just don't forget your old man in all the excitement of your new life."

"I won't," she promised. "Not ever."

Kevin glanced at the clock and tried not to do the math. Unfortunately his brain supplied him with the information. Ten days, seven hours. That's how long it had been since Haley had left Possum Landing. He hadn't heard from her since.

They'd made a deal, he reminded himself. She would go back to her old life and decide what she wanted. If it was him, she would be in touch, if not...

He didn't want to think about that. He didn't want to think about a cold, empty life spent missing her. He'd done the right thing by letting her go, he only wished it didn't have to hurt so badly.

While he knew he wouldn't get over her, he figured the loneliness would get easier in time. He'd accepted the promotion and was now swamped with several field projects he had to coordinate. He had his own office, an assistant and a team reporting directly to him. The pay increase meant that should Haley return they would be able to afford to get a house right off. And if she didn't... he'd have a hell of a nest egg.

In the meantime, he kept busy with his new responsibilities and planning his upcoming trip to California. He and Gage had decided to email their long-lost relatives. They'd found the Haynes brothers to be excited by the thought of new relatives. The date had been set for the big family reunion. Kevin's brother, Nash, was going to meet them there, and Gage was trying to get in touch with his brother, Quinn.

Everything was coming together—except for wanting Haley back.

Just his dumb luck, he thought grimly. He'd finally fallen in love with someone he'd had to let go. Nothing in life was easy, right?

The intercom buzzed. Kevin hit the button. "Yes?"

"You have a visitor. May I send her in?"

Her? Haley? He told himself it wasn't possible, that it was too soon, that she might not still be in love with him... But he didn't want to believe it.

"Sure," he said, telling himself he had to get over expecting her to walk through the door. He stood and waited.

Either his mind was playing tricks on him or the world had stopped turning because twenty seconds later a pretty young woman with hazel-blue eyes and a wide, winning smile stepped into his office. She wore a short denim skirt and a cropped T-shirt that exposed a sliver of stomach and sent need racing south.

Haley closed the door behind her. "You said to go get my life in order. That took about fifteen minutes. I didn't think you'd believe me if I rushed right back, and I thought you had a good point. So I talked to my dad, I made lists, I tried to get over you." She shrugged. "I can't. I love you. So how long do I have to wait until we can be together?"

He didn't remember moving, but suddenly she was in his arms. He kissed her, tasting her, needing her. Loving her.

All the pain of being alone, of missing her, faded. She loved him. She still loved him.

"I love you. I've missed you," he murmured, kissing her cheeks, her mouth, her chin, her nose. "Every damn day has been hell."

She looked at him and smiled. "Compound swearing. I'm so impressed." She touched his face. "I missed you, too. With every breath. I love you, Kevin. How could I not? You wanted what was right for me, even when it hurt you. Isn't that the real definition of love? Wanting what's right for the other person regardless of your own needs? The thing is, *you're* right for me. I know you're not perfect, but that's okay. I'm not perfect, either. And you're the best man I've ever known. I love you so much and I'm proud to be loved by you. I want to be with you always. I want to marry you and go to California and meet your family. I want to make a home with you and have children with you. I want to grow old with you and hold hands and make love until we're old and gray and should probably know better. But we'll do it anyway because we can't resist each other."

She paused. "But I'll wait if you want me to."

He laughed and swung her around the room. "I don't want to wait even a day." When he set her on her feet, he stared into her eyes. "You've said all the fancy words, so I only have those left in my heart. Marry me, Haley. I will do my best to make you happy. I will keep you safe, honor you, love you."

"Yes." She kissed him. "Yes. Of course."

He angled his head and deepened the kiss. Passion exploded between them. It would always be like this, he realized. He would always want her and she would always be there for him. He could see their future as clearly as if it were a movie up on the wall, and it made him humble with gratitude.

"There's just one thing," she said, pulling back. "We

have to go to Ohio because my dad wants to meet you and I sort of said we could be married there. Is that okay?"

"Absolutely. As long as Allan isn't performing the ceremony."

She giggled. "Nope. He's long gone."

"Then Ohio it is. And then Hawaii, for our honeymoon."

"Well, I've been thinking about that. Let's get married and then go to California to meet your family. We can do Hawaii next year."

"I thought that's what had started everything. You were driving to Hawaii."

"It was, until I realized that I'd found my own private paradise with you. It's not about the location. It's about being with the man I love and having him love me back."

"I do," he vowed.

"Forever?"

"Longer."

* * * * *

With special thanks to Jennifer Green
for believing in me and my characters.

HERS FOR THE WEEKEND

Bestselling Author
Tanya Michaels

TANYA MICHAELS

began telling stories almost as soon as she could talk…and started stealing her mom's Harlequin romances less than a decade later. In 2003 Tanya was thrilled to have her first book, a romantic comedy, published by Harlequin Books. Since then, Tanya has sold more than twenty books and is a two-time recipient of the Booksellers' Best Award as well as a finalist for a Holt Medallion, National Readers' Choice Award and Romance Writers of America's prestigious RITA® Award. Tanya lives in Georgia with her husband, two children and an unpredictable cat, but you can visit Tanya online at www.tanyamichaels.com.

Chapter One

Piper Jamieson sagged against the sofa cushions and rolled her eyes at the phone receiver. It could have been a wrong number, a pushy telephone solicitor, an obscene caller even, but nooo, it was her mother. Piper loved her mom, but all their conversations boiled down to the same argument—Piper's love life.

She started to put her feet up on the oval coffee table, but stopped suddenly, as though her mother could see through the phone line and into her apartment. "So, how've you been doing, Mom?"

"Never mind that. I'm more concerned with how *you* are," her mother said. "You don't feel acute appendicitis coming on, right? You aren't going to call us tomorrow with a severe case of forty-eight-hour east Brazilian mumps or something?"

Piper groaned. Although she'd bailed out on all of the family reunions in recent years, she'd used legitimate work-related excuses, never fictional medical ones. But this year she'd made a promise to her grandmother.

This year, there would be no reprieve.

"I'll be there," she assured her mother. "And I'm looking forward to seeing you all." *Mostly.*

"We're looking forward to seeing you, too, honey. Especially Nana. When I went to visit her at the hospital last week—"

"Hospital?" Piper's chest tightened. She adored her grandmother, even if Nana did stubbornly insist women needed husbands. "Daphne told me she was under the weather, but no one said anything about the hospital." As Nana advanced in years, Piper couldn't help worrying over her grandmother's health.

A worry her mother was not above exploiting. "You know what would help your Nana? If she knew you had a good man to take care of you."

Ah, yes—here came the Good Man Speech. Piper knew it well.

"You've always been independent," her mother was saying, "but there's such a thing as being too stubborn. Before you know it, you'll wake up fifty, without anyone to share your life…."

Knowing from experience that it did no good to point out she was decades away from turning fifty, Piper stretched across her couch. Might as well be comfy while she waited for her mother to wind down.

Though she'd escaped her small hometown of Rebecca, Texas, and now lived in Houston, Piper couldn't escape her family's shared belief that a woman's purpose in life was to get married. Piper's sole brush with matrimony had been a broken engagement that still left her with a sense of dazed relief—how had she come so close to spending her life with a man who'd wanted her to be someone different? When her sister, Daphne, had married, Piper thought the pressure would ease, that their mother would be happy to finally have a married daughter. Instead, Mrs. Jamieson was scandalized that her youngest was married, now pregnant, while her oldest didn't even date.

As her mom continued to wax ominous about the downfalls of growing old alone, Piper stared vacantly at the dead ficus tree in the corner of her living room. *I should water that poor thing.* Although, at this point, it was probably more in need of a dirge than H_2O.

"Piper! Are you even listening to me?"

"Y— Mostly."

"I asked if that bagel man was still giving you trouble."

Mercifully, her mother had moved on to the next topic. Too bad Piper had no idea what that topic was. "Bagel?"

Then realization dawned. Her mother must mean Stanley Kagle, vice president of Callahan, Kagle and Munroe, the architectural firm where Piper worked as the only female draftsman. Make that drafts*woman*. In Kagle's unvoiced opinion, Piper's job description should be brewing coffee and answering phones with Ginger and Maria, the two assistants who had been with the firm since it opened. Luckily, Callahan and Munroe held more liberated views.

"You mean Mr. Kagle, Mom?"

"Whichever one is always hassling you at work." She paused. "You know, you wouldn't have to work at all if you'd find a nice man and raise some babies."

Piper could actually *hear* her blood pressure rising. One of only a handful of female students in her degree program at Texas A&M, she'd busted her butt to excel in her drafting and detailing courses, and was now working even harder to prove herself amid her male colleagues. Why couldn't her family be proud of that? Proud of her?

"Mom, I like my job. I like my life. I wish you'd just accept that I'm happy."

"How happy could you be? Daphne says you're underappreciated and that one of your bosses has it in for you."

And thank you so much, Daphne, for passing on that information.

"Daph caught me after a rough week, and I was just venting," Piper said. "I love the actual drafting part." And loved the feeling she got when she was in the middle of a drawing and knew it was damn good, the pride of passing a building downtown and seeing one of *her* suspended walkways. If things continued to go well, Piper was hoping her next review with Callahan would lead to her first project as a team leader.

But better to argue her point in a language her mom could understand. "I'll admit to occasional work-related stress, but are you trying to tell me that marriage and motherhood are stress-free?"

Silence stretched across the phone line.

Aha! I have you there.

Then Mrs. Jamieson sighed as though this conversation epitomized her motherhood stress. "Honey, you aren't getting any younger, and women can't—"

Recognizing the introductory phrase of her Don't You Hear Your Biological Clock Ticking Speech, Piper interrupted. "I'd love to chat more Mom, but..." She thought fast, determined to rescue herself from this black hole of a conversation. "I have to run because I have dinner plans."

"You have a dinner date! With a *man?*"

Did she really want to lie to her mother? Piper gnawed at her lower lip. She'd already told one white lie. Besides, if it would save her from another round of "you'd be such a pretty girl if you just fixed yourself up," why not? Her imaginary person might as well be an imaginary man.

"Yes." Guilt over the uncharacteristic fib immediately niggled at her, but she pressed forward. "It's a man."

"Good heavens. I can't believe you let me go on all this time and didn't say anything about having a boyfriend!"

Boyfriend? She'd only meant to allude to a dinner date to buy herself some peace and quiet, not invent a full-blown relationship. "Wait, I—"

"What does your young man look like, dear?"

Piper blurted the first thing that came to mind. "Tall, dark and handsome." *Oh, very original!* "Dark-haired with green eyes," she elaborated.

"And you'll bring him home with you for the reunion, right?"

"Well, no, I—"

"We can't wait to meet him. I was hoping this weekend would give you the chance to get reacquainted with Charlie, but I didn't know you had a boyfriend."

"Charlie?" Piper would invent a dozen fake boyfriends before she let herself go down that road again. "Mom, I don't want to see Charlie."

Her mother's uneasy silence made it clear that it was too late for Piper to avoid her ex-fiancé.

"You've invited him for dinner or something, haven't you?" What did it take to convince people that she and Charlie were over? Not over in the-timing-just-wasn't-right, maybe-later kind of way. Over in the stone-cold, do-not-resuscitate, rest-in-peace kind of way.

"Piper, he's like one of the family."

More so than she was, it would seem.

"And I don't know why you sound so appalled whenever you mention him," her mother continued. "Charlie Conway is a good man, and he's the most eligible bachelor in the entire county."

That was probably true. Handsome, funny and smart, Charlie Conway had been a fellow Rebecca native and A&M student. He'd been so sought after in high school that Piper had been surprised when he pursued her in college. He'd claimed to love her because she was so refreshingly different from the girls they'd grown up with, and he'd eventually proposed. Their engagement had been strained, however, by his decision to return to Rebecca and carry on the Conway mayoral tradition, and Piper had returned the heirloom diamond ring when she realized that the allure of "refreshingly different" had faded. The longer she'd been with Charlie, the more he'd tried to change her.

"Mom, I don't care how eligible he is. He's not right for me." She'd tried to explain this before, but since she was rejecting the very lifestyle most of her family and childhood friends had chosen, they didn't quite understand. Piper knew they were fond of Charlie—she had been, too, at one point—but she hadn't liked the person she'd become when she was with him. "Promise me you're not going to spend the weekend trying to throw us together."

"Well, of course not, dear—not with this new young man in your life. We can't wait to meet him!" her mother repeated.

"I'll, um, see if he's available." Piper hated the blatant dishonesty, but not as much as she hated the thought of an entire weekend explaining why the county's most eligible bachelor wasn't good enough for her.

"This is so exciting," her mom said. "I can't wait to call everyone and let them know. Oh, and honey, if you're going out tonight, I hope you'll think about wearing a dress for a ch—"

Ding dong!

Piper jumped at the unexpected pealing of her doorbell. "Who—" Remembering that she was supposedly expecting a date, she swallowed the last of her question. "Gotta go now, see you this weekend. Love to Dad."

The doorbell shrilled again as she hung up, and a familiar male voice called through the door, "Piper? You home?"

Josh. Thank goodness, because a day like she'd had called for one of two things: venting to her best friend or a Chocomel, a chocolate-covered bar of caramel-and-nougat-filled nirvana. Talking to Josh was calorie-free.

"Hey," she greeted him as she opened the door. Joshua Weber was a coworker who'd become her best friend after moving into her downtown Houston apartment building two years ago. "Did we have plans tonight and I forgot? I'm sorry, it's been a horrible day, and—"

"Relax, darlin'." His lips curved into the sexy smile that had no doubt been instrumental in seducing many women. Luckily for Piper, seduction wasn't high on her priority list. "We didn't have plans. I just wanted to see if you were interested in going with me for a bite to eat."

"What, no date tonight?"

Women flocked to Josh in droves. With his long lean build, square jaw, lionlike green-gold eyes and thick hair the color of rich chocolate, he was easily the best-looking man in the apartment complex. Maybe the zip code. Or the state.

"Dating can be exhausting." He leaned casually against the doorjamb, his posture matching his informal attire of a faded Astros shirt and jeans going threadbare at the knees. "Sometimes a guy just needs a little peace and quiet."

"So why not enjoy dinner alone in your apartment?" Piper asked.

It was what she'd planned to do. If she had any groceries. She'd been working so many late nights that she'd once again neglected shopping. Other women in her family were prizewinning cooks; Piper barely remembered to keep her fridge stocked.

"Being with you is even better," Josh said. "I don't have to be by myself, but I don't have to be 'on,' either. Besides," he added sheepishly, "I burned the nice dinner I was supposed to be having alone in my apartment right now."

She laughed. "Let me grab my purse and put my shoes back on." As she turned, she patted her French braid to make sure it was still presentable. A few strands fell around her face, but all in all, the braid had survived the day intact.

Good thing she hadn't yet changed from her tailored blue pantsuit into her comfy sweats. Josh probably wouldn't think anything of going out in public wearing a sweatsuit, but the casual look worked for him. For instance, Josh's hair always looked as though it had just outgrown that popular short and gelled style that was slightly spiky on top. Though it was still short, his hair was pleasantly rumpled with no trace of gel. Undeniably handsome when he dressed up for work or an occasionally formal date, he was somehow even more appealing in the rugged laid-back uniform of worn jeans and T-shirts.

The injustice of life. Piper in her oldest jeans was grunge personified, whereas Josh effortlessly resembled a female's fantasy come to life in any clothes. *Probably looks even more like a walking fantasy in no clothes at all.*

She blinked. Thoughts like that were trouble she didn't need, she reminded herself, sliding her feet into a pair of high-heeled navy slingbacks. The shoes were arguably the most feminine part of her wardrobe, but at barely five foot three, she'd take all the help she could get. Especially next to Josh's six foot one.

Grabbing her apartment keys off the coffee table, she stole a look at her tall, platonic friend. Emphasis on the platonic. She was perfectly happy without a guy in her life, and she'd watched Josh back away from enough relationships to know he didn't want a woman in his life. Not long-term, anyway.

And short-term's out of the question. Maybe hot flings with no future worked for some people, but the one impulsive time Piper had flung, she'd found the experience to be more embarrassing than pleasurable. She couldn't begin to fathom how awkward it would be if she constantly saw the flingee at the office.

Shoes on her feet, purse in her hand and lustful thoughts relegated to the dark mental cellar where they belonged, she strolled back to where Josh was waiting. "All set."

Once they'd reached the apartment's parking garage, she turned to ask, "Who's driving?" But she didn't know why she bothered.

He'd already pulled out his keys and was striding toward his two-door sports car.

"It's just as well," she admitted. "I got another ticket today."

"Speeding again?" He shook his head. "I don't know how you manage to even get up *to* the speed limit with traffic as bad as it is, much less exceed it. Do the other cars just magically part for you?"

She climbed into the passenger side. "Hey, you're supposed to be sympathetic about my bad day."

"That's right. You said it was horrible." His low voice was full of teasing mischief as he turned the key in the ignition. "There are ways I could help take your mind off your troubles, sweetheart. You just say the word."

Piper's breath caught, a quiver of expectation in her abdomen. Josh's flirting was nothing new—it was his default mode—but tonight, after her earlier wayward thoughts, there was a split second where she forgot that he meant nothing by it.

Then he spoke again, his tone genuinely sympathetic. "Kagle being a chauvinistic creep?"

Although Stanley Kagle was too business-savvy to do or say anything overt she could formally complain about, his attitude was a constant reminder that she was the youngest and shortest on the drafting team. And the only one with ovaries, which he apparently viewed as some sort of handicap. Thank God for Callahan and Munroe to counter his presence, or she might actually have to brave the job market.

Piper sighed. "No, it's not one of our bosses making me crazy, it's one of our colleagues. If Smith doesn't get me those dimensions for the Fuqua building, my blueprints will be late, and you know who Kagle will blame. Then, of course, the traffic ticket on my way home today. And on top of everything, my mother called and…"

She'd been about to say that her mother was driving her nuts, but it seemed insensitive to complain. At least she had a mom. Josh's mother and father had both been killed in a car accident when he was very young. He didn't discuss his past much, but Piper knew it involved a lot of foster homes and very little stability.

"Grazzio's okay with you?" Josh's rhetorical question was an unnecessary formality. Even as he asked, he was steering his car into the parking lot of their favorite pizzeria.

They ate here an average of five times a month. On nice days, it was close enough to walk the few blocks between Grazzio's and their apartment complex, but on this rainy October night, she was glad for the warm shelter of the car. They hurried through the falling rain to the restaurant, where Josh held the door open for her.

Inside, the leggy brunette hostess greeted them by name, with a special smile for Josh. "Hey, handsome, when are we going out again?"

Josh winked at the woman he'd taken on a couple of dates back in August. "Ah, Nancy, I'd like nothing more than to sweep you off your feet here and now. But you know George from the sports bar is crazy in love with you. I just can't break the poor guy's heart like that."

The hostess shook her head, laughing. "Well, if you change your mind about being noble, you have my number."

Piper thought Nancy would be wise to give up on Josh and give George, the bartender at Touchdown, a call. All over Houston, from the corner sports bar to the Astros' stadium, Piper and Josh ran into women who had briefly been part of his life and wanted to repeat the experience. Piper had been on the receiving end of more than a few envious glares from women, who, unlike Nancy, didn't know Piper had no interest in dating.

Her last relationship, the only one worth counting since Charlie, had ended when her boyfriend gently complained that her work was more of a priority than he was. She suspected that his intent had been for her to change that, but she'd encouraged him to find someone who would focus on him the way he deserved.

Piper and Josh were shown to an elevated booth with blue padded seats, and she stepped up to slide in across from him. An olive-skinned waiter with a mustache and faint accent took their drink orders and left them with a basket of warm bread. The buttery smell reminded her of her mother's kitchen, where something was always baking, and the upcoming weekend. Piper should be thinking of a way to get out of her impulsive lie, but the more she considered it, the more she liked the idea of a human buffer between her and Charlie. Piper knew from her sister that Charlie had most recently dated the town librarian, but he'd broken things off a few months ago, apparently deciding he wanted a more outspoken woman. Specifically Piper, the outspoken woman he hadn't valued enough when he'd been with her.

On her last birthday, he'd sent her jewelry that was too expensive to be justified by their growing up together. She'd returned the gift, but he'd still called her a few weeks later to let her know he was going to be in Houston. She'd told him truthfully that she was too busy trying to meet a project deadline to meet him for dinner and had hoped the reminder of her non-traditional priorities would dissuade him. If it hadn't, she could be in for a very long weekend.

Josh grabbed a roll. "I'm starving."

Lost in her own troubles, she barely heard him. She needed to be ready for her family, and she could think of only one way to do that. "Josh, I need a man."

Chapter Two

Piper's declaration was met with immediate choking on Josh's part. It wasn't often she had the satisfaction of catching him so off guard. Quite the contrary, he normally delighted in shocking her.

He recovered quickly, his grin suggestive. "Why didn't you say so back at your place? Forget the pizza, we—"

She laughed. "That's not what I was talking about."

Having decided that balancing the irritation of dating with her more important career wasn't worth the time and effort, Piper was pretty much living a life of celibacy. Josh's full knowledge of that was probably why he felt safe enough to flirt with her in the first place. No way would he ever actually go out with her. From what she'd observed, he liked to keep women at a certain distance, and he and Piper had passed that point already.

Though she admired plenty of things about Josh, his love life tended toward the...well, *shallow* seemed unkind, but the truth was some of his relationships made mud puddles look deep by comparison. Interestingly few of his dates complained, so Piper supposed it was none of her business. Josh didn't lecture her on her non-dating habits, and she didn't lecture him on the fact that he had the staying power of a— Actually, from the way ex-lovers swooned when they saw him, Piper suspected he had very impressive staying power.

She gulped down some water. "You know I'm going out of town for a few days, right?"

"Yeah. A family reunion." He smiled. "See? I listen."

"Well, I need a guy to go with me." She exhaled a gusty sigh that ruffled her bangs. "I sort of let my mother think I was dating someone, and she's expecting me to bring him home."

His expression turned blank, his mind obviously blown at trying to imagine Piper with a man in her life. "But you aren't seeing anyone."

"Thank you, Columbo. Nothing gets by you, does it?"

"Hey, watch the sarcasm," he said as the waiter returned. "You'll give me indigestion."

"Ready to order?" the waiter asked.

Piper and Josh exchanged guilty glances. Her "need a man" statement had distracted both of them from even opening their menus. As the waiter stood by, they debated what kind of pizza to get.

"We can split it," Josh proposed. "Get half of the pizza made one way and something different on the other half."

"No deal, Weber. Last time we did that, you tried the Jamaican chicken pizza, didn't like it and ate all of *my* half. Besides, I might just get pasta."

"Pasta?" Josh echoed. "Come on, this is the best

pizzeria in Houston. You're going to come here and not get pizza? That makes as much sense as...you having a love life."

The impatient waiter clearing his throat stopped her from snapping a comeback.

"Perhaps I should return in a few minutes?" the man offered.

Glancing from his menu to Piper, Josh said, "I know how much you like the Sicilian specialty. Want to just get that?"

Piper nodded, and the waiter shuffled off, appeased.

Josh immediately returned to the subject of her faux love life. "I don't get it. What made you lie to your mom? You never lie. Having witnessed you turn away persistent men at Touchdown, I would even say that you're some-times *painfully* honest."

Lowering her gaze to the red-and-white checkered tablecloth, she mumbled, "I didn't set out to lie, exactly. I just exaggerated."

"Piper, when was the last time you had a date?"

"Okay, fine, I lied. I had to get off the phone! She called to remind me that I'm the unmarried shame of the family, and I cracked. I told her I had to run because I was meeting someone for dinner."

"And based on a supposed dinner date, she's now book-ing a church and auditioning caterers."

"For a guy who's never met my mother, you have a very clear understanding of her."

"You paint a vivid picture."

Piper bit her lower lip. "I have a real problem here."

"Nah, this isn't serious. A *problem* was Michelle. I can't believe she honestly expected me to remember her cat's birthday. And stalking me for two weeks like that after the breakup—"

"Maybe if you took the time to get to know some of these women before you went out with them, you'd pick up on little things like personality disorders." Piper hadn't meant to sound so snippy, but it annoyed her sometimes to watch Josh waste himself on a string of superficial relationships. Didn't he realize he had more to offer than that?

"Piper, people go out *in order* to get to know each other, and I'm not sure I want dating advice from a girl who hasn't been on one since the Reagan administration."

"Ha-ha. As if my family encouraged me to date as an infant." Though they probably would have if they'd known then how difficult it would be to marry her off.

"What I was saying," he continued, "is that I don't see why this is a serious problem. Let your mom think whatever she wants. Tell them he couldn't make it this weekend. Or that you broke up with the guy. Problem solved."

If only it were that easy. "I would, but Mom said it would really benefit Nana to see me with—" she groaned inwardly "—'a good man.'"

His gaze locked with hers. "How is your grandmother?"

"Hanging in there, but…apparently not doing so well." She swallowed. "Last time we spoke, I argued with her. She was giving me more well-meaning advice on how to live my life, and I told her I was an adult and didn't need or want her interference. I shouldn't have said that."

Josh reached his hand across the table, and it hovered over hers. At the last minute he grabbed the bread basket as though that had been his intention all along.

She wasn't surprised that he shied away. Typical Josh. Weird that he dated and kissed and she-didn't-want-to-know-what-else with so many women, yet simple touches made him uncomfortable. Piper had grown up in a hug-oriented family herself, but she tried to respect the personal perimeter he maintained.

Though she had no trouble telling Josh about the familial reasons for needing a stand-in date, Piper didn't mention Charlie. Josh knew that she'd once dated Rebecca's current mayor, but Piper had downplayed the seriousness of the relationship. She was embarrassed that she, a modern independent woman, had been slowly altering everything from her work schedule to the way she wore her hair. It wasn't something she liked to think about, let alone discuss.

"So." Josh cleared his throat. "You're really going to take some guy home with you?"

"If I can find one," she said as the waiter approached. He set their pizza on the table, and Josh distributed the first cheesy slices. They ate in silence, mulling over her situation. At least, *she* was mulling. For all she knew, Josh was checking out a cute waitress.

To some, asking Josh to accompany her might seem an obvious answer. He'd certainly been willing to do her favors in the past—from free labor on her car to late-night assassinations of Texas-size spiders in her apartment. But this was different. While Josh came across as a people person who could shoot the breeze with anyone, he was intensely private. Piper had watched more than one woman lose him after pressuring him to "open up." A few days of Piper's meddling relatives interrogating him would doubtless be his idea of hell. Besides, how insensitive would she have to be to invite a man who'd never had a real family to a large family reunion?

So, with Josh out of the question, who was she going to ask? Instead of eating with her usual gusto, she nibbled her food, thinking out loud. "Most of the men I know are from work, and I can't ask any of them."

Josh nodded. "They might misconstrue the invitation, and you'd be in violation of the company's fraternization policy."

Plus she couldn't ask any of them for a huge favor when she wasn't exactly Ms. Popular at the office. She couldn't afford to chat in the break room when she was determined to prove herself, to get ahead in a field dominated by men. And she deliberately minimized any feminine assets, which some people had interpreted to mean she was aloof and hard. Though she and Josh had always gotten along professionally, they hadn't truly become friends until they'd run into each other in their building's laundry room.

"You know any nice guys?" she asked.

"I keep in touch with a few frat brothers from college, but I'm having trouble picturing you with anyone I once watched do a keg stand, then throw up on the front steps."

"What about that guy you coach softball with every spring? Adam?"

Josh worked with kids from underprivileged neighborhoods from March to June, and Piper had met Josh's co-coach during last year's district playoffs. Good-looking man, but she and Josh had agreed never to date each other's friends after an awkward situation when he'd broken up with one of Piper's former college classmates—another casualty of the Joshua Weber charm. Piper really pitied those women.

An unexpected thought struck her. Sure, she pitied them now, but how would she feel toward his dates if he ever showed a real attachment to one of them? Her stomach churned, but she told herself it was just the stress of her reunion predicament, nothing more.

"Adam would actually be a great choice for you to take to your parents," Josh agreed, "but he's in Vancouver on an extended business trip until after Halloween. Besides, what would I say? 'You remember my friend Piper—she needs a fake boyfriend.'"

"I have to find someone." She sat back, staring blankly across the table.

What would happen if she just told her family the truth—that she was single and liked it that way? *You know what would happen. Charlie.* The man had blond, all-American good looks and had been born into Rebecca's top social level. Granted, Rebecca wasn't big enough to have many levels, but the point was, he was used to getting his way. He'd seemed more bemused than upset when she'd broken their engagement, and she got the impression he was waiting for her to come to her senses.

Josh swallowed nervously. "Exactly why are you looking at me like that?"

Blinking, she chuckled at his wary tone. "Relax. I'm not asking you to come with me. I just needed a sympathetic ear."

He quickly replaced his guarded expression with a smile meant to be casual, but his relief was so palpable it was practically a third person in the booth. "Hey, here's an idea, what about a man from the gym? You're there every other morning. You've gotta know some guys."

"No, I spend most of my time with Gina. Or working out alone. I avoid eye contact with men so I don't end up trapped on the treadmill, fending off unoriginal lines like, 'Come here often?'"

"I can't help but notice you avoid men most everywhere you go."

"The last thing I expected from you is the Piper-needs-a-man speech." She drummed her fingers on the table. "I get it from plenty of other people."

"Sorry, I didn't mean to imply that. You definitely don't 'need' a guy. You're the most together woman I know." He flashed a wicked smile. "And I know lots of women."

She rolled her eyes.

"Give me something to work with," he prompted. "What did you tell your mom about this mystery man?"

"I told her he had dark hair—"

"Good. Thousands of guys must have dark hair."

"—and that he was tall—"

He laughed. "Compared to you, everyone's tall."

"—and I said he had green eyes." As the words left her mouth, she realized Josh had green eyes. Deep, forest-green with flecks of shimmering gold.

Not that she'd paid much attention.

Hating the sudden warmth in her cheeks, she blurted, "I think green naturally sprang to mind because my own eyes are green."

"Yours are blue."

"Blue-green." She ducked her head. "Close enough."

Okay, maybe she had subconsciously described a man who bore a slight, vague, infinitesimal resemblance to Josh. Made sense. He was the only guy she spent much time with.

It didn't mean anything. Yet her pulse refused to resume its normal rate. She almost pressed a hand over her rapidly beating heart, willing it to slow. After two years of observation, Piper knew that any woman foolish enough to let Josh affect her heart ended up with a broken one.

Josh walked across the nondescript industrial carpet of the main workroom at Callahan, Kagle & Munroe, absently acknowledging greetings from a couple of draftsmen at their respective drawing stations. But his attention this Wednesday morning wasn't really on any of his coworkers—at least none of the male ones. He hadn't been able to focus his attention on work, either, which was why he'd decided to get a soda from the vending machine, motivated more by the chance to stretch his legs than by thirst.

As he approached the break room in the back, he glanced out the floor-to-ceiling window that boasted an impressive view of Houston's skyline. Of course, it would be even more impressive without the ubiquitous road crews and bright yellow machinery below and the gray blanket of smog overhead.

Not smog, just cloud cover. He hoped his cranky mood was due to this being the third consecutive day of autumn drizzle. Because the only other explanation for the irritability that had plagued him since seeing Piper home last night was her dating dilemma.

Her dilemma, he reminded himself. She'd said flat out that she wasn't asking him to go with her, thank God. After the last twenty years of being on his own, Josh wasn't sure he could stomach a weekend of parents and cousins, aunts and uncles all wanting to get to know the man in Piper's life.

Piper would figure out something. She was a determined, resourceful woman. Too bad she was gorgeous, as well. Her intelligence and sense of humor made her entirely too likable, and when combined with the incredible body she tried to hide under severe work attire and baggy weekend clothes—

Incredible body? He was not going there. Not now, not ever.

Except that lately, he had been. A lot. In the beginning

of their unexpected friendship, her no-men oath and his own contrastingly busy love life had been a sufficient buffer, guaranteeing that neither of them would get any ideas about messing up their perfectly safe relationship. So what had changed? She still wasn't interested in romance in any form or fashion, and he still... Come to think of it, he *hadn't* been on as many dates lately. When had he slowed down?

He'd never intentionally set out to break Houston dating records, but it had only taken him a couple of breakups to realize he wasn't cut out for long-term relationships. The emotional distance that had helped protect him while being shuttled from one foster home to another didn't work well in romances, but the loner attitude that had been years in the making hadn't magically expired at age eighteen along with the state's wardship.

Though women might be attracted to him, more than one had decided he wasn't worth sticking around for; he was too used to keeping his own counsel, too guarded for "real intimacy." Maybe he'd been hurt once or twice when a woman walked out on him, but he wasn't complaining about the way his life had turned out. As long as he kept his relationships casual enough that no one heard wedding bells, he could have plenty of fun.

But that "fun" did not and would never include Piper. Their friendship had sort of crept up on him, originally built on a few chance meetings at their apartment complex, some venting about work and a shared affection for baseball and action movies. He wouldn't do anything to jeopardize their friendship—like hit on her.

Entering the break room, he reached for the spare change in his pants' pocket, but froze when he realized he wasn't alone. Clearly, the universe was testing him. Piper stood in the otherwise empty room, bent at the waist and peering into a cabinet below the sink. The short caramel-colored jacket she wore had risen above her hips, and the matching slacks hugged her curves in a taunting way that left him struggling not to look at her caramel-covered backside.

Poor choice of words. The color she was wearing didn't *really* resemble a sweet, sticky dessert topping, he told himself. It was more…well, hell. Women always seemed to have twelve words to describe one color, but he couldn't think of anything but caramel and the thick, sugary taste it left on his tongue.

He wasn't sure if he made a sound or if she'd just experienced that I'm-not-alone-anymore feeling, but she straightened suddenly, glancing over her shoulder.

"Josh! I didn't realize anyone was standing there. Hey, you don't happen to know where the extra coffee filters are, do you? I could have sworn they were in here."

"Uh…coffee filters? No. No idea." No alternate locations sprang to his hormone-impaired mind, but he needed something to distract her from resuming her under-the-sink search. Lord help him if she bent over again. "So, any new thoughts on how you're going to solve your problem?"

She leaned against the counter, her smile rueful. "You mean this weekend? Maybe. I think when I get home tonight, I'll call a few of the guys I've dated here in the city. I might not leave a relationship with *your* finesse and have them come back begging for more, but I think I'm still on speaking terms with everyone."

"Oh." Even though he knew Piper had dated, the thought of her with a guy jolted him. "Well, that's… great."

"If one of them actually says yes," she said. "I just

hope it isn't Chase. I figure I might get desperate enough to ask him, but I won't be brokenhearted if he says no."

"Chase?" The only ex Josh remembered was Bobby. Or maybe it had been Rob. Definitely something in the Robert family.

"Yeah, Chase is one of those people with a strangely apt name. He spent the duration of our very brief relationship trying to get in my—" Suddenly, Piper's expression changed. If he didn't know her and her forthright nature better, he'd say she looked almost self-conscious. "Well, you know what I mean."

Josh's eyes met hers, and he hoped like hell his expression held no sign of the thoughts he'd been having so recently. "Yeah. I know."

Neither of them seemed to have anything to add then, so they stood without speaking, gazes still locked. Though probably not even a full minute passed, the silence stretched on too long to be entirely comfortable.

Piper looked away, glancing at the empty coffeepot on the counter. "I think I'm just gonna grab a soda and get back to work."

He pulled the forgotten change out of his pocket. "Me, too."

They both stepped toward the vending machine, then drew up short. Josh motioned with his hand, indicating that she should go first—mostly because it gave him a chance to regain his composure.

He was glad she was going away for the weekend. Maybe he'd just been spending too much time with her lately. Maybe his dry spell had boggled his thinking and was the logical explanation for the effect Piper was having on him. Sure, that was probably it. And once he found a date for this weekend, and Piper spent some time out of town, Josh would be fine.

He just wished his jaw didn't clench involuntarily every time he thought about Piper spending those days cuddled up to some faceless guy from her past.

Chapter Three

Piper was doomed.

After several fruitless phone calls and a long shower Wednesday evening, she was ready to concede defeat. As she'd rinsed shampoo from her hair, she'd mentally cast about for a last-minute possibility, but the truth was, she'd exhausted all her options. One ex hadn't remembered her, which had been a big ouch to the ego. Chase was busy this weekend, but seemed to think they should get together sometime soon and have sex. Robbie, her last hope and most amicable breakup, had happily informed her he was engaged. Apparently his fiancée would frown on the idea of his running away for the weekend with an old flame. Go figure.

I can't believe he's getting married next month. Has it really been that long since we split up?

Piper pulled on a pair of sweatpants, assuring herself that she didn't mind that her last date had been eons ago. She wasn't one for wasting time, and when you weren't actually looking for a relationship, dating was pointless. Why should she suffer through those pauses in conversation, those realizations that the person seated across from her was never really going to "get" her, when she'd rather be at home with her laptop and computer-assisted drafting software, getting ahead in her chosen career?

She supposed some people dated for companionship, but she had friends she could call on for company. Others might want dating for sex, but her experiences had left her convinced the whole thing was overrated. Pleasant, sure, but worth neither the awkwardness and risks of a casual affair nor the changes to her life to accommodate a relationship.

Maybe it was the guys she'd been with. Maybe a more experienced guy who knew women better, like, for instance, J—

"I do not need sex," she informed her empty apartment and dead ficus tree.

And she didn't need a man, either, she thought grumpily as she towel-dried her hair, then skimmed it back into a ponytail. Maybe she should just stick to her guns this weekend. Tell her family there'd been a misunderstanding—okay, a colossal deception—but that she was single and perfectly happy to stay that way. Of course, they were more likely to believe she was alone because she was pining for Charlie.

She strode across her living room and dug through her rolltop desk for the comfort of a Chocomel candy bar, but came up empty. A knock at her front door ended the sugar search. Given her current luck, it was probably the landlord with eviction papers. She considered her damp ponytail and heather-gray sweatsuit. Wouldn't win any fashion awards, but it covered all the necessary body parts.

When she opened the door, she found Josh, not the landlord. Josh's face was so grim that perhaps *he'd* just been evicted.

"I've been thinking, Piper."

Normally she would have made some joke at his expense, but his scowl discouraged it. "About?"

"You. Your situation, I mean."

He stepped inside, and she backed away with an alacrity she hoped he didn't notice. Earlier, when they'd been in the break room at work, she'd experienced a strange hypersensitivity to his nearness. Now, in the privacy of her apartment, it was magnified. Did he have any idea how good he smelled? A dizzying anticipation fluttered inside her, as if every part of her body was just waiting for the moment when his skin might accidentally touch hers. And she couldn't tell if she was nervous about it or looking forward to it.

Neither. Get a grip on yourself. She gestured toward the living room. It wasn't big, but the square footage there made it a lot safer than the small foyer. "Why don't you come in, have a seat?"

"Sure." He made his way to the sofa. "Did you, uh, did you call any of the guys you used to date?"

Piper perched on the arm of the couch, pleased with the compromise between sitting with him and noticeably avoiding him. "Practically all of them, but then, my list wasn't that extensive."

"Any luck?"

"None whatsoever."

His posture sagged. For a second, his relaxed stance almost suggested *relief,* but then she realized his slumped shoulders must indicate disappointment for her.

He sucked in a jagged breath. "I've come to voluntarily enlist."

Josh wanted to go with her? She struggled to find her voice. "You're kidding."

"I might kid you about a lot of things, darlin', but this isn't one of them."

The familiar endearment stood out today, his warm, husky tone causing her stomach to turn a slow somersault. Her initial surprise and gratitude over his offer gave way to a momentary uncertainty about pretending to be romantically involved with him all weekend. The pretense would involve touching and—and...well, her mind was pretty much stuck on the touching. Her gaze slid involuntarily over his body.

"Unless you've come up with another solution?" he asked hopefully.

"Huh?" Piper blinked. "Oh. No. But are you sure? You sound like a man about to be martyred. You don't have to do this."

Which is why I offered, Josh thought. If she'd asked, he would have said no reflexively. Having no family of his own was almost tolerable as long as he wasn't around someone else's, reminded of everything lacking in his life. But she'd respected his space, reminding him again that she was the best friend he had. The reminder had relentlessly niggled at him, finally goading him into this decision.

His offer had nothing to do with the way he felt whenever he imagined some other man holding her or kissing her, whether the kisses were pretend or not.

"I never had a grandmother to take care of me," he heard himself say. "But you have one you love very much, and this would make her happy. Besides," he added with a smile, "I've never been one to turn down free food. What's a road trip between pals? I mean, it's not like anyone expects us to share a bedroom or anything."

She jumped up from where she'd been sitting, chuckling nervously. "Perish the thought. If we shared a room, Dad would pull out his Winchester and march you down to the courthouse, where your options would be marriage to me or the hanging tree."

"Hanging tree?"

"Sure, the big oak in the town square. They haven't used it in about a hundred years, but they'd happily make an exception for an outsider."

Josh peered up at her. "Gee, you make it sound like such a fun place, how could I not want to go?"

She caught her bottom lip between her teeth. He knew she'd never do that again if she realized it lured a man's gaze to her mouth, to her full bottom lip and the sweet curve of her upper lip. Piper didn't seek out men's attention. She wore her hair back, mostly skipped makeup and probably didn't even own a skirt, but her red-gold hair and turquoise eyes would attract a man even if she wore sackcloth. She applied the same determination at the gym as she did in all other areas of life, and the resulting figure would make any man's mouth water.

Any man's but mine.

With too few people in his life he cared about or trusted, Josh refused to throw away his friendship with Piper on sex. Not even hot and sweaty, mind-blowing, earth-shattering sex with the most delicious woman he'd ever seen. Which would never happen, anyway, because Piper would flatten him with one of her Tae-Bo moves if he ever suggested they hit the sheets.

When he sighed, Piper sat next to him, frowning. "You regret volunteering already."

"What? Oh, no. I was just…making a mental list of the stuff I should pack."

"What about work?" she asked doubtfully.

"I'll call in sick tomorrow and Friday. Don't feel guilty, I haven't taken a sick day all year and I'll lose them if I don't take them in the next two months." And it wasn't as though anyone from the office would guess he was with Piper. Though people knew they were friends, Josh's active dating life was common knowledge.

"You'll really do this?"

"You can count on me." Words that were as ironic as they were true. He'd never encouraged a woman to depend on him because the last thing he wanted was to lead one on. Why pretend he might stick around when goodbye was inevitable?

He'd been left too many times, and it was safer if *he* did the leaving, early enough that no one truly got hurt.

"I know I can count on you. Thanks, Josh." The poignant expression in her aquamarine gaze made him look away.

He stood. "If I'm going to pack, I should do laundry."

"Need any quarters?" She sounded uncharacteristically shy. "I did mine last night and still have some change."

"Nah, I'm good."

She rose then, hesitating briefly before throwing her arms around his shoulders. "Thank you."

Awkwardly, he returned the embrace, immediately recalling the last time she'd been this close to him. A few months ago, at a baseball game. They'd both jumped up, cheering as the Astros battled their way from a tie to a win. At the end of the game, Piper had turned to impulsively hug him.

The clean citrusy fragrance of her shampoo was exactly as he remembered. And the underlying womanly scent of her was the same, too.

He released her abruptly.

Piper shuffled back, her expression apologetic. "I just wanted you to know how much I appreciate this. I owe you."

"How about a lifetime supply of those chocolate chip pancakes you make?" He shrugged off her gratitude with a smile. "It's not that big a deal, really. How bad can one family reunion be?"

"You don't know my family."

"I'm not worried," he said. "And now you don't have to worry about this anymore. This weekend, I'm all yours."

Since all the treadmills were taken Thursday morning, Piper began a brisk lap around the indoor track surrounding the mirrored free-weight area. She supposed it was silly to be here so bright and early—okay, pitch-dark and early—on a vacation day, but she hadn't been able to sleep much after Josh's visit last night. Even after hours to get used to the idea, she was still surprised by his generosity.

On the surface, his favor might seem like a fairly simple thing. It was only a few days, after all, and a few harmless white lies to people who would never see him again. But Piper knew Josh better than that, realized what this would cost him. He'd heard her talk about her relatives enough to know what to expect—a convergence of people demanding to know his intentions and dragging out the details of the life story he hated discussing.

Knowing that she'd apparently underestimated him left her feeling both guilty and curious. If he *was* more capable of opening himself up to others than she'd given him credit for, was it possible that—

You're getting way ahead of yourself.

This was one weekend, nothing more. And Josh's

relationship potential was none of her business, anyway, especially considering she didn't want a relationship. What she wanted was to prove to the people of her hometown that there was more than one type of success in life. Not having a ring on your finger or a significant other to fill your Friday nights didn't mean you were a failure.

As she finished her first quarter-mile, Piper spotted Gina Sanchez off to the side, stretching. A pretty woman with long black hair, a habitually wry smile and a collection of colorful T-shirts—including the one she currently wore that said Lawyers Do It Pro Bono—Gina was Piper's closest female friend. They frequently worked out together and sometimes caught a movie or dinner, but Piper generally turned down her friend's clubbing invitations to popular Houston hot spots.

Piper slowed her pace. "Morning."

"What are you doing here?" Gina stepped onto the track. "I thought you were leaving to go see your folks today."

"Not for another few hours."

Her friend shook her head, sending her dark ponytail swinging. "Ever heard of the concept of sleeping in?"

"Well, in the town I'll be visiting, the closest thing they have to a gym are the three machines in the high school weight room, only two of which ever work at the same time. And eating my mother's cooking for the next few days, I'm sure to come back ten pounds heavier. I figured one last workout would be good for me."

"You're so disciplined."

Piper raised her eyebrows. How was she any more disciplined than her friend, who attended the gym with the same regularity? "You're here most mornings at six, too."

"Yeah, but that's because I want to look good so I can find Mr. Right."

Piper just didn't get it. Her cousins she could maybe understand, since they'd been raised in such an old-fashioned setting where their peers aspired to good marriages shortly after high school. Gina's life was more contemporary than that. An attractive, self-reliant attorney, she nonetheless spent a lot of weekend nights with dates who didn't deserve her, only to agonize the following week over why they hadn't called and whether she would ever meet someone.

Piper knew that with her friend, it was more a case of *wanting* a relationship, not buying into the myth that women needed a man to take care of them. But honestly, why did Gina want something so much when it was usually a one-sided effort that left her grumbling about how there were no good men available?

Friends who'd known Piper post-Charlie had teased her, only half kiddingly, about her militant feminist streak. Maybe she *was* being too cynical, she thought as she pumped her arms in rhythm with her stride. After all, what was wrong with healthy equal partnerships?

Nothing, if they exist.

At first, Piper had thought that's what she had with Charlie, until his little manipulations had added up to one big picture. Never complaining that she preferred jeans to a more traditional feminine look, but buying her skirts for her birthday; insisting that children could wait while she built her career, yet managing to make sure she was holding some cute baby at every possible opportunity, hinting that she'd make a wonderful mother.

Charlie was just one example, true, but she didn't see a lot of counterexamples in the people around her. Gina's attempts to find a fulfilling partnership had yet to yield any convincing successes, and Piper's other closest friend, Josh, actively shunned emotional involvement.

Then there were Piper's relatives, the people she'd grown up watching. One could argue that her mother was happily married, but how happy could a woman really be while doing her husband's laundry and fixing his dinner and voting the way he voted? Personally, Piper would probably gnaw off her own arm to escape that kind of relationship. Her cousin Stella, divorced three times, obviously hadn't found the magic formula for true happiness, either.

Even Daphne, who in the past had echoed Piper's resolve not to end up like their mother, was now married and living in Rebecca, pregnant with twins. True, Daphne taught school instead of following their mom's homemaker path, but what had happened to Daphne's plans to travel and see the world? Her husband, Blaine, had apparently convinced her that staying in town so he could run his family's ranch was more important.

Frustration fueled Piper's gait, and neither she nor Gina spoke as they concentrated on their workout. It was only as they slowed to do one final cooldown lap that Piper caught her breath enough to relay the story of her mother's phone call and the resulting situation.

"You can imagine how shocked I was when Josh volunteered to go with me," she concluded.

Gina regarded her strangely. "Why is it shocking? You spend almost all your free time with the guy already. Is it even stretching the truth that much to hint you're a couple?"

Piper stopped so suddenly she almost tripped over her own sneakers. "Of course it is! You know our relationship is nothing like that."

Stepping off the track toward the free weights, Gina

teased, "What I know is that you're close to a gorgeous straight man who has steady employment, yet you refuse to set me up with him."

Gina and Josh? They were all wrong for each other. They...they...actually, they were two attractive, intelligent people with a compatible sense of humor and similar career drives. Nonetheless, Piper had to restrain herself from snapping a warning that Josh was off-limits.

But she couldn't resist a quick reminder. "I've told you, we promised not to date each other's friends."

"From the way you make him sound and from the glimpses I've caught of him, I might be willing to ditch you as a friend." Gina grinned.

Piper halfheartedly returned the smile. Trying to atone for her inner snarkiness, she said, "It may not seem like it, but I'm doing you a favor by not setting you up with him. Josh is a lot of fun, but he's hell on female hearts. You know how many women I've seen him break up with?"

"Maybe because he hasn't met the right one."

"Won't matter. Josh isn't going to let himself find the right one."

If the right woman dropped into his lap, he'd be too busy running the other way to notice. Not that Piper entirely blamed him for his behavior. With her close-knit—sometimes suffocatingly so—family, she didn't pretend to understand what it must have been like to grow up being bounced between foster homes. People coming and going through Josh's life as if it had some sort of invisible revolving door had probably become the norm for him. His dating habits now simply reflected the pattern.

"So this string of broken hearts, is that the reason you've never gone for him yourself?" Gina asked, surprisingly stubborn this morning. Normally all it took was one of Piper's we're-just-friends pronouncements to change the subject.

"I don't need a reason not to go for him. I'm not looking for romance, remember?"

Gina sighed. "And yet you're the one going away for the weekend with the sexy guy."

Yeah. Piper would love to laugh off her friend's comment—except the fact that she *was* going away for the weekend with a sexy guy was what had kept her awake all last night. How far would she and Josh need to go to convince others they were a couple? The man stiffened whenever she casually hugged him, and lately, she was no better. Yesterday, her entire body had tensed whenever he got close to her. So what would happen if he actually had to, say, kiss her?

And why didn't she believe her own self-assurances that she wasn't secretly dying to find out?

Chapter Four

Josh found Piper in the parking garage. She was loading the trunk of her car and glanced up with a smile when he called out a hello.

"Hi." She took his duffel from him, then unlocked the back door of the car to hang up his garment bag. Shutting the car door, she turned expectantly toward him. "Didn't you bring anything else?"

"Nope. I have everything I need."

"In a garment bag and one small duffel?"

Nodding, he peered through the car window at Piper's luggage. It appeared she'd packed the entire contents of her apartment. Maybe to avoid being robbed while she was out of town.

"I noticed the car was sagging," he kidded her, "but I thought we just needed to fill up the tires before we hit the freeway."

"I have presents to take home for the kids in the family,

plus a gift for my sister, who's pregnant, another for my cousin who got engaged, one—"

His laugh cut her off. "It's your car. Bring as much as you want."

She slid in the driver's side and reached across to unlock his door.

Soon they were zooming down the road and Josh was clenching his fists in his lap. Usually, whenever he and Piper went somewhere, he drove or he took his car and met her there. Or he walked, or did whatever else was necessary to avoid riding with her when she was behind the wheel.

It wasn't just her tendency to drive at warp speed that bothered him; he detested being in situations where someone else was in control. He was a lousy passenger and he knew it. People disliked "backseat drivers," especially stubborn, independent people like Piper who hated to be told what to do.

I am going to keep my mouth shut, he told himself. As far as he knew, Piper had never had a single accident. She didn't need him to tell her how to drive.

His well-intended resolution lasted for about five minutes. Piper's head was nodding in time to the fast-paced song on the radio, her braid bobbing against the collar of her pale yellow shirt, and with each chorus, the car accelerated a little more.

"So," he blurted, "what's the speed limit on this road, anyway? We shot past the sign so fast I couldn't tell."

She glanced at the speedometer and immediately slowed the vehicle down.

He couldn't repress a sigh of relief. It was irrational to get nervous when he was in someone else's car, but for the first eighteen years of his life, he'd had no control whatsoever. He hated not being in charge of a situation.

Usually, he managed to project an easygoing image, but his heart pounded every time he had to fly on a plane or ride with another driver.

For a while, his irrational feelings had even affected his job history, driving him to quit voluntarily before something beyond his power might force him to go. A few months ago, he'd started freelancing his services and it had started to pick up. He was regularly approached with jobs that were big enough to keep him busy, but too small for firms like C, K and M to expend energy on. Lately, he'd had to turn down as many assignments as he accepted, but he never backed too far away from his freelancing—and not because he needed the money. Life had taught him that little was permanent. Not jobs, not families, not lovers. Why get attached to people? Why give someone else the opportunity to leave him? He'd lost enough already.

First his parents, although he'd been so young that he remembered them mostly as faces in the photographs he owned. There'd been a string of foster families he'd stayed with only long enough to start caring before being yanked away and sent elsewhere. Living with the Wakefields had been the last time he'd really dared to hope for a family. After they'd moved, he'd decided becoming close to people was just an invitation to get hurt. He'd once dated a woman, Dana, who had tempted him to try to let someone in. He'd wanted to, he really had, but he'd never been able to adjust to the level of intimacy she'd needed. So she'd become just one more person to walk out of his life without looking back.

Piper zoomed beyond Houston's city limits, and for a moment he silently applauded her speed. Too bad he couldn't outrun the bitterness of his past with the same ease.

Maybe conversation would help alleviate his tension. "Is there anything in particular I should know about you?"

"What?" She sounded perplexed. "You know me pretty well already."

"Well, yeah, but is there something more personal, like you have a birthmark the shape of the state of Louisiana?"

"I do not have any weird birthmarks."

No doubt her skin was as creamy and flawless as her curves were intoxicating. "Okay, then some other obscure detail. Your favorite brand of bubble bath?"

"I'm more the hot shower type."

Her words erased the image he'd been conjuring up of thin, foamy bubbles barely covering her. But the shower comment only made him think of two people intertwined in a steamy tile stall—two very specific people who had no business being naked and wet together.

"Is there any reason you're trying to make me sound like a *Playboy* centerfold?" she challenged teasingly.

"Centerfold?" Cursing his exemplary visualization skills, he battled back an image of Piper scantily clad and provocatively posed.

"You know, those ridiculous interview bios." She adopted a higher-than-normal airheaded tone. "My name's Piper, and I enjoy champagne and bubble baths."

"Maybe my examples stunk. All I meant was, are there little things people might expect me to know about you? Things a lover would know?"

Her gaze shot from the road to Josh, and the word *lover* hung between them like an unfulfilled promise. Or a warning.

After a second, she shook her head. "Convincing my family we're involved is one thing, but trying to convince them we're having a scorching affair would be more complicated, not to mention a little creepy. These are my *parents,* after all. Besides, people may think I'm dating, but I never hinted that the relationship was serious. We just need to take small steps to make it look real. You might have to, um, hold my hand or put your arm around me or something."

"I can do that." Despite all the times he'd deliberately avoided those exact, seemingly simple, things.

"And…" She swallowed. "It might not hurt if they see you kiss me once."

"Kiss you." Her summery citrus scent teased him, and for the second time in as many days he wondered what she'd taste like. Oranges? Sweet? Tangy?

"Just a quick peck or something," she said. "No need for a major kiss."

Showed what she knew about him. If he was going to do it, he would do it right.

"We got off track here," she said a bit breathlessly.

He'd have to take her word for it. His thoughts had strayed so far afield that he didn't even remember the original conversation.

"You were worried about personal trivia," she reminded him. "But no one's gonna quiz you about me. They'll want to know all about *you.*"

His least favorite topic. "Hope I don't disappoint them. I'm not a very interesting guy."

She shot him such a knowing look, he added, "But if there's anything you think you should know to make this more believable, feel free to ask. I don't mind." He ignored her snort of disbelief.

Relief pooled inside him when she didn't call his bluff.

Instead, they lapsed into silence, the kind he would

feel obligated to fill with any other woman. But Piper didn't expect him to be witty or charming. She didn't mind when he was obnoxious and cranky, and she could be obnoxious in return. Gradually relaxing, he leaned his seat back and closed his eyes, letting Piper's humming and the motion of the car lull his nerves.

He didn't wake up until he heard the sirens behind them.

Piper's gaze flew to her rearview mirror, and her heart sank. Ignoring Josh's muffled laughter at her colorful language, she pulled the car over.

She'd been stopped twice in one week! "My insurance company is going to send a guy to break my kneecaps." She rolled down her window, looking up to meet the steel-gray eyes of a very tall patrolwoman.

With her platinum-blond hair and high supermodel cheekbones, the officer was probably a Nordic goddess when she smiled. At the moment, though, she was scowling. "License and proof of insurance, please. Do you know how fast you were going?"

Piper didn't think it would look very good if she admitted she had no idea. Before she could say anything at all, Josh leaned across her, addressing the officer.

"Afternoon, ma'am," he said, exaggerating his normal Texas drawl. "I just wanted to apologize. I'm the one who's got to be somewhere, and my sister was hurrying for me. I shouldn't have encouraged her to drive so fast." He flashed a full-voltage smile. "You should give me the ticket."

Piper mentally rolled her eyes. He was only going to irritate her. And what was he going to say when she asked where they had to be in such a hurry?

But the woman didn't ask. Instead, her cold gaze turned

smoky, and she smiled. "I don't think there's a need for anyone to get a ticket today. Your sister just needs to slow down."

Josh's voice was pure honey. "Thanks so much, Officer—?"

"Blake. Julie Blake."

"I suppose it would be too forward to ask if you're in the Houston phone book, Julie Blake?"

Unbelievable! The previously stone-faced officer actually *blushed*.

If they'd been in Josh's car instead of hers, Piper would have tossed her cookies right there on the dashboard.

After Officer Julie assured them she had a listed number, wished them a good day and sashayed back to her own vehicle, Piper let Josh have it. "What is wrong with you? Are you just one giant gland?"

"Hey, I appreciate the gratitude, but don't get all mushy or anything."

"Gratitude?" She forced herself to drive away slowly. "For what—the lesson in flirting? Thanks, but I've caught the Josh Weber seminar plenty of times."

"I wasn't fl— Okay, I was, but only to try and help save your kneecaps."

"What if your charm hadn't worked? What if you'd just made her mad?"

Josh stared at her. "Have you ever seen my charm fail?"

The question would have smacked of arrogance were it not for one thing: she never had seen his charm fail. Women adored him. Even she, who should know better, had been forced to admit lately that she wasn't completely impervious to his flirtations.

"I think you're jealous," he said, a smirk in his voice.

Exasperated, she almost threw her hands in the air, but decided not to, in the interests of steering. "Jealous? Of the Scandinavian patrolwoman?"

"I don't think 'Blake' is Scandinavian."

"I couldn't care less who you throw yourself at. You and Miss Swedish Cheekbones could—"

"I meant," Josh interjected, "jealous because I'm so much better with the opposite sex than you are. Face it, you're no expert on catching men."

"You make guys sound like fish. Or, more appropriately, a disease. For your information, and my mother's, my sister's and the entire population of Rebecca, Texas, I don't even want a man! So why would I work toward catching one?" *Gee, don't hold back, Piper.*

Though she'd surprised herself with her vehement response, Josh took her overreaction pretty well, simply shaking his head. "You know what? You're right, and I'm sorry."

She bit the inside of her lip. "Oh, great. Apologize and make it completely impossible for me to stay mad at you."

"I do my best. To tell you the truth, I don't even know why I'd say anything about you finding a guy when…"

"When what?"

"Nothing."

Piper risked glancing up from the road, but Josh's face gave nothing away. His eyes were shuttered, his mouth neither scowling nor even hinting at his usual flirtatious smile. In fact, it was almost eerie how expressionless his gaze was. Not vacant, but flat…as though he had no emotions at all.

Well, this trip was off to a fabulous start so far.

She pulled into the parking lot of a gas station. Silence reigned. Even if she'd known what to say, the very set of his shoulders deflected conversation. Not for the first time, she wondered what it must be like to love someone who could shut you out so completely with an instant, invisible wall.

But what must it be like for Josh, trapped on the other side of that wall?

Piper smiled at the ridiculous thought. He lived the life most bachelors dreamed of, and seemed perfectly content with it.

As she slid her credit card through the slot at the gas pump, Josh got out of the car. He crossed the parking lot, and Piper watched a group of college-age girls gape in open admiration. The man couldn't help his own appeal. She shouldn't have called him a giant gland when he was doing her a huge favor.

She was just a little on edge. This was her first trip home in years, and though she'd never admit it out loud, a herd of butterflies was stampeding in her stomach. The idea of pretending to be involved with Josh for the next few days was hardly steadying her nerves.

Still, she couldn't let him know the effect he had on her. Best case scenario, he'd tease her mercilessly until she had to kill him and hide his body on some deserted Texas road. Worst case, she'd make him uncomfortable and ruin their friendship.

She'd just finished filling the car when Josh appeared at her side, a brown paper bag in his hand.

"How about I drive for a while?" he offered. "And before you bite my head off, my offer has nothing to do with you going Mach 10. You know how antsy I get when other people are behind the wheel, and this way you don't have to do the whole trip yourself."

She surrendered her keys, knowing she probably shouldn't drive, anyway, when she was so preoccupied with her dubious homecoming. As she slid into the car and fastened her seat belt, he thrust the bag in her direction.

"I got these for you," he said. "I thought you might need them this weekend."

The paper crinkled as she unfolded the top and looked inside. Half-a-dozen Chocomels.

Piper grinned, the earlier tension between them gone. "You are the greatest, Joshua Weber." She savored the first bite of chocolate. "You know, I got to thinking about what you said earlier. You were wondering if we should know trivial facts about each other."

"Yeah, but you said they weren't important."

"They aren't. Not the trivial ones, anyway. But there are other things that might be. I hardly know anything about your childhood, and my family might think that's odd."

Okay, using her relatives as an excuse to pry was both flimsy and obvious. Luckily, Piper was curious enough not to be picky.

"You know where I grew up. You know I've lived in Texas all my life and went to the University of Texas on scholarship."

She folded her arms over her chest and waited, unwilling to be put off with vague answers.

He sighed. "How specific did you want me to be?"

"Maybe something a little more personal than the state you lived in."

"I didn't expect this from you," he said quietly, the very softness of his tone making her feel as though she'd betrayed him.

Perhaps she had. She'd known beforehand how he'd feel about this.

"Fair enough." She relented. "You don't want to talk, we don't have to. But my family's going to ask you questions this weekend. I'll support however you want to handle them, but you should probably give the matter some advance thought."

A few minutes of silence passed, and Piper turned to watch the flat autumn landscape roll by outside her window.

She almost jumped in her seat when Josh unexpectedly volunteered, "I lived in a total of six foster homes. The last family, the Wakefields, actually looked into adopting me. But they got transferred to Europe before the legal stuff could take place, so I stayed in an orphanage until college. A fraternity contact led me to a job in Houston, and you know the important stuff from there."

For a moment, she couldn't feel anything but surprise that he'd actually shared this with her, but then sympathy crowded out her first response. Six homes and none of them really his. "Josh, I—"

"It was great," he interrupted, his voice way too up-beat. "Like a cruise brochure. See new places, meet new people. Even got my own room once."

But never a family. Losing the Wakefields must've been like losing his parents all over again. "I'm so sor—"

"Don't." His gaze snapped toward her, and she saw the anger in his expression that belied his falsely cheerful tone. "My life turned out fine, and I wasn't looking for your pity. I wasn't looking to discuss this, period. But you're all so insistent."

You're all... Meaning women? Why had she pushed when she'd seen him withdraw time and time again from lovers who'd tried to force him into conversations he was uncomfortable having?

Maybe because you hoped you meant something different to him than those women.

The thought bothered her on many levels. Had she

selfishly pried into a painful past just to prove something? And what was that "something," anyway? Josh was a friend, and they'd never be anything more. If she behaved so insensitively in the future, they might not even remain that.

"You misunderstood my apology," she said. "I'm not sorry for you, but for being nosy. It's none of my business. We all have parts of our lives we don't like to discuss, and I should've respected that."

He relaxed the set of his jaw, but his green-gold eyes sparked in a way that let her know she wasn't off the hook. "So what's the part *you* don't like to discuss?" he challenged.

She supposed she owed him this, and he should hear the whole story before this weekend, anyway. "Charlie Conway."

"Guy you dated in college, right?"

"Yeah." They'd had an instant bond on campus, being from the same hometown, but she'd still been surprised that he'd asked her out. In high school, he'd gone more for the school-spirit, cheerleader type. Piper, captain of the girl's softball team, had chosen shop over home ec. Not that she was the only one—several other girls had decided shop was an excellent place to meet guys.

Piper took a deep breath. "Charlie and I were engaged for six months."

"What?" Josh's head jerked in her direction so quickly that she hoped for his sake Rebecca had a licensed chiropractor.

"He asked me to marry him. I said yes."

"You? You're the most anti-marriage woman I know."

She preferred to think of herself as anti-giving-up-your-identity-for-a-man. For years, she'd shaken her head as her father made the household decisions, swearing she would never be as passive as her mother or some of the other female role models Piper had had when she was younger. In eighth grade, she had felt personally let down when her favorite teacher married one of the junior high coaches and moved to a town where he'd been offered a job, even though the school didn't currently have an opening for her.

Piper wasn't unreasonable; she knew relationships meant making some concessions. Charlie had been her first lover, and she'd viewed their relationship with an excited idealism. The very fact that he'd lavishly praised her independence had made her want to prove she could compromise, too, to make little decisions that made him happy, like taking a class together that he was really enthusiastic about instead of the elective she didn't need but had found interesting. Over time, the issue of a three-hour-a-week art history class she hadn't taken somehow became the issue of how they should spend the rest of their lives.

After their engagement, he'd amended his plan to go to law school and move to a big city, deciding instead he'd run as Rebecca's mayor. The decision itself had shaken her, but more upsetting was the fact that he hadn't discussed it with her at all. He'd simply made the resolution, figuring he could get her to agree to it later. It was sometime after that when she realized just how many things she had agreed to in the time they'd been together. He'd been molding her in small, subtle ways toward the very life she'd said from the start she didn't want.

Had her mother once been the same way? A free-spirited woman with her own goals, who'd sacrificed them one by one in the name of love and compromise? Only it wasn't compromise when just one person was giving in.

As much as Piper loved her dad and her brother-in-law, sometimes she got really angry on behalf of her mother and sister. Then again, Mom and Daphne were adults, and Piper doubted they'd appreciate any interference. She just wished her family would afford her the same consideration.

"I can't believe you were engaged," Josh said, bringing her out of her thoughts. "Why did you wait until now to mention this?"

Why did he sound so accusing? "You're the one who was just saying we all had stuff we didn't like to discuss. Besides, you knew Charlie and I were together for a long time." She'd simply omitted the part about the ring and the short-lived search for wedding gowns.

Josh was quiet, and she wondered what he was thinking. She'd expected him to maybe tease her about her brush with matrimony, but he seemed almost angry.

Finally, he muttered, "I just can't believe you were engaged."

Looking back on it, neither could she. It had been a close call, but at least she could take comfort in knowing she'd learned from the mistake.

Josh squinted in the growing darkness to consult the directions Piper had written down. He'd been following the information on the piece of paper for over an hour now, since Piper had fallen asleep. If not for her deep, even breathing, he might have suspected she was feigning sleep to end what had become a tense conversation earlier.

Although, now that he thought about it, that type of avoidance was really more in line with *his* behavior than Piper's generally outspoken nature.

Of course, for an outspoken person, she'd been

awfully secretive for the last two years on the subject of her engagement. He'd been so startled by her announcement he'd temporarily feared the car would end up in a ditch.

Before, she'd always made what happened with her and Charlie sound like a natural breakup, that they'd both wanted different things after college. The explanation had made sense, but what exactly had happened? And did she harbor unresolved issues that explained why she didn't date now? Was there a chance she actually missed the guy or wanted him back?

Oh, sure, she gave plenty of reasons for her lack of a love life, but Josh was still surprised that she didn't date. Piper might roll her eyes and call him a giant gland, but he'd noticed that she expressed her emotions physically. The hugs she impulsively doled out, the killer workouts she threw herself into when she was ticked about something—judging by them, the woman must be suppressing one hell of a sex drive.

You have no business contemplating her sex drive, he reminded himself. When he and Piper had first become friends, her disinterest in all things romance-and-relationship related had made her "safe." Knowing she didn't want anything beyond a platonic friendship had made her so easy to be with, he'd unintentionally let down his emotional guard. Maybe not enough to be comfortable discussing Dana or his past, but certainly more than he did with other women. Now, however, he regretted the diminished barrier between them, because lately, being alone with Piper seemed about as safe as being locked in a trunk with a swarm of killer bees.

And yet here you are with her this weekend, getting even more involved. Chump.

The sun had dipped over the horizon, but Josh could still make out the white mailbox with numbers matching the address Piper had written down. At the precise second he was realizing what a bad idea this weekend was, they'd arrived.

He slowed the car to turn right, passing over a metal cattle guard that jolted the car.

Piper yawned. "Wh-what is it? Are we lost?" She sounded almost hopeful.

"Nope. We're there. I think." He drove down a bumpy dirt road. "Is this supposed to be the driveway?"

"More or less." She pulled down the visor and makeup mirror, checking her appearance and smoothing her braid. "You'll be able to see the house in a minute."

They crossed a small hill, and a white ranch house came into view. Josh steered the car onto the paved driveway and parked. A screen door clattered shut, and a group of people he couldn't quite get a look at in the darkness ambled down the steps of an old-fashioned wraparound front porch and into the yard, calling greetings.

Wearing the expression of a gladiator going to face the lions, Piper climbed out of the car. It was hard to say which one of them, she or Josh, was currently exhibiting less enthusiasm for the weekend that stretched ahead of them.

The first person to reach them was a man almost Josh's height, with blond hair and a wide smile. He bypassed Josh without so much as a curious glance and pulled Piper into a hug that lifted her off the ground.

"Piper! You're more beautiful than ever." The man kissed her cheek before setting her back down. "I've missed you."

The guy didn't seem to notice how strained her expression was, but Josh took a step toward her, sending what he hoped was a reassuring smile.

She returned the smile, though it didn't reach her eyes. "Josh, meet Charlie Conway."

Chapter Five

Josh disliked Charlie Conway on sight.

Okay, maybe he had already begun disliking Conway before meeting him, but seeing the proprietary way the other man draped his arm across Piper's shoulders certainly didn't help matters.

Before Josh could politely—or not—remind Piper's ex that she'd dumped him ages ago, Charlie had hustled her farther up the yard, toward her parents. And away from Josh, who told himself the chill that rippled through him was due to the evening breeze, not the sense of once again being on the outside looking in.

A dark-haired woman who looked about thirteen months pregnant broke away from the cluster and approached him. "Don't worry, she hasn't thought twice about Charlie since the day she gave back the engagement ring."

Despite having his doubts about that, Josh smiled

at the young woman. "I'm Josh. You must be Daphne Jamieson."

"Daphne Wallace, now." She indicated the bearded man who stepped up behind her. "This is my husband, Blaine."

Josh shook hands with each of them. "Nice to meet you both."

Blaine stared, making no attempt to hide the scrutiny in his brown eyes. "Same here. We've been anxious to meet you. Piper's never brought a guy home before—she must really be crazy about you."

Out of habit, Josh almost blurted, "We're just friends," but at the last moment remembered his role this weekend. "I'm crazy about her, too." His chest tightened as he said the words, and he told himself it was only because sentiment, even fake sentiment, made him uncomfortable.

Piper's mother descended on him just in time to hear his vow of affection, and she wrapped her arms around him in an enthusiastic hug. "I'm Astrid Jamieson."

"Nice to meet you, ma'am. Josh Weber." He had to wiggle away when she seemed reluctant to let go of him.

"Welcome to the family." Mrs. Jamieson winked. "Maybe there will be another wedding before too much longer."

"Mom!" Piper glared. "Try not to scare Josh off by prematurely planning our nuptials, okay?"

Mrs. Jamieson shot a knowing maternal look at her oldest daughter. "When you said you were *finally* seeing someone, I just knew it had to be Josh. The way you talk about him, Nana and I figured out months ago that you were in love with him. So what happened to get you to admit it at long last?"

Piper grabbed his hand. "Josh, I don't believe you've met my father. This is—"

He turned back to her mother. "Piper talks about me?"

"Oh, yes." Mrs. Jamieson was only too happy to answer. "She told me that you two work together, and that you're just brilliant at what you do. And that you're starting your own company!"

"Well," Josh began modestly, "I don't know if you can really call it a company yet, just some work I do on the side, but it turns a steady profit."

Piper's mother beamed. "Then you'll be a good provider. Such an important quality in a potential—"

"Mom! Don't say it."

"Husband." While all eyes were on her, Mrs. Jamieson added one last bit of praise. "Piper wasn't exaggerating when she said you were the best-looking man in Houston. She's been attracted to you from the moment you met."

"I never said that!"

Josh was sure she never had, but he was still surprised at her adamant protest. Didn't she want people to think they were attracted to one another?

Or—the thought struck like unexpected lightning from a clear sky—was her denial more for herself? Josh had never heard of *male* intuition before, but a small part of his mind suddenly seemed to flicker with insight. Even though he had no reason to believe Piper had been wrestling with the same desire he'd been fighting lately, he couldn't help but wonder if that was the case.

Or was he just projecting his own feelings of lust onto her?

Josh abandoned the mental debate as soon as he saw the way Charlie Conway was grinning at her denouncement.

The blond man sized her up as though she were a chocolate-fudge layer cake and he'd just discovered he had room left for dessert. "You mean you *aren't* attracted to him, Piper?"

Josh waited along with everyone else, wondering how she'd respond.

She quickly backpedaled. "Well, of course I am. I just don't think that's exactly what I said to Mom."

"My students would have said he's hot," her sister supplied. When her husband grunted, Daphne added, "I'm not blind."

Mrs. Jamieson continued her recitation for Josh. "She used to mention the constant stream of women you dated, and it was obvious to me that she was jealous of them. Took her long enough to admit her real feelings!"

Piper tugged on Josh's hand and forcibly dragged him away. "You still have to meet my father."

For her ears only, Josh whispered, "But I was so enjoying talking to your mom. This trip has been worth it already."

"Dad, this is Joshua Weber."

At least several inches taller than Josh and backlit by the light spilling from the house windows, Mr. Jamieson glared down at his daughter's suitor. "Son, I have a gun collection and no reservations about using it on you if you hurt my little girl."

"Really, Fred!" Mrs. Jamieson fisted her hands on her ample hips. "Maybe if you didn't scare all the young men off, she would've been married by now."

Daphne and Piper chided in unison, "Mom!" and Charlie cleared his throat, as though trying to remind everyone that *he* hadn't been scared off.

Fred Jamieson reached out to rumple Piper's bangs. "Don't you listen to her. Nothing wrong with taking your time and finding the right guy." He shot Josh an assessing glance, as though trying to determine if this would be the "right guy."

Charlie cleared his throat again. "I'm sure looking forward to one of Astrid's home-cooked meals. Who else is hungry?"

Amid murmurs of agreement, everyone shuffled toward the house. Josh hung back a little, smirking at Piper. "I didn't realize your family had heard so much about me." He was surprised at the warm glow that gave him inside.

Was it really so surprising that over the course of two years, she'd mentioned him to her family? After all, he'd certainly listened to her talk about her relatives plenty of times. But somehow he couldn't help grinning at the thought that he was a big enough part of Piper's life for the Jamiesons to have heard about his freelance endeavors and even his dating habits, although he hoped Piper had given them the G-rated version.

Reality intruded then, eliminating his foolish grin and reminding Josh that he didn't *want* to be a big part of someone's life. Nor did he want anyone to be a big part of his. That led to painful goodbyes.

Piper pressed a hand to her temple. "We've been here ten minutes and I'm ready to go home. This weekend is going to be a nightmare."

"Yeah, we should all have to live such nightmares, forced to spend time with family members who are excited to see us."

She did a double take at his tone, which if not flat-out angry was at least sarcastic as hell.

Where did that come from? He didn't blame her for her surprise or her wounded expression. He'd always been a sounding board and a sympathetic ally, giving her no reason to suspect he'd turn on her like that. Truthfully, he understood why this weekend would be tough for her. Her mom seemed to allude to marriage every few minutes, and what was with the ex-fiancé's cameo appearance?

"Sorry, Piper, what I said didn't come out right."

"You sure about that?" She regarded him shrewdly, and he shifted his weight, feeling fidgety and once again regretting discussing his foster care past with her in the car, even if the conversation had been a short, vague one.

"I'm sure," he insisted. "I was just trying to find the silver lining for you. I mean, yes, parts of the weekend might be irritating, but on the plus side, they're thrilled to see you." Although Conway seemed a bit *too* thrilled.

The sound of Daphne's delicate "ahem" from the bottom porch step drifted through the night air. "Am I interrupting anything?"

"No," Piper and Josh chorused quickly.

His prompt denial stemmed from his relief at the opportunity to end the exchange. He suspected Piper's instant answer and nervous tone came from wondering if her complaints about her family members had been overheard by any of them.

Either way, their speedy "no's" sounded more like guilty yes's, and the porch light illuminated Daphne's face enough for her grin to be visible. "Well, I hate to break up whatever's going on out here, but Mom worries about the food getting cold. She wanted to know if you two would be long."

Josh seized the chance to escape. "I should go offer to help set the table or something, the least I can do to thank your mom for her trouble with dinner. If you'll excuse me, ladies."

He took the steps two at a time. Just as he was reaching for the screen door, he heard Piper ask, "What is Charlie doing here?"

That's what I'd like to know.

Daphne's voice floated through the darkness. "You guys go way back and we all grew up together. Is it so odd he'd like to catch up? Besides, Mom and Dad love having the mayor over to dinner. Makes them feel important. Enough about Charlie, though! Why didn't you call and tell me about you and Josh? I can't believe you'd keep something like this from me."

"It's not really serious, Daph."

"Oh, please…with the way you look at him?"

Even though he figured Daphne was only seeing what she expected to see, Josh still smiled over her words as he stepped inside the Jamiesons' foyer.

The hardwood floor was scuffed in a few places and the blue floral wallpaper was faded, but friendly voices and tantalizing aromas wafted from the kitchen. A real home. He swallowed the unwelcome lump of emotion lodged in his throat and started toward the voices, only to be practically knocked over by Piper, who was walking as fast as she normally drove. The screen door clattered shut behind her and her sister.

"I can't believe no one told me she was here!" Piper declared as she sped by.

A contrite Daphne followed. "I just assumed you knew."

Letting Piper hurry on ahead, Josh asked Daphne, "Everything okay?"

"Nana's inside, and Piper feels bad about not coming in to see her sooner. Nothing would have kept Nana from being here tonight, but the poor old dear just can't handle the nighttime chill."

"How is she?" Josh asked, knowing how worried Piper was about her grandmother.

Daphne wouldn't meet his gaze. "She has her good days and bad days."

They had reached the end of the hall and rounded the corner to the dining room. Though not elaborately decorated, the room possessed homey elegance. Simple lace curtains and a glass chandelier lent the room class, and a plain wooden china cabinet displayed plates and antique heirlooms that had undoubtedly been passed from one generation to the next. A rectangular table matching the cabinet dominated the Jamiesons' dining room.

His gaze moved to Piper, who knelt in front of her grandmother's chair.

She turned at the sound of his footsteps. "Josh, come meet my grandmother, Helen. Nana, this is—"

The white-haired woman lifted the spectacles she wore on a gold chain around her neck. "Step aside, girl. I want a look at him." She squinted her blue eyes and studied Josh so intently he half expected her to ask to see his teeth. Finally she lowered the spectacles. "Virile," she pronounced.

What kind of response was he supposed to make to that?

Nana solved his problem by speaking again before he could. "I expect a man like you knows how to keep a woman happy?"

"I, er, try my best, ma'am."

"See that you do. My granddaughter deserves happiness." She held out her hand as imperiously as a queen, and he shook it, grinning.

Helen Jamieson was not what he'd expected. He'd envisioned a frail woman, covered by quilts. She was small and wizened with age, but her gaze was sharp and lively, as was her gamine smile. If he hadn't known otherwise, he would have guessed this woman hadn't been sick a day in her life.

Piper's mother informed them that dinner was ready, and Josh sat down with the rest of the family. The oak table groaned under the weight of steaming platters and casserole dishes. He was shocked when Mrs. Jamieson made two more trips to the kitchen, bringing out pans and baskets to line the sideboard.

Turning to Piper, Josh whispered, "Who else are we expecting for dinner?"

"Just us."

"You sure? Looks like your mom's feeding a company of Texas Rangers."

She smiled. "Welcome to the Jamiesons'. I hope you brought your appetite. And Josh…?" Though they'd been whispering already, her voice grew even softer as she leaned in closer. "Thank you."

He wanted to say it was no big deal. Hell, he wanted to say *anything,* but his thoughts collided in an indiscernible pileup when he realized how close her face was to his. Her sea-green eyes were wide, as though she'd just made some startling discovery. Her lips were parted gently, and his gaze slid to her mouth. She reacted immediately, her breath coming slightly faster, her cheeks blossoming with pale pink color.

The rosy blush made him wonder how warm her skin would be beneath his hands, but he was jarred from the pleasant contemplation by the sound of a chair being scraped across the wooden floor. Charlie had pulled back the seat on the other side of Piper, but before the man had a chance to plop down his mayoral posterior, Nana spoke up.

"Charlie, come and sit by me, won't you? I had some

questions I wanted to ask you about city business, and my hearing isn't what it used to be."

Hesitating for only the briefest second, Charlie nodded. "Anything for you, Nana."

Piper's grandmother beamed a sweet, almost absent-minded smile at him, but her eyes gleamed with what looked suspiciously like triumph.

The old gal didn't miss a trick, Josh thought. He couldn't help sharing some of Piper's fondness for the family's matriarch.

Astrid Jamieson began passing dishes around, and Josh's stomach rumbled in happy expectation of the chicken-fried steak, mashed potatoes and green beans with bacon. But by the time he was handed the basket of rolls, the salad bowl and the sweet potato casserole, he began to envision the button on his jeans shooting across the room and doing someone severe injury.

Piper's dad blessed the meal, and Josh dug in. After one bite of Mrs. Jamieson's home cooking, he resolved to somehow find room for all of it. It was the best food he'd tasted in his life. Definitely better than frozen pizzas that always turned out soggy in the middle, and microwaved bachelor meals that prompted him to date, just so he had a reason to frequent restaurants.

He smiled at Piper's mom. "Mrs. Jamieson, if the situation were different, I'd marry you."

Charlie raised his eyebrows. "I was under the impression that you weren't the marriage type. Didn't Astrid say something outside about 'a constant stream of women'? Sounds like you'd dated half the female population of Houston."

His jaw clenching at the other man's challenging tone, Josh said, "Probably closer to a quarter of the population. But the benefit of all that dating is that I can truly appreciate what I have in Piper, how special she is. Of course, I don't have to tell *you* that."

The mayor paused in the act of buttering a roll, his blue eyes as sharp and cold as icicles. "No, you don't. I know Piper quite well." The man put as much emphasis on *quite* as he no doubt thought he could get away with in front of her parents, but tempered the insinuation with an innocuous smile. "We grew up together and have such a history, you know."

"Yes, I understand you asked Piper to marry you. It certainly worked out well for me that she turned you down."

Charlie's face reddened, but before he could retort—or lunge across the table to disembowel Josh with the butter knife—Mrs. Jamieson jumped into the conversation, her hearty tone an obvious attempt to dispel the air of hostility that had gathered over the table like the electric atmosphere before a storm. "Glad you like the food," she said, responding to Josh's original comment. "I tried to teach both my girls to cook."

"Piper makes great chocolate chip pancakes," he said loyally.

Eyes narrowed, Charlie glanced from Josh to Piper and back again. "Eat breakfast together a lot, do you?"

Josh floundered for an answer that would shut his adversary up without sending Mr. Jamieson for the famed gun collection.

Piper rescued him. "It's one of the benefits of living in the same building. So, Mom, catch me up on all the local gossip."

Mrs. Jamieson launched into a recitation of what had happened to every citizen of Rebecca since Piper had left home, ending with, "Cousin Stella's latest divorce is final, and she just got back from San Antonio. She had her thighs vacuumed this time. And that nice Beth Ann Morrow you graduated with is pregnant." She glanced at Piper's flat stomach. "Beth Ann's mother is so lucky that she'll have grandchildren."

"Hey!" Daphne sounded as offended as Piper looked. "In a couple of months, you're going to have *two* of them."

Josh looked down the table at her. "You're having twins?"

"They run in Blaine's family," Daphne said with a nod.

Mr. Jamieson harrumphed. "When do you go on maternity leave? I don't like the idea of you working in this condition."

"I'm not fragile, Dad. I'm healthy as a horse. And about the same size as one. But I'm only working till the winter break. They hired someone else to take over next semester, and I'll have all summer at home with the babies before I go back. If I go back."

Next to Josh, Piper tensed in her chair. "*If* you go back?"

Daphne nodded. "Even with Mom's help and Blaine's mother…the twins'll be a handful, and they're only babies once."

"So you're thinking of leaving your students? Of becoming a *housewife?*"

Josh doubted Piper had any idea how shrill her tone was.

"Is there something wrong with being a housewife?" Mrs. Jamieson asked her oldest daughter pointedly.

"I love kids, myself." Charlie spoke up, despite the fact that no one had solicited his opinion on the matter. "How do you feel about children, Josh? See yourself as father material?"

Even though he'd expected this exact type of ambush, Josh faltered. He hadn't allowed himself to think of a real family in years, not since Dana and the realization that he just wasn't cut out for anything permanent. But now, the unbidden image of a child flashed through his mind…a child with aquamarine eyes that looked dangerously familiar. Josh's gaze swung to Piper, almost as though she were responsible for the mental picture and could make it go away.

Instead, his mind simply shifted to different, equally troubling territory. The way she was glaring across the table at Charlie shouldn't be a turn-on, but it was. Her turquoise eyes were brilliant, and her cheeks were stained with color. Josh couldn't help noticing the way her chest rose and fell with each angry breath, either. Did she even know how gorgeous she was, or how much he wanted her in unexpected, undisciplined moments like these?

Piper's laugh was forced. "Charlie, I thought it was Dad's job to interrogate the man in my life, not yours."

She stressed *the man in my life,* but in Josh's opinion, Charlie needed a stronger reminder that Piper was spoken for. At least, spoken for as far as everyone here knew.

Charlie's mouth fell open in a satisfyingly undignified expression, and he didn't seem to know how to respond.

Mr. Jamieson redirected the conversation. "So, Josh, you follow football?"

Josh was more of a baseball fan, but he contributed a remark here and there as Mr. Jamieson and Blaine discussed the Cowboys and the Texans. At least no one was debating a woman's proper role in society or making veiled innuendos about Piper belonging back with Charlie. Finally, the meal ended.

Mrs. Jamieson's attempts to talk everyone into second

helpings were met with moans of protest. "Daphne? You're eating for three now. Piper, you could use a little filling out. Josh? More potatoes?"

Piper cut her eyes in Josh's direction and said sotto voce, "Think I'll clear the table before she starts her Young People Today Are Too Thin Speech."

"I'll help."

Charlie stood immediately. "I can lend a hand cleaning up, help show you where everything goes, Josh. This place is practically my second home."

He might as well have painted the word *outsider* on Josh's forehead in large red letters.

Bitterness burned Josh's tongue. When hadn't he been the outsider? Although surrounded by a roomful of people, for one terrible second he felt completely alone.

As though she understood, Piper rose and touched his arm. The contact sparked through him, melting the sharp loneliness into something warm and full. And risky.

"Just help me get through this weekend," she murmured as they carried dishes to the kitchen, "and I promise you never have to come back."

She rinsed plates, and he stacked them in the dishwasher. Charlie carried dishes in from the adjoining dining room and found frequent excuses to reach between the two of them.

Annoyance simmered inside Josh. "I can't say I'm all that fond of your ex-boyfriend," he said in a low voice.

Piper's expression was bemused as she whispered, "Yeah, I think we all got that. I appreciate the jealous boyfriend act, but you don't have to put quite so much into it."

Though he knew it was irrational, he felt as though she were criticizing him, and thereby siding with Charlie. "If you want, I can drop the boyfriend act all together...."

He trailed off as Charlie carried in a vegetable platter. The man just happened to brush against Piper before finally leaving the kitchen for more dishes.

Josh ground his teeth together. "As I was saying, if there's still something between the two of you that you want to explore, I can—"

"Are you kidding?" Her grimace, complete with eyes rounded in horror, did Josh's heart good. "That's not what I meant at all! As long as you're stuck here, I want you to be able to try to enjoy this weekend and not feel like you had to spend the whole time responding to his barbs, but he is one of the reasons I needed boyfriend camouflage. A big reason."

"Oh." Josh glanced at the doorway, noting that where he and Piper stood was visible to anyone in the dining room. "And your grandmother's fondest dream is to see you in the arms of a good man, right?" Even as he spoke, an internal voice cautioned, *Don't do it.*

"Right."

He took a step toward her and removed the bowl she was holding from her hand. Maybe he shouldn't do this, but how could just once hurt? Only to satisfy his curiosity and help him move on.

Bracing an arm on the counter behind her, he leaned forward, keeping his voice low. "I have an idea that should make your grandmother ecstatic." And Charlie considerably less so.

Piper's oceanic-colored eyes grew so wide he could drown in them. But her lashes fluttered, and her eyes closed as she stood on tiptoe to meet him. Then his lips were on hers.

Fire raced in his blood. As much as he'd tried not to, he had imagined holding her in his arms and kissing her just like this. Now, too late, he realized that the reality was far more devastating to his senses than the fantasy, and his assumption that he could walk away from "just one" kiss unaffected had been a foolish one.

Still, as long as he was making the mistake of kissing her, he should make the most of it.

Chapter Six

Shock zapped through Piper but was quickly replaced by a slow-throbbing desire. Wait, this is not a good idea, she tried to tell herself.

What else but desire could she feel when Josh nipped at her lower lip and teased the corner of her mouth with his tongue? She melted against him, parting her lips, and he deepened the kiss. There was no awkwardness, no bumping of noses, only wanting and a piercing sense of *rightness*.

Why hadn't they kissed like this months ago?

Some part of her seemed to recall that there were important answers to that question, but all she could focus on was the taste of him, the heat of his body against hers. Instead of satisfying any of the sensual hunger growing inside her, his addictive kiss only left her wanting more.

Her fingers went to the top of his shirt, to the button below his collar. She recalled his tight muscles and the sprinkling of dark hair she'd glimpsed a few times when they'd used the apartment pool. Boy, did she miss those summer months…. But she didn't just want to get his shirt off, she wanted—

"Heh-hm." From the dining room, Piper's father cleared his throat. Loudly.

She blinked at the reminder that there were witnesses, and slowly stepped away from Josh. Except that she couldn't get very far away, trapped as she was between him and the counter. A few more seconds of that potent kiss and she might have hopped up on the counter and invited Josh to end her self-imposed spell of celibacy.

What in the world had possessed her? Now that his mouth was no longer seducing hers, she could think more clearly. She wouldn't be doing anything with Josh on kitchen counters or anywhere else. Despite the liquid need pooling inside her and the sweet ache that had settled between her thighs.

"Piper, I—"

"We'll talk later." She averted her gaze, afraid of what she'd see in his eyes and what might still be visible in hers.

She harbored hope that they *wouldn't* discuss this later. What was there to say? He was only a friend. The kiss had been a pretense for her family, part of his favor to her this weekend.

Just because it had been the hottest kiss she'd experienced since…ever, that didn't mean anything. After all, he'd had lots of practice kissing women. Stood to reason he'd be good at it.

She focused on the dishes in the sink, determined to put the incident completely behind her.

Daphne maneuvered her way into the kitchen and set a couple of pans down. She nudged her sister and whispered, not quietly enough, in Piper's opinion, "Not that serious, huh? Looked pretty serious to me."

"It was only a kiss," Piper replied, irrationally riled by her sister's grin.

Daphne hooked one finger through the neckline of her daisy-print maternity dress and fanned the fabric back and forth. "Last time I saw a kiss that hot, it was in a movie." She winked at Josh, and he winked back, looking entirely too pleased with himself. Somehow the cheer the people around her were feeling made Piper's mood even darker.

She actually welcomed Charlie's scowl as he came through the doorway with a stack of plates, which he slammed down on the counter.

"Careful with those," Daphne chided. "They've been in the family forever."

Charlie apologized but still glowered, and Josh muttered, "My work here is done."

Aha! All the proof Piper needed that he'd only kissed her to help convince Charlie she wasn't interested in rekindling the old flame. But the confirmation left her feeling oddly hollow. Dissuading her ex, or any other eligible bachelors her family might try to foist on her, *was* one of the reasons she'd brought Josh with her. So why did she feel almost angry that it was the motivation behind Josh's kiss?

I am not angry. She scrubbed the plate in her hand so hard that the floral pattern almost came off with the food.

Okay, so what was she, then? Confused. Aroused. Curious. Had their shared kiss affected Josh as much as it had her? She could ask him later, but knew she wouldn't. What good would come from knowing that he'd been as turned on as she had? It wasn't as though either of them would ever act on their attraction, and if she'd ever needed evidence that men unnecessarily complicated things, she certainly had it now. She had a career to focus on, with an employer who would dismiss either her or Josh or both if they took the unlikely step of dating.

Of course, there was always the possibility that her worries were for nothing and the kiss *hadn't* shaken Josh as it had her. That prospect didn't make her feel any better.

Once the dishes were taken care of, and Josh and Piper had refused additional offers of dessert, Piper informed her family that it had been a long day and she wanted to go check into the hotel.

"So you and Josh are getting a room there?" Charlie asked. His petulant expression rendered him much less handsome.

"We're getting room*s*," Piper enunciated, "but that's really none of your business."

"I'm just trying to look out for an old friend."

Through gritted teeth, Piper repeated what she had been trying to tell her family for years. "I can look out for myself."

Her mother frowned. "But, dear, you have Josh for that now."

"Actually," Josh interjected, "Piper does great by herself. It's me who needs a keeper. She keeps me organized and focused."

Right then, Piper wanted to hug him more than ever. But it would probably be best if she didn't touch him again until her nerve endings stopped tingling from that kiss. Say, in forty or fifty years.

Everyone but Nana shuffled out onto the front porch and waved goodbye as Josh started the car.

"So," Piper began as he steered the vehicle down the

driveway. "One night down. Think you can still stick it out the rest of the weekend, or do you feel a sudden emergency calling you back to Houston?"

His answering chuckle sounded weary. "I'll stick it out. I shudder to think what you'd do to me if I left you here to face them on your own. Although…"

"What?"

"Well, they do seem crazy about you."

She loved them, too, but it was easier from a few hundred miles away.

It wasn't just her mother's obsession with marriage that bothered her. Or her father's overprotectiveness, or even the occasional feeling that Daphne had defected. It was the hurt that came from feeling they weren't proud of her.

The only previous time she'd visited home after moving to Houston, she'd brought some rolled-up blueprints with her, wanting to show her family the work she did. Her mother never had made the time to sit down and look at the drawings, bustling off frequently to the kitchen to check on whatever was in the oven. Her dad had scanned the drawings, nodded once, then asked her if she was all set financially or needed him to write her a check. They seemed to have completely missed how important her career was to her, how determined she was to show that she could stand on her own two feet.

"Piper?" Josh interrupted her thoughts, for which she was grateful until she realized what he was saying. "About that kiss—"

"It was no big deal."

"No big deal?"

"Right." She wanted to dismiss the topic before he could point out the obvious, that he'd been doing it as part of their act. She knew darn well how he saw her—they were pals, chums, buddies, compadres. Until tonight, Josh had shown no sign of noticing she had two X chromosomes.

He flirted, of course, but that was just Josh being Josh. It had nothing to do with her. And thank heavens for that, because she certainly wouldn't want him to have any feelings for her. The buddy system was working just fine…or would be again as soon as her newly awakened hormones realized that tonight had been a false alarm, and returned to their dormant state.

Determined to downplay what had happened, she summed up the subject before he could. "Suffice it to say, I appreciate the favor. It wasn't too bad, and we might even have to do it again, but only in front of the necessary witnesses, of course."

"Of course." He bit out the words, and she wondered if she should have expressed more gratitude for the way he'd helped her.

Long moments later, as they drove down the dark country road, he spoke again, sounding like his normal self. "I don't mean to disparage your hometown, Piper, but it's creepy out here."

She tore her gaze away from the millions of stars she could see out her window and shot him a questioning glance. "Creepy? I can't believe a man who braves Houston's crime rate would get spooked out here."

"We've been on the road ten minutes and haven't seen a single car. I find that disconcerting."

"Most people around here go to bed by nine."

"Sounds like a fascinating place to live."

"Maybe it's not the most exciting town, but it's clean and friendly and—" It was probably the first time she'd said something nice about her hometown since she'd left.

"Anyway, it's not too bad. It's just not for me, and one of the main reasons Charlie and I broke up."

"When you say 'broke up,' just how mutual was that?"

"Not at all, as you probably guessed by tonight. It was my decision." She stopped there, not wanting to get into a Charlie-bashing session, despite how pompous the man had been this evening.

How could it be fair to catalog Charlie's faults in front of Josh? Charlie had followed in the well-worn path of generations of Rebecca mayors before him, not because he'd ever said convincingly that it was what he wanted, but because it was easier than doing something different. She couldn't imagine Charlie ever striking out on his own or taking initiative the way Josh did with his sideline business, which he ran on the weekends. Besides, even though Charlie was regarded as the catch of the town, she couldn't picture anyone preferring the blond, bland mayor to her wickedly handsome best friend and his lethal kisses. Telling a man with Josh's charisma about Charlie's shortcomings seemed as sporting as letting Babe Ruth come to bat against a Little League team.

So Piper opted to change the subject and give Josh directions instead. He turned the car to the left, and the hotel's blue neon sign appeared up ahead.

"Did you deliberately pick a place this far from your parents?" he asked.

She laughed. "Options are a little more limited out here than in Houston. There are only two real hotels in the whole county, and this one's the best. It won't be the Waldorf, but rates are reasonable and it should be clean."

"Hey, I'm not picky about our digs. I'm just surprised your family didn't insist we stay with them."

"They would have, but I didn't commit to coming for the reunion until my aunt and uncle from Louisiana had already arranged to stay with my parents. They'll get in tomorrow."

As Josh parked the car in front of the hotel, Piper suddenly realized how tired she was. She'd been so tense about coming home that she'd let anxiety wear her down, and she hadn't had a decent night's sleep since she'd first told her mother about her "boyfriend." Now, with the hardest part of the weekend—the first contact—behind her, exhaustion replaced the anticipatory stress.

While they checked in at the front desk, Piper yawned repeatedly, struggling to focus her eyes on the paperwork in front of her. The trek up the staircase to their reserved rooms seemed as grueling as a workout on the StairMaster. She couldn't remember ever being as happy to see anything as the door with her room number on it. Mumbling a good-night to Josh, she shuffled inside, hoping she could make it as far as the bed. She toyed with the idea of not brushing her teeth and just sleeping in what she was wearing.

A sudden knock startled her into dropping a suitcase on her foot. Muttering "ouch" and other words of the four-letter variety, she hobbled toward the door to the hallway, then realized that wasn't where the knock had originated.

For the first time, she noticed another door, next to the bed. She opened it hesitantly and found Josh smiling at her.

Over his jeans, he wore a shirt that was now half-unbuttoned. Her fingers itched to finish the job for him.

"I forgot to pack toothpaste," he said.

"There's a door between our rooms?"

He didn't bother answering the obvious. "So do you

have toothpaste I can borrow in one of those hundreds of bags you brought?"

She kept staring. Under her gaze, he slipped the last few buttons out of their holes and shrugged off his shirt and pitched it into the room behind him. She didn't blame him—damn, it was getting warm in here. She couldn't tell from his facial expression if he was matter-of-factly getting ready for bed or if he was teasing her. Of course, it would be easier to gauge his expression if she actually looked up at his *face*. As it was, she couldn't lift her gaze from the taut planes of his chest. Instead, her eyes trailed downward, following the fine line of hair that bisected his sculpted abs, leading past his navel to the fly of his jeans.

Realizing where she was staring, she jerked her head up to find him watching her. The good news was he wasn't laughing at her. The bad news was enough speculative heat danced in his eyes to warm the entire hotel.

"About that toothpaste?" he prompted. "You never know when minty fresh breath will come in handy."

"Uh, sure…if you want to just go back into your room and finish getting dressed for bed, I can bring you the toothpaste in a minute." Maybe that would buy her time to get her suddenly cardboard tongue unstuck from the roof of her inexplicably dry mouth.

"I don't actually get dressed for bed, Piper. Just *un*-dressed." He flashed a wicked smile. "I could go ahead and do that, but—"

"No! No, that's okay. I didn't realize that you slept n— I mean, I didn't… Just have a seat and give me a sec, will ya?" Maybe if she tried really hard, she could embarrass herself further. Go for some kind of record.

If she'd been more awake at the beginning of this unexpected encounter, she would have handled it more gracefully. At least, that was the story she was sticking to. He sat on the edge of her bed, waiting while she rummaged through her duffel bag. Why couldn't he have used the chair on the other side of the room, next to the window?

So what if he's in my room, on my bed? It's only Josh.

Only? Ha!

She knew instinctively that she wouldn't be reacting to any other man this way. But it seemed something about Josh—lately, *everything* about Josh—made her go as warm and gooey as a Chocomel left to melt in a car on a sunny day.

A strange thrumming sound rang in Piper's ears. Probably her hormones chanting their demands. Well, as she'd explained to Josh before, she had total control over her hormones. She wasn't going to allow some chemical reaction in her body to rule her actions.

Exhaustion and her conflicting emotions impaired her thinking. Then, of course, there was the distraction of the sexiest man she'd ever seen currently lounging on her bedspread—not that she'd need the blanket to keep her warm if he stayed.

She blinked. He was not staying.

"Here." She thrust the tube of toothpaste at him. "Take it. Give it back to me in the morning."

"You want to use some first?"

"I'll skip it tonight, I'm so beat. You just be on your way, and I'll crawl into bed."

He paused in the doorway, where she waited to close the door. His gaze seduced hers, so warm and compelling she couldn't look away. Moving slowly, almost hypnotically, he inclined his head toward her. Her heart beat so loudly she was afraid he must hear it. The people in the room below could probably hear it.

He wasn't going to kiss her, was he? She'd made a point of mentioning earlier that they only needed to keep up the pretense in front of witnesses.

Maybe you need to practice so that it looks natural in front of your family, a small voice rationalized.

But he obviously wasn't listening to a similar small voice. At the last minute, he stopped short and whispered, "Good night, Piper," before backing into the dim shadows of his own room.

She shut the door, replaying the last few seconds in her head, wondering where she'd gone wrong. *Good night, Piper?* She'd been so sure that... *You didn't want him to kiss you, remember?*

Right. It was probably best that he hadn't. Why complicate things further? Besides, despite her attempted rationalization, she knew from their earlier experience in her parents' kitchen that Josh needed no practice. You couldn't improve on sensual perfection.

Time to forget about all that, she told herself. He was gone now, and she was finally free to pull on a long T-shirt and crawl between the clean cool sheets to fall into a restful sleep.

As if that was going to happen. The hotel mattress bore the imprint of Josh's body, and with the subtle spice of his cologne still lacing the space around her, it was easy to imagine him here. With her.

Piper kicked off the sheets, needing air against her flushed and fevered skin. She reminded herself that a love life was almost never worth the time and energy it required. But one with Josh? Okay, so that might definitely be worth something, but not her entire career. She'd worked hard to position herself at C, K and M, and was hopeful that she'd be assigned some big projects after her next review. The last thing she wanted to do was start over elsewhere—especially for a brief fling.

Now if it were for a full-blown relationship... No. She didn't want one of those, either. They were like quicksand. What if she slipped into one and slowly lost her identity before she realized it? What if one day in the future she woke up like Daphne, who also had had plans for her life? What if Piper were the one sitting at the dining room table, announcing to her family that she'd decided to give up her goals and occupation? After all, she'd almost headed down that road with Charlie, and she didn't remember him ever having the magnetic pull on her that she'd experienced moments ago with Josh.

She was just tired. It had been a long day, and this would all look a lot clearer in the morning, after some sleep.

But how was she supposed to sleep when the only thing between her and Josh's naked body was one lousy door so thin she could hear him stretch across his own bed on the other side?

"Remind me what the agenda for this morning is," Josh said as she pulled the car up to the ranch house.

She was guiltily grateful he hadn't asked about the whole day. She hadn't yet figured out how to pass on what her mom had told her last night. Piper had meant to explain about the shower, but that kiss had short-circuited her brain.

"I have to do girl stuff," Piper said, "and you'll—"

"Let me guess. Guy stuff?"

She rolled her eyes. "I figured you could hang out with Dad. Unless you want to go with me to see my cousin's wedding dress and then take Daphne to the OB."

"I'll take my chances with your dad."

"Good choice. Don't worry, it'll be fun. Now, if Dad asks what attracted you to me, make sure you pick an answer that isn't physical." She switched off the ignition. "I mean, don't get too carried away with the whole boyfriend pretense. I'm not saying you're actually turned on by me."

As they climbed out of the car, Josh laughed. "That sounded like a question. Are you fishing, Piper?"

"What? No, of course not." If her slightly raised voice sounded defensive, that was a coincidence.

"Uh-oh. Sounds like a fight." Charlie's unexpected voice came from the porch. "I certainly hope there isn't trouble in paradise."

"As I recall," Josh muttered, "the only trouble in paradise was an uninvited snake trying to cause problems."

Ignoring him, Piper glanced at Charlie, wondering just how persistent he'd be this weekend. She'd expected him to take the hint last night. She managed a smile, but her tone was pointed. "What brings you here this morning?"

Charlie shrugged. "I told your dad I'd come out early and help him load bales of hay to take to your uncle."

"Well, that was…nice."

Behind her, Josh made a small noise.

"It eases my conscience a bit for the way I behaved with you. It sounds trite, but I really didn't know what I had until it…until *you* were gone." Charlie continued as if Josh weren't even with her. "It wasn't all bad, though, right? We had some good times, Piper."

They had, but the last thing she wanted to do was encourage him to dwell on them.

"Some, but that's all in the past. The distant past." Besides, she suspected his continued pursuit was fueled as much by the novelty of his not being able to have her as it was by fond memories. "I'm with Josh now."

To reinforce her words, Josh loyally stepped up behind her, aligning his body against hers and draping his arm around her waist, across the top of her jeans. A dizzy sensation accompanied his nearness. Piper blinked, but then closed her eyes completely when Josh pushed aside her ponytail and brushed a soft kiss to the back of her vulnerable neck. His lips were feather-light on her skin, so how did they wring such a potent response?

The front door banged shut, startling her. She took a step forward, deciding that regaining her sanity was more important than fooling her family at the moment. Daphne made her way down the porch steps, glaring daggers at Charlie. Then she turned to her sister with an apologetic sorry-he-got-away-from-me expression.

Piper smiled. "You ready to go, Daph?"

"Yeah. I appreciate your giving me a ride to the doctor. Blaine didn't want to take off work this morning since he's leaving early this afternoon, and today's Mom's day for helping out at Nana's retirement center. Mornin', Josh. What are your plans?"

"Hanging out with your dad. Piper said it would be fun."

"Uh-huh." Daphne's eyebrows shot up. "If that's what she said."

"Don't worry." Charlie insinuated himself into the conversation. "I'll be here, too. And I can certainly help put Josh at ease."

Piper bit back a sarcastic retort and shot Josh a look asking that he do the same. Open antagonism hadn't accomplished anything, so she was hoping that maybe an if-we-ignore-him-he'll-go-away strategy would have better results.

Daphne offered a weak wave to the guys. "Have a good day. Josh, I'll see you this afternoon at the—" She broke off sheepishly, with a sidelong glance at Charlie. "The, um, thing."

"What thing?" both men asked on cue.

Damn. Piper still hadn't explained about the shower. Well, now was a good time, what with the getaway car so close. She caught Josh's eye and motioned him aside. They walked across the grass toward her parents' barn. "Do you remember me mentioning that my family used the reunion weekend to celebrate a bunch of things at once?"

"Sure." He shoved his hands into the pockets of his khaki slacks.

"Well, the actual reunion is tomorrow, but this afternoon, some local family members and friends of Daphne and Mandy are getting together."

"Should I know who Mandy is?"

"My cousin," she reminded him. "The engaged one, whose wedding dress Daphne and I are going to see. Which leads me back to this afternoon… It's a combination baby shower for my sister and bridal shower for my cousin. A couples shower, and you're my date." She took a breath, praying he wouldn't go nuclear on her.

"I have to go to a baby shower *and* a bridal shower? Any chance you're just kidding to get back at me for past short jokes?"

"Actually, the fact that I'm *not* kidding is my way of getting back at you."

He looked unamused.

"I knew there would be a shower this weekend, but I assumed it was ladies only," she said. "When Mom told me last night it was a couples shower…I should've mentioned it, I know." She'd truly meant to, but she'd become preoccupied with other matters, like not using that door between their rooms to sneak into his bed and fulfill those fantasies she'd had all night.

"Piper, I'm a guy. A guy who watches sports on ESPN from my recliner. I don't sit around baby showers and—I don't even know what it is you sit around doing at baby showers."

"I'll make you chocolate chip pancakes for a year."

He was shaking his head before she even finished voicing the offer. "This is bigger than pancakes." He scowled as though bamboo shoots shoved under his fingernails would be less painful than spending a few hours watching a bride and mother-to-be open some presents.

Piper empathized with his pain. A very small part of her, one she wasn't proud of, was even glad he'd be there suffering alongside her. Probably best not to let him know about that part.

She sent a quick, worried glance toward Daphne and Charlie, who were having their own tense discussion. "Please, Josh? It'll just be one afternoon."

"All right, I'll go." He ran a hand through his dark hair. "But you owe me."

"Anything you want," she agreed automatically.

Chapter Seven

"Anything I want? Well, in that case..." Josh's eyes darkened, the golden glints shimmering with new mischief. "I'm sure that by this afternoon, I'll have a list. I don't suppose any place around here sells flavored body lotion?"

He's only joking, Piper told herself. Josh was teasing her, flirting as always. But it didn't feel that way. The heat she might have expected to be burning in her face was joined by liquid warmth pooling in lower, more intimate places. Since when did she respond to him like that?

But over the last few days, it had become difficult to recall a time she *hadn't* responded this way. He met her eyes then, and his playful smile faded into something more serious, more dangerous than his outrageous teasing had ever been.

Trying to sound amused, she managed a choked laugh. "Flavored body lotion? In Rebecca? Please. You have to drive to the next county just to find a grocery store that sells beer."

"Just as well," he said. "After tasting your kiss last night, I can't imagine there's any part of you that would be enhanced by artificial flavoring."

"Josh!" She'd meant the name to be a warning to stave off further outrageousness, instead she sounded like a woman issuing an invitation. An invitation he intended to take her up on, judging by the way he angled his head toward her.

Her breath mingled with his, but before their lips actually made contact, Daphne called out, "Hey, Piper, I don't mean to interrupt you, but—"

Piper had never been so glad to be interrupted in all her life. "Be right there!" She practically hurled herself in the direction of the car, but she could feel Josh's gaze on her as she retreated. And even the engine coming to life as she turned the ignition didn't drown the echo of his soft, knowing chuckle in her ears.

As Piper drove to the local bridal boutique, Daphne asked if everything was okay.

"Fine." With the possible exception of a pulse so rapid and a body temperature so high that Piper should probably have skipped her cousin's wedding dress fitting and driven straight to the ER.

"You're awfully quiet," Daphne observed. "Did I interrupt an important moment between you and Josh?"

Recalling that moment, Piper found it was all she could do not to melt into a puddle in the driver's seat. "I was just filling him in on the details of the shower."

"About that," Daphne said. "Charlie's going to be there, too."

"He's coming to a couples shower? With whom?"

"By himself, I'm afraid. He wasn't on the original

guest list, despite Mom's urging, but when I accidentally mentioned the shower… What was I supposed to do? He knew Josh was going, and I've known Josh for about twelve hours. I've known Charlie Conway all my life."

Piper sighed. Daphne looked repentant already, and besides, she was right.

"The more the merrier," Piper replied.

Her sister changed the subject. "You sure you want to risk your relationship with Josh by leaving him with Dad all morning?"

"Josh is tough." Plus, she might have been more worried if there was an actual relationship to risk. "He won't break."

"Don't you remember what Dad did when Blaine and I were dating? He said they should spend the day together and discuss Blaine's intentions, man to man. He took Blaine riding and put him on Thunder, for heaven's sake. Poor Blaine was so sore that, for a while, we didn't think he'd be able to father children."

Piper slanted her gaze toward her sister's stomach, which almost reached the dashboard even though the seat was pushed back as far as it could go. "I'd say that worry was for nothing. Besides, wasn't Thunder Dad's paternal retaliation at finding the two of you making out in the barn?"

"And you don't think he saw you and Josh in the kitchen last night?"

Piper's face warmed. "That was just a kiss."

"So you said."

"Why do you sound so skeptical?"

"Why is your face turning bright red?"

It did no good for Piper to try to forget about last night's kiss—it was emblazoned on all her senses, along with today's almost kiss. She could tell herself that there had been witnesses this morning, too, that maybe Josh was keeping up the act for Daphne's sake and helping Piper make a continued point to Charlie. But deep down, she knew better. This morning hadn't been about pretense. It had been about her all but throwing herself at Josh, and his obviously recognizing the need in her eyes.

She refused to ponder what had looked like an answering need in his own. If her resolve weakened, she had a corporate no-fraternization policy and possible notches on Josh's metaphorical bedpost to help bolster it.

"Turn left up here," Daphne instructed, pointing across the street to the bridal boutique.

Today Mandy was picking up the gown she'd be wearing to her January wedding, and she'd insisted Piper drop by to see the dress while she was in town. Six years younger than Piper, Mandy had looked up to her cousin, wanted to be just like her, even saying she wanted to attend A&M university. She'd quit college midway through her degree plan, though, saying that she was spending money needlessly, since her ultimate goal was to help run the family restaurant and raise kids. Piper hadn't seen her cousin in years or met Mandy's fiancé, Donald.

Parking the car, Piper squirmed a little as she thought about the number of times she'd made excuses not to visit her family.

It wasn't that she didn't love them, she thought as she and Daphne entered the bridal boutique. She just didn't want to live the life they'd envisioned for her.

Inside, lacy reminders of that life surrounded her. Veils and cake toppers and tiny wedding favors that made her shudder deep inside. At the handful of weddings she'd attended, she always flinched when a bride promised to "love and obey."

Glancing past the racks of white and ivory accessories

for the ceremony, she saw that the back of the store was stocked with silk nighties and crystal vials of perfume for the wedding night. Her breath rippled out of her in a lusty sigh. Although she couldn't quite picture herself at the front of a church pledging her life to a man, it was disturbingly easy to imagine Josh carrying her over the threshold of a honeymoon suite where they'd make love all night.

Daphne led Piper past a platform surrounded by mirrors to a row of dressing rooms. Mandy stood outside one of the small rooms with her sister, Stella, and their mother.

"Piper!" Mandy rushed forward for a hug. "I haven't seen you in ages!"

Mandy's mother stood to the side, her lips pursed. "We weren't sure you'd make it."

"I said I would."

Her aunt sniffed. "Yes, well. Come on, Mandy. Go ahead and try on your dress."

Mandy happily ducked into one of the dressing rooms, accompanied by one of the boutique's attendants.

"You know," Stella remarked to no one in particular, "I don't even know why she went through the expense of buying a dress. I have three perfectly good ones, and I told her she could take her pick."

Stella was a victim of the warped a-woman-isn't-complete-without-a-man philosophy. As a result, she'd made hasty marital decisions to avoid being alone.

Piper whispered to her sister, "Stella seeing anyone these days?"

"No. Come to think of it, she'll be 'uncoupled' at the shower, too, so Charlie will help round things out. She didn't want to come, but as the sister of the bride…"

Piper started to say that there was no shame in being

single, citing herself as an example, but then realized she couldn't. As far as her family knew, she was with Josh. Still, her feminist ideals refused to be completely contained.

"Has anyone told Stella that there's nothing wrong with not having a man in her life?"

Daphne raised an eyebrow. "Of course there's nothing wrong with not having a man in your life. But think about how happy Josh makes you. Stella just wants that happiness, too. She's lonely."

"Loneliness is no reason to get married three times."

"Well, no, but there are plenty of great reasons to get married. You guys talking about it at all yet?"

"You sound like Mom." Piper had meant it to be a joke, but there was more accusation than humor in her words. And they both heard it.

"Something you want to get off your chest?" Daphne demanded.

This was hardly the time or place, but since it had come up…. "You threw me last night with your decision to stay at home with the twins. That isn't like you."

Her sister scowled. "First of all, I haven't made a final decision yet. Second, as little as you bother to call or visit these days, you don't know what's like me. Third, you're a damn hypocrite."

"Excuse me?" Piper knew her aunt and Stella were shooting curious glances their way, but she was unable to keep her voice from rising slightly.

"You and your talk about women having more choices. Am I only entitled to make choices if they're the ones *you'd* make?"

"Of course not!"

"Really? Because you seem awfully judgmental of anyone who—"

"Okay," a voice from the dressing room chirped at them, "this is it." The door swung open and Mandy emerged, turning to Piper. "What do you think?"

Hardly seeing the dress, Piper made an automatic "it's gorgeous" response. The truth was, she didn't know *what* to think anymore.

Sandwiched in a pickup truck between Piper's father and ex-boyfriend, Josh gritted his teeth as they made their way down what could only loosely be called a street. Mr. Jamieson, claiming there was no use having a truck if you couldn't take the roads less traveled, said the back way would get them to the other side of town faster. Not that Josh was in any hurry to join the Jamieson women at a bridal-baby shower.

At least the shower would mean his time alone with Charlie and Mr. Jamieson was almost over. They'd played a couple hands of poker—during which Josh had been more than happy to win some of the mayor's money— and Mr. Jamieson had then pulled out a family album, showing Josh childhood pictures of Piper, which Josh fully intended to tease her about later. Still, the morning had been uncomfortable. Charlie had inserted a number of observations as he glanced over Josh's shoulder at photographs.

"I remember that picture—a high school dance. In college, we used to go dancing practically every week. Lord, that woman can move. You guys go out dancing a lot?"

Not that Charlie had paused in his Piper-and-I remembrances long enough for Josh to ever answer a supposed question about his own relationship with her. Since Piper's parents, for whatever unfathomable reason, liked Charlie, Josh had refrained from being openly hostile to the mayor while under the Jamiesons' roof. Piper's father had compensated with his own friendly acceptance, but that had only made Josh feel guilty over his lie to her family. Every time Piper's dad called him "son" in that accepting manner, Josh's deception seemed a bit less innocent.

They think I care about Piper.

He cared about her. Just not in that white-picket fence way the Jamiesons thought she deserved. What they didn't seem to realize was that Piper would go stir-crazy behind a white-picket fence. Still, if she ever did decide to let a man into her life, she deserved one who could commit to her fully.

One like Charlie?

The thought was more painful than the bone-jarring jolt of the pickup bouncing through another pothole big enough to warrant its own zip code.

It wasn't only Josh's dislike for the mayor that made him reject the idea of Piper and Charlie. Josh had never felt possessive of a woman before, but the thought of Piper with *any* man… *You never should have kissed her.* It had done nothing to sate his hunger for her.

On the contrary, the incident in her parents' kitchen had only whetted an appetite he'd fought for months to deny. The memory of Piper's kiss had kept him up all night.

A smarter man would have learned his lesson from that kiss, backed away, regrouped—the way he'd tried to last night, when he'd gone back to his own room unkissed and rock hard. But this morning, Josh had found himself once again weakening in the face of temptation, as unwise as a moth darting gleefully into a flame. He'd jumped into the fire with both feet, tormenting himself by teasing Piper. Kissing the curve of her neck? Suggesting body lotions?

He'd behaved with all the self-preservation instincts of a lemming.

A year ago, his flirting with her had been a harmless habit. He reasoned that if he stopped now, she'd know something was wrong. Besides, he enjoyed bantering with her. The flush in her cheeks, the way her turquoise eyes glimmered, never knowing ahead of time whether she'd give him hell right back or get embarrassed... This morning, he would have sworn her reaction had been arousal.

Aroused? The same woman who'd called their kiss last night "no big deal"? Suddenly, a relationship that had always been clear-cut was full of mixed signals and potential land mines.

"So, son," Fred Jamieson began, startling Josh from his frustrated thoughts. "Tell me about this sideline contracting you do."

Josh expounded on his business gratefully, glad to be thinking about more wholesome activities. As he spoke, he became slowly aware of just how successful the free-lancing was, generating so much extra work that it had the potential to become a second full-time job if he let it. Maybe his being so busy with work was why he hadn't dated much lately.

Yeah, you keep telling yourself that, buddy.

Oh, he dated. But at some indefinable point his dates had started ending with alarmingly G-rated exchanges. Maybe an occasional PG-13 slipped in there from time to time, but it had been too damn long since he'd had a really good R-rated evening.

Mr. Jamieson muttered something about having to attend a girls' party, then clapped Josh on the arm. "Hell of a way to spend the afternoon, isn't it? But Astrid would

have my hide if I missed it. I am terrified of that woman."
His tone made it clear he was nuts about her.

"I know how you feel," Josh commiserated.

Piper's father grinned. "I believe you do, son. I believe
you do."

Piper drummed her fingers on the armrest of her green
plastic chair and glanced around the obstetrician's waiting
room, which was full of women with rounded stomachs
and I-could-blow-at-any-minute expressions. Most of the
ladies returned her gaze with friendly smiles. The glow-
ering woman seated next to Piper—Daphne—was the
exception.

Apologizing had never been Piper's strong suit, and it
was even harder to do when she still felt she had a good
point. She knew Daphne had a point, too, though, and
the last thing Piper had wanted was to upset her pregnant
sister, putting her in a bad mood before a party in her
honor.

"Daphne, I—"

"It's okay."

Piper blinked. "It is?"

"I know how much you hate saying you're sorry,"
Daphne said with an unexpected grin, "so I decided to
spare you. Besides, it was my fault, too. Rampaging hormones and all that."

"So we're all right?"

"Yeah."

Yet despite apologies on both sides and exchanged
smiles, the situation still felt strained. Unsure how to set
it right, Piper was relieved when Daphne changed the
subject.

"Do you mind stopping by my place for a minute when
we're finished here? Blaine and I were running late this

morning, and I was in a hurry to go help Mom with those cakes for the shower. I forgot Mandy's gift."

"No problem. I wanted to see the nursery, anyway."

"Great. While we're there, you can rifle through my closet and see if there's anything you want to wear."

Piper fidgeted. "What's wrong with what I've got on? The sweater's nice and the jeans are brand-new." Practically dressy for a small Texas town.

"I'm not criticizing, honest, just trying to save you from an afternoon of Mom following you around, clucking her tongue and—"

"Delivering the When Did Young Women Stop Dressing Like Women Speech."

"Exactly."

"Good point. I'll change." Wanting to seal the truce with her sister, Piper asked, "Do we have a few minutes for you to help me with my hair and makeup, too? You've always been better at that stuff than I am."

Daphne glanced at the clock over the windowed receptionist area. "As long as they get me in to see the doctor soon. The appointment itself will be over in seconds. They're just measuring me and checking the heartbeats, no sonogram today. But I have pictures…if you'd like to see them."

"Of course." She was surprised Daphne hadn't offered sooner. Just because Piper wasn't in a hurry to knit booties herself didn't mean she wasn't excited for her sister. Being an aunt might even be fun.

Daphne reached for her purse, then held out small grainy black-and-white pictures.

"This is from the very first ultrasound." Daphne's tone was thick with unshed tears that might fall at any second. "My sons. Aren't they beautiful?"

"Er, beautiful." *What am I supposed to be seeing*

here? If she squinted, Piper thought she could make out a turtle.

Daphne handed her another photo. "This one they took four months later, the day they told us we were having boys."

"My God." This picture was much clearer, obviously a shot of two babies. Piper could make out profiles of tiny faces and even saw fingers on tiny hands. "Daph, I don't know what to say." Her hand went almost wistfully to her abdomen.

"I know. I'm going to be a *mom*."

"Daphne Wallace?" a nurse in a baggy uniform called out. "The doctor is ready to see you now."

Daphne struggled to pry herself out of her chair and regain her balance. Piper rose, too, following her sister and the nurse. She stood to the side while Daphne's blood pressure and weight were checked.

Piper remembered her younger sister as being so full of dreams. Daphne had talked about wanting to travel, about exotic careers. She'd wanted to be everything from a politician to an artist. Teaching was great, but now Daphne was even talking about giving that up. Was that really what she wanted?

Blaine obviously loved his wife, but Piper didn't see *him* making a lot of sacrifices. He'd inherited the family farm and gone about life as usual, while Daphne was the one bearing his children and possibly losing her career.

Piper watched as her smiling sister chatted with the nurse and described the cribs that had been selected for the twins. Daph hardly seemed filled with regret over any of her decisions. But hadn't she and Piper always said that they didn't want to end up like their mother, who had married at seventeen and never lived anywhere but Rebecca?

Mulling over the choices women in her family had made, Piper accompanied her sister into a cramped examining room where the doctor measured Daphne's ever-growing stomach. Then he pressed a white hand-held device to her distended belly and a small echoing sound suddenly filled the room. *Whump whump whump whump.*

Piper turned to Daphne. "Their heartbeats?"

She nodded, eyes wide with joy.

Maternal feelings Piper hadn't known she possessed welled within her. She must have been channeling from someone else in the building. Okay, yes, there were some really great things to be said for motherhood, but there were other achievements in life, too. Like Piper's career.

Not that her job took her out on her birthday or cheered her up when her day stunk, or watched old movies with her on television. But Josh did all of that. She'd joked before that one reason she didn't need a man in her life was because she had him.

Oh, no. What if Josh *was* the man in her life?

Ridiculous. Hormones were one thing—after this weekend, she couldn't deny Josh aroused her to a degree she'd never thought possible—but lust wasn't love. She needed to keep that in mind for her heart's sake.

Chapter Eight

Mr. Jamieson parked his truck amid the half-dozen vehicles already present outside the community hall. "Well, come on, fellas," he said in the weary voice of a soldier commanding his troops into hostile territory.

As the three men crossed the blacktop, Astrid Jamieson bustled out the main doors. "Fred, you're late!"

"Doesn't start for another twenty minutes," he contended.

"Yes," she scolded as she got closer, "but I asked you to be here forty-five minutes early to help set up, remember?"

"Would you settle for an apology and a kiss?" He scooped her into an embrace that should definitely get him out of the doghouse.

Josh and Charlie both looked away, sharing a moment of mutual discomfort and amusement.

"You guys made it." Piper's voice drifted across the parking lot.

Josh glanced up and immediately did a double take. Her radically changed appearance was like a disorienting blow to the head. She wore a blue skirt that revealed very shapely calves, and a matching sweater that made her eyes glow like the Caribbean Sea. Her hair was loose, curling against the tops of her shoulders and shining red-gold in the sun, and he'd never seen a more beautiful woman. Next to him, Charlie also gaped.

With three long strides, Josh met Piper on the sidewalk. He didn't want the mayor getting any ideas about her. Plus, Piper was *hot*—plenty of motivation for him to grab her by the waist and pull her up against him as he leaned down to kiss her.

The thoughts and feelings he'd been fighting since kissing her last night poured through him, into his actions. He traced her lips with something bordering on reverence, then delved into her mouth with emotions that were much more primal. Everything blended together in a wave of need.

After a slight gasp, Piper kissed him back, and he found the taste of her as alluring as her heady summery scent. Her tongue slid against his in an intimate caress, and desire roared through him. He pulled back slightly to suck on that lower lip he was always staring at. If they'd been alone, he would have—

Oh, hell. They weren't alone. He reluctantly broke off the kiss and looked down at the angel in his arms. She was breathing hard, her eyes unreadable. With effort, he glanced away from her flushed face and tempting lips. Everyone else had gone inside.

"Wow," Piper finally said, the single syllable more a sigh than a word.

"Yeah." NC-17 at least. And that had just been a kiss. Imagine if—no, he should *not* let himself imagine that.

"You look incredible, by the way. I didn't even know you owned a skirt."

"It's Daphne's, actually." She spoke again, her voice more abrupt than dreamy. "Look, Josh, it's great of you to help me out this weekend by pretending we're a couple. Really. You don't have to kiss me like that, though. A quick peck every now and then would probably work."

Not exactly what a man liked to hear. But she was only telling him what he already knew, that they shouldn't fan the flames of the small fire that had sparked between them. He was sure now that she felt the pull of attraction, too—sure enough that he could push the issue, but why? What would happen when things didn't work out between them? And with his track record, what reason could he possibly have for believing they could work out?

He'd lost too many people. If he couldn't have Piper in his bed, he could at least keep her in his life. As long as he kept his hands to himself.

"Don't worry. I won't kiss you like that again." Yet no sooner had the words left his mouth than he found another excuse to touch her. He caught one sunset-colored curl between his fingers, and it slid over his skin like silk. "I've never seen your hair down before."

"In two years?" Her forehead puckered as she frowned. "Of course you have."

"It's always in a ponytail or braid or something."

"That can't be right. I mean, I pull it back for work and the gym, and I wear it up for dressy events, but…I never let my hair down?" She looked startled and disturbed by the discovery.

"Hey, don't get me wrong, it looks great up, too. You just took me by surprise."

"If anyone took someone by surprise here, it was you."

Surprise wasn't the only thing she'd felt, and they both knew it. She'd been as hungry for him as he was for her, but that way lay madness.

She pivoted and began walking back toward the building, her tone as brisk and purposeful as her stride. "Everything go okay today? Dad didn't demand to know your intentions or anything, did he?"

"No. I'm sure he knows you can take care of yourself. He did ask whether we first met at the office or the apartment complex. I told him you picked me up for a one-night stand at a bar."

Her aqua eyes narrowed to dangerous slits.

"The office. I told him the office and that I love working with you. You're the most talented draftsperson I know. Besides me, of course."

A smile flirted at the corner of her mouth. "You think I'm talented?"

"You know you are." He held the door open for her. "You're the best. C, K and M is lucky to have you."

"Thanks." She sighed. "A girl likes to hear that every once in a while. This way—the room we rented is down on the left. So what did you guys do?"

"Played poker. I made thirty-six bucks. Your friend Charlie is the only politician I've ever met who can't bluff. Then your dad showed me some pictures, told me stories about you, about how a lot of your classmates went to the small college in the next county. Said that at seventeen you were ready to leave home and take on the world, that they tried to talk you into staying closer for a year or two, but you have a stubborn streak that makes mules look indecisive."

She stopped dead in her tracks, hurt in her gaze. "Are they still angry that I left?"

"I didn't get the impression that they were ever angry," he said, "just worried about you and reluctant to let go."

Did she really think her father had said anything derogatory about her? Even the mule comment had been made with paternal pride.

Piper took a deep breath. "With Mom, Dad and Daphne, I've always…I mean, the three of them… Come on, I told Mandy I'd help set up, and we're not getting anything done out here in the hall."

He followed, thinking about how ironic life could be. As he'd been shuffled from one home to the next, he'd stopped reaching out to people, stopped letting others reach him. He'd decided it would just be less painful to accept not fitting in. Was it possible that even with her close-knit family, Piper had felt like an outsider, too? Given their very different pasts, he'd never expected to have that in common with her. Didn't she know how much they cared about her?

Shaking his head, he stepped through the doorway and discovered a room decorated with balloons and crepe paper wedding bells. A garish papier-mâché stork the size of a condor hung from the ceiling, looking as though it might swoop down and attack guests.

Despite all his male instincts prompting him to flee, Josh forced his feet forward into the spacious rectangular room. At the center were several round tables. Against one wall were two tables piled with presents, and in the opposite wall was a small doorway that must lead to a private kitchen. Women of various ages entered and exited every few minutes, piling food on a large table positioned right outside the door.

Piper hurried in that direction, saying her help was needed, and left him to fend for himself. She must really trust him if she didn't think he'd make a run for it as soon as her back was turned.

Blaine and a few other men sat huddled around one of the round tables, and Josh expelled a sigh of relief as he ambled in their direction. Fellow Martians on a Venusian planet. Pulling out the chair next to Blaine, he introduced himself to the others. Name tags sat in the center of the table, but none of the other guys wore a baby-bottle-shaped adhesive badge, and Josh didn't plan to be the first.

He was so relieved to be around other men that he didn't even mind too much when Charlie finished carrying a cooler for Mrs. Jamieson and joined them at the table. No guy—not even the irritating mayor—deserved to be cut adrift in this bastion of estrogen. Besides, as long as Charlie was hanging out with them, he wasn't in the kitchen, trying to corner Piper.

Blaine, who had just introduced Mandy's fiancé, asked Josh, "Have you and Piper RSVPed to the wedding yet? I was thinking that you two could stay with Daph and me instead of at a hotel. Unless you don't want twin newborns underfoot, which we would understand."

Josh gave a noncommittal smile, unbalanced by a sense of loss at never seeing these people again. Mrs. Jamieson and her great cooking, Blaine and Daphne who had warmly accepted him, Mr. Jamieson who called him "son." If his fictional relationship with Piper had actually been real, then…

He ground his teeth. Hadn't he learned long ago to stop wanting relationships? A family? Love?

If you don't want it, you can't be hurt when you don't get it. A sound outlook, but it was damn near impossible *not* to want Piper.

* * *

Piper stood at the lace-covered buffet table. All the guests had arrived, and people were filling their plates with food. She breathed in the sweet, tangy smell of pineapple from the fruit salad and the zesty aroma of horseradish from the shrimp cocktail. But her stomach was still doing somersaults from that kiss in the parking lot, and she wasn't sure she could eat anything.

Darting her gaze toward a smaller table, she watched as Josh poured them both glasses of iced tea. How was it that she'd known him for so long, yet felt as though she were seeing him for the first time? She studied his profile with admiration, her knees slightly weakened by the sight of his strong jaw and teasing smile as he responded to something one of her cousins was saying. His dark hair, though not messy, was unruly above his face, as if he'd been running his hands through it. Or maybe she'd tousled it herself while they were kissing.

She shook her head, trying to forget what had happened. Yeah, right. With enough effort, she might be able to put it temporarily out of her mind, but for how long? Especially now that she knew with an unwanted certainty that their kiss last night had been anything but a fluke. She'd tried to convince herself during sleepless hours early this morning that the spontaneous combustion between them probably couldn't be duplicated a second time. But the way he'd kissed her in the parking lot had left her hot and wanting more.

Fantasies haunted her. Josh kissing her, undressing her, sharing her bed back at the hotel. It would never happen, she assured herself. But here, away from her no-men life in Houston, away from the women Josh had dated...for a second, it seemed almost possible.

Wishful thinking, prompted by hormones. She wasn't

going to kid herself that a couple of steamy kisses had changed anything. Maybe if she were a different type of person, she could allow herself a weekend fling. But how could she bare herself so intimately—literally—to him, then just pretend nothing had happened when she saw him at the office on Monday? She wasn't risking their friendship, or her job, on something so brief, even if she knew the sex would be nothing short of fantastic. Somehow, though, looking around at the happy people around her—Daphne grinning at Blaine; a couple from Piper's high school class who had married after graduation but still acted like honeymooners—it was tough to remember why relationships were such bad things.

"If it isn't the Pied Piper," a voice behind her boomed. "Still short, I see."

She spun around. "Hey, Uncle Joe. Still bald, I see."

Mandy's father crushed her in a hug that must've looked to the casual observer like a mutation of the Heimlich maneuver. "I always did like you, girl. Spunky and smart. Your dad tells me you're doing pretty well for yourself up in the big city. We're all proud of you."

This was news to Piper. "I thought I was the spinster blight on the Jamieson good name?"

Before her uncle could answer, Josh reached her side, balancing a small paper plate filled with food, and two plastic cups. Piper took one of the drinks and introduced her uncle.

"Piper's mom has told us a lot about you. Pleased to meet you," Joe said, slapping Josh on the back so heartily that he lurched forward. "Let me give you two a tip—if you decide to tie the knot, *elope*. If there's one thing my daughters have taught me, it's how complicated weddings are."

Elope? Wedding? For a second, Piper's head swam.

The idea of Josh settling down with *anyone* was unimaginable, much less settling down with her.

Oblivious to the mental chaos he'd caused her, her uncle glanced across the room. "If you'll excuse me, I think I'm just going to go check on your grandmother, see if she and her friend need a ride back to the nursing home when this is over."

Josh made a teasing observation about Nana's adhering to the couples theme and bringing an octogenarian suitor with her, but Piper barely heard him.

"Piper?"

She started, Josh's questioning tone interrupting the blurred, soft-focus matrimonial images that still filled her head—the traditional garter worn beneath her gown, Josh slowly rolling it down her leg, trailing his fingers against her skin…. "He was just making conversation," she said quickly.

"Hmm?"

"My uncle. The elopement advice. It was just small talk. Believe me, I didn't say anything to make my family think we were headed for the altar."

"I didn't think you did." He examined her closely. "You seem horrified by the idea. Completely appalling, huh?"

She bit her lip. If she admitted that at odd times today she'd secretly found the idea *appealing,* he'd walk straight out the door and hitchhike back to Houston.

"Yeah, well, you know. I'm not one for romance."

"Right." After a moment, he added, "We definitely see eye-to-eye there."

Once all the guests were seated and eating, Mandy and Daphne went to the front of the room with their husbands, who wore matching pained expressions. Clearly the "couples shower" concept had not been devised by men. As friends and relatives ate, Mandy unwrapped the usual bridal presents—towels and small home appliances. Then Daphne took her turn, pulling tiny baby clothes out of gift bags.

When the last package had been opened, Piper leaned closer to Josh, trying not to think about how warm and inviting his scent was as she whispered, "I don't know about you, but I'd rather not participate in the who-can-make-the-best-wedding-veil-out-of-toilet-paper games."

"That's really what women do at bridal showers?" he asked, a half smile on his face.

"In mixed company, anyway. If it were just us girls, we might still make the veils, but we'd probably also have a few drinks and encourage the bride with bawdy sex stories."

His eyes widened, but his surprised expression was almost instantly replaced with one of prurient interest. "So what's your favorite bawdy sex story?"

"Um…" Currently, the only thing that came to mind in connection with sex was the man staring back at her. "Never mind that. Let's volunteer for dish duty and escape to the kitchen while everyone else is engaged in the diapering-the-baby-doll relay or whatever."

"Sounds good to me." He stood first, pulling her chair back for her.

How many times had Josh reached past her to open her car door, or stood by as she locked her apartment? She'd noticed how tall he was on those occasions—hard not to, when he was teasing her about her own height—but this weekend she was aware of his body in a whole new way. The heat that emanated from him when he stood close, the width of his shoulders, the leisurely confidence he moved with, neither hurried nor self-conscious….

"Piper, we're kitchen-bound, right?" His tone was

puzzled, and he obviously wondered why she wasn't following through on her own plan.

"R-right." They were off to wash casserole plates and punch glasses, and she wasn't going to dwell on the last time they'd done dishes together, when they'd ended up kissing. There was nothing intrinsically sexy about liquid detergent, no reason to think the incident would be repeated. Unfortunately.

Later, as she took her frustration out on a large plastic bowl coated with remnants of nacho cheese, Piper realized she needn't have worried about the sexual tension that would arise when they were alone. Josh kept himself busy loading things into the cooler at the opposite end of the kitchen or retrieving empty serving plates off the buffet table. Then Stella appeared, holding the blender Mandy had received and explaining that most of the older guests were leaving and the remaining younger ones wanted margaritas.

She mixed the first batch, delivered them and returned to make more. With her cousin's intermittent presence as unlikely chaperon, Piper managed to quit fixating on Josh long enough to finish the small pile of dishes near the sink. Finally, they were done, but Piper was in no hurry to return to the land of happy coupledom in the other room and the uncertainty it had filled her with earlier.

Option B was to stay here with Josh. Stella had left the kitchen after making her last batch of margaritas. Piper had turned one down, figuring the drink would only jumble her thoughts further. Now, however, she was reconsidering.

Josh seemed to be enjoying his. Clearly content to be away from the shower festivities, he was leaning against the industrial-strength refrigerator behind him. Next to a very sturdy counter, she couldn't help noticing—one that would easily accommodate two people's weight and withstand vigorous activity.

She swallowed, wondering when she'd developed this strange countertop fetish.

Her gulp attracted his attention. He lowered the glass and met her eyes, the corner of his mouth quirked up in the sexy half grin she knew so well. "If I didn't know this weekend was a pretense, I'd never guess the look on your face was an act."

No chance in hell she was going to ask "What look?" because she knew he'd tell her. Instead, she turned the tables on him. "Just like no one would have guessed that kiss in the parking lot was an act?" She'd meant it to be a statement, not a question.

"Are you asking me if it was real?" He set his glass down and took a step closer to her. "Did you want it to be?"

Yes. No! Maybe—in a different reality. "I think we should get back out there."

"It was your idea to come in here."

"Well, yes, but not to be completely antisocial, just to escape the standard games."

"And is this another escape attempt?" He punctuated his question with an eyebrow raised in challenge.

"Escape from what, you?" She willed herself to laugh, to smile at least—anything to make light of his uncomfortably accurate insight. But she couldn't.

"Yeah, me." Stopping directly in front of her, Josh folded his arms over his chest. His stance should have relieved her, since it meant he had no immediate plans to reach for her, but she didn't feel relief. She felt like a firecracker with a fuse slowly burning down to the detonation point.

How did the man project so much untamed sensuality simply by standing there?

She forced a soft laugh. "You make it sound as if I should be scared of you." When it was really her own actions she feared. "But you're, um, perfectly harmless."

Yeah, Josh is to harmless as lion is to fluffy kitten. Any chance he hadn't noticed the quaver in her tone and the blush she could feel in her face? She braced herself for him to mention those very things, but instead he sighed.

"Well, you're right about me not harming you, anyway." His voice softened. "I would never want to do anything that could end up hurting you, Piper."

"I know you wouldn't."

Affection knotted her chest, a deep tenderness that was more disconcerting than the rampant lust. The lust she could try to attribute to months of abstinence. The wellspring of emotion wasn't as easily waved away.

He gazed at her with searing intensity, then turned to grab his margarita. "Maybe I needed the reminder myself."

As he gulped the frozen drink, Piper envied him the icy coldness and the tequila. She could use both.

Lowering the glass, he suggested, "Let's get out of here."

She followed him to safety, pondering the way he'd unexpectedly backed down. After two years of teasing her outrageously, pouncing on opportunities for innuendo, he'd let her off the hook just now. Why? Because he'd glimpsed her nervousness and was protecting her?

Or was it because their teasing had become so real that he needed to protect himself?

She had the impression that the more superficial and less genuine his relationships, the more comfortable he stayed. Instead of being relieved that they'd dodged a metaphorical bullet—or at least the mistake of getting hot and heavy among the pots and pans—she felt inexplicably sad.

Out in the main room, four couples along with Charlie and Stella remained, seated around two tables that had been pushed together. At the other end of the room, Piper's mom and aunt picked up wrapping paper and ribbon and exchanged gossip. Piper and Josh sat with the twosomes.

Daphne smiled. "Welcome back, sis. You're just in time."

"For what?"

Her sister pushed a large bag across the table to Mandy, who sat in her fiancé's lap. "We wanted to wait until it was just close friends, but we have a few presents left for Mandy and Donald. For the honeymoon," she added with a wink.

There was good-natured laughter as Donald extracted a pack of condoms with the words *Just Married* on them. Mandy retrieved the next item—a heart-shaped bottle of flavored body lotion.

"Hey!" Josh swiveled his head toward Piper. "You told me this morning we couldn't get any flavored body lotion here."

Piper felt the blood drain from her face. She imagined she was as pale as Josh had suddenly gone. Clearly, he hadn't thought before speaking. And now that all speculative gazes were locked on the two of them, he wasn't speaking at all.

Charlie reddened and said it had been nice seeing everyone, but he had to go. Stella offered to walk him out.

Daphne gave a discreet cough that no doubt covered up a laugh. "Actually, you can't buy it in Rebecca. But there's always the web. We're not so small-town that we don't have internet access."

"Right," Josh mumbled, his eyes fixed on the table. "Good to know."

Josh Weber, king of the suggestive insinuation, was actually *embarrassed.* Charmed by his unexpected and endearing reaction, Piper impulsively slid her hand on top of his before recalling his aversion to displays of affection. He surprised her by flipping his hand over and interlocking his fingers with hers.

Mandy once again reached into the wicked gift bag, then held up a complicated red-and-black lace contraption that perplexed Piper. How did someone who wasn't a contortionist put it on? Where did all the straps go? However one wore it, it couldn't possibly be comfortable.

But then she made the mistake of looking at Josh's face, and decided that any discomfort the garment caused would be worth it in exchange for the passion it aroused. His eyes locked with hers as he slowly traced her wrist with his thumb. He moved his fingers, sliding them up and down between hers.

Her breathing grew shallow, and she knew he could feel her pulse jumping under his thumb. He gifted her with a warm, lazy smile so intimate it made her feel as though they were the only two people in the room. When he lifted her hand and kissed it, self-preservation kicked in. She tried to pull her hand back without being too obvious.

Equally subtle and stubborn, he refused to let go.

She tugged again, and his grin widened.

"I have to go to the bathroom!" she announced loudly, yanking her hand away and springing to her feet.

Daphne stood. "I'll go with you."

Together they left the room, with Piper desperately hoping her sister wouldn't—

"So, he likes flavored body lotion?"

Oh, well. It had been an unlikely hope.

"I'm not answering that," Piper protested.

"Fine." Daphne grinned as she pushed open the door to the ladies' lounge. "I'll just have to speculate. I bet he's an incredible lover. And he's so tall, with those really big hands, that I bet—"

"Daphne!"

"Oh, come on. My hormones are in overdrive and being this pregnant is not conducive to a love life. Let me live vicariously through you."

"To tell you the truth, Josh and I haven't…explored that area of our relationship."

"Ooh. I thought you only said you'd booked two hotel rooms to keep Dad off the warpath." She sighed deeply. "This is even better."

"Better? I thought you wanted to hear lurid descriptions of his sexual performance."

"Better for you, I mean. Don't you love this part? The long kisses that make you wonder how good his mouth will feel in other places. Staring at his hands, wondering how they'll feel against you. The anticipation that's both wonderful and maddening."

Maddening. The perfect word to describe this trip so far.

When Piper had left home on Thursday, she'd had a job she liked and a best friend who conveniently lived in her building. She hadn't been confused. No lying awake at night thinking about the way Josh kissed; no staring at sonogram pictures and trying to imagine what it would be like to have her own child growing inside her; no bridal showers where she wondered if it would really be so bad to be married.

This is why I left town in the first place, she thought as she washed her hands. *The brainwashing.*

Daphne finger-combed her dark hair and studied her reflection in the mirror, then applied a coat of lipstick. "What are you guys doing tonight? A few of us are going to that bar outside town. I may not be as light on my feet as I once was, but I can at least sit out on the deck and enjoy the music. A band from Austin's playing."

Piper hadn't thought that far ahead, but it was a sure bet she didn't want to hang out at the hotel with Josh in the adjoining room. "A night out sounds good to me if it's okay with Josh. I don't see why he'd turn down cold beer and a few hours dancing when he was willing to attend the shower."

"He was a good sport this afternoon," Daphne said approvingly. "Blaine grumbled about having to be here, and half the gifts were for us! The way Josh looks at you, he'd follow you to the end of the world."

Piper lowered her eyes, not meeting her sister's gaze in the mirror. She hated deceiving Daphne.

Oblivious to Piper's guilt, Daphne continued, "I know you said the two of you haven't discussed marriage or anything, but I doubt it will be very long before—"

"We aren't even dating," Piper confessed, desperate to shut Daphne up before her sister asked to be maid-of-honor at a nonexistent wedding. "Josh isn't my boyfriend."

Her sister turned, leaning against the marbled vanity. "That's ridiculous."

"I told Mom I had a date just to get her off my back, and she assumed I was seeing someone. So Josh, who is a good friend but *nothing more,* agreed to come with me this weekend and be that 'someone.'"

"You're kidding."

"I'm really not."

"You lied to me?" Daphne's eyes clouded with hurt. "I know Mom can get carried away and drive you nuts, but we used to be really close. Why didn't you just tell me the truth?"

"I'm sorry."

Her sister sighed. "It's okay. It might've started as a fib, but from what I've seen between you this weekend, I guess you're a couple now. Ironic, huh?"

"No." Her family gave new definition to the word *stubborn*. "Hear what I'm telling you, Daph. We're *not* a couple, so there's no irony." *And Dad says I'm mulish?*

"This is your sister you're talking to. I see how you look at him."

Not this again—Josh had been remarking on the same thing in the kitchen. "All right, you caught me. He's easy on the eyes. Can't a girl do some harmless ogling?"

Daphne stared at her, a faintly pitying you-really-don't-know-do-you expression settling over her features. Then she laughed. "Not that part, the other kind of looking. Piper, you're in love."

Chapter Nine

Hours later, Piper still couldn't get the ridiculous claim out of her head. Darn Daphne's overactive imagination. *You're in love.*

"I am not," she assured her reflection.

The woman staring back from the hotel room mirror didn't look convinced.

Forget about that and just finish getting ready. Easier said than done. Everyone had been too full from the food at the shower to handle a sit-down dinner, so she and Josh had had more than enough time to return to the hotel and get ready to go out tonight. At least, it would have been enough for a woman who hadn't applied, washed off and reapplied her makeup, not to mention changed clothes a ridiculous number of times.

She could blame Daphne for that, too. When they'd stopped at Daph's place earlier, her sister had given her several like-new outfits. Piper had laughingly argued that Daphne would probably fit into these again someday, even if it didn't seem like it now, but her sister had said the clothes would be out of style by then and besides, this gave her an excuse for future shopping. Now, Piper had entirely too many wardrobe choices.

Recalling Josh's blatant admiration this afternoon, she had first toyed with the idea of wearing a skirt tonight. Then annoyance had seeped through her system like a noxious liquid. That kind of change, though admittedly small, had been how things started to go wrong with Charlie. And at least he'd been willing to spend his life with her. She rarely knew ahead of time if Josh would be spending his lunch hour with her.

Discarding the skirt, she'd tried to split the difference by putting on comfortably worn jeans but wearing sexy makeup and her hair loose. Then she'd realized that was stupid. Even though the covered patio-style bar would be nice and cool tonight, dancing would warm her up considerably and possibly have her makeup smudged and her hair limp. Besides, did she really think it was a good idea to do anything that could be construed as sexy? No.

What a sorry state she was in—she didn't want to attract Josh, but apparently wanted to look noticeably great around him, all the same. Weird twisted female logic.

Not as twisted as the idea that you might be in love with him.

Well, she wasn't, she told herself as she yanked her hair up into a bouncy ponytail. Luckily, the cheerful, curly end result didn't reflect the mood she'd been in while styling. She limited her makeup to some color around her eyes and shiny gloss that promised "kissable lips." Just a figure of speech, written by some schmo in a marketing department somewhere. It had nothing to do with the course of her evening. For clothes, she went back to the jeans she'd started with this morning, accompanied by a snazzy little red sweater with cap sleeves and a scooped neckline that had more of a dip than her usual tops. She had the benefit of feeling sexy, but could still tell herself she hadn't gone to any extra trouble. The sweater was simply a smart choice for not getting overheated in the crowded bar.

Just as she was telling herself she'd finally achieved the right look—casual hotness—a knock sounded at the door, the safe one that led to the hallway.

"Be there in a sec." She crossed the room and opened the door.

Josh was a study in contrasting denim. His long-sleeved shirt looked soft to the touch and was much lighter than the dark blue jeans cut from a heavier material. A look well-suited to the bar they were headed for, but did he have to wear a button-down shirt? All she could think about was the night before, watching him unbutton those last few buttons and wishing she'd been the one to do it for him.

"Hey." His smile and tone were the same ultracasual he'd adopted on the drive to the hotel. "Ready to go?"

After they'd left the shower, conversation between them had been constant and trivial—a lot of talk with absolutely nothing said. But they'd avoided enigmatic silences, difficult topics and flirting of any kind. He was standing by his earlier retreat in the community center kitchen. A wise course of action.

And she was a fan of wisdom, Piper reminded herself as she followed him down the hotel staircase, observing that men like Josh were the reason jeans had been invented. She was wise enough to know that she wasn't in love, anyway. What had happened this weekend was an anomaly, easily explained. She and Josh had been spending too much time together lately. He was a sexy man, and her repressed hormones were rebelling. Seeing him here, at her home, around her family, lent an intimacy to their relationship that hadn't been there at ball games or the local pizza joint. All of that was circumstantial; it wasn't love. Except…

She bit her lip as he unlocked the car doors. Hadn't she been the one to think that he should find a nice girl, that he had more to offer than a few nights of fun? Yet the thought of him settling on one woman made her skin crawl. Josh and Gina were two of her very favorite people, but earlier this week, the idea of the two of them together had hurt.

You're just afraid of being displaced if he ever found a lasting relationship.

Maybe that really was what bothered her, she told herself moments later, as they drove down the dark rural stretch of highway. She *was* jealous, but not in a sexual or romantic sense, simply a possessive he's-my-best-friend-and-I-don't-want-to-lose-him way. Funny, but she didn't think she and Charlie had ever had that.

There'd been the thrill of falling in love and the thrill of her first sexual exploration, but there'd never been deep friendship. In retrospect, the best part of their physical relationship, for her anyway, had been the sense of discovery, the short-lived novelty of feeling that she was somehow more fully a woman. Sex had been okay, but she hadn't experienced a burning desire for her fiancé. Not like the desire she'd been feeling for Josh the last few days.

She might try to tell herself Josh was just a friend, but she'd never wanted anyone the way she wanted him.

Gina's words from earlier in the week taunted her. Her friend seemed to think Josh just hadn't found the right woman. Was that true? And if so, did Piper want to be that woman?

Glad for the nighttime that hid her pensive expression, she said, "While we're alone, I just wanted to say thank you again for coming with me this weekend. I hope it's no trouble."

"Nope. And you're welcome." The glowing dashboard panel illuminated his quick smile, his teeth flashing white.

"I can't believe you were even free...what with working your sideline projects. And all your dating."

He didn't say anything, and Piper experienced a moment of self-loathing. What was she doing here? Shamelessly fishing?

She knew there had been dozens of women in his life; she just didn't know what part they'd played. Had he slept with all of them, or did some of his dates end platonically? Hard to believe, when the man oozed the promise of sexual fulfillment. Had he loved any of the women he'd known? Had he ever been hurt by a woman?

The truth was, all Piper had were unsubstantiated guesses based on his teasing remarks and the roster of female Houstonites who accosted him while he was out in public. But the fact that she saw Josh almost every single day, considered him her best friend and didn't know much beyond Michelle had a cat and Nancy wanted to see him again reminded Piper of how private he was.

Suddenly, she needed more information. "I was just wondering...you *do* date an awful lot."

"That isn't a question."

He didn't sound angry, so she pushed bravely—or stupidly—forward. "Well, you do, don't you?"

Another grin flashed, this one quicker than the last before it dissolved into the darkness. "I figure I have to date enough for the both of us in order to maintain cosmic balance."

Classic Josh Weber answer—entertaining and evasive. This was what he did, kept people at bay without their even realizing it, smiling and cracking jokes the entire time.

Piper didn't want to be kept at bay anymore. She wanted to know what the risks were, wanted to see his life with open eyes so that she could determine if there was room in it for another person. And so she could force herself to accept the situation once and for all if there wasn't.

"I know you're going to say this is none of my business, but I...I care about you, as your friend. If you want to be left alone, why do you date all the time? And if you do want to be with someone, then..."

"Then what?" he countered, his tone a defensive challenge.

"You're going to have to change."

He swiveled his head to look at her, and she couldn't see the anger in his expression so much as feel it. "Funny. Most women like me the way I am, Piper."

Ain't that the truth. "I'm surprised you can conclude how they feel about you, given your tendency not to stick around."

"Where do you get off implying that I can't be there for someone? I'm here now, aren't I? And I believe I've commented before on the irony of you giving me dating advice. At least *I'm* not hiding in my work."

Ouch. Of all the people in her life, she'd thought Josh had some idea of how important her job was to her. "I'm not hiding! If anything, you're the one who's hiding—in plain sight, as the saying goes. You give the illusion of going from one relationship to the next, but you don't let people get close to you, so you're actually more alone than I am."

Josh couldn't help flinching, but he doubted she'd noticed. She seemed to be on quite the roll. He didn't know what the hell had brought this on, but whether she'd meant to hit such a raw nerve or not, he wanted her to stop. Immediately.

"Are you finished, or are you auditioning for your own talk show? 'Do as I Say, Not as I Do' with our host, Dr. Piper."

"That's not fair."

"Neither is ambushing someone you call a friend. What do you know about being alone, Piper?"

She had friends in Houston who met every need, from workout buddy to this lunatic weekend of fooling her family. And then there was her family itself. Sure, her relatives could be overbearing at times, but they adored her. They all seemed so happy that she'd finally come home that he half expected a parade in her honor. The first person Josh had ever truly considered spending his life with, Dana, was now a bittersweet memory; the first person Piper had ever considered spending her life with was still hanging around hoping she'd change her mind.

"I—"

He couldn't take any more of this. "It was a rhetorical question." To make sure he got his point across, he flipped on the car stereo, letting the angry cadence of a hard rock song stoke his indignation.

This was what he got for kissing her—being talked to death. Didn't they have a good time as friends? Didn't she enjoy his company and know she could count on him? Why wasn't that enough? Women. What was with the quest for details, the need to have a man spill his emotions? Thank God he hadn't slept with her.

Yet even as he had the thought, he was forcibly reminded of the arousal he'd been fighting. As ticked off as he was at the moment, the unique scent of her teased him—as did the thought that sex after an argument could be the best sex of all. Sure, making love to Piper would be a huge mistake, one he'd managed to so far avoid, but if the opportunity really presented itself, he didn't think he could pass it up. Mistake or not.

True to form, Piper ignored his attempted retreat. She reached out and switched off the radio. When he glared in her direction, he saw the stubborn set of her jaw and the way her arms were crossed over her chest. It was a crime to flatten breasts like hers.

Despite himself, he almost smiled at her feisty demeanor. At the moment she was being a real pain in the ass, but the way Piper refused to back down was something he lov— He admired that in her. "You had something you wanted to add, no doubt?"

"Yeah. An apology. I keep telling my mom to butt out of my love life—"

"You don't have a love life." He hadn't yet forgiven her enough to pass up the small jab.

"Anyway, if I'm happy single, why shouldn't you be? What a hypocrite I turned out to be."

Josh wondered if she even knew how wistful her expression had grown at the bridal shower earlier. For just a minute, she'd seemed enchanted by the idea of her own wedding. Or maybe she'd just been enchanted by the idea of a well-deserved vacation on the beaches of sunny Cancun, the bride and groom's honeymoon destination. Hard to believe Piper might really want to get married, but until a few days ago, Josh wouldn't have believed she'd relentlessly pry into his private life, either.

"Are you happy?" he asked. "Being single, I mean?"

She studied his face in the darkness. "Aren't you?"

"Absolutely."

"Yeah. Me, too."

There was quite a crowd gathered at the bar. People were in the mood to appreciate the live music and semi-outdoor venue now that the sweltering Texas summer had finally ended. Also, Piper supposed that, for anyone who had already seen both movies showing at the cinema and didn't feel up to some Friday-night cow-tipping, there weren't a whole lot of social alternatives. The bass from the band shook the ground beneath her feet as she followed Josh across the small, overflowing parking lot. Trucks with four-wheel drive and tires equipped for "mudding" had made their own parking in the field next to the building. Patrons waiting in line outside chatted and laughed, some tapped their feet to the boisterous George Strait classic being played. In contrast, Josh's perfunctory smile was subdued.

She'd hurt him. For just a second, even in the darkness of the car, she'd glimpsed actual pain in Josh's eyes. She never should have said that to him about being alone. He wasn't someone who held a grudge, but things hadn't been the same between them since their earlier conversation. Whatever she'd been trying to accomplish—and she was fuzzy on that in hindsight—she'd failed.

When it was their turn in line to pay the cover charge, she pushed a ten across to the cashier, waving away Josh's five. "It's the least I can do." She wasn't sure whether she meant she owed him for this weekend or for her earlier outburst.

They walked inside, through the smaller interior of the club, where the rectangular bar took up the center of the room and customers shot pool or played darts. Beyond that was a door leading out to the oversize deck area and covered dance floor. A band played on a dais, and tables were scattered off to the sides along gazebo-like trellises. Piper opened the door, scanned the crowd and finally spotted Mandy, once again perched in her fiancé's lap.

"This way," Piper told Josh, taking a shortcut across the edge of the oval dance floor underneath the strings of multicolored lights.

The twang of the guitars in the band and the mingled scents of cologne and beer filled her with nostalgia. She'd left Rebecca too young to get into any of the area bars, but no self-respecting Aggie graduated from A&M without going to a few beer joints and dance halls.

Mandy beamed in greeting. "I'm really glad you're here this weekend, Piper. The rest of my family's been driving me nuts."

"I know the feeling," Piper said.

"Stella's after me to ask this man we barely know to be a groomsman just so she has an excuse to get close to him, and my mother is speculating about everything that could go wrong with the wedding. I swear we should elope."

Donald patted his fiancée's hand. "It'll be all right, dumplin'. In a few months, the wedding will be behind us, and we'll be in Cancun."

Piper nodded. "Wise man." Even if he did call his bride-to-be 'dumplin.'"

"Piper!" Daphne was winding her way through the crowd at a rapid clip, her grimly determined expression incongruous with the lively atmosphere. As Blaine caught up with her, Daphne explained breathlessly, "I was trying to hurry. I wanted to warn you that—"

"Hi there." Charlie Conway's voice, melodious enough for public speaking, was beginning to sound to Piper like fingernails on a chalkboard.

"Too late," Daphne muttered.

Piper sighed. "Hello, Charlie."

He pushed past Daphne and Blaine, sparing Josh a civil nod before extending an upturned palm in Piper's direction. "I was hoping for a dance."

Why couldn't he accept that there would never be anything between them again? Was it simply because Rebecca's golden boy wasn't used to taking no for an answer? "You know I'm here with Josh."

Charlie managed to look wounded. "And he won't let you share one dance for old time's sake?"

Let? She had to give Charlie credit—he knew which buttons to push. Then again, why wouldn't he? Toward the end of their ill-fated relationship, he'd pushed all the wrong ones.

But in their years together, they had shared some good times. Given the high points of their past and the nostalgia she'd been feeling, it seemed churlish to refuse one simple dance. She glanced toward Josh, who didn't meet her gaze. If he was still angry about her earlier comments in line, maybe some distance would do them both good. She owed him some space.

"*One* dance," she finally agreed.

Flashing a dimpled smile that made him look nineteen for a second, Charlie took her hand to lead her onto the floor. Strange that there had once been a time when he... what—made her heart race? Piper wondered. Try though she might, she couldn't recall ever feeling the exhilaration, frustration and sheer desire a single glance from

Josh could incite. Had she ever truly loved the man she'd once planned to marry?

She absently matched his movements, not needing to concentrate to do so. The two of them had shared so many dances that she knew instinctively when he would turn and what steps he would take.

"We still move together as if we were one person," Charlie murmured in what was probably supposed to be a seductive, husky whisper. But he was trying too hard. Real seduction was inexorable, deriving its very power from a sense of inevitability, not effort.

She moved back, putting distance between them. "It's not very hard to predict what you're going to do, Charlie. You haven't updated your moves since you were a teenager."

"Don't be so sure." The way his thigh brushed hers as they turned was probably not an accident. "I've got some more adult ones now."

Piper almost laughed. His forced attempts at flirtation bordered on the comical when contrasted to her time with Josh.

Speaking of Josh…she shot pleading glances over Charlie's shoulder. She'd thought that a quick dance and a stroll down memory lane would be bearable, but now she wanted to flee. Josh had always been fairly well attuned to what she was thinking—maybe he'd help her out.

Or not.

Blond and beautiful Rosalyn Granger, a woman who'd been in the same grade as Piper, stood by Mandy's table, introducing herself to Josh. Piper could see the interest in the woman's eyes even from this distance. Josh smiled, said something that was no doubt charming, and Rosalyn laughed. Then she touched his arm—the universal sign of a woman flirting.

Piper wondered if the two of them would go dance together. *I'll bet Roz won't start telling him how to live his life, and tick him off.* Even though Josh hadn't made a move in Rosalyn's direction, the image of him taking her into his arms on the dance floor was imprinted so hard on Piper's brain her head hurt from it.

Rosalyn finished whatever she was saying, then touched his arm again. Really, had the woman no shame?

"Could you excuse me, Charlie?" In a complete breach of etiquette, Piper abandoned her partner in the middle of a song. She hurriedly crossed the room, skidding to a stop between Josh and Rosalyn.

Pasting the biggest possible grin on her face, Piper exclaimed, "Roz! What a nice surprise to see you here! You look great." Dammit.

Rosalyn's answering smile lacked enthusiasm. "I saw you out on the floor with Charlie. You two still make the cutest couple. We've all been wondering when you'll get back together."

When hell freezes. "Charlie and I are just old friends. My heart belongs to Josh here." She squeezed his hand for emphasis.

"Hey, Roz, is that you?" A guy just walking through the doorway called out a greeting, and with one last sultry smile for Josh, Rosalyn ambled away.

"Piper, about my hand," Josh said. "You're cutting off the circulation."

Disgusted with herself, she promptly let go. He wasn't really her boyfriend; no reason to act like a possessive lover.

"Sorry," she muttered. Her gaze collided with Daphne's, who watched from her seat at the table.

Her sister glanced from Josh to Piper, then smirked.

I am not *in love with him,* Piper broadcasted the message with sibling telepathy and a strong glare. *We are just friends.*

Sure you are. Daphne's sarcastic thoughts were as easy to read as the neon blue beer sign blinking on the latticed wall behind her.

Glancing away from her sister, Piper looked up at Josh and wondered at the source of his fierce scowl. Was he angry that she'd run off Rosalyn? Or still annoyed about their earlier conversation?

"What's wrong?" she asked him.

"You tell me." He crossed his arms. "I'm not the one who barreled over here to snap at an old school buddy. Looked to me like you were jealous."

"Jealous? Ha! You're clearly not getting enough oxygen to your brain." She tilted her head back. "The air you're breathing way up there must be too thin. If I seem annoyed, it's just because we had a deal." Lowering her voice, she added, "Our relationship might not be real, but I'd appreciate you not picking up other women in front of my family."

"Rosalyn was just keeping me company while *you* were out there in the arms of your ex-fiancé."

His tone was so biting, so un-Joshlike, that she blinked. Despite the accusation he'd tossed at her, was it possible *he* was jealous? And if he were, what did that mean?

Not this again. Honest to heaven, she wasn't one of those women who stood around analyzing men and feelings and relationships. At least, she never had been before. Grinding her teeth, she recalled times she'd congratulated herself on not obsessing about a guy the way some women did. How the mighty had fallen.

She needed a distraction. "Let's dance."

"Fine." His hand around hers was gentle enough, but his posture suggested they were about to enter into hand-to-hand combat instead of the Texas version of the waltz.

Chapter Ten

Despite Josh's customary grace and her vast experience dancing, they trampled each other's toes and risked banging into each other whenever they turned corners.

"I thought you knew how to dance," she grumbled.

"I do." He shot her such a pointed look that she bristled.

"Are you saying I don't? If you'd been watching when Charlie and I were dancing, you'd know that—"

"Charlie let you lead. Say what you want about me and my need for control, Piper, but I'm not the only one."

"I…" Dammit, he was right.

Not just about the dancing, either. She liked being in charge of her life, dreaded the thought of a man trying to muscle in. She guarded her autonomy by keeping men at arm's length.

But this was just a dance floor, for heaven's sake. Surely she wasn't such a control freak that she couldn't let Josh lead? Inhaling deeply, she forced herself to relax and follow him. As it grew easier to move her body in rhythm with his, she began to enjoy the physical give and take, the way their movements brought them closer together and then apart just long enough to make her yearn to be against him again.

Gradually unwinding, Piper smiled up at him and even hummed along with the band. Josh grinned back, obviously taking her sacrificed lead as the apology it was. When the song ended, Josh's fingers, interlocked with hers, loosened their grip slightly, and he hesitated.

Piper tilted her head back. "I'm game to stay out here a while longer if you are. I love to dance." Which was true, but more than that, she needed the physical outlet for the emotional frustration she'd been feeling.

The dancing couldn't help alleviate the sexual frustration, though. That only grew worse as Josh pressed his other hand against her hip to guide her in a turn. They did several tight spins together, his long legs grazing hers, the denim he wore making a raspy whisper. When the music shifted to a ballad, Piper's heart fluttered. Slow dancing with Josh seemed a dangerous idea, but she'd just finished saying she didn't want to quit anytime soon.

They both stilled for a second, and Piper stared at his shirt, not wanting to meet his gaze. Then he pulled her closer to him, so that she could have rested her cheek against his chest. Josh lifted her hand, moving it so that it cupped his neck, and dropped his own hand to join the other at her waist. Plenty of couples around them had adopted this exact stance, but that didn't keep the situation from feeling blatantly intimate. Arms around him, she scooted closer, moving her feet absently, mostly just swaying now. With every brush of their bodies, Piper's blood heated. Her breasts pressed lightly against him, just enough to tease her senses, and lower, between her thighs, the part of her that so desperately wanted to be pressed against him, ached with damp need. It occurred to Piper that with her fingers laced behind the nape of his neck and his hands at her hips, resting at the sensitive space just atop the curve of her bottom, she and Josh were nearly in the same position they'd been in when they'd kissed earlier.

All she had to do was look up.

Josh swallowed. "I know you wanted to dance, but… it's gotten kind of crowded out here."

She clung to the excuse to escape. "Yeah, everyone comes out for the slow stuff."

"How about we take a break? I could grab us a couple of cold beers."

She nodded in prompt agreement. Then, eager to sit for a while, she rejoined Daphne at the table.

"Hey," her sister said. "We were just debating how much longer to stay. I tire out pretty easily these days, and I want to conserve energy for all that shopping tomorrow."

Piper grinned. Tomorrow afternoon was the reunion picnic, and most of her relatives would be at the Rebecca Fall Festival in the morning. But Blaine, Piper and Daphne had attended dozens of past festivals, and Piper had suggested the four of them visit an outlet mall a couple of counties over instead. Daphne had been thrilled by the suggestion of one last pre-baby shopping spree; Blaine, while not as thrilled, had the good sense to humor his heavily pregnant wife.

They'd be back in time for the reunion, and this way Piper wouldn't spend the day on old-fashioned carnival rides with Josh. If she couldn't even wash dishes with the man without wanting to peel his clothes off, then she had no business going through the dimly lit Tunnel of

Love with him, or being seat-belted into the cozy seat that would take them to the top of the Ferris wheel.

As though Daphne knew exactly who Piper was thinking about, she asked, "Where's Josh?"

"Grabbing us a couple of beers." She glanced around to make sure he was still out of earshot. "I don't know what to do about him, Daph."

"Jump him." her sister offered helpfully. "I did mention my hormones are in overdrive lately, right?"

Earlier that day, Piper would have protested that the idea was crazy. She and Josh were friends. He left a wake of broken hearts as wide as the Rio Grande. And the last thing she needed was a man complicating her life. So why wasn't she scoffing at Daphne's suggestion?

Instead, the suggestion took on a life of its own in Piper's imagination. Josh kissed with a slow, sure thoroughness that suggested he knew how to show a woman a good time. An unselfish, unhurried, uninhibited *very* good time.

He arrived at the table just in time to catch what Piper was sure was a fire-engine-red blush, but he didn't say anything as he handed her a frosty brown glass bottle. His fingers brushed hers, and heat swelled in her body, making her feel tight and full in places she'd almost forgotten about until this weekend.

She quickly gulped her beer, but it didn't help. She guzzled a bit more than she intended, and choked.

Josh handed her a napkin. "Are you all right? You're…"

Acting like a lunatic, she silently finished for him. Prying into stuff they never discussed, swooping down on Rosalyn like something out of *Fatal Attraction,* insisting he dance with her, then fighting with him over who got to lead.

To say nothing of the way she kept undressing him with her eyes.

"I'm fine." Piper sipped her beer. Slowly.

Fine? She was tense around the one person with whom she'd always been able to relax. This was Josh, the guy who let her vent about work and constantly borrowed her fabric softener because he liked the brand, but didn't want to be seen buying a bottle with a teddy bear on the label. Couldn't they go back to that—to the easy camaraderie they'd shared? She so desperately wanted to say the right thing, to restore the normalcy of their comfortable relationship.

Preparing for the casual one-liner or friendly observation that would point them in the right direction, she cleared her throat, opened her mouth to speak. But nothing came out. She was at a loss.

Seeking inspiration, she turned to face him. Her gaze locked with his, and his green-gold eyes sent shivers up her spine. The only things she was inspired to do had nothing to do with conversation. Openmouthed with nothing to say, she nervously cleared her throat again and gave a little cough.

"You sound like you're coming down with a sore throat," Josh commented solicitously. He looked almost hopeful, as though illness and a possible fever would explain the way she'd been acting.

Talk about a blow to her pride. Only moments ago she'd been thinking about this man in strictly sexual terms, while he looked ready to run right out and buy her a box of tissues and a bottle of vitamin C.

"N-no, I'm healthy as a horse." Now she was comparing herself to livestock? Good thing she'd made a conscious choice to be celibate, because she clearly lacked feminine wiles.

"Piper?" Charlie Conway approached the table. Nuisance though he was, his presence at least put an end to her making a fool of herself. For now. "You walked off, so we never really had our dance. I thought maybe now—"

"Sure." Anything to get away from the sexy man sitting next to her, confusing her so much that white-jacketed men with butterfly nets couldn't be too far off in her future. But this time, she was going to use the opportunity to set Charlie straight.

Thankfully, the band was playing a fast song, which allowed her to move constantly and not get too close to him.

He licked his lips nervously. "Piper, I've realized nothing I say is going to convince you that we belong together. So I'm not going to try to convince you with words." He stopped suddenly, leaning in.

She realized with a sort of detached horror that he was lowering his head to kiss her. *The only man I want kissing me is Josh Weber.* Even though Daphne had tried to warn her, the truth was so forceful that for a moment Piper couldn't move. *I love him. I'm in love with Josh.*

"Stop!" Belatedly mobilizing herself, she shoved Charlie away. "Enough is enough. I didn't want to have to be rude about this because we're old friends, but I don't want you. You don't want me, either. You want the perfect Rebecca housewife next to you during your mayoral campaigns."

"That's not true," he protested. He rocked back on his heels, running a hand through his blond hair. "I'll admit, maybe it was at one time. I did try to change you, but I'm older now, Piper. Smarter. I know what I lost. I've had plenty of time to find 'the perfect Rebecca housewife,' but that's not what I want."

Unfortunately, we don't always get what we want. "I'm with Josh now." She'd repeated that sentence, or variations thereof, so many times this weekend. Only this time did the irony bite her on the ass. She *wasn't* with Josh, but she wanted to be.

Charlie regarded her for a long moment. "You care that much about him?"

Lord help her, she did. She'd always imagined that love made a woman less, somehow, but thinking about all the times she'd spent with Josh, she realized he made her feel more. More confident when they discussed work, more attractive when he flirted with her, more powerful when she felt him respond to her kiss. Happier, sexier, even angrier. But never diminished in any way.

"Never mind," Charlie said. "I can see the answer in your expression. But are you sure he's the type who will stick around? I got the impression… Can he give you what you want, Piper?"

She decided to treat the question as rhetorical, since she was certain the answer was no. "Charlie, I'm sorry."

He didn't say anything when she turned and made her way back to Daphne. Josh was talking to Blaine and Donald about baseball, and Piper scooched onto the bench seat with her sister, her voice a dazed whisper.

"Daph? You were right. I am in love with him."

Daphne fluffed her dark hair. "I always was the smart one. Piper, every time you call me, we end up talking about Josh. And with the way you smile at him, it's so obvious."

"How obvious?" Her heart pounded against her chest. "Do you think he knows?" Even Charlie had said her emotions were evident in her expression.

"No, men are clueless," Daphne assured her. "When

it pertains to them, they're always the last to know. But you should tell him."

Piper sneaked a glance in his direction. The sight of him made her heart flip-flop, and she wondered if it would ever be possible to get tired of looking at him. "Tell Josh? Are you kidding? The only person in the Lone Star State more antirelationship than me?"

"I don't think of you as antirelationship, Piper. You just hadn't found the right guy to have a relationship with yet."

Piper had to admit that her views about couples and love had certainly been changing over the last few days. Still, she wasn't entirely at peace with the idea of a man taking a major role in her life again, not yet. "Daphne, if I tell you something, promise not to get mad at me?" The last thing Piper wanted was a hostile exchange like the one they'd had at the bridal shop.

Daphne waited, having had too many years' experiences as a sister to agree to a blanket promise.

Piper sighed, grateful for the thumping music of the live band that helped keep their conversation private. "You've said before that I don't want to turn out like Mom, and you're right. I respect her, and I'll admit she seems happy, but I couldn't be happy with her life."

"So who asked you to be? Falling in love doesn't need to change you into Mom or anyone els—"

"I thought it changed *you.*"

"What?"

"Well, when we were growing up, you didn't sound as though you wanted to be a Rebecca housewife, either. You talked about being an artist or a politician or traveling. Then you gave it all up because of Blaine."

Instead of sounding offended, Daphne surprised her by laughing. "Piper, you took off to college when you were

seventeen, and I'm almost four years younger than yo
Sure, I wanted to be an artist at one time. If you'll recall,
I also once wanted to be an astronaut. And I think you
missed the year I wanted to start my own all-girl band.
Blaine didn't change me, I just grew up, figured out what
I wanted."

Piper blinked, thinking of all the times their father had
expressed an opinion to which their mother had immediately agreed. Piper had imagined that Blaine and Daphne's
relationship was similar. "You're not unhappy?"

"Do I *look* unhappy, you twit?" Daphne chuckled
again. "Once I took some college courses, I realized
teaching is my calling. I love making a difference to these
kids. Plus I get summers off," she added with a teasing
grin.

Piper felt confused all over again. "Then why are you
talking about quitting teaching?"

"I don't plan to stop forever, just maybe take some time
off while the babies are young. But even if I do turn over
my classroom for a year or two, I'll still work occasionally
as a sub and stay in touch that way."

"So Blaine isn't trying to turn you into some throwback
from the '50s." Piper felt about six types of stupid. She'd
jumped to conclusions about her brother-in-law just because of the way Charlie had once tried to change her.

"Are you serious? Blaine likes our being a dual-income
family, trust me. Piper, I don't know how you see my marriage, but if I still wanted to get into politics, my husband
would personally organize my campaign against Charlie.
And as for wanting to travel, we plan to, once the kids
are a little older. He's not holding me back."

Piper bit her lip, afraid to open her mouth again and
stick her foot any farther down her throat. Leather sandals

might be great for showing off the toenails she'd painted earlier, but they made lousy snack food.

Daphne shook her head. "Mom does a lot for Dad, and you've always thought that made him some kind of chauvinist. I'm the first to admit that some of the people in this town are a little old-fashioned, but I think your view of our parents is skewed. Mom loves to cook and do things around the house. It's her domain, and she insists on controlling it. She's like you—she likes to do things her way."

Piper and her mother were alike?

"She's pushy and stubborn, but Dad's crazy about her. Half the time when she goes along with him, it's because 'his' idea was hers in the first place. You think it was Dad's choice to spend yesterday at a bridal-and-baby shower?" Daphne smiled. "Or Blaine's idea to spend tomorrow shopping? You had a bad experience with Charlie, but that's not Dad's or Blaine's fault. Or Josh's. Tell him how you feel."

Fear crowded Piper's chest, tightening her lungs. "I get that you're trying to help, but trust me, keeping this to myself is for the best. I know Josh. I understand him." And she understood he was unwilling to form any deep emotional attachments that might make him vulnerable.

Daphne arched an eyebrow. "Well, let's just hope you understand *him* better than you 'understood' my marriage."

Josh lay on his side, staring at the avocado-and-gold-paisley wallpaper illuminated by the streetlight spilling through his window. He could always pull the curtains shut, but the light outside wasn't what kept him awake. Thoughts of Piper were torturing him.

Probably just the proximity of her being curled up in bed on the other side of this wall.

Ha! She could move to Canada and he'd still be aware of her. And to be honest, it wasn't the hotel wall that separated them.

What was happening? First they'd snapped at each other earlier this evening, then she'd been so quiet on the ride back to the hotel. She'd been strangely contemplative ever since her second dance with Charlie Conway, and it made Josh uneasy. Was that why he hadn't asked what was on her mind on the return drive—fear that she was thinking about Charlie? He'd seen changes in her this weekend, despite her comments about staying single. She wouldn't reconsider Charlie's offer, would she? The mayor was downright irritating…but also apparently loyal, a more than capable provider, perhaps appealing to women and with family roots that went deep into the town's history.

She'd be miserable here. Wouldn't she? He felt as if he couldn't predict Piper as easily as he once had. Not that she'd ever been completely predictable. Banishing all nightmare-inducing thoughts of her back with Charlie, Josh stared harder at the wallpaper. Still 118 ugly swirling paisleys, same as the last four times he'd counted.

When that blonde in the bar—Rose? Robin?—had flirted with him, he'd smiled the way he normally would when an attractive woman was showing interest in him. But he'd been on autopilot, not really seeing her, attuned instead to Piper in her ex-boyfriend's arms. Charlie wasn't right for her.

But Josh wasn't right for her, either. From his business practices to his dating life, he'd remained more or less a loner, keeping his contact with others casual and as enjoyable as possible for the limited time it existed. It wasn't a bad life, so why rock the boat now? Why not just accept the unusual opportunity this weekend presented, and let it go at that?

All weekend he'd been free to do what he normally wouldn't, or couldn't. Not just kissing Piper, but holding her hand, as he had earlier today. As long as what they did here fell under the guise of pretending for the benefit of others, he could selfishly indulge in this time with her. Dancing, kissing, teasing, even sharing her family. But if it ever became something real, beyond this weekend, he'd lose her when they broke up.

The few women he hadn't dumped first had left him because he was too "emotionally inaccessible." And they were right. He'd been able to admit that, even as he hadn't really felt their loss. Until Dana. He'd really tried, dammit. He'd wanted to be what she needed, wanted to show her how he felt about her. But he'd learned too early in life not to make himself vulnerable to others to unlearn it now. Piper deserved a man who could love her unreservedly.

Too restless to stay in bed, he stood, absently registering the creaky groan of mattress springs at the shift in weight. He paced the small room. If his reluctance to commit was the only thing keeping them from a real chance at happiness, he might have a problem. But everything from their shared workplace to her celibate lifestyle meant friendship was the most logical relationship for them to have.

Yet logic didn't stop the way he'd felt when he'd watched her dance with Charlie. Logic couldn't ease the intense desire that rocked Josh each time he kissed her. And logic certainly hadn't helped him fall asleep hours ago instead of thinking about her all night long.

He pictured her in the blue skirt she'd worn earlier,

her legs shapely and seductive beneath. In a baseball cap, jumping up and down and whooping victory at an Astros home game. Deep in concentration as she worked, oblivious to everything but the angles and lines of her drawings. In a mischievous mood, her aquamarine eyes sparkling like the ocean. In his arms...

Worse, she was in his heart. The truth he could no longer ignore was that he'd have to be an idiot not to want Piper.

But allowing himself to act on that would just mean more pain when it was over. Why let someone in when he'd still be alone in the end?

The words Piper had spoken blew through his mind like a cold, hostile wind. *"You give the illusion of going from one relationship to the next, but you don't let people get close to you, so you're actually more alone than I am."*

He was worried about being alone in the end?

"I'm alone now."

The truth dawned unpleasantly, shedding light into corners of his life he'd rather not examine. He'd told himself he lived a good life, and while that might be true in some ways, it was also a hollow life.

Piper could fill that hollowness.

Panic immediately radiated through him. Better to ignore the emptiness than risk their friendship. But... ignoring it wasn't working anymore.

Admittedly, the majority of his past relationships had been meaningless. He'd designed them that way so that no one would be hurt when either party walked away. But it was Piper who consumed his thoughts now, and his feelings for her, two years in the making, weren't shallow or easy. For the first time in his adult life, he couldn't just pick up and walk away. *So what do I do?*

Pursue a woman who scorned romantic attachments even while the thought of such an attachment still scared him?

Well, nothing else had worked. At least this way he could maybe follow up on those kisses they'd exchanged and ease the throbbing sexual need that had him so turned around he could barely think.

"Wow." Josh stood in the hall outside her hotel room, his wide eyes and gaping mouth making it clear that this wasn't his usual offhand flattery. He looked flummoxed.

Despite Piper's grim mood and the sleepless night she'd endured, she was happy to be responsible for the flummoxing. When she'd finally abandoned all hope of sleep and crawled out of bed a few hours ago, she'd decided she needed to look her best today. Falling in love with Josh was such a stupid thing to do that she'd needed some salve to her pride. A good hair day was about the best she could come up with on short notice.

In a pair of snug, cowgirl-cut jeans, which she'd only packed in a fit of nostalgia, and a high-collar shirt with a peekaboo cutout above her cleavage, she felt sexy in a uniquely Texan way. And with time to kill since she'd climbed out of bed so early, she'd curled her hair so that it spilled over her shoulders in soft waves. She'd even dabbed on some makeup.

Quite a change from the Piper of French braids and business suits. "The people at work would sure be surprised if I started showing up like this, wouldn't they?" Despite her words, Josh's was the only opinion she cared about.

He grinned down at her. "You go into the office looking like this, darlin', you won't get anything done with all the men hanging over your desk and drooling on your blueprints."

The exaggerated compliment actually deflated her. *He's just being Josh.* Still, as she turned to grab her purse from off the bed, she resolved to match his every teasing comment. No way would he ever guess that her heart was as cracked as a faulty foundation.

"Maybe I've been too focused on work, anyway," she drawled, walking toward him. She stepped outside the room and shut the door behind her before he had a chance to move back, forcing them to share personal space for just a second, bodies brushing. "There's something to be said for having a good time, don't you think?"

Too bad the man she wanted to have that good time with was so off-limits.

He swallowed. "Definitely. I'm all for a good time."

And not much else, she was afraid. Josh deserved so much more than the shallow relationships he allowed himself, but Piper couldn't force him to accept love he didn't want.

Subdued, she followed him down the carpeted hall. The plan was to grab a bite to eat from the continental breakfast buffet downstairs, then meet Blaine and Daphne near the town picnic grounds, where they'd return for the reunion after shopping. On the one hand, Piper looked forward to joining the other couple, since they could help alleviate some of the tension she felt around Josh. On the other hand, being around her happily married sister and brother-in-law would sting a little, too. Piper had always felt a twinge of pity for her sister, who'd never escaped Rebecca, but today she envied the love Daphne and her husband shared.

Today, Piper's pity was only for what she and Josh might have shared if circumstances were different.

* * *

Piper studied the wooded picnic area crowded with generations of Jamiesons and their families. A group of men were gathered around a cooler of cold beverages, while some younger members of the clan played Frisbee and catch. Still others sat at the tables, looking over photo albums and exchanging news. She was sure her name was being mentioned frequently. They were probably all still shocked that she'd attended, much less brought a man with her.

In retrospect, her lie hadn't been worth it. It would have been easier just to tell her mom she wasn't interested in dating than to deal with the confusion she felt now. Josh had been extra-attentive all day, his previous aversion to physical affection nowhere in evidence when he'd dropped his arm around her shoulders in the back seat of Blaine's car. When the four of them had been shopping, Josh hadn't come right out and said so, but she got the impression he wanted to be alone with her to talk about something. Although it was cowardly of her, she'd pretended to miss his signals, using Daphne's and Blaine's presence as a shield. Piper had meant what she'd told her sister—letting Josh know about her feelings was a *horrible* idea, the surest way to lose his friendship. Unfortunately, she wasn't sure how long she could conceal them if she was alone with him.

Walking next to her, Josh observed, "You have a really big family."

"Yep, my dad was the youngest of five kids." She looked up in time to catch the yearning in his eyes, and felt ashamed of all the times she'd griped about her relatives. She didn't need Josh to tell her that as a kid, he would've given anything for a family.

"Come on," she said gently, "I'll introduce you to

everyone." They mixed and mingled among her cousins, then stopped for lemonade. As Piper turned to introduce him to more relatives, she was heralded by her great-aunt Millie.

"Piper!" Millie barreled forward, a determined expression on her wizened face. Not only did Millie always speak her mind, but, since she was mostly deaf, she usually spoke it loudly enough to be heard down the coast in Corpus Christi.

This afternoon was no different.

The thin, elderly woman stopped in front of Josh. "This must be your stud-muffin."

Piper tried to ignore the many heads that swiveled in their direction, as well as her great-aunt's unexpected—and somewhat disturbing—use of the term. "Josh, this is Great-Aunt Millie. Millie, Josh Weber."

He kissed Millie's hand, causing her to blush so becomingly that she looked years younger for a moment.

"Have you two set a date yet?"

"Uh, no," Piper said, "not yet."

"Well, don't dawdle," her great-aunt scolded. "A woman your age can't afford to wait. Only a few prime breeding years left." As though Piper were one of the heifers Millie and Great-Uncle Earl had once raised.

To avoid saying something she'd regret, Piper merely sipped her lemonade, wishing it were spiked.

Then Millie glanced at Josh and cackled. "But I'll bet you could still give her babies. A strapping young fellow like yourself is probably shooting more than blanks."

Piper choked, determined not to further commemorate the moment by shooting lemonade out her nose.

Millie shuffled off to terrorize other members of the Jamieson clan, and Piper apologized to Josh. "I swear that after this weekend you never have to see these people again."

"So you've said. Numerous times."

"Don't worry, I mean it."

He followed Millie's progress with his eyes. "The women in your family seem to get even more outspoken as they age." Grinning, he turned back to Piper. "Lord knows what you'll be like in forty or fifty years. Look out, world."

"Are you implying that I'm outspoken?"

"No, you're quiet and meek. And tall enough to be a supermodel, too." At her mock glare, he added, "Your not being a supermodel is a big loss to the men of the world. I don't know a woman sexier than you."

Oh, she wished he'd stop saying things like that. And she wished her imprudent heart wouldn't speed up when he did. "Josh, you're doing it again."

"Doing what?"

"When it's just you and me, you don't have to flirt."

"I've always flirted with you," he pointed out. "Long before this weekend. What's different now?"

Now I'm in love with you, and it hurts.

"Besides," he pressed, his expression growing alarmingly serious, "how do you know I *don't* find you sexy?"

"Because we're friends?" What was he trying to tell her? She knew from their kisses that he wasn't indifferent to her—she wasn't an idiot—but did he honestly want to act on the feelings growing between them?

"You think being your friend means I can't notice how funny and attractive and smart you are?" he challenged.

"Well…" Being friends certainly hadn't stopped her from noticing all those things about him. As she glanced away, trying to gather her thoughts, her gaze landed on a small, spry figure energetically winding up to pitch in the family softball game.

Nana? Yep, that was her grandmother—the very picture of health. In fact, as Piper watched her grandmother throw a fastball, she realized Nana looked to be in better shape than some of the much younger players on her team.

"I've been had." Piper practically growled the words. It had occurred to her that her mother might stretch the truth about Nana's condition, but to lie outright?

With Josh trailing after her, Piper stalked over to where Blaine and Daphne stood in the shade. "I want an answer. Are you people so desperate to get me married off that you let me believe someone I love was seriously ill?"

Blaine glanced guiltily to where Nana was in the process of striking out someone half her age. "Don't get mad at Daph. Nana *was* sick. It started out as just a cold, but when she developed some complications, she went to the hospital for observation. So when your mom said Nana had been ill, she wasn't lying. She just played it up because she knew you'd be more likely not to back out. And more likely to bring Josh for all of us to meet."

"I didn't know until just before you got here that Mom made the situation sound so dire," Daphne added hastily. "And Nana doesn't know at all."

"But that business about her not coming outside to meet me because she wasn't well?" Though definitely relieved about her grandmother's condition, Piper was plenty irritated.

"She's supposed to avoid the night air while she's still recovering from her respiratory infection," Daphne said. "Dad will drive her home early tonight so she doesn't catch a chill. Piper, you have every right to be annoyed with Mom. Just keep in mind that sometimes we lie to the people close to us, without even planning to, because we think it's what's best for them."

Piper flushed at the subtle jab. How angry could she get with her mother for the deceptive exaggeration when Piper herself was guilty of comparable tactics? Maybe Daphne had been right last night about Piper and her mom having some traits in common. Besides, there was no point in staying mad at her mother when the universe was sure to pay Astrid back for the deception, anyway.

If Piper had learned one thing this weekend during her masquerade with Josh, it was that even the simplest white lies had a way of becoming complicated.

Chapter Eleven

Whatever else happened this weekend, Josh could honestly say he'd never been so well fed. Sitting at the picnic table, reflecting on the array of home-cooked food he'd enjoyed today, he knew he should feel mellow and full now, but mellow was difficult with Piper so close to him. Though he'd been trying—unsuccessfully—to get a few moments alone with her all day, her family's presence did have one current benefit. With everyone squished together on the bench, Piper was pressed into him from shoulder to thigh, her softness a tantalizing weight against him.

Her arm brushed his as she gestured during her conversation with Daphne, and his body hummed with awareness, like a generator kicking on, sending electricity to all the pertinent points. But this was nothing compared to a few moments ago, when Josh had reached past her and accidentally grazed her breast. They'd both frozen, and she'd stopped talking to her sister, turning to look into his eyes.

They were leaving tomorrow, and unless Josh seized the moment soon, he was going to lose his chance. The odds of their exploring the attraction between them, of finding out if they could be more than friends, were greater here. Once they returned to Houston, it would be too temptingly safe to fall back into their old routine, regardless of the passion he knew they invoked in each other.

"Hey." He tapped Piper on the shoulder, and she tilted her head back to look at him. "How about you and I go for a walk? Just the two of us," he added, lest she try to draft anyone else.

Seeing the uncertainty in her expression, he quickly appealed to the workout guilt she had to be feeling by now. "I figured we could burn off some of the calories we've been packing on all weekend."

"Well…" She frowned. "I guess we could."

They both stood, telling her immediate family that if they didn't see them later, they'd meet up with them in the morning for breakfast. Then they headed for one of the park's hiking paths, into the surrounding woods. The breeze carried the sounds of crickets chirping, owls hooting in the distance and armadillos scurrying in the underbrush.

"You were right," she told him, her brisk pace at odds with the cozy chat he'd been hoping to have. "I do need to burn off some calories."

"No, that was me trying to get you alone. Your body's perfect as is."

Her laugh was rueful. "Then you haven't been looking hard enough."

The hell he hadn't. "Tell you what. Strictly as a favor to you, I'm willing to make a more thorough evaluation. Clothing optional."

After a moment, she broke down and smiled, shaking her head. "Cute."

"I was hoping for 'irresistible,' but cute's a start."

"You know you're irresistible," she muttered.

Hope flashed as brightly as a shooting star. The very fact that she sounded a bit ticked off made him think that her statement was more than an offhand remark. "You don't seem happy about it."

"Well, I…it's not important."

How she saw him was vitally important—high time he let her know that. But telling her the truth, even hinting at what the last few days had meant to him, what she'd come to mean to him… He took a deep breath, knowing that if he delayed much longer he'd fall back on the banter that was nothing more than a mask, and never take this chance.

"Piper, the last couple of days have been some of the best of my life."

She chuckled. "Oh, sure. With my mother practically measuring you for a tux, and me acting like I've developed multiple personality disorder—"

"Piper." He stopped walking, turning so that he stood in her path. "The last couple of days have been some of the best of my life." His tone brooked no argument, not even the playful kind, and she didn't respond. He took advantage of her rare speechlessness while he could. "Because of you. But don't get me wrong. In some ways, this weekend has been damn uncomfortable, too. Cold showers, for instance—zero fun. Plus, they're not much of a long-term solution."

"S-solution?"

"Yes." He bluntly stated what they'd danced around since their first night in Rebecca. "Our lusting after each other and not doing anything about it has definitely become a problem."

That had lacked the eloquence she deserved, but with the effect her nearness was having on him right now, he was lucky to be saying anything besides "you woman, me man." The way she was looking up at him, her lips softly parted, her eyes reflecting wonderment in the moonlight...

To hell with figuring out what to say to her. Who needed words? He gripped her shoulders with his hands and drew her closer, using less finesse than he normally managed, but Piper didn't object. She raised up on her toes to meet him, to kiss him for the first time with no witnesses. No excuses, no pretense, just their naked need for each other. His lips found hers, worshipping, ravishing, promising her a night she'd never forget.

His hands ran down the curve of her spine to cup the swell of her bottom, pulling her tighter against him, groaning at the friction of her body against his erection. No turning back now—they'd definitely passed the point of platonic. They just weren't as far past it as he'd like.

"Piper, if this isn't what you want, if you think we should stop—"

"No! I—I mean, I don't want to stop." She leaned back, looking around their wooded surroundings with wide eyes. "Delay, maybe. Can we go back to the hotel?"

Tiny lights exploded behind his eyes. Piper wanted to have sex with him! He was actually, finally, going to make love to her. Her ready acceptance left him speechless and feeling like the luckiest man alive. But, damn, he wished that hotel were closer.

He laced his fingers with hers. Though she walked with a quick stride, his legs were longer and he had to force himself not to drag her to the parking lot. They reached the car, but instead of unlocking the doors, Josh pressed her up against the side, seeking her already up-turned mouth.

A soft breathy sound escaped her, somewhere between a sigh and a moan. "Keys."

He fumbled in his pocket for the key ring, then handed them over to his favorite speedaholic. "You definitely drive. The less time this takes, the better."

Skirting around the front of the car, she shot him a wicked smile. "Then we're not thinking along the same lines."

He meant to laugh, but groaned instead, realizing just how much time he wanted to take exploring, tasting her body. If the drive to the hotel didn't kill him.

When he said as much, she chided, "Patience," but the urgency in her eyes was unmistakable and immensely gratifying.

"*Patience?* I've been waiting for this since the day I met you. It just took me awhile to realize it."

She shot him a look of such melting adoration that he wanted to reach across their seats and kiss her. She also hit the accelerator.

Piper didn't know what to say. His admission that he'd wanted her for so long took her breath away. She'd been fighting so fiercely to contain her desire for him, never believing she'd have a chance to act on her feelings, never thinking he'd let her that close.

At the hotel, she slammed the car into Park, and he rushed out to open her door for her. After they'd hurried up the stairs like impatient newlyweds, he unlocked the door to his room and swept her into his arms, carrying her inside. She felt like a bride going over the threshold, but the matrimonial analogy didn't bother her as it once might have. In fact, she experienced a twinge of wistfulness, but it was quickly replaced by the heady sensation of being in Josh's arms.

Fumbling one-handed with the small lamp on the nightstand, he set her down beside his bed, his mouth already on hers before her feet touched the floor. The deft way he kissed her, like a man who knew all her secrets, sent desire spiraling through her. His hands were at her waist, pressing her against him, and she mentally cursed the layers of clothing separating them. She smiled inwardly, though, at the chance to finally unbutton his shirt and slide it off his shoulders. When she'd dreamed of doing this, she hadn't realized her hands would be shaking.

She laid a palm across his bare chest, tracing her fingers over the smattering of hair and the muscles toned from recreational weight lifting. "I've imagined this, you know."

"Really?" He sounded pleased that she'd pictured being with him, but then he laughed. "Please tell me your fantasy didn't stop here."

Their kiss muffled her answering laugh. She explored his mouth, then slowly lowered herself from her tiptoes to kiss his jaw and run her tongue over his collarbone. Her fingers went to the waistband of his jeans, but he lightly encircled her wrist, stopping her.

"Wait. I want to see you." He met her eyes, his gaze hypnotically sensual, as he released each button on her shirt with much more dexterity than she'd exhibited. "You're not the only one who's thought about this."

Cool air hit her skin as he pushed the material of her shirt away, but the appreciative gleam in his eyes more than kept her warm. He skimmed his fingers along her rib cage, trailing upward, seemingly in no hurry, though his breathing grew more labored. He cupped her breasts, his fingers grazing their already stiff peaks through the lace of her bra. A spasm of need went through her midsection, leaving her light-headed.

Tugging gently at his hand, she sat on the bed before her legs gave out beneath her. Josh followed, kissing her again, building the waves of feeling inside her until she thought she'd drown. The possibility of losing herself in the undertow was exciting rather than frightening. She sank back against the mattress, pulling him with her, wanting his weight above her.

When he broke off their kiss to remove her bra, she moaned in protest, but it quickly turned to a sound of approval as he bent his head and took one hardened nipple between his lips. He turned his attention to her other breast, and Piper gripped his hips with her hands, undulating her body against his in an instinctive attempt to assuage the slow burn she felt.

Again her fingers went to the waistband of his jeans. He made no move to stop her this time as she lowered the zipper with some effort, her task made more difficult by his blatant arousal. She tugged the jeans and briefs down together, her eyes widening at his impressive erection. Knowing how much he wanted her gave her an electric rush, filling her with a tingling, ultrafeminine satisfaction. She curved her fingers around him, sliding over the smooth rigid length.

His breath hitched. "You're amazing."

Piper couldn't find her voice, but she silently returned the sentiment. She'd never experienced this before. Not the fiery driving physical sensations and not the maelstrom of emotions, either. Happy and nervous and calm all at once. Nothing had ever felt more right.

Moving together, they fumbled with her remaining clothes, and she wriggled free of them, desperately needing to be flesh-to-flesh. He traced one strong, lightly callused hand down over her abdomen and between her thighs, resting the heel of his palm on her. The contact, slight and unmoving, teased her senses. Tense with a sweet pain only Josh could ease, she moved against him, seeking more. His response was to scoot down the bed, replacing his hand with his mouth, kissing her intimately.

Unused to feeling so vulnerable to another person, exposed in a way not even being naked could approach, Piper stiffened at first. But she'd already given Josh her heart. She wanted to give him her body now. She relaxed, surrendering herself to the man she loved and the dizzying heat of desire. His tongue moved on her, and her involuntary sounds of need mingled with the pounding of her own heartbeat in her ears. Soon her entire body pulsed with that rhythm. She climaxed in spasms that left her clinging to his shoulders, somehow utterly replete and yet feeling empty, wanting him to fill her and complete what they'd started together.

He moved away only long enough to deal with a condom, then aligned his body with hers. When he entered her, the oxygen left her lungs in a whoosh, but she didn't need air. Only Josh.

And he gave himself to her, as generously and thoroughly as she ever could have imagined. Over and over, until the swells of passion crashed through her, propelling her forward into a second orgasm. Her body clenched, drawing him even more tightly into her. Glancing up, she watched his face, taut with desire, as he found his own release.

They held each other, their ragged breathing and thundering hearts the only sounds in the small room. Piper wasn't sure she'd ever be able to think or speak coherently again, so she was glad that it took Josh at least a few minutes to regain his composure, as well.

Rolling slightly to the side, he leaned close, framing her face with his hands, pushing back slightly damp strands of hair. "That was incredible."

Instead of giving her a chance to find her voice, he kissed her. Perhaps that was for the best, because the only thing she could think of to say right now was "I love you."

So say it, she told herself later, when they both lay on their sides and Josh had his arm around her. She snuggled against him, enjoying the way he idly traced one hand up and down her back. But not even the closeness of the moment gave her quite enough courage to bluntly state her feelings. It was such an irrevocable admission, and not knowing how he would respond ate at the edges of her perfect contentment.

Josh's breathing eventually deepened, and she realized he'd fallen asleep. She envied his relaxed slumber. Moments ago, she'd felt weightless and carefree. Now she worried that even after knowing him for two years, and the intimacy they'd just shared, she still couldn't guess what his reaction to her feelings would be. No question that he saw her as more than a platonic friend…but how much more? Perhaps she should have thought to ask these questions earlier, but thinking had been the last thing she'd wanted to do.

As her intoxicating afterglow faded, Piper realized there was a lot she didn't know. Such as what they were going to do about their relationship once they got back to Houston and a shared office where they weren't supposed to *have* a relationship? And would Josh even consider this a relationship?

She grimaced at the tension slowly knotting her muscles. She would have thought her sated body would stay relaxed and boneless a little longer. After all, she'd just had the best sex of her life.

She only hoped great sex wasn't all it had been.

Chapter Twelve

Josh stifled a yawn, the conversation around the Jamiesons' dining room table momentarily receding to a dull buzz. After breakfast, he and Piper were headed back to Houston, and for once he wouldn't mind if she wanted to drive. Considering all his missed sleep last night, he'd be happy to doze in the passenger seat on the return trip.

Around two in the morning, he'd awakened from a dream about Piper to the reality of Piper. The naked, warm satiny reality. He'd brushed aside her citrus-scented hair and kissed the back of her neck, still drowsy enough that his intentions weren't truly carnal. But then she'd stirred, moving her softly curved bottom against the one part of him that was fully awake. They'd ended up making love a second time, teasing and exploring each other almost in slow motion, with the kind of delicious languor that made the interlude seem more fantasy than reality once morning broke.

Except that fantasies didn't rob him of his sleep. Or leave a tiny bruised love bite above Piper's collarbone that had forced her to change shirts twice this morning so her family wouldn't see it. Though the mark had been unintentional, Josh couldn't help taking a small amount of satisfaction in the physical proof that Piper was…

What? His? Piper would never belong *to* any man, so the most a guy could hope for was to make her see that she belonged *with* him. Josh frowned inwardly, absently pouring syrup into a thick, sticky puddle over a homemade Belgian waffle, wondering how Piper viewed last night. This morning, they'd overslept and had rushed through getting ready so they could check out of the hotel and be on time for breakfast. He'd kissed her and she'd kissed him back, but they hadn't talked. He supposed they could have in the car on the way to her parents, but neither of them had mentioned it.

Just as well. Josh didn't know what to say.

Last night had certainly shown him the rewards for letting someone into his life. He couldn't remember ever being as happy as he'd been. But he did remember the last two times he'd dared hope for true happiness—the day the Wakefields had told him they'd be adopting him and the day he'd told Dana he loved her.

"Josh?" Mrs. Jamieson's worried voice seemed to be coming from far away, and he blinked to bring her into focus. "You okay? You seem exhausted this morning."

His gaze slid involuntarily to Piper, who guiltily stifled a yawn of her own as her mother spoke.

He grinned, his mood improved by Piper's sleepy expression. "I'm fine, ma'am. Just thinking that the weekend went by too fast."

"You can come back soon for the wedding, though," Blaine said. "I'm tired of being the only guy for Piper and Daphne to abuse verbally. This way, we're evenly matched."

"Two women pitting wits against two guys isn't an even match," Josh said with a chuckle. "We'll get slaughtered." But his joking was forced. Would he see any of Piper's family again?

An hour later, breakfast was finished, the dishes were in the kitchen and the Jamiesons had trooped outside to bid Piper and Josh farewell.

Piper hugged Daphne goodbye, and Josh couldn't help noticing a new easiness between the two sisters, an affection that was more relaxed than it had been when he and Piper arrived. The weekend in Rebecca seemed to have helped her work a few things out.

"I wish I could be here when the twins are born," Piper said.

"Me, too," Daphne agreed. "But a due date is as far from a sure thing as a lottery ticket. You could always drive down when I go into labor, but I don't really want you trying to make the trip between Houston and Rebecca at three in the morning."

Piper laughed. "Well, maybe you'll be one of those women no one ever hears about, one who goes into labor at a respectable hour, like 9:00 a.m., instead of the middle of the night. And if not…I'll just have to come home for Christmas and spend time with you and my new nephews then."

For a moment, silence reigned, then her family all began talking at once.

"You make sure to bring Josh with you," Nana instructed, so commanding that he wondered how he or Piper ever could have believed she was frail. "I'm so glad you finally found a good man to take care of you."

"Honey, you're welcome here anytime," Mrs. Jamieson

assured her daughter. "Whether you have a boyfriend with you or not. We don't care."

Piper did a double take. "You don't?"

"No." Her mother shot Josh an apologetic look. "Not that we wouldn't be thrilled to have you over for Christmas, of course."

"What about all those lectures?" Piper demanded. "The ones about how I wasn't getting any younger? The pressure to marry Charlie?"

Mrs. Jamieson winced. "I've realized this weekend how much I love having you visit…and how much I've driven you away. I didn't mean to put so much pressure on you, it's just that marrying your father and having you and Daphne made me so happy. I wanted you to be that happy."

"Even if what makes me happy is work and friends, not a relationship?"

Mrs. Jamieson glanced from Piper to Josh. "Well, sure, honey. But you have found a great relationship."

"Right," Piper agreed quickly. "It was more a hypothetical question."

"A moot point is what it is, " Nana said. "You and Josh will be here in December. I'll get started on his Christmas quilt."

"Quilt?" Josh parroted.

Piper glanced over her shoulder. "Jamieson tradition."

And Nana wanted to include him in the family custom? The dangerous longing he'd been suppressing since he was sixteen welled within him—the desire to belong.

They aren't your *family. They include you because of Piper, and you don't even know if the two of you have a future.* The dark voice in his head was one he knew well, the same one that had talked him out of hope before. Not a cheerful voice, granted, but it had saved him from further pain and disappointment.

Today the voice seemed darker than ever, and Josh was torn. He wanted to change, he really did. He wanted to be sure of his feelings for Piper and hers for him, wanted to hope for the best. Despite parents being killed, foster families getting transferred to Europe, girlfriends walking out because of his inability to connect, happy endings *did* happen sometimes, right? It worked out for some people.

For some people, maybe, the voice conceded. *But for you?*

By the time Piper looked through the windshield and saw the Houston City Limits sign, she'd reached an unpleasant but inescapable realization: she was a big fat coward. Okay, given the strict gym schedule she subjected herself to, maybe the fat part wasn't necessary. But she'd definitely shown a lack of courage during their drive from Rebecca back to the city. Why hadn't she said anything to Josh about last night?

Because it was difficult to express what last night meant to her when she had no idea what it might have meant to him. She supposed she could ask about his innermost feelings and thoughts. Yeah, because that strategy had always worked really well for women in his past.

"We're almost there." She didn't even want to think about how inane she sounded—pointing out that he was about five minutes from his own home in case he'd somehow missed that—but she'd needed something, anything, to temporarily slice through the silence of everything they weren't saying.

Josh nodded, but didn't pry his gaze from the window he'd been staring out of for the past few hours. First, he'd shown an inexplicable fascination with watching miles of pastureland and the occasional cow. The bucolic landscape had given way to the slithering freeways and overpasses of Houston. Now he stared unblinkingly at the coppery reflection of the setting sun across the buildings of the city skyline.

Despite the awkward way time was dragging inside the car, Piper still felt that they were nearing their apartment complex much too soon. One more street to go, then their weekend would officially be over. Surely they weren't just going to have sex after two years of platonic friendship, then ignore it. Was she supposed to pretend that nothing had happened, hop out of the car, hand Josh his luggage and tell him goodbye?

Don't be melodramatic. The man works with you and lives one story above you. It's hardly goodbye.

So what was it, then?

"Josh—" *We need to talk.* She stopped herself just in time from uttering the dreaded phrase. Gee, maybe if she thought really hard she could come up with something even more trite to say that would send him hurling himself from a moving vehicle even faster.

Something in her tone must have penetrated the invisible wall of self-isolation he'd been projecting all day, because he turned to briefly meet her gaze. "Is this about last night?"

She tried not to ponder how many times he may have had about-last-night conversations with other women—or how those conversations had ended. "Yes."

"I'm sorry, Piper."

The pit of her stomach began sinking like the post-iceberg *Titanic.* "You're sorry we made love?"

"No! I'm not sorry we— I was apologizing for the awkwardness today, not what happened last night. I didn't know what to say, so I thought I'd take the easy way out and just take my cue from you."

Her laugh bordered more on a nervous giggle. "Figures. The one time I decide to follow a man's lead." She steered her car into the parking garage.

"Can I help you carry in your stuff," Josh offered, "or would that offend your feminist sensibilities?"

"Maybe I can make an exception just this once."

After she parked the car, they divided the bags and rode the elevator up together. She unlocked her front door, and Josh followed her inside, setting down her stuff and shifting his own luggage from one hand to the other.

"I hate to not eat and run, but I should get upstairs," he said. "Unpack, check messages, get my laundry done before work tomorrow."

"Yeah, I should do all that, too." Doing everyday tasks seemed surreal—how could she just go about her normal, mundane tasks when so much had changed for her this weekend? "Well...thanks for everything."

"My pleasure." The perfect opportunity for an outrageous comment or at least a wicked gleam in his eye to give his words double-entendre emphasis, but Josh simply rocked back on his heels.

They stood in awkward silence, him like a bellhop waiting for a tip and her like a hotel guest who just realized she didn't have any cash on her.

He turned toward the open door, but then paused. "Piper, have dinner with me tomorrow night."

Her heart fluttered. "Dinner?"

"Yeah. A real dinner date, not just a shared pizza at Grazzio's."

Thank God. Piper breathed a sigh of relief. What they'd shared had been more than a weekend fling out of town. She just had to be patient. Even if Josh felt the same way she did, he would probably be more skittish about expressing it. The man's entire life had been people leaving him. Wouldn't the best way to encourage him to change be to demonstrate she was willing to modify her ways, too?

And she did mean *modify*—a willing compromise that she'd thought of herself, not a complete reinvention to satisfy another person. She'd learned something this weekend, and although her relationship with Charlie had taken an unhealthy turn, doing something for someone you cared about did not make you a spineless throwback to the fifties.

She wanted to show Josh she was giving this her all, make some sort of gesture. "Dinner sounds great. But instead of going out, what if I cook here?"

For a moment, he looked stunned, then his gold-green eyes glinted with amusement. "Want me all to yourself?"

She grinned. "Come over tomorrow and find out. Just let me know what time works for you. I'd planned to stay a little late at the office to catch up, but—" Good grief. The office. How had she forgotten? "What are we going to do about work?"

The humor in his gaze disappeared, like a light going out, leaving his expression dark and carefully blank. "You mean the no-dating policy?"

"Yeah."

"No need to decide that right this second, is there?" He was trying to sound nonchalant, but his tone was as guarded as his features. "We keep everything to ourselves for now, and if this develops into anything, we'll figure out what to do later."

If it develops? Didn't they at least rate as "something," already? Nice to see they were both giving this their all.

"Piper, maybe that didn't come out right."

"No, it's okay. I know what you meant." She used her best worldly, unhurt, I'm-a-big-girl tone.

"Do you? Because you look upset. I didn't mean that this *wasn't* anything, only that…" He shoved his hands into his pockets. "Men just aren't good with words."

You are when you're trying to seduce women. It was only after the seduction had been accomplished that the charmers didn't know what to say.

Josh was so happy to see Piper Monday night that it startled him. After all, they'd been in the same office all day. But he hadn't said two words to her there. He didn't waste time with words once she opened the door to her apartment, either.

Instead, he lowered his free hand—the one not holding the bottle of wine—to her waist and pulled her to him for a kiss hello. His greeting apparently took her by surprise, because at first she was simply soft and pliant beneath his mouth. Then she brushed her tongue against his, kissing him back with enough heat that he almost dropped the merlot.

In what seemed like the far distance, the elevator beeped, signaling that the doors were about to part. Josh realized that he and Piper should probably step into her apartment before they took this any further.

He pulled away reluctantly, smiling down at her. "You look great." She'd come to work today dressed as a hybrid of Houston Piper and Rebecca Piper. Neither braiding her hair back nor letting it fall completely free, she'd instead pulled the sides up with delicate barrettes. She'd also skipped the usual pantsuit in favor of a muted-red sweater over a knee-length black skirt. "I've been wanting to tell you that all day, but I figured I'd save the hitting on you until after work."

She grinned. "Better late than never."

Following her inside, he thought to himself that he might have been the only one on the drafting floor who hadn't hit on her today. Even Smith had lingered near her workstation after they'd finished discussing some specs on a new building. Josh had itched to storm over there and stake his claim, but of course he hadn't.

Quite the opposite. He'd stayed as far away from Piper as possible. Now more than ever, it was important to keep up a professional appearance. His reward for keeping a businesslike distance was enjoying her company tonight.

He trailed her into the galley-style kitchen and set the wine on the pale green counter. "I hope red is okay, I wasn't sure what we were having."

"Lasagna sound good?"

"Sounds great." Not that he was here for the food. "Anything I can do to help?"

She picked up a small container of cottage cheese and emptied it into a white plastic bowl, cocking her head toward the refrigerator. "You can make a salad, if you like. I hit the grocery store on the way home, so there are actual vegetables in there that were grown during our lifetime."

"If it's green, grab it and chop it up. If it's fuzzy and black, pretend I didn't see it. Got it."

She shot a mock glare over her shoulder before turning back to the bowl. She added ricotta and blended the contents with an electric mixer. Josh found the salad ingredients, taking them and a small wooden cutting board over to the corner apartment management generously designated "the breakfast nook." He sat at the table chopping, but couldn't help glancing in Piper's direction every couple of seconds, despite the danger to his fingers.

God, she's beautiful. Just looking at her made him ache inside. The fact that he'd pushed for this dinner gave him hope, because the truth was, when they'd arrived back in Houston, he'd wanted to run like hell. Away from her and away from the emotional devastation she'd wreak when she left.

If. If she left, he tried to tell himself.

Piper finished layering pasta, meat sauce and cheese in a pan and placed the lasagna in the oven. Then she pulled out two glasses and a corkscrew.

"How about some of that wine now?" she asked, opening the bottle.

He carried the salad into the kitchen. "Sure." He started to pour some of the merlot into a glass for her, but almost spilled it when she leaned forward to rest her arms on the countertop. Obviously she didn't realize that he could see straight down her loose sweater.

Or—he noticed the sly, secretive curve of her lips—maybe she knew exactly what she was doing. He stole a second glance at the lacy black bra she wore. Piper was just full of surprises tonight.

She straightened, sipping her wine. "Missed you at work today."

"I was there." He tried joking it off. "I was the guy you couldn't see from behind the overflowing pile in my in-box."

"I guess so. I mean, I know it's my fault you're backed up, but maybe we can have lunch together sometime this week."

He drank his wine, stalling. The last thing he wanted to discuss was their work week. He'd told Piper last night that there was no reason to figure out a way around the no-dating policy just yet, but she was too forthright a woman to accept deception as a long-term solution. Josh couldn't wrap his mind around the alternatives.

Would Piper quit her job because of a man? No chance in hell. And when he considered quitting...it was such a drastic move. Too permanent for a guy like him. He couldn't alter his life like that without knowing for sure that the person he was doing it for would be around for the long haul. And how could he ever be sure?

"Josh. Did I lose you?"

"Sorry. I got preoccupied by this incredibly sexy woman."

"Oh." She smiled up at him, flirting from beneath her lashes. "You're forgiven."

"You're no fun at all." He set his wineglass on the counter and reached out to take hers from her hand. "I had very specific plans for how I was going to earn your forgiveness."

The delicate pulse in the hollow of her throat quickened. "I take it back, then. You're not forgiven. I predict it's going to take considerable work on your part to appease me."

He leaned in without yet touching her, letting the anticipation build for both of them. "Guess I'd better get started then."

She stretched up to reach him. Josh lowered his head, but then stopped.

"Wait. I have a better idea." He turned and lifted her so she was sitting on the edge of the counter, solving their height difference.

Her lips met his in a deep, openmouthed kiss, rich with the heady flavor of the wine. He braced one hand on the countertop next to her and cupped the other behind her head, his fingers tangled in the silk of her hair. Josh kissed her like a man experiencing water for the first time after days lost in the desert. He wanted to drink in everything about her—her sweet taste, each breathy sigh and sensuous movement.

Dropping his hands behind her, he lifted the hem of her sweater and ran his fingers over her bare back, tracing her spine. She quivered beneath his touch, and he continued to kiss her as he slid his hands around to her flat abdomen. He slowly worked his way up to the lace cups of her bra.

He traced his thumb over one pebbled nipple, and she

kissed him with growing ardor, meeting the thrust of his tongue. He felt her hands at the front of his shirt and smiled against her mouth when he realized she'd popped one of the buttons off in her zeal to get him out of his clothes.

Luckily, he had no buttons to contend with. All he had to do was draw back for the ten seconds it took to whisk the autumn-colored sweater over her head. She sat on the counter, a temptress in her unlikely attire of barely-there black bra and black skirt that revealed nothing yet seduced the imagination.

"That's a good look for you," he said, his husky tone probably a truer indication of his desire than the compliment.

Running a hand over his chest, she lightly raked her fingernails against his skin. "Is this still part of your apology for not listening? If so, feel free to tune out as often as you'd like."

Under other circumstances, he might have laughed, but at the moment he was too aroused. Piper dropped her hands to his waist, slipping her fingers through the belt loops of his pants, tugging him closer. Then she moved to the zipper, lowering it millimeter by millimeter, leaving him hard and aching for her touch.

Josh stepped out of his pants, kicking them across her tile floor. She scooted closer to the edge of the counter, trying to press her body to his. A whimper of frustration escaped her when the narrow skirt got in her way. He bunched up the fabric, caressing the satiny skin of her thighs as he did so, and stood between her legs.

The tiny black lace panties she wore nearly sent him over the edge. It wasn't just the lingerie that affected him, or even the surprise of finding them on a woman who normally didn't indulge in lacy, feminine clothes. The real turn-on was how well he understood her, how right he'd been about her. He'd realized months ago that beneath the genderless pantsuits and supposed disinterest in sex existed a fiercely passionate woman, a woman Piper didn't let others see. But she'd chosen to reveal that side of herself to him.

"Nice," he told her, tracing the lacy edges of the panties, brushing his hand over the short curls concealed underneath. "But I hope you don't mind if I take them off."

She wiggled her hips to accommodate him. "If you insist. But the panties and the bra are really a matching set...."

"I see what you mean." He reached up to flick open the delicate front clasp, filling his hands with her.

She was so perfect, so responsive. He stroked one nipple, watching her face as he rolled the bud between his fingers. When she arched her back and offered herself up to him, he lowered his head to her breasts, paying lavish homage with his mouth

"Did you want to move this to your bedroom?" Because if she did, they should head that direction *now*.

She locked her legs around his waist, as though trying to prevent him from going anywhere. As if there was anyplace he'd rather be. "No. Here."

The sexy rasp of need in her voice made him almost lose it right there. He grabbed a condom from his pants pocket and started to put it on. Brushing his hand away, she unrolled the latex over him slowly, squeezing just hard enough with her fingers for his breath to catch.

Grasping her hips, he sheathed himself inside her. Piper pulled back slightly, angling her body so that he slid in deeper. Her gaze met his, her eyes filled with love and rapture he couldn't believe he deserved. Couldn't believe would last. He'd never felt so connected to anyone, and the intensity overwhelmed him. Emotions he never let himself feel rushed at him, and, for a fraction of a second, panic eclipsed the ecstasy of being inside her.

He closed his eyes, trying to find a safe distance. He wanted to ignore the emotion and the risk it represented, and lose himself in their physical connection, use the incredible sensations to shut out his fear and pretend that his heart wasn't hers for the breaking. Wordlessly apologizing to her with his body, he made love to her with slow smooth strokes that took all of his self-control and wrung pleasure-drenched moans from her.

She gasped. "That is s-so good."

He rocked his hips, Piper hot and tight around him. "You mean right...there?"

"Mmm, yes. *Right* there."

Another motion of his hips caused another soft gasp, this one slightly louder and more ragged. Wanting to make this perfect for her, wanting to atone for that piece of himself he was deliberately withholding, he moved inside her, holding back until her nails dug into his skin. She shattered around him, her muscles working to push him to his own shuddering release.

Her head rested against his chest, her body rising and falling as she tried to catch her breath. He hugged her to him, his own breathing too labored for him to form words. Even if he'd been able to speak, he knew he wouldn't voice the thought screaming in his head: *I love you.*

He hadn't said it in years—not since he'd forced himself to tell Dana as she was leaving. But it had been too little, too late, and she hadn't even turned to acknowledge the stricken admission. She'd simply walked out the door, out of his life, and he'd sworn then and there never to be hurt like that again.

It wasn't the memory that hurt so much as the realization that his love for Piper was harder won and ran much deeper. The pain of losing her would be excruciating. So he choked on the words he knew she deserved to hear.

Chapter Thirteen

Four days later, they'd made love in Piper's kitchen, her shower and, just now, rather athletically, on the floor of her living room. They'd made love in her bed last night, after already having sex bent over her desk, but Josh hadn't been able to sleep. And she hadn't complained when he'd awakened her.

Now he tilted his head back from his seated position on the floor, sprawled against the base of the sofa. Piper sat above him on the couch, wearing his shirt. "You know, we should really try to make it to the bed more often," he stated.

"I know what you mean." She leaned down to kiss him, laughter in her voice. "I think I have rug burn…but it was worth it."

The sex had been incredible—when wasn't it?—but it was the only time he felt at peace, able to push his doubts away. In the week since they'd returned from Rebecca, he'd had some of the most intensely wonderful moments he'd ever experienced. But also some of the scariest, and the anxiety was wearing on him. Josh lived in a constant state of waiting for the other shoe to drop.

Today, he'd tried to prove something to himself. He'd survived plenty of other goodbyes in his life, and if he and Piper ever parted ways, he could survive that, too. To illustrate the point, he'd avoided her all day, told himself that it wouldn't kill him to go without talking to her, touching her. He could be fine without her.

He'd noticed her questioning glances at work, but she hadn't approached him. She'd given him his space, which had made staying away that much more difficult. He'd tried to appease his conscience, and his need to reach out to her, by sending her an email that said he was swamped and would be staying late, but would love to see her over the weekend.

Then he'd blown the whole thing by knocking on her front door an hour ago and asking if she wanted to watch the last half of a football game with him. Clearly, his little "self demonstration" had been a complete failure.

He reached up now, running his hand over the smooth muscle of her calf. "I'm sorry I…was so busy today."

"No problem." But her smile didn't reach her eyes, and she quickly looked away, glancing at the ignored television set, where football had been replaced by a syndicated sitcom. "Sorry you didn't get to see any of the game."

"Really?"

This time the smile was genuine. "No. Not really. Given the same situation, I'd seduce you all over again. Besides, football's not my thing. Just a way to kill time until baseball season."

Next spring. Thinking that far into the future caused a dizzying nausea.

She entwined one arm around his neck and tousled his

hair with her other hand. "Hey, if you'd like to give that bed thing another shot—"

"As tempting as that sounds, I can't stay." Holding her last night should have been bliss. Instead it had been hours of tossing and turning and second-guessing. Besides, he shouldn't have come down here tonight at all.

"Oh. You're going?"

He could tell by her tone that she was hurt, and annoyance crept into his voice—only she wasn't the one with whom he was annoyed. "I stayed last night."

"I know. I just…"

"I'm still way behind. My sideline stuff doesn't magically take care of itself."

She rose from the sofa. "There's no reason to get condescending. Hold on. I'll go change so you can have your shirt back."

Regret bubbled up in him. "I don't have to leave this second."

"No, you should. The sooner you tackle that work, the sooner you'll get caught up." But her blue-green eyes said she wanted him gone. He'd hurt her, and she was ready for him to be on his way.

"Unless your plan isn't to get caught up," she muttered as she walked toward her bedroom.

"What's that supposed to mean?"

She paused at the doorway, turning to glare at him. "You think I haven't noticed how busy you suddenly are at work?"

"I've always been busy at work. So have you."

"Exactly. And yet we've still had time to talk for a minute in the break room or grab lunch together. You've been ignoring me, Josh."

The knot of fear in his chest tightened. Four days, and she was already unhappy. Fragments of conversations with Dana came back to him: *"I can't reach you, Josh...I need someone who's really there for me..."* Had it started so soon?

"What about this? Just now?" He spread his arms to encompass her living room, where items of clothing were still strewn about.

"You mean dropping by to have sex? Isn't that what's referred to as a booty call?"

The disdain in her voice sliced through him, and he felt cornered. "I didn't hear you complaining a few minutes ago."

She opened her mouth, but then stopped, holding up a hand. "You know what? Let's not do this. It's been a long day, and we were both busy. I'm glad you came by, Josh, I am. And I don't want to fight."

"Me, neither. Piper—"

Shaking her head, she interrupted, "Just give me a second to change. It's okay." But she didn't turn away quickly enough to hide the bright sheen of unshed tears.

And he couldn't help noticing that, even though they'd spent most of their time this week naked together, when she went into her room to change, she firmly closed the door behind her.

I've had it. Piper stomped into the gym locker room the following Wednesday morning, knowing that she had to talk to someone or she was going to lose her mind. She hung her work clothes from the hook inside her locker, then slammed the door hard enough that the resulting metallic clang reverberated throughout the room.

She'd seen Gina last week, but for some reason hadn't shared any of the details of what had happened between her and Josh. Instead, she'd simply told her friend that she'd reached a new understanding with her family and would probably be seeing them again at Christmas. At the time, Piper had made excuses for her silence, such as it would be embarrassing to tell Gina that she and Josh were having a red-hot affair after all the times she'd insisted they were just friends, or the relationship was so new that she was savoring it before telling her friends. But the truth she could no longer escape was that she hadn't told Gina anything about Josh last week because, deep down, Piper knew things were wrong between them.

On the surface, the situation looked pretty good. In Rebecca, she had concluded that she loved the man and wanted more than platonic friendship. They'd taken their relationship to a new level, and had been spending a lot of their free time having phenomenal sex. Although twice now he'd left shortly after the phenomenal sex.

Where was the problem? She'd never been clingy, and she wasn't about to start now. She wasn't the type of woman who *had* to have a man stay over. But she couldn't ignore her gut feeling that Josh was the type of man who had to leave. In reality, while their lovemaking might be the stuff of erotic legend, she didn't want a legend. She wanted her friend back.

It was an odd paradox, but the closer they got physically, the more she felt she was losing him emotionally. It seemed as though they barely talked, and she missed that. She supposed she could have passed on the sex at any given time, but she wanted it as much as he did. She just wanted more with it. Was she being too greedy? Too hypersensitive? She needed a second opinion.

Ready to talk to Gina about the problem, Piper left the locker room, hoping her friend was already upstairs. She took the carpeted steps two at a time, the loud, familiar cadence of weight machines in use not as soothing today as she normally found it. Though the main workout floor was hardly deserted, there weren't enough people that Piper had trouble spotting her friend. Eye-catching in a bright red *I Object* T-shirt, Gina stood near the water fountain smiling at a dark-haired man who looked as if he was trying his best to overcome any objections she might have.

A pang of guilt jabbed Piper. Though not intentionally condescending, she had never understood Gina's yearning to find someone. Now she did. Piper had been saying for months that she was content with her life—her job, her family, her friends—but she'd realized that she wanted more than contentment. She wanted passion and laughter, someone who could share her triumphs and defeats.

No, not just "someone." She wanted Josh. She didn't know who Gina wanted, but Piper hoped her friend found him.

Gina glanced up with an acknowledging smile as Piper approached. "Hey, lady."

"Hey." When her friend's dark-haired admirer returned to his workout, Piper added, "Am I glad to see you this morning. If you don't mind listening, I could use a friendly ear."

"Don't mind at all. Makes it worth my showing up. I almost slept in this morning. Some days I just can't get excited about the thought of hitting the treadmill."

Suddenly Piper felt exactly the same way. She'd told herself that maybe exercise would help clear her mind, but that was ridiculous. She and Josh had already shared enough aerobic activity this week to elevate her to a Zen-like state of clarity.

"What if we ditch our normal disciplined routine?" Piper suggested rebelliously. "Let's get out of here, and I'll buy you a doughnut."

"Doughnuts over discipline?" For a moment, Gina

seemed as though she might lay her palm against Piper's forehead to check for fever and delirium. "Since when do *you* do what's tempting instead of sensible?"

Piper bit her lip. "Funny you should ask."

"I can't believe it." It was probably the eighth time Gina had restated that sentiment since Piper had filled her in, but who was counting? "I really can't believe you did it."

"Yeah, I'm sensing that." Piper leaned back in her U-shaped, overstuffed chair, thinking that the furniture in the coffeehouse might be even more comfortable than what she had at home. "Just let me know when you get past the whole Josh-and-Piper-slept-together part, so we can figure out what I should do."

"I might never get past that part!" Gina brushed powdered sugar off her hands, still shaking her head in disbelief. "Do you know how many times you lectured me about you and Josh just being friends?"

"I didn't lecture, exactly." People who'd never met Piper's mom had no idea what a lecture was. "Besides, we really *were* just friends. But that, um, changed over the weekend." Into what, she didn't know.

"At least now I understand why you refused to set me up with the guy."

"No, that's not—" Piper broke off, realizing Gina was kidding. Mostly. "All right. I get it. You told me so. I've been denying the truth to myself and everyone else, yada yada. You were right, I was wrong. But now what?"

Gina's smirk faded into a more empathetic expression. "You feel like he's using you for sex?"

No, that wasn't it.

Was it?

"It's more that I feel like…when we're not having sex,

he's shutting me out. But I don't know how to say any-thing to him without sounding like one of those needy women whining about how she wants more attention. Especially when I think he's trying. Considering Josh's track record, this could be the most serious relationship he's ever had. But that track record makes me nervous. I half expect to come home to a note on my door telling me he's joined the French Foreign Legion or something."

"You think he'll find an excuse to leave."

He had with every woman before her. Piper would love to think she was different, special, but had he given her any real reason to believe this would last? And did she even want it to last if she couldn't have Josh both as her friend and as her lover?

"I never considered myself insecure," She said, "but how can I feel good about this when we're actually less close than we were before?" She lowered her voice just in case the background sounds of chatting customers, per-colating coffee and rustling newspapers weren't enough to blot out the finer points of her sex life. "It seems like we traded our friendship for kick-ass orgasms. And the truth is, the orgasms aren't worth it."

"Easy for you to say. Those of us who can't remember our last 'kick-ass orgasm' might feel differently." When Piper didn't respond, Gina sighed. "I hate to see you upset, but I'm not sure I can help."

"That's okay. Just talking about it has been helpful. I'm glad I told you." It had certainly been easier to admit her concerns to Gina than it would be to spell them out for Josh. Piper was afraid he wouldn't want to hear them.

But if he was too reticent to voice his feelings for her, assuming he had some, and she was too aware of the fate of his ex-lovers to broach the subject, what would keep their relationship from deteriorating to nothing more than cheap sex?

"I can't believe you made it this long without telling me the two of you have been hitting the sheets," Gina said. "I don't know whether I'm annoyed or impressed at your ability to keep a secret. But, Piper, it's not me you need to be having this conversation with. You've got to talk to *him*."

"I was afraid you were gonna say that."

As soon as Josh opened his door Friday evening, he understood that the moment he'd dreaded had arrived. One glance at Piper's face told him everything. She looked like a woman trying hard to appear nonchalant about something that was vitally important to her. And she looked unhappy. He wasn't making her happy.

Even back in Rebecca, he'd known he wasn't the right guy, couldn't give her what she needed, but he'd foolishly hoped he could have everything, anyway.

"Hey, Piper. Come on in."

"Thanks." She flashed an unconvincing smile, and he thought about what a pair of actors they were. First with her family. Now, miserably, with each other.

Glancing away from her fake smile, he told himself he was no better. His voice was full of forced cheer. "I just got home from the office." He jerked his thumb over his shoulder to indicate the kitchen. "I was about to get a drink. You want one?"

"Sure. If it's no trouble."

Right. Because pouring a second soft drink was going to be the difficult part of this confrontation.

In the sanctuary of his kitchen, he clenched his fists, fighting the rising tide of impotent rage, the recognition that once again he was losing someone. He hadn't seen the end coming quite so clearly with Dana, but he'd acquired more practice in the last several years. His stomach rolled over, and he felt as though he was sixteen again, just hearing the news that the Wakefields were going to Europe. Without him. Well, he wasn't a boy anymore. If he was losing Piper, he would take it like a man.

He walked back into the living room, where she waited on the sofa. "Here you go." Settling his weight on the arm of the couch, he handed her one of the cold drinks.

"Thanks." She took the glass, but immediately placed it on the scuffed-up coffee table, an antique he'd bought at a garage sale with plans to restore. It was actually quite a nice piece, given some work, but people so easily threw away belongings.

"What brings you up here?" His edgy mood made his voice abrupt. His words weren't rude, but his tone was chilly. Already detached.

Her eyes widened, and she drew back almost imperceptibly. Some would have missed the slight motion, but Josh was already watching for signs of withdrawal. "Do I need a reason to come see you? Although, now that I think of it, we don't spend any time in your apartment."

It was easier to be in someone else's. Easier to leave someone else's. "No, you don't need a reason. But I think you have one."

"Fair enough." She wouldn't meet his gaze. "I wanted to talk to you. You remember when I asked you what we were going to do about work?" She looked up then, but he had trouble reading her expression. Or maybe he didn't want to understand what he saw there. "You suggested we wait and see if we were going to develop into anything."

"Are you upset about that? I told you it didn't come out the way—"

"Josh. I'm not here to pressure you or guilt you or complain about the way you worded something. You don't even have to tell me right now if we've 'developed.' But when do you think you might know?" She rose, fidgeting nervously with her hands. "I didn't like ignoring you at work these last two weeks and feeling as if we're having some illicit, sordid relationship."

He wanted to believe it was only the work situation bothering her, but he'd already met his quota of self-delusion for the month. "You say you're not pressuring me, but you sound like you're hinting at some sort of ultimatum." The best defense was a good offense.

Her angry glare wasn't as worrisome as the resigned expression that almost immediately replaced it. "You know what? Maybe I am. It's not fair to you to give you a timetable or try to force some kind of commitment, I admit. But it's not fair to me to keep going on like this."

He wanted to say "Like what?" but, dammit, he knew.

He'd been the one to close his eyes when she was staring deep into his because it had been the only way he knew to save his soul. He'd been the one who barely spoke to her at work, telling himself that it was professionalism, not fear. He'd been the one who left her after making love because holding her while she slept would just cement how much he loved her, something he dared not voice because he wanted to defend whatever tiny part of his heart could still be protected from her leaving.

She deserved more. So had the other women who had broken up with him for this very thing. *You never should have touched her,* he reminded himself. *You knew better.* She should be with a man capable of sharing his whole heart with someone. Josh feared he'd lost that ability somewhere between foster homes four and five. Or maybe five and six. Who could keep count? *Do the right thing and let her go.*

He was going to lose her, but he wasn't going to negotiate with her the way he had with Dana, attempting to find inside him whatever it was she wanted. Even if he said the right words today, they were only words. They wouldn't change who he was or what she needed. It was best if she left now, before this hurt him, either of them, any worse.

"I agree with you, Piper."

"You do?" She blinked, looking surprised and hopeful.

"We *shouldn't* go on like this. It isn't fair to you."

"Ah." The cautious hope flickered, and a light went out in her eyes. The quick understanding in her disappointed expression was testament to how well she knew him. "You mean we shouldn't go on, period."

"It's not that I don't...care about you."

"Oh, God, this is actually it, isn't it—the Josh Weber goodbye? The it's-not-you, it's-me, you-deserve-more, let's-still-be-friends brush-off you give all your women?"

Anger slammed through him, not at her but with himself. All his women? Piper thought she was one of a crowd, and it was his own fault she didn't know that he'd never loved anyone this way, probably never would again. But how could he convince her she was special, when he couldn't convince himself that he deserved her?

"Yeah. I guess that's my goodbye," he told her. A *real* goodbye. Despite the let's-still-be-friends comment she'd hurled at him, he couldn't stomach a superficial friendship like those he maintained with some former lovers. Not with Piper.

"You're unbelievable." She looked enraged, but hadn't made any move toward the door yet. Didn't she know the adhesive bandage approach was best—just rip it off fast and hard? Taking one's time only increased the pain. "I don't even rate my own special brush-off? After the week we had? No points for creative positions or being extra limber?"

Her furious tone didn't keep him from seeing the calculating gleam in her eye. By reducing what they'd shared to crass terms, she'd given him the chance to protest that it had meant more.

He needed her to get out. Now. Before he begged her not to leave him. Pleading hadn't stopped people from abandoning him before, and he was too old to try it now.

"It was great sex, Piper, but it was just sex."

He almost flinched for her. Josh had *never* said something like that to a woman, not even when it had just been sex.

Piper opened her mouth, probably to call him a liar or a bastard, both of which would have been true. But then she silently pivoted…and left him.

Chapter Fourteen

Just sex? Piper wanted to kick the crap out of someone—Josh, for instance—but figured she'd make do with a punishing exercise regimen instead. So she returned to her gym's weight room for the second time that day. Though rusty on breakup procedures, she guessed she was due to be back home now, crying her eyes out and stuffing her face with Chocomel bars. She preferred embracing her anger.

Stay mad as long as possible, she instructed herself while she increased the weight resistance for her leg curls. Because as soon as the anger started to taper off, the pain would probably obliterate her.

Just sex. The words didn't bother her. After studying him very closely, plus the emotions he'd tried to keep out of his expression, she was certain Josh knew exactly how special their connection had been. She suspected that very connection was why the king of cordial separations had ditched his usual finesse in favor of finality.

No, what bothered her was that he'd deliberately run her off, rid himself of another woman, another relationship. A conversation she'd had with Gina rang silently in Piper's ears.

"He's hell on female hearts. You know how many women I've seen him break up with?"

"Maybe because he hasn't met the right one?"

"Won't matter. Josh isn't going to let himself find the right one."

And Piper had been the right woman for him, she was sure of it. Just as he was the perfect man for her. *That's* why this hurt so much, not because of something stupid he'd said to get her to leave. After the childhood he'd had, one would think he'd grab at the chance for happiness. But she couldn't force him to accept her love if he was too scared to give them a chance.

He wasn't the only one afraid, her conscience reminded her. Piper had been walking on eggshells since the first time they'd made love. She'd wanted to talk but had found excuses to avoid it so that she wouldn't lose him.

My fear was justified. I did lose him.

Yeah. But if she looked at it that way, his fear was justified, too. He'd lost her.

That was his own damn fault...wasn't it?

He'd pushed her away, sure, but she'd let herself be pushed. Piper slowly brought her legs back into the starting position and leaned against the padded, black vinyl seat, confusion condensing into an excruciating headache behind her eyes. After a moment, she realized that the pounding anger that had driven her to the gym had receded. Time for those Chocomels now, she figured as she stood.

Maybe she'd call Daphne and try to sort this out. But by the time Piper reached the locker room to retrieve her purse, she'd discounted that idea. Daph might have good advice, but Piper was too miserable to talk to half of a happily married couple right now. Gina, then? No, Gina was a great listener, but as she'd pragmatically pointed out last time they'd spoken, she couldn't actually do anything about the situation.

Come to think of it, Piper had been entirely too willing to let someone else solve her problems. She'd put off instigating a real conversation with Josh, and even this evening when she'd finally gone to see him....

"Oh, hell!" Her exclamation of self-disgust drew curious stares from the employees at the check-in desk, but she ignored them as she walked out into the cool evening air.

She'd gone upstairs today looking for a way to get Josh to admit to his feelings, to connect with her emotionally, but she'd guarded her own feelings. The man had lost everyone he'd ever loved, starting with his parents—a relationship most people, including Piper, took for granted. Josh couldn't take love for granted, couldn't let himself trust it.

I should have given him a reason to trust.

Maybe she still could. It would have to be convincing, though. She couldn't just call him up and tell him she loved him and wasn't going anywhere. He wouldn't believe her.

She needed to do something that would make a statement he could have faith in. Something that would prove she wasn't so easy to get rid of, that she was sticking around. Something big.

Piper took a deep breath, raising her fist to knock on the door of her boss's office. At just after seven-thirty on Monday morning, none of the other draftsmen had come in yet. Maria was here already to brew coffee and read the paper in the empty break room, but mostly, the place was deserted. It was a well-known fact, though, that Callahan, the founder of C, K and M, often put in early hours and was even here most weekends. Piper wanted to talk to the man before anyone else got to work.

"Come in." Callahan's gravelly voice was booming even through the door. She supposed someone who didn't know him might find him intimidating, but he'd always been her favorite of the three partners.

"Good morning, Mr. Callahan," she said as she entered the office.

"Piper." His bushy eyebrows arched upward. "You're here early today."

"I needed to speak to you, sir." She still couldn't believe she was quitting her job over a man. It was the complete opposite of what anyone would expect from her, but that's exactly why she thought it might penetrate Josh's thick skull. Or the thick barriers around his heart. She loved him enough to leave C, K and M, solving the fraternization problem, if she could convince him to fraternize again.

And if she couldn't…well, working here and having him banter meaninglessly with her the way he did with Nancy from Grazzio's would be unbearable.

"Please, have a seat," Callahan invited.

She glanced at the two straight-back chairs available, but she was feeling too restless and edgy to sit down. "Actually, if you don't mind, I'll stand. Might make this easier. Sir, I've enjoyed working for C, K and M." A what-the-hell-I'm-quitting-anyway brand of honesty allowed her to add, "Well, working for you, at least. But I've given this a lot of thought over the weekend, and I'm afraid I have to turn in my resignation."

He leaned back in his office chair, regarding her silently for a long moment. Nervousness made her feel a little shaky, and she regretted not having sat down.

"I see. I'm sorry to hear it, of course. Do you mind if I ask if this is the result of anything one of the partners has done, or could have done differently?"

"No, sir. I'm leaving for personal reasons."

"That's a shame. You're one of my most promising employees...and C, K and M will be shorthanded now that Mr. Weber has quit, too."

Well, that did it. She sank into the nearest chair. "Josh quit? When?" Had he arrived at six-thirty instead of seven o'clock? After mulling this over for the past two days, she'd thought she'd calculated her exit perfectly.

By the time Josh arrived at work today, she figured she could tell him she was leaving and it would be too late for him to talk her out of it. She could also tell him that her feelings weren't going to disappear because of an argument they'd had in his apartment, that he should call her if he was ever ready for a real relationship and the emotional risks it entailed.

Only Josh wasn't coming into work today, she realized.

"He stopped by on Saturday," Callahan said. "Told me that those sideline jobs have grown plentiful enough that he's going into business for himself, and he hopes there aren't hard feelings. I hate to lose him, but I remember what it was like to want to make a name for myself. His workload must be impressive, because he made his resignation effective immediately."

She knew Callahan was studying her, but she couldn't lift her gaze from her lap. It felt too heavy. Everything felt heavy. "I suppose he thought a clean, quick break would be best."

Josh had run away. From her, from what they could have together. It wasn't the same thing she was trying to do at all. She half wondered if he was making plans to move out of their building. *Why did I think I could make this work?* On the plus side, he'd never cared enough to run from previous relationships. He'd been very casual about his breakups until now. She felt herself smile for the first time that morning.

"Well, I'm happy to give you two weeks," she told Callahan. In fact, it gave her more time to make phone calls. She'd picked up business cards and interested contacts over the years and had plenty in savings to get by for a couple of months, but it wasn't as though she had a brand-new job lined up yet. "After that, I can wrap up a few things from home if you need it."

"Can I make a counteroffer, Piper? Why don't you take a personal day, maybe two, and reconsider? As a favor to me. You started out at the appropriate level here at C, K and M, but maybe we didn't advance you as quickly as we should have. Your review is coming up soon, or was, and I had planned to increase your leadership responsibilities then. Perhaps I should have done so before now."

He was making her a project manager. She'd wanted this, but she wanted Josh to share it with even more. "I… my quitting was not an attempt to force your hand, sir."

He nodded. "I understand."

She rather feared he did, and tears pricked her eyes, making her blink. All this energy she'd put into her job, all the times she'd insisted she didn't need or want a man in her life. No wonder they said be careful what you wished for.

In the end, Piper did accept a personal day to rethink her decision. Given what she'd learned about Josh in her meeting with Callahan, it made considerably less sense to leave C, K and M, but she could use some time to clear her head. Driving back to her apartment, she reevaluated her other plans, as well. Should she still try to convince Josh of her feelings?

Yes. If she didn't, she'd be letting fear control her as much as he was letting his past control him. She'd talk to him, but not today. It wasn't even 9:00 a.m. when she stepped back inside her apartment, but she already felt as if she'd been put through the emotional wringer.

After taking a restless nap on her couch and watching some really bad afternoon television, which almost made her feel better about her own life, Piper decided she'd wallowed enough. Since she had some unexpected free time, she might as well use it for something besides looking around her apartment at the places she and Josh had made love during their brief but intense relationship.

Silencing a distraught soap opera grande dame with a well-aimed remote control, Piper rose from the sofa. Laundry was a top priority; she'd been going through workout clothes faster than normal lately. Then maybe a trip to the grocery store. She was also going through a lot of Chocomel bars since she'd been home. After she'd gathered a hamper of clothes and a pen and pad to make a shopping list, she walked out to the elevator in her socks.

As she approached the laundry room, she heard the rhythmic rumble of a dryer. She turned the corner, and her heart stopped at the sight of Josh sitting in one of the blue plastic chairs. His shoulders were slumped, and he was running a hand through his hair. Not for the first time, judging by the unkempt furrows in the dark mass. Yet he still looked heartbreakingly sexy, she thought, her eyes sliding from his strong, achingly familiar profile to his leanly muscled torso and the denim-clad legs stretched out in front of him.

He straightened as soon as he realized he wasn't alone, turning toward her with a friendly smile that was replaced by a much more sincere look of shock when he saw it was her. "Piper! What are you doing here?"

Josh couldn't believe his eyes. He'd been thinking of her nonstop since he'd last seen her Friday evening, and now she was standing there as though she'd simply walked out of his imagination. Except in not one of his mental images had she been balancing a white clothes hamper against her hip and scowling at him.

"You thought I'd be at the office." She made it an accusation.

"Well, it is the middle of the day on Monday." Which was precisely why he was here now. He'd solved the seeing-her-at-work problem, and figured with some effort to avoid her in the building, they could both live in the same apartment complex for a while. "Why *aren't* you at the office?"

She stepped forward, dropping her hamper on a low table with an angry thud. "Same reason you aren't. I quit."

Regret pooled inside him, churning in his stomach. Not only had he been a jerk, he'd screwed up her job for her. "You shouldn't quit. You don't need to quit. I—"

"Beat me to it. Yeah, that's what Callahan said. I don't know why I was even surprised. You leave relationships, you leave my apartment, you leave the company."

He managed not to flinch at the reproach in her voice. "All for the best."

She snorted, hands planted on her hips. Any other time, her feisty demeanor might have made him smile.

"It's not for the best. It's nuts, you know that? This could be great. *We* could be great."

For a second, he was too stunned to say anything. He'd hardly expected her to speak to him again, much less argue in favor of their being together. Was there a chance she still wanted him, a chance he could give her what she needed if she did take him back? He squelched the unexpected hope before it could hurt someone.

But he couldn't squelch Piper. She narrowed her eyes and made a decidedly unromantic vow of affection. "I love you, you idiot, and I'm pretty sure you could love me if you'd stop screwing this up for both of us."

I love you. Though some part of him had known how she felt, her declaration rattled him nonetheless. He'd known Piper didn't take sex or their friendship lightly, and while maybe their night in Rebecca could have "just happened," she never would have continued with their fling if she didn't have very strong feelings for him. But it had been a long time since anyone had actually said those words to him, even longer since someone had truly meant it.

She was right about his feelings, too. He'd probably started falling in love with her the night he'd moved into his apartment and had encountered her in this very room, dancing to a rock ballad on the radio while her darks were on spin cycle.

"Piper, I—"

"No." She held up her hand. "I let you say things that weren't true on Friday, let you push me away, and I'm not giving you that chance again. You're not pushing me away now, Josh. I'm leaving of my own accord so that you don't do the guy thing and say more stupid stuff you can't take back. Just think about this, okay? Think about what it would be like to finally have something that lasts with someone who loves you."

Without even pausing to collect her clothes, she pivoted and marched toward the doorway, and he knew what her hurry was. He'd heard the tremor in her voice and hated himself for any tears he'd caused her. But the shakiness with which she'd spoken didn't mask her conviction in what she was saying, a bone-deep certainty he envied. He didn't think he'd ever let himself be sure of anything he couldn't control, never let himself trust in an emotion that completely.

She'd offered him love that lasted. Was it really within his grasp?

That dark voice inside started to tell him no, of course not, but Josh shut it out. He'd shied away from hope and clung to fear, and where had it landed him? Alone and miserable without Piper. A future of missing her stretched before him.

You couldn't do anything about your past. But you can *do something about this.*

And if he didn't, then she was right. He was an idiot.

Josh stepped off the elevator and into the hall, but the walk to Piper's front door had never seemed so long. It was almost comical how hard his heart was thudding against his chest. How many times over the last two years had he traced this very same path? She'd told him a mere hour ago that she loved him, so why was he still so scared?

Because maybe she's come to her senses by now.

He ignored the pessimistic thought and knocked on her door. "Piper, it's me, Josh."

After the way he'd behaved, he wouldn't have blamed her if she refused to answer. If all else failed, maybe he could ransom the hamper full of clothes she'd abandoned in exchange for her hearing him out. But she opened the door, swinging it wide with a wary expression on her face. She was dressed the same as she had been earlier—ponytail, sweatpants, T-shirt. Somehow the contrast between the nondescript clothes and her own beauty made her even sexier than if she'd been wearing something obviously attractive.

"You really are beautiful." That hadn't been how he'd planned to start the conversation, but how could he go wrong with an opener like that?

"If you came down here with empty flattery, I'll break a vase over your head." But she sounded more uncertain than her bravado implied. She was trying to decide why he was here at all, and not quite allowing herself to hope. He knew the feeling.

"There was nothing empty about what I said. Can I come in?" He held out the green-cellophane-wrapped cone. "I would have been here sooner, but I wanted to get you these."

She glanced at the clusters of baby breath peeking out. "Flowers?"

"Not exactly."

She looked down inside the wrapping and laughed. He wondered if she'd ever seen a Chocomel bouquet before. It had certainly been a first for the surprised florist.

"I figured it was a good start toward groveling for forgiveness." His body tightened as he recalled playfully seeking her forgiveness on their first date, making love with her in her kitchen. He'd like nothing more than the physical reassurance of holding her close and making love now. But they had to talk first.

Glancing up from the bouquet to meet his gaze, Piper smiled. "I love you."

He didn't think he'd ever get used to hearing it. "I—" Paralyzing fear gripped him, but it wasn't as strong as what he felt for this woman. The words had gone unsaid too long. "I love you, too."

Her expression blossomed, full of tenderness and radiant joy. The Chocomels fell to the floor as she moved forward to wrap her arms around his neck. She pulled him closer and proceeded to kiss him breathless.

Stepping inside her apartment without breaking the kiss, Josh nudged the door closed behind them. He nipped her lower lip, but then angled his head away from hers. "We have to stop."

"Maybe we should take a vote on that," Piper told him, nibbling the side of his neck.

Need trembled through him. She had to know it was about more than just the sex, though. "We can vote just as soon as we've talked."

Her arms slid to her sides as she glanced up at him in shock. "Really? You'd rather talk?" She didn't look so much disappointed as optimistic, and he was reminded of how badly he'd botched things up during the past week. He was also reminded of everything he wanted. Love. Commitment. All the things he'd been afraid to hope for, but that now seemed possible with Piper beside him.

"Yeah. You deserve to know how you make me feel." He took her hand, leading her over to the sofa, determined to get it all out before he regressed. "I know you just needed someone for the weekend, Piper, but... You know better than anyone that I wasn't looking for someone to share my life, but over the last two years, you've become so important to me. I can't really imagine you not being there in the years to come. Actually, I *can*. That's what I've been doing the last few days, and it's been awful."

She squeezed his hand, but didn't say anything, and

he took the silent encouragement to go on. He wanted to be with her, but she should know what she was getting.

"I love you—I can't believe how good it feels to finally say it—but I'm probably going to screw this up in dozens of ways."

Her voice was thick with unshed tears. "Then you'll make it up to me in dozens more. Josh, I know you. You're kind and giving and passionate. You have more capacity to love than you think."

Her faith in him was humbling. He framed his face with her hands. "Maybe you just bring it out in me." He leaned forward to kiss her, his body raging with the need to show her physically how much he cherished her. But he stopped himself, worried about one other thing and determined not to rush into sex just because it was so much easier than talking. "I'll support your decision if it's what you really want to do, but I wish you hadn't quit your job. Not because of me."

He'd quit for the wrong reasons initially, but the fact of the matter was he looked forward to the challenge of building his own business. Piper, on the other hand, had been determined to prove herself at C, K and M and had done good work there. He hated that she'd left.

Leaning forward, she brushed her lips against his in what was less a kiss and more a promise of things to come. "Don't worry. Callahan and I are negotiating for me to return. I might even get a raise out of this, so you did me a favor." She shot Josh a sheepish smile. "Speaking of past favors… You're prepared to deal with my family in order to be with me?"

"I love your nutty relatives almost as much as I love you." He touched his tongue to the soft spot just below her earlobe, and she shivered. "You think you can handle my not being used to sharing my emotions with anyone?"

"Don't worry. You'll get better with practice, and I'm not giving up on you."

Not giving up on him. God, he loved her.

She ran her hand underneath the hem of his shirt, her fingers skimming up his chest, resting near his heart. "You're okay with the fact that I can barely cook anything besides chocolate chip pancakes and lasagna?"

"That's what takeout's for," he answered, loving her touch against his skin. "You should be aware, I'm pretty certain I snore."

"Worth it to have you in my bed," she assured him.

He pulled her closer, lifting her from the couch to straddle his lap, groaning at the friction of her sweet, sexy weight atop him. Their mouths met, and he'd never been more hungry for a kiss, wanting to greedily lap up every joy this woman could bring to his life. Wanting to give her the same joy.

She pulled back slightly, her smile as full of mischief as it was adoration. "So would *now* be a good time to vote on whether or not we should make love? All in favor—"

"Aye."

* * * * *

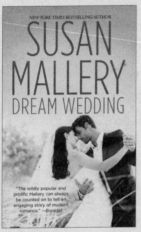

New York Times and USA TODAY bestselling author

KRISTAN HIGGINS

Turning thirty has its ups and downs...

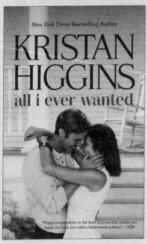

For Callie Grey, coming to grips with her age means facing the fact that her boyfriend-slash-boss is way overdue with a marriage proposal. And that she's way off track, because Mark has suddenly announced his engagement to the company's new Miss Perfect. If that isn't bad enough, her mom decides to throw her a Big Three-Oh birthday bash…in the family funeral home.

Bad goes to worse when Callie stirs up a relationship with the town's single—yet not so warm and fuzzy—veterinarian, in order to flag Mark's attention. So what if Ian McFarland is more comfortable with animals? So what if he's formal, orderly and just a bit tense? Friendly, fun-loving and spontaneous Callie decides it's time for Ian to get a personality makeover. But, dang—if he doesn't shock the heck out of her, she might actually fall for Georgebury, Vermont's, unlikeliest eligible bachelor….

Available wherever books are sold!

Be sure to connect with us at:
Harlequin.com/Newsletters
Facebook.com/HarlequinBooks
Twitter.com/HarlequinBooks

Coming next month from reader-favorite author
Teresa Southwick

FINDING A FAMILY...AND FOREVER?

Kidnapped as a child, Emma Robbins heads to
Blackwater Lake to find her birth family.
In the process, she becomes the nanny to
Dr. Justin Flint's young son. The handsome
widower is unwillingly attracted to the lovely
newcomer, who loves the boy as her own, but
secrets and lies may undermine the family they
begin to build.

*Look for the latest in the
Bachelors of Blackwater Lake miniseries next
month from Harlequin® Special Edition®,
wherever books and ebooks are sold!*